Secret

June Francis' sagas include *Step by Step*, *A Dream To Share*, *When Clouds Go Rolling By*, *Tilly's Story* and *Sunshine and Showers*. She had her first novel published at forty and is married with three sons. She lives in Liverpool.

Also by June Francis

Look for the Silver Lining
A Place to Call Home
The Heart Will Lead
Another Man's Child
Someone to Trust
Shadows of the Past
It's Now or Never
Love Letters in the Sand
Many a Tear Has To Fall
Memories Are Made of This
Walking Back to Happiness
Where There's a Will
For Better, For Worse
Friends and Lovers
Flowers on the Mersey
It Had To Be You
Hers to Have and to Hold
Secrets and Lies

The Victoria Crescent Sagas

Step by Step
A Dream to Share
When the Clouds Go Rolling By
Tilly's Story
Sunshine and Showers

JUNE FRANCIS

Secrets and Lies

CANELO

Penguin
Random
House

First published in the United Kingdom in 2025 by

Canelo, an imprint of
Canelo Digital Publishing Limited,
20 Vauxhall Bridge Road,
London SW1V 2SA
United Kingdom

A Penguin Random House Company
The authorised representative in the EEA is Dorling Kindersley Verlag GmbH.
Arnulfstr. 124, 80636 Munich, Germany

Copyright © June Francis 2025

A CIP catalogue record for this book is available from the British Library.

Print ISBN 978 1 83598 337 9
Ebook ISBN 978 1 83598 339 3

Printed and bound in Great Britain by Clays Ltd, Elcograf S.p.A.

Look for more great books at
www.canelo.co | www.dk.com

CHAPTER ONE

LIVERPOOL

MARCH 1958

The train from Birmingham left the tunnel and was chugging into Lime Street station as, trembling with anger and apprehension, thirty-eight-year-old Olive Jones gathered her belongings together. She gazed through a window at the large clock high on a wall, where she used to meet her very first boyfriend when she was fifteen; they had split up when she had spotted him with another girl, pretty and petite, coming out of the Kardomah café on Church Street, laughing and giggling as he kissed her neck. Olive's slender face creased in a deep frown, puzzled as to why she should be thinking of that day now, when she had enough on her mind to make her feel unwanted and lonely. In the pocket of her coat was the letter sent to her from her brother Peter's wife. It had shocked her to the depths of her being, because her sister-in-law Eleanor had asked why she had not attended her father's funeral.

The question had been like a slap in the face. Olive loved her father dearly. They had been close. He had taught her to swim and ride a bike – and made her a football rattle to cheer on Everton when they were playing at Goodison Park, their home ground. And then the last time she was home he had let her in on his big secret – the numbers he used to fill in his football pools. Her mother did not approve of gambling in any form, even raffles at the church Christmas Fayre, where small things such as talcum powder and bath cubes or a box of chocolates were donated by people for prizes.

As she stepped down from the train onto the crowded platform, she was almost knocked over by a sharp elbow, and instead of an apology, she was told to look where she was going; she had been gazing at the other clock, beneath which were the times of trains and their destinations, but could not see the names clearly. Her eyes were filled with tears, and she had been attempting to mop them away. Her father had told Olive a while ago that in future he wanted her to do the pools using his numbers. She had thought it odd because as far as she knew his numbers had never come up. Still, she had done as he asked, not knowing he was sick and the prognosis was not good. She bumped into a woman carrying a baby and Olive apologised as she mopped her eyes again, considering how her mother must have known her father was seriously ill the last time Olive returned to her place of work at an airfield in Oxfordshire. Why had she kept it from her. Why?

And why hadn't Olive's daughter Joanna written to her? Or had she presumed her grandmother would have done so? Even so, Joanna could have got in touch with her as soon as her grandfather's illness was showing signs of being serious. Olive had so wanted to tell her father that his numbers had come up trumps at last; not to the sum of £75,000 he'd have liked, but enough money to buy a house where she and Joanna could set up a home of their own. If Joanna was willing, that was. Part of the reason Olive had answered the government's call for women to

2

work on the ground at airfields, towards the end of the war, was due to her separation from her husband, Theo. Her daughter had been deeply hurt and had blamed Olive for the split. Olive paused, as a person in front of her in the queue came to a sudden halt only a short distance from the ticket barrier.

As the woman moved on into the bustling station, Olive paused and took out her ticket, aware of a blast of cold air coming through a side entrance opposite the Adelphi Hotel in the street outside. Then she noticed a man standing to the left of the barrier, in a queue opposite her. She blinked and rubbed her eyes. He reminded her of Theo, with his neatly trimmed sideboards and almost invisible fair eyebrows and eyelashes. He was fumbling in his jacket pocket and took out a sheet of paper, which he perused. Then he lifted his head and folded the paper, staring at the people in the queue waiting to go through the ticket barrier. His eyes widened and she realised he had recognised her. She wished she could vanish into thin air, as she was in no mood to pass the time of day with him. She had believed he was in London. But maybe he had been informed about her father's funeral by her daughter, Joanna. Olive felt hurt and angry.

'Ollie!' he yelled. 'So you did get my letter. You're just the woman I wanted to see.'

'What letter? And don't call me Ollie, you know I hate it!' she exclaimed.

Her husband's expression altered. 'Oh no! Then we need to talk right away.' He squeezed between a man and a woman and managed to seize Olive's arm.

'Don't touch me, you're pinching me and you're holding up the queue.'

'Sorry,' he said, but did not release his hold on Olive. 'I never could get used to you being so tall. Glenys is petite compered to you.'

The man the other side of him shoved him several feet away. 'Beat it, mate, before I knock your block off.'

Olive freed herself and tossed her ticket to the railway attendant, then she was finally through the ticket barrier and quickened her pace, dodging round people and heading for the entrance at the far end that led to Lime Street. But Theo managed to catch up with her and forced his arm through hers. 'Come and have a coffee and cake. I've something important to talk to you about,' he shouted in her ear.

'I'm not interested,' she said, although his mention of Glenys, who was an old flame of his, caused her to guess it was about the other woman. 'And don't make me laugh. We were married long enough for you to get accustomed to my height, although you having named me "your dear giraffe" was something I never could forgive you for, you… you shrimp! My height came in useful for changing light bulbs and reaching shelves you couldn't.'

'I'll ignore that remark. Come with me and I'll explain,' he said, hanging on to her. 'I won't keep you long.'

'You better hadn't. I'm on my way to see Joanna and Mam.' She glared at him. 'Have you seen my daughter lately?'

'Yes, I was at your dad's funeral. Why weren't you?'

'So she did write to you.' Olive attempted to free herself and this time she managed to.

'She said your mam was writing to you.' His brow puckered. 'Why, is she short of money? I did send her last month's allowance. The last lot of money she'll be getting from me.'

4

Olive came to a standstill. 'Why is that? Has the price of slate plummeted?'

He shook his head. 'No, but I want to remarry and it's a matter of some urgency.'

Olive took a deep breath and then exhaled. 'So, this letter you mention had nothing to do with Dad?'

'I was sorry to hear about his death.' He took hold of her arm again. 'Let's get a move on to Lyons and then you can go your way, and I can go mine.'

Olive allowed herself to be dragged through the noisy crowds out of the station and along Lime Street to the café facing the Forum Cinema. As soon as they were seated and had ordered, she said, 'I presume it's Glenys and she's pregnant?'

'She has just presented me with a son,' he said in a self-satisfied tone. 'More than you ever did.'

'My daughter gave you plenty of love, even though you always made your desire for a son obvious to most who knew you well.' She wanted to spit in his face, but instead added, 'A son to inherit your shares in Jones and Sons Slate Company.'

'Joanna was never my daughter, but I was a good father to her. You tricked me into marriage.'

'You wanted to marry me. You wanted a son and made no bones about it a month after we'd been seeing each other and seemed to get on well,' Olive reminded him. 'We agreed it would be convenient to both of us to wed, and you persuaded me into your bed.' She paused. 'When did you realise Joanna wasn't your daughter?'

'When I returned from London in '44 and you'd named her Joanna instead of Lydia, as my father suggested, after my sister who had died of diphtheria.'

'Joanna Jones sounded much better than Lydia Jones, and Joanna is in the Bible as well.'

'But not such an important woman. It reminded me of GI Joe and that there were Yanks camped in Aintree Racecourse.'

Olive reached for her coffee and gulped a mouthful. 'You never said,' she murmured a few minutes later.

'She was a beautiful baby, and I was no saint. Besides, Glenys was in prison.'

'Poor Glenys! Did you go and see her and tell her about Joanna?'

'You mean at the time?' He frowned. 'She laughed and told me it served me right, because I had let her down, and then she cried.'

'Did you feel bad?'

'Not at the time because I believed she'd let me down, but since then I've seen her a few times after bumping into her accidentally in London.'

Olive smiled cynically. Her friend Eliza had already filled her in about Glenys and Theo working at the Foreign Office, knowing they had worked for the Secret Service during the war. 'Have they taken her back on at the Foreign Office now the war is well over?' She wanted to see if he'd tell her.

'That's none of your business,' he said. 'Anyway... So, what about a divorce?' He reached out and covered her hand on the table with his.

She stared at him from narrowed eyes. 'I'll think about it.'

He raised her hand and carried it to his lips. 'Pretty please.'

'You old smoothie! What about Joanna? Are you going to tell her the truth? She thinks a lot of you.'

'Are you?' he asked, letting her hand slip.

Olive sighed and glanced at her wristwatch. 'I'll need to go soon; I wanted a walk to the Pier Head for some exercise and fresh air after the journey before heading for Mam's.'

'Well, eat up and let me know when I'll have your answer. I'm sorry about your dad,' he repeated. 'He was a good man.'

'Thanks.' She reached for a chocolate cupcake and crammed it into her mouth.

He took a cream horn. 'Did your parents know about the Yank, and you being pregnant?'

'Good God, no,' she spluttered, spitting out crumbs.

Theo pulled a face. 'Your mam would have gone through the roof.'

'Too true! She was bad enough about us separating and me leaving Joanna with her.' She took out a handkerchief and wiped around her mouth and hands. 'It's Alfie's seventeenth birthday in May. If there's a party, will you be there?'

'I'd like to know your answer about the divorce before then,' he said vexedly.

She smiled and stood up. 'All right, keep your hair on. I'll drop you a line.'

Theo pushed his chair back and stood. 'You will hell, I'm coming with you now and I'll have an answer before we part.' He tossed a banknote on the table after glancing at the bill and, taking her elbow, he ushered her outside.

'You can let me go now,' said Olive, gazing straight into his blue eyes. 'I'm not going to run away. Besides, you know where I'm going.'

His grip eased and she wasted no time heading towards the Mersey, although she stopped now and then to glance

7

in the shop window of the Scotch Wool shop on Church Street and other windows in Lord Street. There were still signs of devastation here and there, it occurred to her that there was something missing and realised it was the clang of trams. Last year the buses had taken over. It felt strange, but at least the Liver birds and the Mersey ferries were still to be seen, and she took several deep breaths of the fresh, salty air as seagulls wheeled on the breeze.

She ignored Theo as she stood on the landing stage and watched the vessels of all shapes and sizes coming and going. Her thoughts drifted back to the day when she and her mother had come to meet her mother's younger sibling, David, but he was not at the meeting place. They'd waited and waited for two hours but still he had not arrived, so her mother found a telephone kiosk and phoned his lodgings, only to be told there had been an accident on a ship that was in dock and in need of repairs. David had gone immediately to help, and that had been at least four hours ago. Olive remembered the colour draining from her mother's face and how she had been in a terrible state. She was never the same again after being told he had been killed when he had fallen down an open hold and been crushed by a heavy plank of wood.

Olive had been seven years old at the time, and up until then her mother had taken her out and about, but after David's death her mother didn't want Olive's company and had never stopped grieving for her brother in the years that followed – even throughout the war years and after, when her own son, Peter, had married and provided her with two grandchildren. The family had thought she might buck up when Joanna moved in with her in the wake of Olive leaving Liverpool after hers and Theo's separation. She felt that familiar guilt at leaving her daughter behind and hurried from the landing stage, forgetting about Theo. She made her way to the bus stop and caught a bus that would take her close to her mother's home. She leapt aboard just in time. It was only then she became aware of her name being shouted and remembered her husband. She caught sight of him running after the bus. She groaned and waved to him. 'I'll be in touch,' she called. He slowed down and shook his fist at her. She went upstairs, dragging her baggage, and sat down with a sigh of relief, hoping Theo would not follow her to her mother's home that evening. She had enough to cope with having to face her mother.

When she arrived at her mother's house, there was no answer to her knock. But she still had her key, and she let herself in. She built up the fire and put the kettle on and noticed a letter behind the clock. She removed it and saw it was addressed to her, and it had an American and an English stamp on it. She would have opened it there and then if she had not heard the key in the lock and female voices. She placed the letter back behind the clock and turned to face her mother and her daughter, who was growing into a real beauty, with long flaxen hair and blue eyes. Both looked completely taken aback and their voices were not welcoming.

Olive poured out three cups of tea and suggested Joanna visit the chippie, handing her a pound note and half a crown. Then Olive went and took out plates and cutlery before sitting opposite her mother, who was tight-lipped.

'So, why didn't you inform me about Dad's illness and death?' demanded Olive in a quivering voice.

Flora glared at her in a way that reminded Olive of a snake ready to strike.

Her mother sipped her tea and glanced into the fire.

'Look at me,' said Olive. 'And answer my question, please?'

'He didn't want you worrying about him being ill,' replied Flora, removing her headscarf to reveal a head of greying hair fastened in pipe cleaners.

'What's your excuse for not telling me he had passed away and when the funeral was?' said Olive in a choking voice.

Her mother stared at her coolly over the rim of her teacup as she took a mouthful of tea. 'I didn't want you there. You'd had enough of him, and I wanted all of him at the end.'

'What do you mean?' asked Olive, astonished.

'You know what I mean,' sneered her mother. 'Going to the football matches with him, knitting him a blue and white scarf.'

'You didn't want to go,' said Olive. 'Since Uncle David died you hated doing anything that could be fun. You refused even to go to the flicks or to listen to the band playing in the park.'

'It wouldn't have been fun without David,' insisted her mother, draining her cup. 'Anyway, what brings you home?'

'A letter asking why I wasn't at Dad's funeral,' said Olive as the kitchen door opened. A shivering Joanna entered and withdrew the packet of fish and chips from inside her coat, where they had kept warm against her chest.

Instantly, Olive was distracted by her entry and hoped her daughter had not caught what she had said. 'They smell lovely, is there any bread to make chip butties?'

Joanna glanced at her but made no comment. She took a crusty loaf from one of the shopping bags she had placed on a chair, went into the back kitchen and reappeared with a block of Stork margarine.

'How long are you stopping, Mam?' she asked, slicing the loaf.

'I'm back in Liverpool for good,' replied Olive. 'I'm planning on finding a job and somewhere to live.'

'What about here?' asked Joanna.

'I sense your Nan doesn't want me,' said Olive, reaching for a chip and biting it in half. 'Besides, I want my own place.'

'What about Dad's place?' asked her daughter. 'He's in London most of the time.'

Olive took a deep breath and steeled herself to reply. 'Theo has asked for a divorce. He wants to marry someone else.'

'You should never have separated, Mam,' snapped Joanna. 'Or gone away.'

Olive said, 'His job is there and no doubt he will either sell the house here or rent it out. He met a woman who works in London, someone he knew years ago, or so Eliza told me. Worked for the Secret Service during the war. Then she got involved in some family trouble in Liverpool and Wales, broke the law and ended up in prison. They split up but he still has feelings for her.'

'But you mustn't agree to a divorce,' said Joanna, leaning across the table towards Olive. 'He might change his mind about her again.'

'She has his baby. A boy,' said Olive quietly.

'Which means he's an adulterer,' interjected Flora. 'But he's got what he's always wanted, a son.' She reached out for a handful of chips and put them on a plate. 'A little bastard, that's why they want to marry.'

'Mother!' cried Olive. 'Do not use such language. The marriage is to do with the shares in the slate quarries,' she added, her eyes filling with tears at the expression on her daughter's face, thinking if she knew the truth about her real father, she would hate them both. 'You know, like Alfie inherited his Welsh father's, Bryn Jones, who was killed in the war.'

'You mustn't agree to a divorce,' repeated Joanna, kneeling in front of Olive and resting her head on her lap.

Olive stroked her flaxen hair, so like Joe's. 'It's what Theo wants, and if this was wartime, he'd go through a form of marriage without a divorce, many men did.'

Joanna lifted her head and stared at her mother. 'You mean Dad would have committed bigamy?'

'He'd run two families and keep them secret from each other.' She sighed, wondering if Joe would have done the same if he had known about the baby, but she hadn't given him the chance and Josh had promised not to tell him. She'd met Josh first, in the Grafton. He had picked her up off the floor where she had been shoved when a fight had broken out between Brits and Yanks. She'd been trying to escape. She had thought he might have asked her to dance but he had taken her outside and suggested the flickers just along the road. He had also told her that he was married so she did not have to worry about him trying it on, he had come looking for a mate at the dance hall but had now changed his mind. Then it seemed he had forgotten about the flickers when the friend she had gone to the dance with had turned up and insulted him, calling him a liar, and dragged her away. Olive did not see him again for a while until they met in the Blue Anchor pub near Aintree Racecourse. Joe had been there too, and set his cap at her; he'd made no mention of being married, and he was a bright spark with the gift of the gab.

'Enough of this talk,' said Nan. 'You can stay here for tonight, Olive.'

'You're too kind, Mam,' said Olive. 'I'll go up soon, if you don't mind. I'm tired out after the journey.'

'Don't give me any of that lip or you'll be out on your ear,' said Flora. 'And you've got a hope finding yourself a house in this climate, although there's always a prefab.'

It was not until Olive had climbed into bed and snuggled beneath the covers that she remembered the letter behind the clock, but she was too tired to get it straightaway. Besides, she'd be better not going downstairs while her mother and daughter were there, although she hadn't had her share of the fish and chips. Maybe she should make that her excuse. She was about to throw back the covers when there was a knock on her bedroom door.

'Is that you, Joanna?' she called.

'Yes,' whispered her daughter. 'I've brought you some chip butties, half a fish and a cup of cocoa.'

'Come in,' said Olive. 'Thanks, love.'

Joanna carried in a tray and placed it on the bed in front of her mother. She also took an envelope from her pocket. 'There's also this,' she said, placing the letter on the tray. 'It came a fortnight ago and has an American and an English stamp on it. Who do you know in America?'

'I'll find out in the morning. I'm starving right now.' She placed the envelope on the side table and reached for a chip butty.

'Aren't you curious, Mam?' said Joanna, reaching for the envelope and fiddling with the flap.

'Stop that,' said Olive. 'You'll get grease on it. It's from one of the girls from the airfield in Oxfordshire who married a Yank, I should think.'

Joanna clicked her tongue against her teeth. 'How boring,' she said. 'Don't worry about the tray, Mam. I'll take it down in the morning.'

–

At seven o'clock the following morning Joanna decided to get up and make her mother some toast and a poached egg, as well as a cuppa. She planned to take it up to her, that way she might discover the contents of the letter. She was on the way downstairs when she heard the letterbox clatter and took the stairs two at a time. Thinking it was a bit early for the postman, she called out, 'Who's there?'

'Is that you, Joanna?'

Recognising the voice, she hurried to open the door to Theo. 'Is that you, Dad?' she whispered.

'Open the door and let me in,' he demanded. 'I need to speak to your mother.'

'At this hour? She's still in bed and asleep.' She smiled. 'It must be important. Have you changed your mind about a divorce?'

'She told you, did she?' he said loudly, brushing past Joanna. 'I don't suppose she told you that I'm not your father too.'

'You're lying!' Joanna flung the words in his face.

She steadied herself against the doorjamb, thinking she must have misheard him. She turned on her heel and stared after him as he raced up the stairs. 'Will you be quiet, Dad,' she called in a sibilant whisper. 'You'll wake Nan, and we don't want that.' She caught up with him on the stairs and seized his coat, but he shook her off as he reached the landing. 'Which is Ollie's bedroom?' he whispered.

'I told you she's asleep. She was tired out.'

He shouted, 'Let's speak to your mother and we'll see who's the deceiver.'

Joanna wasted no time leading him to her mother's bedroom. 'Mam, Dad's here and wants to speak to you. It's not true, is it, about him not being my father?'

'How could you break it to her in such a hurtful way, Theo?' said Olive, before facing her daughter. 'I'm sorry you should find out like this, love. We'll talk about it later, as I said. You go and bring up my cup of tea.'

Joanna hesitated and her gaze passed from her mother to Theo.

'I'm not your father,' said Theo. 'You heard me.' His voice softened. 'I know it's hard for you to hear but there it is. I love someone else, and she needs me.'

Joanna's bottom lip trembled, and she did not move. 'Mam, is it true?'

'Everything will be all right, love,' said Olive. 'Life goes on – you're young, and there'll be lots to look forward to.' She turned to Theo. 'You can have your divorce. You'd better see a solicitor and so will I. Joanna, will you see that man out and, please, bring me up that cuppa?'

As Theo rushed down the stairs, followed by Joanna, the girl wondered if the letter with the American stamp was from a Yank and could prove that Theo was not her father. Maybe that was why Olive didn't want him in the bedroom, in case he spotted the envelope. She felt sick to her stomach, knowing she was going to confront her mother and demand the truth about her paternity.

She slammed the door shut after Theo had left the house, remembering he had always wanted a son.

When she entered Olive's bedroom, she thought her mother looked scared, and noticed that she had opened the envelope.

'Here,' Olive said. 'Read this and forgive me if you can.'

Joanna took the envelope after handing the cup of tea to her mother and placing the plate of food on the side table. She removed a large sheet of paper and began to read.

> *Dear Olive,*
>
> *I am writing to you with the latest news of Joe and enclosing an envelope from him. He changed his mind about sending it, but I thought you might want to know what he has to say.*
>
> *Forgive me for not keeping your secret. I'm sure you'll understand when you read the letter.*
>
> *I am seeing to it that my son Jay gets it. He was in Europe with the air force during the Berlin Blockade and played a part in the airdrop. He is now in Britain and has been visiting family in Scotland.*
>
> *I have asked him to deliver this to a friend of yours and mine, as I don't have your parents' address.*
>
> *I pray that both you and your daughter are well.*
>
> *Warmest wishes,*
>
> *Josh*

Joanna looked at her mother and said tersely, 'So, it's true. Am I allowed to read the other letter?'

'Of course,' replied Olive, squaring her shoulders and handing a smaller envelope to Joanna. 'It very much involves you.'

Joanna read the address first and saw that it was in San Jose, California, and the date was last year. Then she began to read.

> *Dearest Olive,*
>
> *No doubt you think I have no right to address you in such a way after the way I deceived you and did not treat you with the respect you deserved. My only excuse is that I fell in love with you at first sight and the times we spent together were some of the happiest in my life. You looked so lovely and were so understanding about a soldier's needs. Josh warned me off and I wondered if that was because he liked you himself, but although we were all friends, he was aware of how much you and I were in love.*
>
> *I regret we never got to say goodbye. I wish I could have danced at your friend's wedding, and you had told me that you were having our baby instead of unburdening yourself on Josh.*
>
> *Now the reason for this letter. I am going blind and would like nothing better than to see my daughter before I lose my sight, but I don't have much time. If she and you could see your way to forgiving me and coming over to California, I could refund her the cost.*
>
> *I did not tell you all those years ago that I was married because my wife was an invalid, and we had a small son. Sadly, they were killed in a car accident on the way to her parents' shortly after I*

discovered I was losing my sight. I was in a poor state afterwards and could not drive them myself, but my wife insisted our son could do the driving and I stayed at home.

Much love, Joe

'So, what do you think of that?' asked Olive, turning over the letter from Josh and seeing Eliza and Jack's address on the back. 'Just as I thought: his son delivered it to Eliza's.'

'You mean Josh's son? The one who was in the Berlin Blockade put in place by the Russians? I heard they just wanted to make life difficult for the ordinary German people,' she said, without pausing for breath.

Olive shook her head. 'The British and Americans were flying in supplies to their troops and to help the ordinary German people who were in a bad way. Also, the Americans don't like Communism and are determined not to see it spread.' She paused. 'But changing the subject, how curious are you to meet your natural father?'

'He doesn't offer to pay your fare, Mam. I wonder how much two tickets would cost.'

'Perhaps he can't afford two plane tickets,' said Olive. 'Although, I don't think there are civilian flights.'

'We'd have to go by liner,' said Joanna. 'I thought all Americans were rich.'

'You've been watching too many movies,' said Olive. 'Anyway, I don't need his money. I have my own and, besides, I won't have the time to go travelling if I'm to find a home for me, you and my friend, who doesn't want to go and live back home with her mother. She's fed up with her going on about her finding a fella and getting married. Iris offered to pay me a fair rent.'

'Nan's not going to like it,' said Joanna, only half-listening. 'She treats me like a kid when I'm sixteen and one of the oldest in my class. So can you speak to the Head and ask for permission for me to do my final exams earlier and for me to have time off to go to America? I need to know when I'm going, Mam. We need to sort that out.'

'I'll do that. As for Nan, she shouldn't have kept Dad's illness from me, or the date of the funeral.' Olive reached for her cup of tea and sipped it. She pulled a face. 'It's gone cold. I'll get up and make a fresh one, and I'll warm up my breakfast. I want to go into town soon and visit the travel agent's and possibly see about passports. I also need some new clothes.'

'I wish I could go with you to town,' said Joanna. 'I need a bra, and Nan won't let me have one. She insists I wear a liberty bodice.'

'Don't you have school today?'

'Yes, but it's the Easter holidays the week after next. We could go then.'

Olive said, 'Okay, let's go to town then. And I'll write a letter to your head mistress and explain the situation and Joe's blindness, but not say he's your father but a close relative.' She paused. 'I need to go to the bank and the Labour Exchange to register for a job. I also want to buy flowers and visit Dad's grave. I presume you know where it is.'

'Can I have a new dress? And are we taking Nan when we eventually go to town?' asked Joanna.

'She won't want to come if she knows we're going to the Labour Exchange up Renshaw Street. It's quite a walk.'

'I presume we'll go to Marks and Sparks for underwear. We'll cross at the traffic lights outside the railway station and then cut through past the back of the market and then the Playhouse theatre. They still have puppies and kittens for sale at the back of the market. I asked Nan could I have a puppy for my birthday, but she said no, that it would make a mess and leave hairs everywhere and need walking. I told her I would look after it, but she just laughed.' Joanna sniffed back tears. 'It's not fair, I do lots of work around the house, as well as washing the step and back yard.'

'I'll buy you one when I get my house,' said Olive.

'You're serious about that?'

Olive nodded and her daughter did a little dance around the room.

'I wonder what my natural father will have to say about my having had another dad called Theo. And what about his relations and friends? What will they think of me being his bastard child?' Tears welled in her eyes. 'And what will they think of him having an invalid wife and carrying on behind her back? He'll go down in their estimation.'

Olive placed her arm around her daughter. 'Some will say he's not the first. They certainly won't blame you. You're the innocent in the matter. No doubt some would like to set eyes on me because it's often the woman who gets blamed, saying she seduced him.'

'But you loved each other,' said Joanne, wiping her damp face.

Olive toyed with her necklace and sighed, thinking of Josh now and wondering about his wife, the mother of Jay. How much had she missed her son while he had been in Europe? And he was now in England instead of going home as soon as he was demobbed.

'I wonder what Da— Theo will say about you buying a house,' muttered Joanna, a choke in her voice. 'He'll wonder where you got the money from. Although, he gets an income from his shares in the slate business, so he's not hard up. I wonder if we'll get to see his baby son, who'll inherit the shares. It's not fair that the females in the family miss out.'

'You'll inherit stuff from me,' said Olive. 'My house – and I'm thinking of going into business for myself. He'll just have to wonder how I can afford it. I'm not going to tell him, or he could expect half of my winnings in the divorce settlement.'

'Winnings!' cried Joanna, staring at her mother in amazement.

'Using your granddad's pools numbers – and lower your voice. It'll be yours and my secret. I need you to swear on the Bible, 'cos you'll be tempted to tell those close to us.'

'Don't you trust me, Mam? Is that why you didn't tell me about Joe earlier?' There was a sob in her voice.

Olive shook her head and placed an arm about her daughter. 'No, it was because I thought you would hate me and be ashamed of me.'

'At least Joe wants me,' said Joanna, her head drooping on her mother's shoulder.

'I always wanted you,' said Olive huskily. 'And I'll look forward to going shopping with you when the school holidays start.'

CHAPTER TWO

Joanna linked her arm through her mother's as they left the bus in Lime Street. Olive gazed across the road at St George's Hall. She noticed a young man in uniform leaning against one of the blackened lions not far from the Cenotaph, which had been built just after the Great War. He looked familiar but at that moment Joanna tugged her arm and said, 'Time to go, Mam.'

Before she could speak, Joanna hustled her along the pavement in the direction of the traffic lights. Olive continued to stare across the road and saw that the young man was still there, so she suggested they cross immediately as she had seen someone who looked familiar near the Cenotaph.

'It's not safe, Mam,' said Joanna. 'We'll walk to the lights and wait for them to change, then cross and walk back on that side.'

'He could have gone by then,' said Olive impatiently.

'Who is it?' asked Joanna.

'I could be mistaken, so let's do as you suggest and cross at the lights.' Olive dragged her daughter along the pavement, then hurried her across the road and to the lions, only to find the young man had vanished. If she had not rushed, she might have noticed him crossing towards the railway station. Disappointed, she gazed about her as she and her daughter crossed a different road which led to the entrance of the Mersey Tunnel; on one side was St John's Gardens and on the other side there was a way to the shops, including a side entrance to Marks and Spencer's and the lingerie department.

Joanna not only wanted a bra to replace the liberty bodice that her nan insisted on her wearing, but also a suspender belt to replace the thick elastic bands that Nan gave her to keep her stockings up. Olive purchased a pair of knee-length pants and a blouse, as well as dresses for Easter for her and her daughter. For herself she also bought a nightdress and stockings. A short while later, when she passed the flower girls in Clayton Square, she remembered that she was going to the cemetery and so she bought flowers.

'Granddad is buried in Anfield Cemetery, and we can catch a bus there to get home,' said Joanna. 'We could also shop for more food in Breck Road.' She hesitated. 'I'm hungry and thirsty now, Mam. Would it break the bank if we went and had a cup of tea and a scone in Lyons?'

'Right,' said Olive. She was still disappointed at not discovering who the young man was, and she was not ready yet to return to her mother's house; besides, she was also thirsty and hungry. As well as that, she had not been to the Labour Exchange in Renshaw Street, or the bank, or looked in the windows of estate agents. She would also have to find herself a solicitor. But first Lyons and then, lastly, the cemetery.

It was while they were waiting for their order, at a table near the window, that Joanna spied Alfie, Eliza's son, passing. He was not alone, but with a young man in uniform whom she had never seen before. Joanna wasted no time leaving the café and hurrying out to follow them. Olive gazed after them and was sure it was the young man she had seen earlier. The fact he was with Alfie strengthened her conviction that he could be the son that Josh had mentioned in his short note. It was a fact that Josh had met Eliza and her husband Jack on their wedding day, when he brought the message from Joe for Olive, saying he would not be able to go to the wedding with her. It was the last time she had seen Josh, but she had sent him a Christmas card, along with the one from Jack and Eliza, as they had exchanged addresses. She had kept quiet about hers, as she did not want her mother being nosey if he sent one to her address. But he had continued to write to her care of Jack and Eliza until she and Theo had married, and no doubt she must have told him about them separating. She felt for his letter and the one from Joe. She wished Josh hadn't encouraged Joe to send the letter. She was all a dither and decided not to wait for Joanna to return with Alfie and his companion and instead went to the ladies'.

–

Joanna was furious when she returned to the table and found her mother absent, having left their shopping unattended. The waitress was standing there, holding a tray with their order on it. Joanna took it from her and asked if her mother had said anything to her. 'She said she needed to go to the ladies'.'

Jay said, 'She mustn't want to see me.' He paused. 'Mom told Pa he shouldn't interfere and that he's given Joe enough assistance. And she's never forgiven Joe's wife for turning her help down.' He shrugged. 'Ma and Pa are always disagreeing over something, and I heard her saying that she was considering doing what granddad said and getting a divorce; he's a lawyer and could arrange it.'

'Josh obviously believes it'll be good for Joe to see Aunty Olive and meet Joanna,' said Alfie.

Jay nodded. 'Speaking of her, how about introducing me and the young lady,' he said.

Alfie looked embarrassed and did so, and apologised.

'Hi,' said Jay, holding out his hand.

'Hello,' responded Joanna, shaking his hand. 'Glad to meet you. You're wrong about Mam. Those letters came as a shock. She'd only just discovered Granddad had passed away and Nan hadn't told her, so she'd missed his funeral.' Joanna switched her gaze to Alfie. 'Then she met Theo by chance at Lime Street station and he wants a divorce as soon as possible to marry again. He's got the son he always wanted.'

Alfie whistled. 'Theo wants a divorce. I hadn't heard that. And Mam's made no mention of it to Amelia, who you must know is Theo's dead uncle's wife. Theo's not coming to my birthday party. He'll be down south.'

'It seems odd that should happen when the letters from America have just arrived. I've read them and am considering whether to go to America, Mam's after buying a house over here, so I doubt she'd allow me to go on my own, and she also needs to sort out time off with school, and altering when I sit my exams if necessary.'

Alfie and Jay exchanged looks.

'Have you received the invitation to my seventeenth birthday party?' asked Alfie. 'If you, your mam and Nan come, Jay could explain everything to your mam.'

'And to you,' said Jay, gazing at Joanna thoughtfully. 'I hope you can come to California. It'll buck Joe up and Dad is looking forward to seeing you as well.'

'I'll look forward to the party,' she said, thinking he was almost as attractive as Alfie, but older, with a nice American accent and a crew cut. 'When is it?'

'You should know my birthday,' said Alfie.

'But is the party on the day?'

'It's written on the invitation, which has been posted off,' he said. 'We'll have to be going or we'll be late for the tennis match. See you and Aunt Olly at my birthday party.'

'Don't call her that,' said Joanna. 'She hates it, makes her feel like Popeye's girlfriend.'

'Sorry,' said Alfie, winking at her. The two waved and left.

A few minutes later her mother turned up. 'So, what did they have to say?' asked Olive.

'It's Alfie's birthday soon and we're invited to the party.' Joanna poured tea into her mother's cup. 'The fella with him is Jay, Josh's son. Alfie introduced us. He'll be there but Theo won't.'

'Alfie's birthday is in May, there's plenty of time,' said Olive. 'He was born the week of the May blitz.'

'We've been sent an invitation card,' said Joanna. 'Jay's nice looking, with good cheekbones.'

'He's like his father, then,' said Olive casually. 'It was him I spotted by the lions outside Saint George's Hall.'

'Why didn't you tell me?' asked Joanna.

'I wasn't sure, and that's why I wanted to cross the road. The uniform was a different colour.'

'Jay will explain things better at the party than any letter,' said Joanna. 'I was told something I didn't know. But I'm unsure whether to tell you.'

'Don't be so mysterious,' said Olive, sipping her drink. 'If you've been told and haven't been sworn to secrecy, then you should tell me.'

'Joe is Josh's wife's cousin.'

Olive put down her cup and freed a long breath. 'Does Eliza know?'

Joanna shrugged. 'I don't know. Alfie does. But most likely Jay talked to him about it. They've grown close. It's not important, is it?'

'Does it mean anything to you?' Olive was wondering if money was tied up in the relationship that connected the two families. If so, would it affect Joanna, as Joe's daughter?

'Eliza must have known about Joe being your father,' said Olive, annoyed. 'Why didn't she say something to me?' Could Josh have told her? She hated the thought that he might have broken his word. But why should he have told Eliza? Unless he had spoken to Jack about it over a drink, thinking the couple would support her if matters got tough.

'Probably Eliza thought you'd tell her if you wanted her to know. She probably thought you'd be home for Granddad's funeral and the pair of you could have talked then.'

'Which you now know I knew nothing about. I didn't even know he was ill.' Tears filled Olive's eyes.

Joanna patted her mother's hand. 'I can't understand Nan. Uncle Pete and me and Aunt Eleanor believed she'd told you.' She paused. 'Anyway, we'd best eat up and drink our tea if we're going to the cemetery, right?'

'But first the Labour Exchange and then the bank and a quick look in some estate agents' windows. I won't be bothering with the tourist agency. I've already discovered there's no flights to America across the Atlantic. It'll have to be by ship, but it doesn't take too long,' said Olive.

'So, your heart's still set on buying your own house before the trip to California?'

'Even more so now. I don't want to be staying under your nan's roof for much longer.'

Joanna sipped her tea. 'Are you still undecided about going to California?'

'I'm more interested in finding a house,' said Olive. 'How do you feel?'

'I'm curious. At least Joe wants to see me, unlike Theo.' Joanna paused. 'Alfie was telling me that Theo spotted Jay on Newsham Drive, talking to Amelia, who shares her house with Uncle Jack and Aunty Eliza. He left a note apologising that he wouldn't be at the birthday party, as he would be in London. He didn't mention the divorce; I wonder why not.'

Olive gnawed on a fingernail. 'Most probably Theo didn't want to get drawn into talk about the divorce. Theo is Amelia's dead husband's nephew.' She sighed. 'And he is related to Alfie, whose father Bryn Jones was killed in the war.'

'Alfie gets on well with Theo and Jack,' said Joanna.

'I'm fond of Alfie,' said Olive.

'Me too,' said Joanna. 'Maybe I could travel with them if you find a house.'

Olive was not so sure about that, thinking of moonlit evenings on board the ship; although she trusted Alfie with her daughter, she was not so sure of Jay. She swallowed the last morsel of scone and washed it down with her tea, then wiped her hands on a paper napkin, checked the bill and placed some money on it before calling over the waitress.

Joanna stood up and followed her mother out of Lyons, having picked up all the shopping. They visited the branch of Lloyd's bank, where Olive opened an account, deposited her pools cheque and withdrew some money. Then they visited the Labour Exchange and Olive registered her name but could see no jobs that appealed on the noticeboard. They then caught a bus that would take them to North John Street and gazed in the windows of various estate agents, seeing what kind of house Olive could buy for the price she wanted to pay. She then remembered she needed a solicitor but decided it could wait until another day. They needed to visit the cemetery and shop for food. She was glad it was not raining as she and her daughter entered the cemetery, as it would have felt more miserable. She was also relieved that her daughter and not her mother had accompanied her She could not remember a time when her parents had ever been lovey-dovey or sent wedding anniversary cards. Had their marriage been one of convenience? Had there ever been another fella in her mother's life? She supposed she would never know.

'This way, Mam,' said Joanna. 'It hasn't got a headstone yet. Nan said she couldn't afford one.'

'But it must have his parents' names on and his sister's, because he'll have gone in the same grave as there was room for one more.'

'Uncle Pete said that, but Nan said she didn't have the money to pay a stonemason to inscribe the necessary words. Pete said he'd pay for it if he were ever to get a rise, but money was tight, what with the two kids to feed and clothe.

'I overheard him say if Eleanor got a little part-time job once both kids were at school they could save to buy a house.'

'I'll pay for the stonemason,' said Olive. 'But don't you go telling anyone about my winnings. I'll tell them I've been saving for when you go to university.'

'I won't. Does your friend who's going to lodge with us know?'

'Iris. It's been difficult keeping quiet, but I learnt to hold my tongue and keep a secret years ago. I told her in the end, and she said that she'd still pay rent to me.'

Joanna halted, thinking, *I was that secret.* 'We're here, Mam.'

Olive gazed down at the grave and then lifted her eyes to the gravestone in white marble with gold lettering. She brushed back her tears and said, 'Hiya, Dad, I'm sorry I never got to kiss you ta-ra. I can say thanks for your football pools numbers, which came up trumps.'

She turned to her daughter, but Joanna had already gone to fetch water for the flowers and so Olive placed them in the vase and promised that later in the year she would come and plant bulbs so he would never be without flowers in spring. She said a prayer and then softly sang 'Thine Be the Glory'. Joanna came back and linked her fingers through her mother's and hummed the tune. Then they turned away and called in at the office on the way out, where they asked the woman there for the name of a stonemason to inscribe words on the family stone.

'Do you feel better now, Mam?' said Joanna.

'Better than I did. Now we're best going shopping for food and tomorrow I'll call on the stonemason and make a few other phone calls.'

–

Flora had a face on her when they arrived home and placed the shopping on the table.

'What's all this?' she demanded. 'Where've you been?'

'I left you a note,' said Olive, flopping on the sofa. 'I'm desperate for a cuppa and to take me shoes off.'

'You could have asked me to go with you,' said her mother in a sour voice.

'Up hills and down dales, Mam, you'd have been exhausted.'

'Mam went to sign on at the unemployment,' said Joanna, putting the kettle on. 'That was quite a walk along Renshaw Street from Lime Street, and then we back-tracked and ended up getting the bus to Anfield Cemetery to place flowers on Granddad's grave.'

Olive cleared her throat and said, 'When I saw Dad's name and details were not on the stone, I decided to contact a stonemason and have them inscribed. I thought I owed you both that for caring for Joanna while I have been working for King and Country.'

Flora spluttered. 'You should have asked me first about what to have written on it.'

'I thought you'd allow me that privilege, seeing as how I couldn't be at the funeral because I wasn't told about it.'

'All right, we will leave it at that. Our Peter will be pleased. The way that wife of his spends his money.' Flora stood up and went over to the table and flicked open one of the bags. 'So, what have you been buying?'

'Don't be nosey, Nan,' said Joanna, seizing the Marks and Sparks bag that contained her new underwear.

'I've bought steak and kidney pies for this evening's meal, and Joanna popped in the chippie for chips and mushy peas and a bottle of tomato ketchup,' said Olive. 'I love tomato ketchup on chips.'

'What's wrong with malt vinegar?' said her mother.

'There's some on the chips,' said Joanna, removing the newspaper wrapping. 'Don't they smell good, Nan? I asked for plenty of vinegar, knowing you liked it. Aren't I thoughtful?'

'You don't have to soft-soap me,' said her grandmother. 'You might get around your mother, but I know you better than she does.'

'I'd say Granddad knew me better than you, Nan. We had fun together.'

'Football matches,' spat out Flora. 'Bad language and goodness know what else.'

'Enough, you two,' said Olive, 'The food will be getting cold.'

'Sorry, Mam,' said Joanna, 'I'll make the tea.'

Olive fetched cutlery and placed the food on plates after removing the bags containing the clothes she had bought and taking them upstairs to the bedrooms. When she returned, Joanna was pouring tea into cups.

Flora was inspecting her pie. 'Where did you buy these?' she asked, cutting hers in half and examining the contents.

'Marks and Sparks. I also bought three chocolate eclairs and some strawberry jam and a crusty loaf.'

'What was in the bags you took upstairs?'

'Clothes. I wanted them out of the way so they wouldn't get greasy fingers on them.'

'That makes sense, doesn't it, Nan?' said Joanna, forking a mouthful of pie into her mouth.

'I'd like to see what our Olive bought you.'

'I'll show you after,' responded Joanna. 'I've wanted them for ages. I'm almost grown-up after all. Girls a year younger than my age could get married in the olden days.'

'What's that to do with now? You haven't been messing with boys up the back jiggers, have you?'

Olive glared at her mother. 'What a thing to say, Mam!'

'Chance would be a fine thing, anyway,' said Joanna. 'I hardly have a minute to myself. If I'm not studying for exams, I'm washing dishes or peeling vegetables or scrubbing the front step. It was different when Granddad was alive and well. He'd take me to the match or to the flicks or the park, where we'd row on the lake. You never wanted to come.'

'Enough of your cheek!' shrieked Flora. 'Blame your mother. It's she who went off and left me to care for you.'

'I paid you for it,' said Olive. 'And if you were short, Dad would have seen you right. Anyway, any clothes I've bought for my daughter is up to me, and the sooner we can get out of here, the better it will be for the three of us.'

'Fat chance you've got of getting a house,' sneered her mother.

'That's what you think,' said Joanna. 'Mam has—'

Olive turned on her, 'Shut up, Joanna! We don't want people knowing our business or there'll be no university place for you.'

Joanna sniffed and dug her fork into a chip. 'Don't say that, Mam. You promised. Or is it that we're both going to America instead? California has a very good university – Stanford. I'm sure my real dad will pay for me.'

Flora yelped. 'So that's what that envelope from America was about. Your mother messed around with the Yanks? No doubt it's why Theo wants a divorce.'

'That's where you're wrong. He wants to marry his old flame. She's given birth to his son. I told you that, Mother, and you called him an adulterer,' said Olive. 'Now let's have some peace and quiet. I want to eat my food before it gets stone cold.'

A lump of coal shifted in the fire and was clearly heard as silence fell. Then came the sound of cutlery scraping plates. Olive rose and went to switch on the wireless, and the sound of laughter filled the room. She said, 'That's Ted Ray. It must be "*Ray's a Laugh*".'

'Appropriate,' said Joanna, standing up and collecting the plates. 'Anyone ready for another cuppa and a chocolate eclair?'

'I want an apology,' said Flora.

'Don't start, Mam,' said Olive. 'The only thing on offer is tea and a chocolate eclair.'

'I'll wash the dishes and then we can wash our hands and faces and go upstairs and show off our new clothes. Agreed?' said Joanna.

'If you say so,' chorused Olive and Flora.

Half an hour later they were gathered in Olive's bedroom. The contents of the bags were emptied on the bed in two separate heaps. Olive showed off hers first, starting with the nightdress of flower-sprigged cotton trimmed with lace, then three-quarter-length red trousers, which Flora expressed disapproval of, and a pink linen blouse.

Flora's jaw dropped even further when her grand-daughter produced the flesh-coloured silk brassiere edged with lace and matching briefs and a suspender belt.

'There's hardly anything of them,' she gasped. 'You'll catch your death of cold, playing hockey in them drawers.'

'I would wear my navy-blue knickers over them for games, Nan. I must. It's a school rule.'

'I should think so, too,' said Flora. 'What about your top half? You'll wear your liberty bodice?'

'Not on your nelly! I'll be warm enough in my bra and sports shirt, which is nice and thick. And the big girls won't laugh at me when we get changed,' stated Joanna.

'I blame this on the flickers and the suffragettes,' said Flora.

'You should blame it on those who brought in stays and corsets. There's probably many a woman who could have died because they affected their breathing,' said Joanna.

'Too right,' said Olive, nodding vigorously. 'Tell the truth, Mam. Admit that wearing a corset was like wearing armour.'

'You felt protected,' admitted her mother with a reminiscent smile.

'From whom?' asked Olive. 'Not Dad?'

'Don't be personal,' said her mother, hunching a shoulder. 'Anyway, what's this about going to America? Who's going to look after me?'

'You'll have to begin being nice to our Pete and Eleanor. You could offer to look after their kids so they could go out together, and you'd have a free meal and could play happy families,' said Olive.

'No thanks. Me and her have never got on. I've another plan, so you don't have to worry about me.' She left the bedroom with barely a glance at the remaining clothes on Olive's bed.

Joanna exchanged looks with Olive. 'Do you think she's really got a plan or is she trying to make us feel sorry for her?'

'Only time will tell,' said Olive. 'Now take your clothes. I want to go to bed. We can talk about California another time.'

Joanna left her mother's bedroom with her new clothes, determined to bring up the subject in the morning.

Olive called, 'God bless and sweet dreams.' She put away her clothes, put on her nightgown, then climbed into bed.

CHAPTER THREE

Olive slid out of bed, took off her nightgown and threw it over the board at the bottom of the bed. Then she dressed, before tiptoeing downstairs and washing her hands and face in the back kitchen sink, after going to the lavatory in the back yard. Then she made a pot of tea and poured out a cup.

She wasted no time crunching some toast and washing it down with the tea. After cleaning the breakfast things and putting on her outdoor clothes, she found her handbag and crept to the front door. She was about to open it when she heard footsteps on the stairs and Joanna calling down, 'Where are you going so early?'

'For milk. We're nearly out of it.'

'I can go for that after we discuss going to California.'

'Lower your voice. You'll wake Mam up,' whispered Olive, pulling the front door ajar. 'There's probably enough for your cereal and a cuppa for Mam. I've made a pot of tea.'

'What's the rush then? You said we'd talk. We must decide soon if I'm to get there before Daddy Joe goes blind,' said Joanna, having reached the bottom of the stairs.

'I want to find us a house before California,' said Olive.

'I thought you'd be dying to see Joe, if the pair of you were madly in love. His wife is dead and you're getting a

37

divorce. It seems as if it's meant to be, and if you were to get married, we'd live over there, wouldn't we?'

'Now who's rushing ahead of things,' said Olive, running her fingers through her curly copper hair. 'We haven't seen each other or even written to each other for sixteen years. He doesn't even mention missing me in his letter, or that he still loves me. I'm not convinced I still have such strong feelings for him either.'

'But he's lost his son and that could hurt more than losing his wife and could be why he wants to see me so much. I'm blood of his blood and flesh of his flesh,' she cried.

'You're being melodramatic,' said Olive. 'This is all Josh's fault for breaking his promise and telling Joe.'

'You shouldn't be thinking the worst of him. He was just thinking of his friend,' said Joanna earnestly. 'But how is it Josh writes to you if he has a wife who's aware of your existence?' She sat down on the bottom stair.

A visible tremor quivered through Olive. 'How do you know that?'

'Jay mentioned it. Apparently, Josh's wife told him to keep out of it.'

'I wonder if he ever told her that he met me first, but it didn't go anywhere because he was honest enough to remember he had a wife back in America. Not in those exact words, but near enough.'

'But Joe didn't?'

'His feelings for me ran away with him, and life can't have been easy for him, having a crippled wife.'

'Which shows he has some good points,' said Joanna.

'Enough,' said, Olive. 'I'm not rushing into a decision. And if I see a house I like, I'll buy it. Besides, I mightn't like America, whereas I love my country and Liverpool, even more so when she's been battered to the ground, and I have friends here.'

'But California, Mam. Hollywood, film stars! Sunshine! Swimming in the Pacific!'

'Sharks,' said Olive.

'Are you going to see Aunty Eliza? I'll come with you.'

Olive shook her head. 'I'll see her at the birthday party. That's another reason for me to go out. I'll need to get Alfie a birthday present, and I also need to visit the stonemason. Now go and have your breakfast.'

Olive gazed at her daughter, thinking she looked apprehensive. 'What is it?'

'Did you ever consider getting rid of me before Theo asked you to marry him?'

'Blood of my blood, flesh of my flesh,' she answered.

Joanna freed a heavy breath, then said accusingly, 'You just made that last bit up. Admit it!'

'Why should I? You're not the only one with a way with words.' Olive turned her head, so her daughter could not see her expression, as she remembered overhearing some women gabbing in the street years ago about ways of getting rid of a baby. She had been in her early teens and shocked to the roots of her hair. They'd all had too many kids as it was; one had enough to have her own football team.

She left the house and caught a bus into town, and as the bus went along Dale Street where the Town Hall was situated, she thought about her conversation with her daughter and decided to write down in her own words something other than blood and flesh, such as, *I knew you were a precious part of me as soon as I was aware of your presence.* She would buy a pretty card and write inside it and place it on Joanna's dressing table.

In the meantime, she would go inside several estate agents, tell them her requirements and ask them to put her on their mailing list. As for a solicitor, no doubt they would recommend one. She was aware that some specialised in different aspects of the law and that she could find names and details in a telephone directory. When it came to the divorce, she didn't want Theo knowing of her winnings. Anyway, she had a lot to think about and she realised that it was likely that Jay could now have informed his father that a divorce was on the cards between her and Theo.

Over the following week, she was able to see two houses. One was near Sefton Park, but a couple were already after it, and the other did not have three decent-sized bedrooms. One good thing was that Joanna was delighted with what was written in the card that Olive had placed on her daughter's dressing table.

–

The weeks were flashing past, and a letter arrived from Josh, asking if her divorce had gone through and how much longer would matters take, as Joe was beginning to think Joanna did not want to meet him. Still, Olive could not make up her mind whether to go to California. She encouraged Joanna to write to Joe and tell him that she was in the middle of exams and that once they were over, it would be Alfie's birthday, and she could not be away for that.

Then halfway through April, Olive was sent details of a semi-detached house in Waterloo, situated between Seaforth and Crosby, not far from the seafront. 'It sounds perfect,' said Olive. 'I must go and see it before someone else gets in before me.' She wasted no time getting in touch with the estate agent, who told her that the owners wanted a quick sale and there was someone else interested. Olive was aware that a cash buy could enable her to get ahead of the couple who were interested, although it would leave her short of money to buy herself a ticket for America. She dithered for a few minutes, but then bought the house, without even having a surveyor check pipes, electrics and the roof, she just prayed that all would go well, even as she knew her daughter would hit the roof. As for her mother, she was still moaning and saying that they couldn't depend on her leaving them anything in her will, as she was going to spend it all on a cruise.

CHAPTER FOUR

A week before Alfie's birthday, Olive remembered she still had not bought his present and knew she had to go into town that day. She knew her daughter was vexed with her, but she had promised to come with her to choose Alfie's present. So far only her mother, Joanna and her friend Iris knew about the house. She was dreading the truth coming out; it had been bad enough when news of the divorce had broken. She had found herself a solicitor at the beginning of April, having received another letter from Theo's solicitor. Of course, Theo was taking responsibility for the breakup of their marriage, having committed adultery, so not before too long Theo would be able to wed his lover and make their son legitimate. Olive had received more legal papers to sign. If they were not for the house, they were to do with the divorce.

Olive knocked on Joanna's bedroom door and asked, 'Are you coming with me? I've still to get Alfie's present.'

'I don't need to ask why you've left it so late,' said Joanna, opening the bedroom door. 'Your head's been full of other things.'

'True! I've written to my friend Iris and sent her a photo of the house,' said Olive as they crept downstairs. 'She's hoping to get to Liverpool in three weeks' time. And I really do want you to see the house.'

'So, it's definite you won't be going to California,' said Joanna. 'I'm determined to go, whether you like it or not.'

'We'll see,' said Olive. 'The divorce has not been finalised yet either.'

'What's that to do with anything? You weren't intending to marry Daddy Joe anyway.'

'I don't need another husband,' said Olive. 'I'll get along without one.'

'You say that now but who's going to do all the jobs around the house?' whispered Joanna as they left the house, leaving a note on the sideboard for Flora.

'I'll find an odd-job man who's in need of earning a bit of extra money,' said Olive confidently. 'Besides, I have a brother and there's plenty of women who can wield a paintbrush or hammer in a nail and change a plug.'

'Is your friend Iris one of them?'

'As far as I know, and I'll soon learn,' said Olive, 'Anyway, that's enough. Here comes a bus. We'll go into town first and I'll buy Alfie's present.'

'Have you thought of anything?'

'I know he likes classical music.'

'Not just classical music, but I thought you said you were going to buy him something that he could keep.'

'You're right. I did.' Olive started to give it a thought but when they reached Lime Street, she was still none the wiser.

Joanna dragged her across the road as she wanted to look in a jeweller's window.

'What are you looking in here for?' asked her mother.

'I like looking at the shiny rings.' Then Joanna spotted some gold cufflinks. 'What about them for Alfie?' she suggested.

'He might lose one,' said her mother, but continued to gaze in the window. Finally, she said, 'I think I'll buy that for him.'

'What's that?' asked Joanna.

'The gold St Christopher on a chain,' replied Olive. 'I think it's a suitable gift from a godmother.'

Joanna was silent but followed her inside the shop, where she watched and listened with interest as her mother purchased the St Christopher medallion and chain. She was especially interested in the cost, wondering not for the first time just how much her mother had won on the football pools and how much the house had cost. She was aware that Olive still had to purchase furniture and pay solicitor's fees, as well as tuition fees if she went to university – just how much money did her mother have left? It seemed apparent to her that her mother really would need to find a job.

They did not linger long wandering around the centre of the city but went to Central station. They caught the Southport train to South Road, Crosby. Olive told Joanna that was the closest shopping centre to the house, although there were also shops on Liverpool Road and St John's Road, but South Road led down to the promenade and the beach. 'Is there a bus to Waterloo?' said Joanna, gazing towards the main road.

'Yeah, but I thought you might prefer walking close to the front. On the bus we'd need to get off near Rougemont Avenue. It's named after a chateau where some of the fighting during the battle of Waterloo took place. There's even a replica building. Most of the houses are Victorian, Edwardian or even Georgian, and they are large, as some of the well-off from Liverpool moved out this way. I think one of the Gladstones did towards the

44

Seaforth end. You've heard of Gladstone Dock, haven't you?'

Joanna nodded, noticing there was a Woolworths and a Boots, and further down cafés and a couple of pubs, and close to the bottom a small place that sold ice cream and lollies. 'So, how far are we to the house you've bought?'

'About a mile. I'm not that good at measuring distances, and there are shortcuts one can take,' said Olive. 'It's a nice walk, anyway.'

They walked in silence along a pavement for a while. On their left-hand side were attractive terraced houses decorated with wrought iron palisades each side of the front door and small front gardens. On the first floors were wrought iron balconies, and then they came to an opening and could see larger houses. They turned off the main road and stopped in front of a corner house: the garden was walled and had a side gate as well. Olive opened it and led the way inside; taking a bunch of keys, she opened a door which led into a large kitchen. There was a lounge, which had two windows, one overlooking the side garden and the other the back garden. The parlour gazed over a smaller space that was mainly lawn. There was a lobby and a cupboard under the stairs that led to a large cellar, whose walls were whitewashed. There were several shelves, but it was empty, except for a makeshift single bed and a small table. It was lit by electricity, as was the rest of the house.

Joanna led the way upstairs and opened all the doors: the two rooms at the back were a good size and looked over the roofs to catch a glimpse of the sea as well as the parkland. She decided to go up to the next floor, and it was there that one could get a decent view of the sea as far as the horizon. She could just about see a ship and wondered if it was a cargo ship or the Irish ferry or even the Isle of Man boat. If she lifted herself and gazed left and down, she could see the Wirral, and if she lifted her head slightly Snowdonia became visible. Her spirits rose.

She would ask her mother if she could have this room. After all, she had younger legs for climbing stairs. Besides, her mother and Iris would want the larger bedrooms and the floor where the bathroom and lavatory were situated. Later, she was to discover there was an outside lavatory, a washhouse and a coal shed.

'So, what do you think of it?' asked her mother as they seated themselves on a well-worn bench outside the kitchen door.

'I've chosen my bedroom,' replied Joanna.

'The attic one where you can see the sea,' said Olive. 'So, you won't be staying in America?'

'I never intended to.' She stretched out a hand to her mother. 'I wish you were coming. But I can see you're going to be busy. Aunt Eleanor will be green with envy.'

'She can come and stay, or the kids can, and I'll take them to play on the beach while she and Pete have some time to themselves.'

'What about Nan?' asked Joanna, gazing down the garden. 'I wonder what your neighbour is like?'

'I'll find out sooner or later.'

'Will you be getting yourself a gardener?'

'I'll borrow a book from the library and have a go myself. Iris will probably give me a hand. As for Ma, you heard her. She's going on a cruise.'

'Do you think she'll go on her own?'

'Who can she go with? She's got no friends who could afford to go on a cruise.'

'She might find herself an old fella on the cruise. They're the ones who have the money.'

'We'll see,' said Olive. 'She's going to need new clothes, which will cost her. Unless she finds something decent in Great Homer Street Market or buys some material and makes her own.' She paused. 'I'm going to have to make curtains for the windows here.'

'Can I choose my own material?'

'You mean before you go away?' asked Olive.

'We could measure for the curtains now and choose the material today. My windows won't need much. They're not that large.'

'We'd best get going. We can go to that shop in Stafford Street. We'll probably get a bargain there.'

'I was thinking of George Henry Lee's,' said Joanna.

'You can forget there, unless you've money of your own. Anyway, who's going to see them all the way up there?'

'I will,' said Joanna.

'Tough luck! I'm having to watch my money if you're going to university.'

So, without another word, they locked and left the house and caught a bus to London Road, where they purchased some orange and cream material for Joanna's bedroom, as well as cotton thread and other necessary items in Stafford Street.

CHAPTER FIVE

Towards the end of the first week in May, Olive, Joanna and Flora set out for Alfie's birthday party. Olive was wearing a royal blue rayon dress cinched at the waist with a waspie belt, Nan wore a pink twin set and a check skirt, and Joanna the dress her mother had bought her. They set out in good time with their presents to catch the bus that would take them close to Newsham Drive, where the Molyneux family lived. The evening was cloudy but reasonably warm.

They were among the first to arrive, and their coats were taken from them and carried upstairs to one of the bedrooms by Milly, who was a close friend of Eliza and another of Alfie's godmothers. She had twins, Mary and John, who were two years older than Alfie.

Alfie's younger sister Beth was helping her mother in the kitchen, where Alfie was snaffling sausage rolls from a tray for him and Jay to take to the back garden, and asked Olive and Joanna to follow them. Flora was talking with Amelia, who was a writer of romantic fiction, and they had gone into the sitting room.

Olive and Joanna sat on a garden bench and gazed at Jay. Alfie had returned to the house.

'Well?' said Olive, her arms folded across her chest. 'Although we know most of it from reading your dad's and Joe's letters.'

'Then you are aware that Joe's had a tough time. His wife and son were killed in an automobile accident. Joe wasn't with them because he had an appointment he couldn't miss. He has an eye problem and could be blind by fall. He'd like to see you both before that happens.'

'Why does he want to see me?' asked Joanna.

Jay glanced at Olive. 'Pa told him he had a daughter, because Joe was so down, almost suicidal.'

'Josh gave me his promise not to do so.' Olive paused. 'Joe deceived me.'

'But he had a right to know about me,' said Joanna, pressing both hands hard against her cheeks. 'You deceived me and Theo.'

'Theo and I married for convenience.' Olive gulped. 'He was trying to get over a love affair that went wrong.'

'You should have told me earlier,' Joanna whispered, shifting a foot or more away from Olive.

'I thought you'd hate me,' croaked Olive.

'I'll leave you two to talk,' said Jay quietly.

'What's the point of that?' snapped Joanna. 'You know all there is to know. So how am I going to see Joe before he goes blind?'

'Your father gave me the money for your fare,' said Jay, producing a wad of banknotes. 'If your mom wants to come, she'll have to pay towards her own fare. Joe's not loaded.'

'Just like that,' said Joanna, glancing at her mother.

Jay looked embarrassed. 'Joe hasn't had a proper job for years. My pa's lending him the money and would help you out with money when you're there as he's played a part in this whole affair. He'll be disappointed… He was looking forward to seeing you.'

'I can't go. I've just bought a house. Why couldn't he have come here?'

'Have a heart,' said Jay, having made no move to leave them alone. 'Joe's not fit.'

'My mother is old and recently widowed,' said Olive.

'I see. So, you don't care about Joe,' said Jay.

'I didn't say that,' said Olive. 'It's Joanna who wants to meet him, but I'm worried about her going without me all that way, and about the gun laws in America.'

'Have you finished, you three?' interrupted Alfie, standing in the kitchen doorway. 'It's my birthday party, remember.'

'Sorry,' said Jay, his expression brightening. 'Coming! I hope you've saved us some grub.'

'We'd better go inside as well,' said Joanna. 'Although, I thought we'd come to a decision, Mam.'

Olive followed her daughter into the kitchen. 'I had.'

'You've shocked and confused me,' added Joanna angrily.

Eliza gazed at Olive and Joanna as she placed vol-au-vents on a plate. 'Did Jay tell you where he and Alfie went today?'

A loud buzz of conversation as well as the music of the Everly Brothers singing 'Wake Up Little Susie' could be heard coming from the sitting room.

'No,' replied Joanna. 'Where did they go?'

'They climbed Snowdon,' said Eliza. 'Jay does a fair amount of trekking back home, apparently, and Snowdon was a mountain Alfie wanted to conquer on his birthday.'

'Good on him,' said Joanna, 'It's a wonder Jay didn't join the marines instead of the air force.'

'We'd better go and find Mam,' said Olive.

'You don't have to worry about her. She's talking to Amelia,' said Eliza.

'Even so, she'll be wanting to know how we got on with Jay,' said Olive.

'She asked me how long he'd been here,' said Eliza, offering them a vol-au-vent. 'I told her a while, but as she'd just been widowed, I thought it best if Jay just posted the letter to you. I remember his father well. Nice chap.'

'You could have written to me,' said Olive, biting savagely into the vol-au-vent. 'Gosh, that tastes good.'

'I thought I'd see you at the funeral,' said Eliza.

'I didn't know about it. I hadn't even been told Dad was ill,' said Olive, tears welling in her eyes.

Eliza placed her free hand on Olive's arm. 'We all thought your mam would write to you.'

'She said that Dad didn't want me to know he was ill, that he didn't want me upset.'

'It could be true,' said Eliza.

'You'd have thought she'd have wanted me with her to help her with the arrangements.' Olive wiped her eyes with a scrap of cambric. 'Anyway, it's too late now. Let's go and join the party.'

The young ones were bopping, and most of the older guests were huddled in groups chatting. Just then Eliza led a man to where Olive was talking to Milly and Jack.

'Here's Alan, here to pick up George.' She paused. 'Alan, you remember Olive, don't you?'

Alan's eyes surveyed Olive's face. 'Not the Olive who gave up on me after two dates?' he said.

She flushed. 'You had all the girls chasing you. You didn't need me.'

'But you were the one that I wanted,' he responded.

She shrugged. 'I heard you'd married.'

'I hear you're divorced,' he said as the others moved away.

'Marriage isn't for everyone,' she commented, wondering who had told him that. 'I believe you have a son.'

'George,' he said. 'He and Alfie go to the same school.'

'He must be a bright lad.'

Alan nodded. 'He's a good lad. He's going to go on to a technical college. He's going to be an engineer.'

'Good for him.'

'I'm not going to have him ending up in a dead-end job like me.'

'There's been a war. Life was different when we were young. I heard you ended up volunteering for the army.'

He nodded. 'Joined up with one of me mates. He was blown up on D-Day.'

'Sad.'

'Unlucky! Just like my wife, Dot. She was killed in the Blitz.'

'Your son survived, though.'

Alan nodded. 'The grandparents all wanted him, so I had to sort it out when I was demobbed and home for good.'

'That must have been difficult,' said Olive.

'Eventually I decided George and me would have our own place, and I managed to get us a prefab in Sheil Park.'

'Lucky you,' she said. Then she noticed her mother looking their way, so she excused herself.

Flora said, 'Who's that bloke you were talking to?'

'He worked in munitions and then went in the army.'

'So, what's he doing now?'

'His wife was killed in the Blitz, leaving a son, and Alan lives with him in a prefab.'

'I'd love to see inside his prefab,' said Flora. 'Perhaps you could ask him.'

'You have a house. The Corpie aren't going to give you one. They're more likely to ask you to take in a lodger.'

'I've already got you and Joanna,' said Flora. 'I could make more money if you two moved out.'

'You know I've got my own place,' said Olive, standing up. 'Do you want me to bring you something to eat?'

'You do that while I think,' said Flora. 'Then you can tell me what the Yank had to say.'

Olive left her mother sitting and staring in Alan's direction and wondered what she was plotting. She tried to keep her eye on her, but it was busy at the buffet table. When she returned, it was to find Joanna sitting with her and sharing the food on her plate.

'So, is it true what she's told me?' demanded Flora. 'She's not Theo's daughter but a Yank's, who wants the pair of you to go and join him in California?'

'I'm sure I've already told you, Mam. Joe wants to see his daughter,' said Olive. 'I'm not going.'

'You should be ashamed of yourself,' said her mother.

'That comment is why I never told you,' said Olive. 'Keep your voice down.'

'Kept it from your dad and tricked Theo into marrying you.'

'He's no saint,' said Olive.

'And you're a slut and have no taste in men,' sneered her mother.

'Nan,' whispered Joanna. 'There was a war on. Mam wasn't the only one, I bet.'

'Trust you to stick up for her! And who's looked after you, providing you with a roof over your head and food in your tummy?'

'Granddad and Theo,' said Joanna. 'Anyway, you won't have to put up with me much longer. I'm off to America. My natural dad is going blind and wants to see me.'

'He just wants to use you, and Theo wanted a son. He only put up with you.'

'Enough, Mother!' said Olive.

'I want to leave,' said Flora, as Joanna moved away from her. 'I've had enough of this racket. Give me the old tunes, any day!'

'It's all right by me if you want to go home now, but Joanna and I will stay a bit longer. I'll call you a taxi.'

'You could come with me and leave Joanna here. She's young and enjoys this racket.'

'I don't fancy her making her own way late at night and I wanted to have a good chat with Eliza.'

'I bet you told her,' the old woman sniffed.

'Well, you wouldn't win your bet. I didn't. Do you want me to call a taxi?'

Flora's lips tightened and she remained silent for several minutes before saying, 'I don't want to go home on my own, even in a taxi. I want to go with you.'

'I'll see what Joanna has to say.' Olive turned away and went over to her daughter and repeated the conversation to her.

'We'd better go with her or she'll have a worse face on her.'

So, they gave their apologies and left in a taxi, and made the journey in silence.

As soon as the taxi drew up outside the house and the driver opened the rear door on Flora's side, she hurried up the step and into the house. She would have slammed the door behind her if Joanna had not been too swift for her and let in the bedraggled dog huddling in a corner.

Olive followed her daughter and mother as quickly as she could, after standing in the rain on the pavement while paying the driver.

When she entered the living room, the dog was curled up in front of the low burning fire and her mother swore. 'I believe you don't want us here, Mam,' said Olive, removing her sodden hat.

'Go, the pair of you, and don't come back!' Flora stood up and kicked the dog that had sneaked in from the rain.

'Nan, you wicked witch,' cried Joanna, picking up the dog.

'Don't you call me names,' roared Flora. 'I won't soil my lips naming what you are.'

'Let's go to bed,' said Olive, ushering her daughter before her and up the stairs.

They went into Olive's bedroom and Joanna snuggled beneath the bedcovers, putting the dog on top of the coverlet. Mother and daughter were trembling, their teeth chattering. Olive patted Joanna's back. Gradually, both quietened and fell asleep.

CHAPTER SIX

Olive woke up feeling confused because she had been dreaming that she was in a tree-lined street and could spot Joanna hiding behind a tree. And across the road was a man concealed behind another tree with a gun. And further along another man with a rifle. Horror had seized her, and she tore herself out of the dream and fell onto the floor, clutching the dog, which licked her hand. She crawled across the floor and let the dog out.

Olive decided she needed fresh air and a walk. The nightmare was still on her mind; all was quiet in the house and the rain had stopped, and the air smelt fresh. She put on her coat and hat. The dog had disappeared. She walked until she reached the main road, then turned right and continued to walk, unaware of where she was and how far she had walked. She was unheeding of her surroundings, but aware the sky was brightening.

She looked about her and realised she was in Walton and could see the steeple of St Mary's Church on the hill. Across the road she could make out a policeman. She thought she recognised Eliza's husband and called his name as she began to cross the road.

He called, 'Olive! What are you doing here at this time of the morning? And look where you're going. There's a cyclist coming. Get back onto the pavement.'

She looked about her and watched a cyclist pass along the main road from the safety of the pavement. She stood, waiting for a break in the traffic. Then she heard a rumbling noise and a warning shout, and something hit the back of one of her ankles and she fell. Shocked and hurt, she struggled to get up, searching for something to lean on, and then she caught sight of a worried young face who said, 'Sorry, missus, it just ran away with me, and I lost control.'

'Out the way, lad,' said a familiar male voice.

Two strong hands gripped her shoulders and carefully lifted her, freeing her from the steering cart with the help of two schoolboys, one of whom had hold of the rope attached to it. The other was shaking as he stared at the policeman. 'I didn't mean it, sir,' he said.

Olive noticed the hole in the navy-blue hand-knitted jumper and felt sorry for him. 'I'm sure you didn't,' she said, a tremor in her voice. She was aware several people had gathered.

'Dangerous things,' said a quavering voice belonging to an old woman in a black astrakhan coat and a headscarf, carrying a paper-wrapped loaf of bread.

'Fun, though,' said a couple of men in working clothes and boots.

'Clear the way now,' said Jack, having managed to get Olive upright. She gazed into his exasperated face as the gathering slowly moved aside and he lowered her onto a wall and carefully removed her shoe and bloodstained ankle sock. She winced and said, 'It doesn't hurt too much. I don't need to go to the hospital. I can just go home.' She felt herself slipping and seized the pocket of his jacket.

He sighed. 'I'll decide that when I get you into the back of the police car. You can lie down, and I can get a proper look at the injury.' He hoisted her higher and looked for the two schoolboys. 'Your hides need tanning, but I haven't time now. Write down your names and addresses and I'll make sure the local bobby visits your dads.' He handed them a small notebook and a pencil.

'I haven't got a dad,' said the smaller boy, who had apologised. 'He was killed in the war.'

'It wasn't my fault,' put in the larger boy. 'You took my steery without asking.'

'You gave Jerry a turn.'

'He's me mate and older than you. You stole it.'

'He's me brother and left it on the pavement outside our house.'

'Enough!' said Jack, placing a hand on the steering cart. 'I'm confiscating this.'

The owner protested. 'That's stealing.'

Jack said, 'Don't be hard-faced. I'll leave it at the local police station where it can be picked up by a parent. Now, write your names and addresses and beat it.' He held out a hand. The smaller lad gave him a paper from the notebook then shot off as quick as a flash, while the other boy sulkily threw the notebook in Jack's direction, but it fluttered downwards. Olive managed to catch it before it landed in the gutter.

She handed it to Jack and asked, 'What are you doing here?'

'I've been to Walton gaol to talk to a prisoner. It took longer than I'd reckoned on.' He paused. 'Anyway, let's get across the road. The quickest way would be for you to get in the steering cart and I pull it.'

She smiled. 'You are joking?'

'No, I can put it in the boot and drop it off at the local police station.'

'It'll take time. Eliza will be worrying about you,' said Olive, accepting his help into the steering cart and clinging on while avoiding the stares of passers-by as they hurried across the road.

When they reached the other side of the road, he helped her into the back of the police car and placed the steering cart into the boot. It did not take them long to reach the local police station.

'I'll phone Eliza from inside the station. You're best waiting here,' said Jack. 'Then I'm taking you to the hospital. Your wound could go putrid if not treated properly. I'll take you home. I need to talk to you, anyway.'

She sighed and watched him enter the station with the steering cart, wondering how much he would tell the policemen inside about what had happened. He was back in a quarter of an hour.

Once he had made himself comfortable and started the engine, she asked him, 'Did you tell them about wheeling me across the road in the steery?'

'They said I was no gentleman, but I told them you were a good sport and saw the funny side of it and waved to people as if you were the Queen.' He grinned.

'Fibber!' she said, smiling. 'Did you phone Eliza?'

'She sends her love and prays you'll get better swiftly.' He took a deep breath. 'Jay told me about your conversation at the party.'

'I see.' She hesitated. 'What do you think of the American gun laws, Jack?'

'Jay didn't talk about them?'

'No, but I worry about them. I had a nightmare last night.'

He shook his head. 'You've watched too many Westerns and gangster films.'

She let out a long breath. 'You're most likely right. Even so, one hears bad things. I'm asking myself whether I should allow Joanna to go all the way to California without me. Innocent people can be caught up in the crossfire.'

'You should talk to Jay,' said Jack. 'I gather he and Alfie did mention to you that they climbed Snowdon yesterday. It's been an ambition of Alfie's for a while, and Jay enjoys mountain climbing and does a fair bit of it back home.'

Olive pondered on his words and then said, 'Are you telling me that you and Eliza are allowing Alfie to go to America with Jay to climb mountains? Don't they have mountain lions and poisonous snakes?'

'I believe so, and no doubt Jay will carry a Bowie knife and a gun. Jay has lots of common sense and has been in the forces, and Alfie is not a child. They'll look after Joanna better than you can if you were able to go with them. Talk to Joanna. I hear that her father is an American soldier, and he wants to see her before he goes blind.'

'Who told you?' she murmured, her heart seeming to turn over.

After he pulled up outside Walton hospital, he said, 'I did wonder when Josh appeared at our wedding, and you married Theo so soon after, and then Joanna arrived early...' He gave her a sidelong glance. 'But you'd be better staying home after your accident.'

Olive wondered if Eliza had thought the same in both cases. If so, she could have spoken to her about it – or was it possible Josh had told Eliza? She felt a spurt of anger. But no, surely he wouldn't have, despite the family keeping in touch and a friendship developing between Alfie and Jay, and the latter turning up on their doorstep with Josh's and Joe's letters for her.

'I should have told Eliza at the time, but I was ashamed and trusted Josh to keep my secret. We were friends.'

'I believe that Josh is truly fond of you,' said Jack. 'I'm not so sure of this Joe.'

'But Josh was married, and he told me so from our first meeting at the Grafton. You're thinking it was just a physical attraction between Joe and me, and that was partly true, and he made a play for me. Josh was just friendly, and we talked a lot. But as I knew he was married there was no smooching. Not knowing Joe was married, I let him closer.' She glanced out of the window and reached for her handbag and her shoes, with her ankle socks stuffed inside. 'Anyway, enough said. Let's get into the hospital.'

Jack helped her out of the car and into the hospital and was told at Reception to grab a wheelchair from nearby and follow the sign to A&E. Fortunately, it was not crowded and a nurse attended to her without much delay. She cleaned the wound and smothered it with an antibiotic cream; then she bandaged her heel and ankle, before producing a special shoe of leather and canvas that not only protected and supported her ankle, but also her foot and leg that had been jarred on impact. Olive was prescribed a few pills so the discomfort and pain would not keep her awake. She was advised to visit her GP regularly so he could keep his eye on how the healing progressed.

It was Jack who thought of asking whether she could borrow a wheelchair, only to be told there was a shortage so she could borrow one for a week and then she would have to make do with crutches that she could pick up when the wheelchair was returned; although Jack was handed a pair of crutches and was told that they could come in handy in the early days for getting up and down stairs and steps.

After exchanging thanks and goodbyes, Jack and Olive left the hospital, and they discovered the truth of coping with steps with a wheelchair. Once they reached the car, the wheelchair was folded up and placed in the boot, as soon as Olive was settled in the back seat with the crutches lying behind her on the sill of the back window.

CHAPTER SEVEN

When they arrived at her mother's house, it was to find Joanna alone. Her first words to Olive were, 'What were you thinking of, going out so early in the morning?' She seized Olive's arm and added, 'Were you hurt that bad you need crutches?'

'I have a wheelchair as well but it's in the boot,' answered Olive.

Joanna stared at Jack. 'Did she go all the way back to your house? It's nearly lunchtime and Nan's gone missing.'

'Did she say where?' asked Olive. 'We've been to the hospital. Is there any lunch? We're starving. Jack's been out longer than I have. He needs to phone Eliza again.' Jack had already picked up the receiver and dialled.

Olive stepped back, not wanting to appear to be listening. The conversation seemed to be going backwards and forwards, and he was frowning.

'What's wrong?' she asked.

'Alan is at our house with George. He suggested that—'

'Are Jay and Alfie there?' interrupted Olive.

Jack lifted the receiver to his ear again and listened. 'They all want to come and see you. Alan says he'll bring them.'

'Why?' Olive gasped, taken aback. 'I'm worn out. I don't mind seeing Eliza and the boys, but that's all. I want to speak to them. Why on earth does Alan want to come?'

'Your mother was talking to him at the party,' said Jack.

'Oh Lord,' said Olive. 'What's she said to him?'

'I'd better check the biscuit tin,' interjected Joanna. 'And the milk.'

'Stop worrying,' said Jack. 'I'd be more concerned about where your mother is. I'd have thought she'd be here, knowing you were out of the house so early in the morning.'

'Nan is annoyed with me and Mam,' said Joanna. 'She's probably gone to have a moan with one of her old cronies and stayed for lunch.'

'Do they live far?' asked Jack.

'She hasn't kept in touch with any friends from the old days since her brother was killed,' said Olive.

'What about your brother and his wife?' asked Jack.

'She and Pete's wife can't stand each other,' said Olive.

'It's sad,' said Jack. 'Families should support each other.'

'Mam was different before her brother was killed.' Olive sighed.

'What about your father's relatives?' asked Jack.

'His brothers and sisters were very clannish, and she felt an outsider,' said Olive. 'I heard her accusing him one day of caring about them, especially his younger sister, more than her. Saying he slipped her money whenever she came to him with a sob story of her husband keeping her short by spending half the housekeeping going to the pub.'

Jack shifted uncomfortably. 'Maybe your mother felt the sister got money she should have had.'

Olive shrugged. 'It says in the Bible that money is the root of all evil.'

'No, it doesn't,' said Joanna. 'It says the love of money is the root of all evil. Which is a different thing all together.'

'Whatever,' said Olive. 'Dad was always careful with money but not tight.'

'Let's change the subject,' said Jack. 'I presume your mother is cross with the pair of you because of the trip to America to see Joe?'

Mother and daughter nodded. 'But things will change now,' said Olive. 'Don't put the phone down, Jack. I want to talk to Eliza and for her to pass on messages to Jay and Alfie, as well as Alan.'

'I can guess why,' he said, handing her the receiver.

'Hi, Eliza,' she said. 'Sorry, I can't cope with visitors today, I'm whacked. Besides, Jack needs to go home now, as he's exhausted. I'll take a taxi on Monday morning to drop in on my sister-in-law and then go on to yours. I'll be bringing Joanna with me, and we'll want to talk with Alfie and Jay. Could you also ask Alan if I could call in to see his bungalow on Monday evening if it's convenient?'

'Fine,' said Eliza, 'See you then.' The phone went dead.

Olive turned and gazed at her daughter and Jack, who was putting on his cap.

'I'll see you out,' she said.

'See you Monday, then,' he called as he left the house, but as he reached the front gate, he said something else she couldn't make out.

Joanna was bent over by the front door, stroking the stray dog. Olive said, 'Did you catch what he said?'

Joanna straightened up with the dog in her arms. 'Something about Josh's wife being Joe's cousin. It means me and him are related.' She rubbed her chin against the dog's head. 'Are you going in, Mam? I thought you were hungry and, besides, you need to get off that leg and rest.'

'I'm resting against the doorjamb.' She shivered and accidently shoved the door open with her shoulder and one of her crutches slithered on the doormat inside.

Joanna moved swiftly and the dog jumped from her arms. She made a grab for her mother's sleeve, managing to save her from falling over the dog. Olive gasped and burst into tears as her daughter placed an arm around her waist and drew her against her. 'Don't cry, Mam. We've got each other.'

'Let's get into the kitchen,' sniffled Olive. 'You're right. I need to get off my feet.'

Swifter than she imagined, Joanna half-carried her mother to the sofa and lay her carefully down, placing a cushion beneath her feet and another beneath her head.

Breathing heavily, Joanna said, 'Cup of tea or coffee, Mam?'

'You sit down, love, and get your breath back. I can wait.'

Joanna sat on a chair and after a few minutes said, 'So, what happened, Mam? How did you fall and how did Uncle Jack find you? Why did you go out so early?'

'I needed to think and wanted some fresh air, so I just walked and walked until I came to my senses and realised I was in Walton. I saw a policeman across the road and recognised Jack. I called him and started crossing the road, but he shouted to get back on the pavement because a cyclist was coming, so I did. Then I heard a rumbling and a warning shout and a nasty pain and whack in my ankle, and I fell.'

'What was it?' Joanna's eyes were wide with astonishment and curiosity.

'A steering cart driven by a schoolboy who looked terrified and was apologetic, even more so when Jack turned up in his police uniform, almost at the same time as the owner of the steering cart. The boys started arguing while Jack inspected my injury and told them to shut up.' A giggle escaped her. 'He told them he was going to confiscate the vehicle, and the owner accused him of being a thief. Jack told him not to be so hard-faced and that the steery was going to the local police station where it could be picked up by their fathers. The younger lad said his father had been killed in the war, then he took off at a rate of knots, determined to escape the bigger boy. By then I was really in pain and Jack insisted on taking me to the hospital, but we needed to cross the main road, so he shoved me in the cart and wheeled me to the police car, where he lifted me into the seat. Then he placed the cart in the boot and took it to the police station, before driving me to the hospital.'

Joanna was laughing by the time her mother finished and had sagged against the cushion. 'I'll make the tea and fetch a meat pie from Sayer's. You must be starving. Hopefully, by then Nan will be back.'

She left after removing Olive's special shoe, at her request, and the bloodied bandage. Blood mingled with ointment, but the wound had almost stopped bleeding. 'Should I put a clean bandage on it straight away, Mam?' she asked.

'No, let the air dry it up,' said Olive. 'And you can bet your nan will want to look at it when she comes in.'

But Flora had still not turned up after Joanna had returned with meat pies and cream cookies. The two women ate them and drank two cups of tea each. Then Olive dozed off and when she woke up on the sofa, covered by a blanket, she saw that it was gone five o'clock and was told by Joanna that her mother was still not home.

She decided to phone her brother. He did not sound surprised to hear that she was at their mother's house, and he wasn't even surprised to hear that she was back in Liverpool for good. But he told her that he had spotted their mother talking to a St John's Ambulance Brigade bloke by Goodison Park football ground, and that he had been at their dad's funeral. 'His name is Dougal Kennedy, and he knew Dad when they were boys.'

Olive felt like hitting the roof. 'Interesting, but why didn't she mention him to me?'

'Ask her when you see her,' he said. 'She's bound to come home sooner rather than later.'

'That's a joke,' she said. 'Anyway, I thought I'd drop in on Monday and see the kids.'

'See you then,' he said. 'Ta-ra!'

Olive told Joanna what Peter had said, and her daughter muttered, 'Bloody hell! What a family! Are you hungry again, Mam? I fancy some chips from the chippie, have chip butties.'

'Okay, I don't mind that. Pass my handbag and I'll give you the money. Get some dandelion and burdock as well.'

A quarter of an hour later, Joanna was back, and they stopped worrying about Flora and put the television on. They enjoyed their chip butties and dandelion and burdock, while talking about the difference between British and American comedy.

It was not until the ten o'clock news was on that they heard a key turn in the front door. They exchanged glances and switched off the news as footsteps approached. Joanna went and put the kettle on and returned in time to see Flora enter the room followed by a man who had a head of pure white hair.

'Where've you been, Nan?' asked Joanna. 'We've been worried about you, being out all this time. And who's this?' she added a few seconds later.

'I think I know who it is,' said Olive. 'Dougal Kennedy, and he was at my father's funeral, which I wasn't told about.'

Dougal glanced at Flora, who had paled. She said, 'I told you she couldn't get away, being in the WRAF. Besides, he didn't want her to know he was seriously ill,' she stammered.

'He would have wanted to see me,' said Olive, tears glistening in her eyes.

Joanna decided to intervene. 'Don't get yourself upset, Mam. Granddad loved you and he mightn't have recognised you at the end. Can we change the subject? Cocoa, Mam? I'd like to know why Mr Kennedy is here now. Perhaps he's heard I'm going off to California to meet me dad with Jay, who I'm sort of related to.'

'Florrie did say that she would have a room spare, and I'm searching for new lodgings,' said Dougal. 'I knew your granddad and Florrie years ago. We lived in the same street. I was told your granddad was ill by your uncle Pete because I used to see him and your granddad, before he took ill, at the match when I was on duty with the St John's Brigade.'

Olive and Joanna pretended to be struck speechless, but that did not last long once Dougal had departed, after that brief introduction.

Flora said, 'You're not going to America travelling unchaperoned at your age. You would end up in trouble like your mother, who looks in trouble again. That's what comes with going out alone so early in the morning to meet a man.'

'You've a dirty mind, Nan,' shouted Joanna. 'Mam had a fall and Jack found her and took her to the hospital in his police car.'

'A likely story! How did he know where to find her? I bet they arranged to meet, and *him* her best friend's husband,' she sneered.

'How dare you, Mam! Dirty dogs know their own tricks. How long have you been meeting the man you've just brought here? And you invited him to Dad's funeral. You must have been seeing him while Dad was ill,' said Olive, a sob in her voice.

'He's a decent and generous man, unlike your father,' Flora screamed. 'You've both got a nerve speaking to me the way you have after all I've done for you.'

'He knew you were married, then,' said Olive. 'And lower your voice. I'm not deaf. I was hurt and you haven't even asked how I am. Instead, you spit out filth and make plans to have your manfriend living under this roof, convinced that me and Joanna would both be going to California, but then you realised, when you noticed my special shoe, that I really had injured myself. I know I'm no saint, but I do pray that you're not making a mistake and he's using you, Mam. At least he was honest with us, saying he… was looking for new lodgings.' Her words came to a faltering finish as she took in the hurt expression on her mother's face. It was then she realised that comments had been expressed that would not be forgotten or forgiven for a long time, if ever. Olive knew that she would not be able to continue living in her mother's house once Joanna left for America; she would make the move she had been dreaming of since she had won on the football pools. 'I'm going to bed,' she said, putting on her shoe and picking up the crutches. 'See you in the morning.'

Joanna followed her a quarter of an hour later, after going down the back yard to the lavatory and saying, 'Good night, Nan, sleep tight.' Beneath her breath, she added, 'I hope the bugs bite.'

She hurried upstairs and knocked on her mother's bedroom door. 'Can I come in?'

'Of course,' Olive answered.

Joanna entered and saw that her mother was already in bed, snuggled beneath the bedcovers. 'I won't stay long. Are you comfortable?'

'Not too bad, but can you get me a drink of water? I need to take a tablet. You'll have to give me a hand sitting up. I don't know what I was thinking of, snuggling down so soon. I haven't even read me Bible notes or finished me library book.'

'I'm sure you know my head is still reeling. I can't wait to get on the ship to America. I just wish you were coming with me.'

'I can't. Not just because I'd be a burden on you, but because I've plans.' Olive felt a spurt of excitement.

'Moving into your house?'

'I can't do that right away,' said Olive. 'I've been thinking further into the future than that. I'd like my own business.'

'Doing what?' asked Joanna excitedly, resting her hands on the wood at the foot of the bed.

'It takes some thinking and you've enough to think about now. Go and fetch me a glass of water like I asked, please? After you sit me up gently.'

Joanna did that and turned the bedcovers up at the end of the bed to check on her mother's foot. She took a spare pillow from the wardrobe and placed it in a position to protect her mother's ankle and heel, before going downstairs as instructed. She was aware of her grandmother approaching as she pushed open her mother's bedroom door with the glass of water.

'Good night again, Nan,' she said.

'Good night,' said her grandmother, leaning against the wall next to the bedroom door. 'Is our Olive comfortable?'

'As can be expected.'

'I could take that water in for you,' said Flora, reaching out for the glass. 'I can have a look at her foot.'

'Why the change of tune, Nan?' Joanna drew the glass out of her reach.

But Flora seized her wrist and twisted, spilling some of the water.

'Stop it, Nan,' cried Joanna. 'You're hurting me.'

'Then let me have the water! I want to help.'

'Stop messing about, Mam,' called Olive. 'Is it that you've remembered what your mother told you? Never let the sun go down upon your wrath?'

'Shame you didn't remember it yourself,' said Flora.

'Enough,' said Joanna, stamping her foot before going into the bedroom and taking the water over to Olive, who took it and swallowed the tablet she'd been holding in her clenched fist.

'Peace,' murmured Olive, dragging the bedcovers over her head. 'Get to bed, the pair of you.'

Nan said, 'Not before I tell you that Dougal's promised he'll be paying me rent.'

'I'm glad to hear it. Now let me sleep.' Olive was asleep in no time.

CHAPTER EIGHT

By the time Olive was roused by Joanna the following morning with a cup of tea, sunshine was flooding the bedroom, she could hear pigeons cooing under the eaves and the sound of church bells, and she realised it was Sunday. It had been a month or so since she had attended morning service, and she was in the mood to have a good sing. Then she felt a stinging in her heel.

'Are you all right, Mam?' asked Joanna, placing a tray on the bedside table.

'My heel and ankle are stinging. What do they look like?' She reached for her cup of tea and cautiously sipped it.

Joanna sat at the bottom of the bed and lifted her mother's leg. Placing her foot on her lap, she slowly unwound the bandage and removed the dressing so she could have a good look at the damage. She wiped away the ointment and traces of blood and was aware of Olive wincing and attempting to withdraw her foot.

'It's barely bleeding, and I should think it'll dry up completely in a day or two if you keep off it, but I'm no nurse.'

Olive sighed. 'You're doing well, love, and I should expect it to hurt still.' She paused and gazed towards the window. 'It's a lovely day.'

'True. And you'd like to go out.' She smiled.

'I'd like to go to church,' said Olive.

'Drink your tea and eat your breakfast.' Joanna handed the bowl of Weetabix to her mother with a spoon and took the teacup from her. 'And if you're good I might be able to help you there.'

'Well, I would need your assistance to get along, even with the crutches,' said Olive, taking a mouthful of food.

Her daughter beamed at her. 'Jack turned up with the wheelchair, but he didn't linger, because I told him you were fast asleep.'

'That's brilliant!' Olive swallowed and placed the breakfast bowl on the tray and clapped her hands. 'Did he set it up?'

'I helped him. He said I'd need to know how to do it.' She frowned. 'Now, if we're to get to church on time, you need to finish your breakfast, have a wash, and dress, and I must put on fresh ointment, dressing and bandage.'

Without any more delay, Joanna fetched all that she needed while Olive gobbled down the rest of her breakfast and threw off the bedcovers. With her daughter's help, she got into a position where she could tend her injury with the least difficulty. Then, after being washed and dried, she dressed and combed her hair. Her special shoe and ordinary one was put on by her daughter, who passed the crutches to her and assisted her out of the bedroom and to the top of the stairs.

'I didn't expect you to be up and dressed,' said Flora from her bedroom doorway. 'I was going to bring you up a cup of tea.'

'I'm going to church, Mam,' said Olive. 'Jack brought the wheelchair, which was in the boot of the police car.'

'So, we'll manage without much trouble,' said Joanna.

Olive noticed her mother's hurt expression and, putting a lid on the anger she still felt over her words and actions, said, 'Do you want to come, Mam? And would you mind carrying one of my crutches until I get downstairs, please?'

'Give us it here,' said Flora, taking the crutch. 'And I don't mind taking a turn pushing you. It's not easy getting a wheelchair on and off pavements. I did a fair amount of it when my dad had to have one of his legs amputated.'

'I didn't know about that,' said Olive, grasping Joanna's elbow. 'Was it because of the First World War?'

'No, it was some medical condition, and he would have died if it hadn't been removed.'

Joanna shivered. 'That's awful.'

'He survived, but it wasn't easy for Mam. She was having twins at the time, and one died. He was Jonathan.'

Olive wondered if the twin who survived was David, and saw her mother in a different light. She remembered when her uncle David had died, and her mother had never been the same since; she even stopped going to church for a while.

'It might do us all good to get out,' said Joanna, taking the first step down sideways and leaning against the wall. Olive tightened her grip on her daughter's elbow and, using the other crutch carefully, she followed her down slowly and reached the bottom of the stairs safely.

'That was a bit scary,' said Joanna. 'I worried a couple of times I might have been going too fast for you, and you'd slip.'

'You'd have stopped me fall,' said Olive, still clinging to her daughter's arm and moving forward out of Flora's way, towards the wheelchair parked in the lobby. Joanna shifted the wheelchair and lifted several coats and hats from hooks on the wall.

'But she could have slipped,' said Flora. 'And you'd have both fallen and hurt yourselves and I'd have had to phone Dougal, who'd know if we needed an ambulance.'

'Why Dougal?' asked Olive, staring at her mother as she took a russet-coloured coat from her granddaughter.

'He knows a lot about first aid and he's picking me up this afternoon. We're going to Southport.'

'Hope you enjoy yourselves,' said Olive, forcing a smile. 'Anyway, nobody fell downstairs. Don't look on the dark side, Mam.' She paused and looked at her daughter. 'Can you help me on with my coat, love?'

Joanna picked up her mother's grass-green coat, which was belted at the waist and then flared out. She helped her on with it and watched as she took from a pocket a dark green beret and placed it at an angle on her copper-coloured hair. Then she shoved a ten-shilling note in her pocket for collection. The girl then slipped on a light pale blue jacket but did not bother with a hat, then helped her mother into the wheelchair as Flora held it steady. Then the front door was opened, and Olive clung to the sides of the seat as her daughter and mother eased it onto the path. Flora closed and locked the front door while Joanna pushed the wheelchair to the front gate and stepped out onto the pavement and headed for the parish church on School Lane. Olive was thinking that perhaps later if the weather was still fine, they could have a walk down by the Leeds Liverpool Canal, if Joanna was in the mood. She felt certain that her mother would choose to go straight back home.

It did not take them long to reach the parish church, despite Flora doing little to help with the wheelchair. A fact that Joanna pointed out. Fortunately, the sidesman on duty helped and asked Olive what she had done to herself, while Flora left them and went to sit down in a pew. Olive was kept talking by members of the congregation who recognised her.

After the service, Flora surprised Olive by saying, 'There was a nice atmosphere in there today. Down to the new vicar perhaps.'

'And the sunshine,' said Joanna. 'The sun coming through the stained-glass windows and painting coloured patterns on the floor was magical. I hope the weather is good when I cross the pond and you go on your cruise, Nan, and Mam moves,' she added.

Olive held her face up to the sun. 'I hope it's like this tomorrow.'

'Money,' muttered Flora. 'All this travelling and moving about costs money.'

'You can't take it with you, Nan,' said Joanna. 'Do you know the Americans call the Atlantic the pond?'

'At least I'm not crossing that, but I'll be close to the Irish Sea when I move,' said Olive.

'But how is it you can afford to move to a bigger house?' asked her mother. 'You've never supported yourself.'

'That's a lie. Anyway, Iris will pay rent,' said Olive. 'And I've got money in the bank.'

'Your dad never left you any money in his will,' said her mother. 'I suppose he sent you a postal order.'

Olive smiled grimly. 'He thought a little more of me than that,' she said.

'What about Joanna?' asked Flora.

'I'll see she won't go short,' said Olive. 'We won't need to cadge from you, Mam. I presume Dad left you all that he had in the bank when he died?'

Her mother's eyes narrowed. 'I should think he did. He was tight-fisted enough when he was alive. Anyway, I won't go short, and I plan to go on a cruise soon. You two have had enough from me so I'm going to spend my nest egg on myself.'

'You've already told us that,' said Olive. 'Good luck to you, Mam. Will you be going alone or with Dougal Kennedy on your cruise?'

'None of your business,' said Nan.

Olive shrugged, wishing her mother had not said what she did about Dad and spoilt things. 'I'll call a taxi and go and visit Eliza tomorrow.'

'What about Alan? Are you going to see his prefab?' asked Flora.

Olive nodded. 'I'm as curious as you are. But I won't be encouraging him to drop by at your house to see me. I'm not looking for another fella.'

Joanna said, 'Can I come with you to Aunt Eliza's? I need to speak to Alfie… and Jay as well, if possible.'

'I thought I said you could come the other evening,' said Olive. 'Do you want me to bring something home for supper tomorrow, Mam?'

'Are you trying to soft-soap me like your father?' said the older woman. 'I can tell you it won't work.'

'It's a treat,' said Olive. 'Be nice!'

'Bitch!' said her mother.

'Woof woof!' Olive could not resist saying, shocked by her mother's further rude behaviour and glad that they were nearly back at the house, having forgotten to suggest going for a walk along the canal. Just as well, because no doubt Joanna was tired, doing all the pushing, so much for her mother giving a hand. 'You're home, Mam! Be happy! It won't be long before you're rid of us, and you have Dougal lodging with you and paying you rent.'

–

Yet when Dougal arrived an hour or so later, Flora was as nice as pie to her daughter and granddaughter in front of him. She spoke of Olive's bravery and Joanna being such a help, the three of them going to church and people making a fuss of them, as well as Olive singing the hymns beautifully.

Dougal offered to have a look at her foot and Olive did not want to appear ungrateful, so welcomed his offer and told him that Joanna had cleaned it that morning and re-dressed it. Joanna said that she would be pleased for him to inspect it, as he was an expert and she was an amateur. She went and fetched all that was necessary.

So, Olive sat on the sofa and placed her foot on a clean towel spread over a pouffe and watched, along with Joanna and Flora, as with clean and gentle hands, Dougal dealt with her injured heel and ankle. She freed a gasp only once, and that caused him to pause for a few seconds before resuming mopping away ointment and a little fresh blood. Then he re-dressed it and suggested a tot of sherry for the patient.

'I don't have any sherry,' said Flora with a shudder. 'Mother didn't hold with strong liquor.'

'I have a bottle of sherry upstairs in the bottom of the wardrobe,' said Olive. 'I was given it as a farewell present when I left the WRAFs. I've hardly touched it. I had a tot when I heard that Dad had passed away.'

'I'll go and get it, shall I?' suggested Joanna.

Olive nodded and her daughter left the room.

'Is giving Olive strong drink a good idea?' murmured Flora, glancing at Dougal.

'A tot isn't much, and she will enjoy it, and it will help with the pain,' he said. 'It's not as if she's a drunken football hooligan.'

'No, of course not,' said Flora. 'I beg your pardon. I'll go and put the kettle on.'

'I'll enjoy a cup of tea,' he said, as he dried his hands on a towel, after having washed them again.

'You're not having a drink of sherry?' she asked.

'No, I enjoy the odd tot of Irish whiskey and a couple of pints of beer with family and friends, but that's all.' He unrolled his shirt sleeves and took Flora's hand. 'What about us having that cup of tea and then heading off to Southport and leaving the girls to watch a film on the telly in peace.' He kissed her lightly on the lips.

Olive guessed he had forgotten she was there, but she found herself thinking the better of him and remained silent until Joanna bounced into the room, clutching the bottle of Bristol Cream sherry. Olive asked her to get four small glasses and pour half a glass for Joanna herself.

Immediately, Flora spoke up. 'She's underage and should not drink strong drink.'

'It's only a couple of mouthfuls,' said Olive. 'Scarcely more than she would drink of red wine at Holy Communion – and did you know, Mam, in the olden days most people, including children, drank ale because water could make you ill or even kill you.'

'Moderation in everything,' said Joanna, 'including food.' She opened the sherry bottle and poured a small amount of the tawny liquid into two glasses, before lifting the bottle in a salute to Dougal and Flora, who shook her head. 'I signed the pledge when I was twelve.'

'I didn't,' said Dougal. 'But I'll do without, lass. I'm having tea, which didn't become popular in Britain until the seventeenth century, when it was brought by the East India Company from India or China. It was very expensive at first and only the rich could afford it. Charles the Second's wife, who was a Portuguese princess, introduced it to the ladies of the court.'

'You are clever, Dougal,' said Flora, beaming at him and rising to her feet. 'I'll go and pour out our tea.'

Olive said, 'I knew about the East India Company but not about the Portuguese Catherine of Braganza introducing teatime to England.'

'Tea never seemed to catch on the same in America,' said Joanna. 'I'll ask Jay how come they prefer coffee, when I see him tomorrow.'

'I'd like to go with you both tomorrow,' said Flora. 'I'd like to see Alan's prefab for myself.'

'Did he ask you, Mam?' asked Olive, and she took a sip of her sherry and smacked her lips. 'That's lovely that. Just what the doctor ordered.'

'I doubt it,' said her mother. 'Especially not with sleeping tablets.'

'That was hours ago,' said Joanna. 'And Mam only had one, with plenty of water.'

'And I don't intend taking one tonight,' added Olive. 'I know not to and, besides, I want to get up early, as I'm going to see Eliza.'

'Spending money on a taxi,' muttered Flora, topping up her tea.

'It's my money, and I'm going to drop in at our Peter's too and see Eleanor and the kids on the way to Eliza's. I'm not seeing the prefab until evening.'

Flora pulled a face. 'You could phone him and ask if I could come as well.'

'I don't want to. I have a life of my own. I don't know what time I'll get there, and you don't know where it is.'

'You could pay for a taxi for me, seeing as you can afford to buy your own house.' Flora glanced at Dougal. 'Wouldn't you agree?'

He gazed into his teacup. 'I'd like another hot cup of tea and after that I think we should make a move if we're going to Southport.' He stood up and made as if to go to the back kitchen.

Flora scrambled to her feet and went over to him to take the cup from his hand. 'I'll do it. You sit down.' He stared at her for several minutes, before returning to his chair and making himself comfortable.

'Are you going to have a ride on the big dipper?' asked Joanna.

'I might, but it'll be a miracle if I can persuade your nan to join me. She'd never go on it with your granddad and me when we were kids. She feared heights. She liked the waltzer, and the merry go-round and she was a dab hand at the coconut shy.'

'What about the haunted house and the helter-skelter?' asked Olive.

'She would pay for her brother David to go on the helter-skelter. She said she was too old for it. He liked the haunted house, but she didn't. Your dad and me would pay for him and take him inside while she was trying to win a prize on the hook-a-duck. He was a good kid, was David, but she'd never leave him alone.'

'Did you have any brothers and sisters?' asked Joanna.

'Too many,' said Dougal. 'Mam loved babies but then they started coming in twos – that was number five and six. Dad said we couldn't afford any more and went off somewhere without telling us where he'd gone, leaving me and Mam to look after the young ones.'

'That wasn't fair of him,' said Olive. 'How did you and your mam manage?'

'He sent me money once a month, saying he had left Liverpool and found himself a better paid job, but wouldn't be coming back.'

'So, did you give the money to your mam?' said Joanna.

Dougal said, 'I gave her a certain sum a week and asked our Bridget to make a shopping list.'

'I take it from that your mam wasn't a good manager,' said Joanna.

'She'd got herself in debt several times.'

'Where's your mam and brothers and sisters now?' asked Joanna.

'Don't be nosey,' said Olive.

'I don't mind,' Dougal said. 'They live in Ireland with Mam's sister and family. Don't talk about it to your mam, though. She couldn't stand our Bridget, because your uncle David fancied her, and she caught them kissing once.'

The subject was dropped when there was the rattle of cups and the sound of footsteps, and Flora entered the room. Soon after, Dougal and Flora left the house.

–

'Phew!' exclaimed Joanna. 'Imagine having six kids.'

'Giving birth to one was enough for me.'

83

'So, is there anything in particular you want to do this afternoon?' asked Joanna. 'Or shall we do what Dougal suggested and watch a film, if there's a decent one? I know it's a lovely day, but we will be going out tomorrow.'

'Agreed,' said Olive. 'I nearly passed out when Mam suggested my asking Alan could she come with me.'

'She needs to watch what she says when in Dougal's company or she could lose him.' Joanna rolled her eyes.

'Let's change the subject and have a look what's on telly,' said Olive, picking up the Sunday newspaper and turning the pages. Then she stopped and read out loud, 'You have two choices; *The Hound of the Baskervilles* with Basil Rathbone or *Rob Roy* with Richard Todd, which is a Walt Disney film.' Olive added, 'I like Sherlock Holmes.'

'I've seen it before,' said Joanna. 'Let's see what the reviewer says about the Walt Disney film.' She took the newspaper and checked channels and times. 'We could watch one of them and part of the other.' So they watched the whole of *Rob Roy* and the latter part of *The Hound of the Baskervilles* on the other channel.

CHAPTER NINE

The following morning Olive and Joanna wasted no time leaving the house as soon as the taxi was outside. They were arm in arm and Olive managed to make as little noise as possible with her crutches. Her mother had the front bedroom, and they did not want to wake her and have her make a fuss. Joanna had taken tea and toast up and left it on the bedside table by her radio, not expecting the radio to switch on the alarm, nor had she expected the milkman and the taxi driver to have a talk on the front step loud enough to cause Flora to come to the window, throw up the sash and shout down for them to shut up. The two men got on with their jobs just as Joanna was helping Olive clamber into the cab. Flora shouted down at her daughter and granddaughter, swearing and shaking her fist at them.

'She's making a show of us,' said Joanna, even as the taxi driver closed the door.

'Don't let it worry you, girls. The milkman was telling me that a neighbour said she's got herself a fella. Got plenty of dosh tucked away, has she?' asked the driver.

'She's going to spend it on a cruise,' said Olive. 'We're off to visit a friend.' She gave him the address, then settled back as comfortably as possible.

'We won't have to put up with it much longer,' whispered Joanna, snuggling up to her mother.

'We do owe her, though, for what she has done for us in the past,' said Olive in an undertone.

'Yeah!' Joanna sighed. 'But she made me work for every mouthful.'

'It's been a long time coming but she's got what she wanted now.' Olive paused and whispered, 'She never loved Dad. She only ever cared for her brother who died. Let's pray she finds some contentment with Dougal, if she behaves herself.'

'She'll need a lot of prayer,' murmured Joanna.

They both fell silent and then Olive suddenly remembered she was meant to be visiting Peter's before Eliza's, but if she did that, she wouldn't see him because he'd be at work. She would have to alter her plans and go straight to Eliza. Having made that decision, she closed her eyes and tried to relax.

Within half an hour the taxi pulled up outside the house in Newsham Drive and, as soon as the driver stepped out, Eliza appeared at the front door and hurried to greet them and provide a helping hand.

She and Joanna took one side of Olive each, once she had paid the driver, and helped her into the house.

Eliza was pleased to see them and put the kettle on immediately. Once they were seated and drinking tea and eating freshly baked fairy cakes, Eliza asked, 'How are you, Olive? Is there anything I can do for you?'

'I wanted to see Alfie and Jay,' said Joanna. 'But they don't seem to be here.'

'And I want to use your phone if that's okay?' said Olive.

'Fine. Is your mam's out of order?' asked Eliza, topping up their tea.

'No, but I don't want her listening in.'

'We've had a row,' said Joanna, reaching for a fairy cake. 'What's it over?'

'A man, to start with. And she's planning on giving him my room,' said Joanna.

'He can have mine,' said Olive, 'now I've bought a place of my own.'

'Bought!' exclaimed Eliza. 'What with?'

'I've money in the bank,' Olive chuckled.

'Tell her, Mam. She's your best friend.'

Olive said, 'I took Dad's advice and Lady Fortune smiled on me better than she did in my love life. Anyway, I wanted a house with at least four bedrooms, a bathroom, a decent-sized garden, a large kitchen, and a dining room and living room.'

'You must have a lot saved,' said Eliza. 'Houses that size cost more than a few bob.'

'I know.' Olive beamed. 'I'd love a house the same as yours, but I doubt I could afford it.'

Joanna said, 'George and his dad live in a prefab rented from Liverpool's Corporation in Sheil Park.' She paused. 'He says that although they might appear small from the outside, they have all mod cons and a garden, two bedrooms, a bathroom, a decent-sized kitchen and a living room.'

'There'll be a waiting list for them,' said Eliza. 'You must know there's still a shortage of houses since the war.'

'I've heard about it,' said Olive.

'Your friend Iris will be made up with you taking her in as a lodger, Mam,' said Joanna.

'Tell me about Iris,' said Eliza.

Olive told her briefly but omitted the plan she had for Iris. Instead, she swiftly moved on to ask Joanna if she was going to stay and wait for Alfie to return.

'He's gone downtown,' said Eliza. 'He's meeting Jay and going to the outdoor shop to buy some clothes and equipment, despite Jay telling him he'd get them cheaper in America and without the bother of taking what he buys all that way, but there's no telling my son. The thing is that he has money of his own from his shares in the Jones family slating business.'

'He can probably borrow what he needs when he gets there,' said Olive.

'Jay said the same, but Alfie wants his own and to buy British.' Eliza sighed. 'He's very patriotic.'

'I wonder what Josh thinks of Alfie going out there,' said Olive. 'I must write to him and tell him I'm not coming. If I was going, I'd tear a strip off him for breaking his promise to me. I would like to do so face to face but I need all the money I've got left.'

'What promise was that, Mam?' asked Joanna.

'Never mind,' said Olive. 'It's done now and most likely he thought he was doing the right thing.'

'Maybe he'll come back over here again one day,' said Joanna. 'Jay said they have kin in Ireland. He was going to go over with Mary, Milly's daughter, at Easter when she visited her gran in Dublin.'

'But he didn't go, since he changed his plans and decided to go home earlier with you and Alfie,' said Eliza. 'Anyway, he would have had to rush his visit.'

'So, what are you going to do now, Joanna?' asked Olive.

'I could take the dog for a walk in the park,' she offered.

'If you don't mind, you could take Beth with you,' said Eliza. 'The outing would do her good. She's been stuck in too long with measles and she's no longer infectious.'

'Fine, I'll enjoy her company,' said Joanna, although if truth be told, she'd enjoy Alfie's more.

Once Beth and the dog were ready, they crossed the road outside to Newsham Park. 'Now we can have a good chat without big ears listening in,' said Eliza. 'So, tell me truthfully how you feel about missing out on going to America and seeing Joe after all this time?' she asked, offering another fairy cake.

'Relieved,' replied Olive. 'I have no desire to meet up with Joe, but I can understand Joanna wanting to meet him, and if he is willing to support her through university, I'd be pleased. He owes her that much.'

'Has Alan coming back into your life changed your feelings towards Joe?' asked Eliza with a twinkle.

'No, and that's all I'm saying,' retorted Olive, biting into the fairy cake. 'I just hope that Joanna doesn't fall for any fellas in America. I want her home.'

'I feel the same about Alfie,' said Eliza. 'Although, I can't see him wanting to leave his position in the slate company over here.'

'How d'you think he feels about Mary?'

'He's known her since he was a baby and she's older than him. Besides, I think she fancies George.'

Olive stretched and yawned. 'Well, we can't live our children's lives for them. Besides, I made a bit of a mess of my own. Not that I'd do without my daughter, and I look forward to being a grandmother.'

'Me too,' said Eliza, 'but I'm in no hurry.'

'At least we survived the war,' said Olive.

'Anyway, when are you going to phone Alan?'

'What for?' asked Olive.

'To give you a lift to his house,' said Eliza. 'You'll soon run out of bobs if you keep getting taxis.'

89

Olive hesitated and then lifted the receiver. She let it ring for a while and was about to give up when a voice gave Alan's number.

'Alan, this is Olive. Have you a few minutes for us to talk?'

'Sure! What is it you want? Do you need a lift somewhere? If so, it'll have to wait until this evening.'

'That's kind of you, but no, I was wanting to see inside your prefab. Mam was interested in what it was like inside.'

'You're welcome to,' he said warmly. 'But for what reason?'

'I'm moving out of my mother's house, and she's asked me to have a look at your prefab. I wonder if a prefab would be better for her and her man friend. She's finding the stairs a problem.'

'I see. Do you know where I live? It's a bit of a way from your mother's house.'

'I know. Eliza has told me.'

'If you're not doing anything this evening, I could pick you up. I'll come straight from work.'

'Thanks, but I'm at Eliza's,' she replied.

'Good, I'll see you then. Ta-ra!'

'Ta-ra!' Olive put down the phone.

'What are you up to?' asked Eliza.

'I want to see inside the prefab, I was being honest,' said Olive.

'You told him you were here.'

'I thought you wouldn't mind me and Joanna staying on here until this evening. Although I'd like to go into town before then, and you must come with me and then visit the house I've bought. We'll leave the shopping there.'

'All right, I'd like that,' said Eliza.

'I'm going to oversee my life and make my own decisions.'

'So, you don't have it in mind to marry Alan?'

'I don't have it in mind to marry anyone,' said Olive.

'Sad!' Eliza sighed.

'No, it's not. I could change my mind if an exceptional bloke took my fancy.'

'You'll be lucky,' said Eliza. 'Now, how about a look at the back garden?'

'Okay, I'd like to pick your brains.'

Olive enjoyed her turn around the garden and asking the names of various flowers, looking forward to the time when she would arrange her own garden. While she was admiring the shaggy white head of a dahlia, the door at the bottom of the garden opened, and Alfie and Jay entered. Greetings were exchanged and Jay told them that they had been to get tickets for the ship to America. 'I booked one for Joanna for a single cabin. We're sailing a fortnight today, so I hope she has her passport.'

'She had her photo taken weeks ago and we visited the passport office in the Liver Building shortly afterwards,' said Olive. 'I got mine at the same time, although I'm not going with the three of you to America this time around. She'll be glad to have a date because we need to speak to the headmistress. Again. It's mainly about sitting her exams that she's anxious about, and university.'

'Jack thought you wouldn't,' said Jay, not appearing to have heard what Olive said about the headmistress and exams. 'Not with you having an accident and buying a house.'

'You never know,' said Alfie, 'You could go travelling in the future. But you mentioned her headmistress, I hope all will be well there. We'll be away mainly during the summer hols. I should have discussed that with her earlier, only nothing was certain.'

'I understand,' said Olive. 'We should have got a passport for Mam at the same time we did because she told Joanna and I that she was thinking of going on a cruise.'

'Has she said where she fancies going and who with?' asked Eliza. 'What about the man you mentioned?'

Olive shook her head. 'She's being very secretive. Anyway, I hope she enjoys herself. She's made it obvious that it's her dream of a lifetime and she has done enough for us,' she said.

'Joanna could go to Liverpool Uni,' said Alfie. 'She could live with you then and it wouldn't cost so much.'

'She could get a grant if she wanted to go away,' said Eliza.

'Joe should be willing to support her if she decides to stay in California,' said Jay. 'I hear Stanford is a good university.'

'Enough said,' murmured Olive. 'She might change her mind about continuing her studies.'

'True enough,' said Eliza. 'She could want to marry and have children.'

'Don't talk about children. Dougal, Mam's would-be-lodger, is one of six.'

Eliza's mouth fell open. 'What does your mam think of that?' she asked.

'I suspect she doesn't like the family. They're all younger than him. He helped bring them up after the father left, but they've gone with the mother to live in Ireland with their grandmother and some other relatives.'

'Dad's relatives in Ireland are from big families,' said Jay. 'He's determined to go and see some of them this year. Mam says they're common.'

'Has she been to Ireland?' asked Olive.

'No, but some of them came to California for the wedding a few years before I was born, and one family live in New York. I've only met them once.'

Olive said, 'The Irish certainly gets around. Anyway, I'm hungry. Where's the nearest chippie and will you go, Alfie, and fetch some fish and chips, please?' She dug into her handbag and took out her purse. 'My treat, if anyone else wants some. Put up your hands and get some for the girls. They'll be back from the park soon.'

After eating the fish and chips, Olive and Eliza excused themselves and caught a bus into town. Olive, using her crutches, led the way to George Henry Lee's, arm in arm with Eliza, and the pair headed down to the basement, where Olive inspected curtain material and purchased several lots she liked. Then they took the Southport train.

'How far out are you?' asked Eliza after they had passed Seaforth.

'Not far now,' replied Olive, gathering her shopping together. 'Next station.'

'Crosby,' said Eliza.

'Crosby and Waterloo,' Olive said. 'Our Peter's two are going to love visiting the beach and hopefully so will your Beth when she comes to visit.' She led the way down to the front, where there was a slight breeze, and then along in the direction of Waterloo, aware that her friend was inspecting the houses.

'You can't see the sea from here,' said Eliza.

'No, but it's close.'

It was not long before they turned, and Eliza was able to see the larger houses. She smiled at Olive and asked, 'You can see the sea from the higher windows?'

Olive nodded. 'And it's only a short walk to the beach. But come and see inside the house.' She led the way and Eliza said, 'But your front door doesn't face the sea.'

'No, but there are three entrances, with it being a corner house, and plenty of garden at the front, side and back.'

'It must have cost you a fortune. How did you manage to get a mortgage with you being a woman?'

'I haven't got a mortgage,' said Olive. 'I won on the football pools. I told you. Dad gave me his numbers and asked me to carry on doing them.'

'Didn't you think that was odd?' said Eliza, following Olive into the house.

'I just thought he'd tired of doing them week after week,' she said, taking out two small bottles of Coca-Cola from her shopping bag and handing one to Eliza, then perching on a low windowsill. 'I need to buy a kettle and some saucepans and a frying pan and crockery and cutlery, teapot and tea, sugar and milk, and order some furniture for next time I come here.'

'I should think you would. You're going to need help.'

'I know, but I don't want Alan knowing this address until after my friend Iris arrives. I think he could prove a nuisance, otherwise.'

Eliza frowned at her. 'Then why are you going to see his bungalow?'

'Just curiosity, and to see how he is with his son. Joanna says he's a nice lad but reckons his father walks all over him.'

'There's nothing you can do about that, especially as you don't have any intention of marrying Alan. Besides, he has two sets of grandparents to keep an eye on him.'

'I know that, but I heard they squabble over him.'

'He's missing his mother,' said Eliza. 'Anyway, let's see the rest of the house.'

'Come on, then,' said Olive. 'Do you want to go upstairs first to see the view?'

'Okay, I can tell you're dying to show me it. Have you ever seen the view from the top of the Liverpool Anglican Cathedral? It's fantastic.'

'One day,' said Olive. 'Now follow me.'

They went upstairs and Eliza stared out of the window. 'Lovely. I'd want this room for myself.'

'Joanna has claimed it,' said Olive, joining her at the window. 'I can get to the beach quicker and see who's at the front door from the first floor.'

'Okay, then show me your bedroom and the bathroom.'

They went down one flight of stairs and entered a room overlooking the road and the front step and gate. 'It's a better size and shape,' said Eliza.

'And can take a larger bed,' said Olive.

'Which you need, being quite tall for a woman.'

'Something a lot of men don't like,' Olive said. 'Mam didn't like it either because I was tall as a girl, and she complained of it costing more money for my clothes. I liked it then, especially when me and Dad went to the match and I could see over people's heads.'

She showed Eliza the rest of the house and then suggested they'd best head back, after her friend had expressed her approval.

They walked to Seaforth and took the bus as far as the Rotunda, where there had once been a theatre which had been bombed during the Blitz. It was now a wasteland, which they crossed to catch a bus that would take them to Belmont Road, close to where Eliza lived.

They hadn't been there long when Alan turned up. He offered Olive his arm and assisted her into the car. It only took minutes to arrive at the prefab and Alan wasted no time opening the car door and hurrying to open the front gate wide. Olive did not immediately move away from the car but rested against it and gazed at the prefab.

'What do your parents think of you and George living here?'

'Dad says that it makes sense. It's easy to keep clean and has all mod cons. What more do a father and son need?'

'I bet your mam said they need a woman,' murmured Olive.

Alan grinned. 'You hit the nail on the head. She believes the males of the species can't get collars white enough.'

'Did George tell her they can go to the laundry?'

He nodded. 'She said it'll cost more money. I said that lots of women send their whites to the laundry, and they iron them lovely.'

'What about cooking?' Olive smiled.

'His other granny taught him to cook and do a certain amount of baking. Although nothing beats George's jam roly-poly or homemade rice pudding with golden skin on top.'

'Delicious,' murmured Olive. 'You must invite me to a meal when George is the chef.'

Alan pulled a face. 'I can cook as well.'

'Sounds good,' she said. 'Can we see inside now?'

'I thought you'd never ask,' he said, and took her hand.

'I'm a big girl now,' she said, gazing down at him.

'You don't have to remind me,' he said.

As soon as they stepped inside, they could smell cooking, and they followed their noses to the fitted kitchen, where George was at the sink cleaning saucepans.

'Cottage pie,' said Alan, 'with baked beans in the mix.'

'Dad used to have it in the army,' said George. 'He told me less meat is needed.'

'Good idea when meat was rationed,' said Alan. 'Is there enough for our guest?'

His son nodded and Alan went to a drawer, took out cutlery and began to set the kitchen table before taking Olive through into the sitting room, where there was a fire burning in the grate. He led her to a deep armchair.

'A glass of sherry?' he asked, taking three glasses and a bottle out of the sideboard cupboard.

The cream sherry was good, thought Olive, sipping it slowly, Alan sat the other side of the fireplace, and she met his gaze. He lifted his glass as if in a toast and for a moment she thought he was going to say, 'Here's to us!'

Instead, he said, 'Here's to a peaceful future.'

She murmured agreement, adding, 'You must have been relieved that your boy was too young to fight.'

He nodded. 'He's a good lad, despite having no fight in him, and he goes on about his mother. She spoilt him.'

'He must miss her,' said Olive.

'He never stopped talking about her when I first came home, went on and on about how she'd dance with him around the kitchen, and they'd laugh and laugh.'

'How did that make you feel?'

'How do you think?' he asked, raising his eyebrows.

She flushed. 'Am I being too nosey?'

'I could ask you how you felt when your Yank left you here, yearning for him?'

'That's different,' she retorted. 'Besides, I coped and accepted that my dream was dead in the water. You had what you wanted, the woman you fancied and a son.'

'She was second best,' said Alan. 'I allowed myself to be tricked into marriage.'

'Lower your voice,' she whispered. 'He'll hear.'

'He's aware of what his mother was,' he said under his breath. 'A good-time girl. Her mother knew it and made sure George knew it, but she was a fool, because he loved what her mother hated in her. He loved her gaiety. And he knew she loved him.'

Olive almost wished she had not come and had kept her mouth shut. She drained her sherry glass and attempted to stand up, only to stumble and fall back into the chair. She tried to get up again. 'I won't stay for dinner. I need to get home.'

'You'll upset him if you don't try his cooking. He's started taking an interest in girls. He likes your daughter, you know, and Mary.'

'Too young for him,' she said, wondering how she was going to get out of this chair, having left her crutches in the kitchen.

'What's up?' asked George, who appeared in the kitchen doorway. 'Dinner's on the table.'

'Nothing's up,' said his father.

'It looks like our visitor is trying to get up. Dinner's ready, so why don't we help her, Dad,' said George.

Olive stared at Alan, who grinned. 'I was just going to do so,' he said smoothly, making a move towards her.

He placed an arm about her, so his fingers rested just beneath her breasts, and if it weren't for George, she thought Alan would have tried to have a fondle. She pulled away from him and clasped George's shoulder. The lad led her to a place at the table and drew out a chair. She slid onto the seat and gazed at the food on the plate. She picked up the knife and fork and waited until father and son were seated before digging in. The cottage pie was extremely tasty, and she realised how hungry she was and was glad that she had stayed and would be able to compliment George on his cooking.

She smiled across at the young man. 'Have you ever given thought to becoming a chef?' she asked.

Before he could reply, Alan spoke up. 'What are you asking him that for, when I've told you he wants to be an engineer? It is more of a job for a man and will pay better.'

'He's a good cook,' said Olive. 'He has a gift for it. You must appreciate him.'

'Of course,' Alan said. 'It's how he pays his way. Otherwise, I'd have to pay the woman who comes in and cleans to prepare meals for us.'

George surprised her by speaking up. 'I'm glad to do the cooking, Mrs Jones. I enjoy it and, as Dad says, it's a way for me to pay my way. It mightn't be so enjoyable if I did it for a job.'

She felt herself flush. 'Sorry I opened my mouth,' she said, picking up her knife and fork again.

'So you should be,' said Alan solemnly.

'I appreciated what you said, Mrs Jones,' said George. 'It made me feel good about myself.'

She smiled and continued eating until she had cleared her plate.

Alan said, 'Want seconds?'

She shook her head. 'I've had an elegant sufficiency.'

Alan stared at her. 'What's that supposed to mean?'

'It was something my gran used to say when she was more than satisfied,' said Olive, glancing at the clock. 'I should be going. Mam will be wondering where I am.'

'Won't Joanna have told her?' asked George.

'She could still be at Eliza's.'

'Alfie told me she might stay in America,' George said. 'I wish I could go with the three of them. I've never been out of Britain.'

'You might get your way,' said Alan. 'You could end up fighting the Commies.'

'Don't be horrible,' said Olive. 'There won't be another world war, not with both sides having the atom bomb.'

'I wouldn't be so sure,' said Alan. 'Look at Korea, and what about Vietnam?'

'I'd rather not look at them,' said Olive.

'Then there was trouble over the Suez Canal, which resulted in Eden resigning. We've lost India, and there's trouble in Kenya and Cyprus.'

'I've had enough of this,' said Olive. 'I must go home.'

It was at that moment the doorbell rang, and George went to see who it was. Olive pricked up her ears and caught the sound of Joanna's voice, mingling with Alfie's.

'It sounds like I mightn't have to disturb you to take me home,' said Olive.

Before he could protest, George entered the room with Joanna, who said, 'George said you were ready to leave, Mam.'

'I am,' she responded swiftly, before thanking George for the excellent dinner and Alan for showing her the prefab.

'You didn't get to see all of it,' said Alan. 'You must come again.'

'Yes, you should, Mrs Jones,' said George. 'You never got to have a pudding.'

She smiled at him. 'I won't forget.'

Joanna hustled her out at the sound of Alfie's voice telling them to get a move on.

Once Olive was made comfortable on the back seat, she said, 'I really appreciate this, Alfie.'

'Didn't you enjoy yourself?' asked Joanna. 'You were so keen to see the prefab, I convinced myself that it was an excuse to see Mr Biggs in his own setting.'

'You're partly right,' said Olive. 'I saw that he hadn't changed from the person I knew years ago, but I got to know George better and liked him. He's an excellent cook and a hard worker. Alan would miss him if he left home.'

'Why should he leave home?' said Alfie. 'He's planning on going to technical college and there's one in south Liverpool where he can study engineering.'

'He told me he wished he was going to America with the three of you. He'd like to travel.'

'He should train to be a marine engineer and go to sea,' said Alfie.

'Let's change the subject,' said Joanna. 'We've enough to think about and there's not much time before we catch the liner to California.'

CHAPTER TEN

Olive was sitting in a shelter along the front in South-port, eating fish and chips and gazing out across the sands towards the far horizon where the sun dazzled on the Irish Sea. The ship that she had seen Jay, Alfie and Joanna depart from Liverpool on was stopping at Cobh in Ireland to drop off and pick up other passengers sailing to America. Jack, Alfie and Jay had lifted all the luggage out of the boot of the car and carried suitcases, rucksacks and knapsacks down to where the liner was moored in the Mersey, trailed by Olive, Joanna and Eliza. Kisses were exchanged and tears shed, and good wishes and safe journeys spoken before final hugs were given and the travellers went on board.

'Look after her, Alfie, love,' Olive had called after them.

'You know I will,' he had shouted.

'Both of us will,' Jay had added as they leant over the side of the ship, blowing kisses.

The three on land had waved, and so had those aboard, as the ship's hooters sounded.

Olive wiped her damp face with an embroidered handkerchief and wondered if the liner had arrived in Ireland yet. She thought of her mother and decided to phone her later to let her know she was safe and would be back soon, but for now she needed to be alone and have a rest after the trauma of the last few days and saying goodbye to her daughter. She could not tell her mother the truth; she could not cope with her shouting and arguing and swearing on and on. Olive felt a sudden chill and deposited the chip paper in a bin and made her way slowly to the bed and breakfast where she was booked in and went to bed. After praying again for a safe journey for her daughter, Alfie and Jay, she drifted off into a dreamless slumber and did not wake until a ray of sunshine painted a shaft of golden light on the bedspread through a gap in the curtains. Her headache had completely vanished, and she felt refreshed, so she decided to book into the B&B for another night, before returning to Aintree. She had forgotten to phone her mother last evening, but she would do that this morning. She should also phone her brother and apologise for not turning up when she had said she would.

Should she tell her mother where she was? She decided she'd only share that information if asked. She had a bath and dressed and went downstairs and had breakfast. Only then did she phone her mother.

'Where were you last night?' asked Flora.

'I'm in Southport,' replied Olive. 'And I'm staying another night, so you don't have to worry about me. I needed a break.'

'With someone, are you?' asked her mother.

'No, I'm on my own.'

'A likely story.'

'It's the truth,' she said quietly, holding on to her temper.

'That Alan Biggs phoned and wanted to speak to you.'

'Well, I don't want to speak to him right now,' said Olive. 'I'm through with men.'

Her mother huffed. 'Anyway, when am I going to see this house you've bought?'

'When I get the front door key,' lied Olive.

'Fair enough,' said her mother.

'How's Dougal? Have you seen him since that Sunday?'

'Yes, we went to the flicks. There's a letter for you here from America. Do you want me to open it and tell you who it's from?'

'No, I'll open it when I arrive home tomorrow. Ta-ra, Mam! See you then, and perhaps we can discuss you going on a cruise…' She put the phone down, that would give her mother something to think about.

Taking a notebook and pencil from her shoulder bag, Olive made some calculations and decided she could afford to give her mother fifty pounds towards a cruise, as she did not want her to use all her nest egg on the holiday that was her dream. Would she go alone, or would Dougal go with her?

–

Olive was physically exhausted when she got off the train at the Old Roan the following afternoon, so she called a taxi to take her to her mother's house. She was prepared to go straight to her bedroom after tea and to read the letter from America there, but her mother spoilt that idea when she told Olive that Alan said he'd call in straight from work.

'You should have put him off, Mam,' she said. 'I don't want to see him. I've a lot to think about and don't want to be disturbed.'

'I thought you'd like company, seeing as Dougal and me are going to the Empire to see a show. We didn't want you moping now Joanna's gone.'

'I'm not moping,' said Olive. 'I've lots to look forward to, and if I want help to move stuff, I can ask Jack and our Peter.'

'No doubt,' said her mother. 'Anyway, you owning your own place gives you a sense of security. No worries about not being able to pay the rent man and being turned out.'

'There's still rates to pay.'

'Have you taken them into account?'

'Of course. And I've also some money for your cruise in appreciation for giving Joanna a home.'

Her mother looked taken aback. 'How can you afford it?'

'Ask no questions and I'll tell you no lies.'

'You didn't meet a rich fella while you were in Southport, did you?'

Olive shook her head and glanced at the clock. 'What time will Dougal be in?'

'Soon, he knows we're going out. He'll just have a quick sarnie and a cup of tea, and we'll go. He's going to take me for a Chinese afterwards.'

'Enjoy yourself,' said Olive. 'I'm going upstairs.'

'Do you need help?'

Olive shook her head.

'Night, Mam!' Olive wasted no time dragging herself upstairs, clinging on to the banister rail with both hands. She changed into clean pyjamas and gazed at the writing on the flimsy airmail envelope. She pressed her lips tightly together before slitting open the envelope with a finger.

> *Dear Olive,*
> *What's this I hear about you NOT coming to*
> *the States despite your divorce having been final-*
> *ised at last. What's going on? Jay mentioned a*

guy you knew years ago returning home after the fighting in Europe. Anyway, I'm crossing the pond sometime this year and will drop in and see you. I've been meaning to visit kin in Ireland for some time. They live near the coast and skin-dive, which I enjoy too. I'm planning to travel by ship and so will have room to bring my equipment. They dive for scallops and mussels. I like seafood. Looking forward to meeting your daughter.

See yer!

Yours, Josh

It was at that moment she heard the front door open and the sound of voices. She recognised Alan's and swore under her breath. Swiftly, she placed the letter under her pillow, and snuggled beneath the bedcovers, closed her eyes and pretended to be asleep.

There were footsteps on the stairs, but they were not her mother's. Could they be Dougal's?

A man asked if she was asleep. Stupid question! She recognised Dougal's voice and said, 'Is it Alan at the front door?'

'Yeah! Do you want me to chase him?'

'Best not, if Mam's invited him. I'll get up.'

'Okay!'

His footsteps retreated and soon she heard the front door close. She sat up, presuming her mother and Dougal had left. Then there came footsteps again, so she slithered out of bed, got dressed and opened the bedroom door.

They stared at each other. Alan looked disappointed. 'Your mam said you'd gone to bed.'

'I got up again.'

'What are you playing at?' he rasped.

'What are you?' she responded.

'Your mam thought it would do you good to have company.'

'Just as I thought,' she said. 'We've only just met again after goodness knows how long since we went out on two dates and then I discovered you were seeing Dot and within a short space of time you married her.'

'She tricked me into marriage.' He moved towards her.

'Don't try any tricks,' she said. 'You were a flirt then and I believe you haven't changed that much. I now know it was a mistake asking to see the prefab.'

'I suppose because George was there,' he said.

'I like your son. He's a nice lad.'

'You could be a mother to him.'

'How many times do I have to tell you, I'm not interested in us getting together.'

'You used to be, and I think you should give us another chance.'

'This is a stupid conversation,' she said, picking up one of her crutches.

He lunged for her.

She managed to dodge out of the way, seriously worried that there was a danger of one of them falling down the stairs. 'I want you to leave, Alan.' She noticed a sweeping brush leaning against the wall and seized it, threatening him with it. 'Now beat it and go and find yourself another woman, before I really lose my temper.' She thrust the bristles in his face.

He spluttered and backed off and then turned and headed for the stairs. 'You're mad,' he yelled.

She prodded him lightly and he thundered down the stairs and opened the front door. She heard the stray dog bark at him and then she heard the gate clang; a couple of minutes later came the roar of the car engine.

She lowered herself onto the top stair and laughed until she cried, then went downstairs on her bottom, invited the dog inside and gave him a slice of ham and a drink of water, before returning to bed and re-reading Josh's letter. She imagined him swimming underwater across the Irish Sea and into the Mersey. Men! They were selfish and crazy! Suddenly, she remembered Captain Webb, who had been the first man to swim the English Channel. What had she been thinking of allowing her daughter to visit Joe? But at least she had Alfie with her as a chaperone. He was like a brother to her. Although he and Jay would be climbing mountains. She doubted Joe would be climbing, or even going rambling, unless Josh went with him and Joanna. What about Josh's wife? Was she into the great outdoors?

She turned over and was determined to go to sleep but she was still awake when she heard her mother and Dougal come in, and the dog bark. She decided she had best go and rescue it. She went downstairs on her bottom to find that her mother and Dougal were arguing, and realised Dougal was fond of dogs and was in favour of it staying.

Her mother turned on her. 'What were you thinking of allowing this scruffy mongrel in my house?' She glared at Olive.

'It was Alan's fault. It got in when he left,' she said. 'Anyway, it won't be bothering you much longer because I'm taking him with me to my house. He'll be company and a good guard dog. I'm not going to waste my time worrying about Joanna while I wait for news, I'll busy myself putting my house in order, ready for when my friend arrives. I'd also like to take the doll's house Dad bought me for Christmas when I was ten. I got enormous pleasure playing with it, and I'm sure Brenda and Beth will too when they come to visit me. I'll ask our Pete to pick it up and drop it off at my place.'

'When are you planning on leaving?' asked Flora.

'Sometime in the next month or so, and when the house is ready, you and Dougal can come for lunch,' she said, picking up the dog. 'I'm sure you two will manage without me.'

'We'll miss you,' said Dougal.

'I won't miss that dog,' said her mother. 'And with her own place, she can get married.'

'I don't want to get married,' said Olive. 'So you can stop encouraging Alan. I want my independence.'

'How are you going to support yourself and Joanna, when she comes back?'

'I've told you before, Mam. I've got savings, and I'll get myself a job.'

'I bet your dad's been sending you a postal order every month since you went away.'

'You're wrong. It's true he used to give me half a crown for pocket money when I was at school. I always saved some of it.'

'Leave the girl alone, Florrie,' said Dougal. 'We don't need her money.'

'She gave me fifty pounds towards the cruise. How can she afford it?'

'It's none of your business, Mam. Now I'm going back to bed. I'm meeting Eliza tomorrow.'

—

'What's the rush? You and your mam are getting on better now, aren't you?' Eliza refilled their teacups and offered Olive another scone.

Olive nodded. 'And Dougal is fitting in fine and manages to prevent her from interfering in my life too much, without upsetting her.'

'In what way?'

'He's twigged that I don't want Alan visiting day in, day out. It helps that he's suspicious of him,' said Olive.

'That's odd when you think how you didn't trust Dougal when he first came on the scene.'

'I found a photo of him and Dad in an old tin box. They were most likely in their teens, but they were grinning and were obviously friends.'

'Right,' said Eliza. 'But why have you gone off Alan?'

'He wouldn't take no for an answer.' Olive's eyes flashed with anger, and she told her about the previous evening. 'So will you come into town with me?'

'All right, but what about your mam, wouldn't she like to go with you?'

'She'd go on about getting stuff cheaper, but I used to love going into Lee's basement and looking at their materials. Like we did the other week. It's furniture I need now.'

'You mentioned Waring and Gillow's. They are dear.'

'I know, and I'm not saying I could furnish the whole house from there, but I'd love to see what they've got. As for beds, Benson's will do me. They stock different names, and I'll buy a Silentnight double for me and two singles for Joanna and the guest room.'

'When is your friend Iris coming?'

'In a fortnight.'

'Are we going to have lunch in town?'

'I've been thinking of just coffee and cakes, and a trip to the flicks.'

'What did you want to see?'

'*The Ten Commandments*, starring Charlton Heston. It's on at the Gaumont. Apparently, it's been showing for weeks, so must be good.'

'You're on,' said Eliza. 'It could be that Jack will want to see it.'

'If he does, he could take Beth.' Olive finished her scone and drank the last of her tea. 'We'd best be going if we want to do all that we suggested.'

Eliza said, 'I hope Amelia has done her writing quota for the day; otherwise, she won't be available to look after the kids.

Fortunately, Amelia was free, so out Olive and Eliza went. They took a taxi into town, firstly, they checked the time the film started, then they went to Waring and Gillows and looked at bedroom suites. They went to the haberdashery department and bought more curtain material for the sitting room. Then Olive decided enough was enough, as she was tiring and ready for a break. They would stop for cake and coffee, before heading for the cinema, as it was possible there just might be a queue. Eliza agreed and off they went to Lyons. She spoke to Eliza about that first sighting she'd had of Jay and how she had thought he was so like his father in appearance. Instantly, she recalled Josh's letter and tears welled in her eyes.

'Are you all right?' Eliza asked. 'You're not worrying about Joanna, are you? They'll have landed in America by now.'

Olive shook her head. 'I was thinking of Josh. I received a letter from him yesterday.' Olive carefully wiped her eyes with a handkerchief.

'Do you want to tell me or keep it to yourself?' Eliza covered Olive's hand, which rested on the table, and squeezed it gently.

'I liked him, I still do, but I'm cross with him for telling Joe about Joanna. And then he mentioned something about a guy I used to know years ago – how does he know about that?'

'Jay probably asked questions about Alan, what with him taking an interest in you and offering you a lift… And I probably told him that you went out with him years ago, and goodness knows what George might have been told by his mother about you and Alan. Sorry!'

'Even so, he had a nerve questioning my behaviour and then signing "Yours, Josh" when he's married,' said Olive. 'After all, he knew Joe was married with a son.'

'I liked him, so did Jack. We thought him a nice bloke.'

'I wonder what his wife's like,' said Olive. 'He never talked about her.'

'They argue a lot, apparently. So Jay told Alfie,' Eliza said.

'What about, I wonder,' said Olive.

'Jay just shrugged when Alfie asked.'

'Perhaps when they realise he's listening, they shut up,' said Olive, reaching for a jam doughnut.

'Enough said,' murmured Eliza. 'We'd better stop talking and eat and drink if we're going to get to the flicks in time.'

Olive agreed, although she was thinking that Josh and his wife couldn't have been arguing in the years he'd been away fighting during the war; had they only started when he returned?

She kept her thoughts to herself and wondered what his wife thought about his plan to visit Ireland. He had made no mention of her accompanying him. Was he coming on his own or was Jay coming with him? Perhaps he would stay in America to keep his mother company.

'Time we were going,' said Eliza. 'Hurry up and finish that doughnut.'

'Some cakes can't be rushed,' said Olive. 'I'll pay the bill and finish it on the way.'

They moved as quickly as they could, but Olive told Eliza to go on ahead and save her a place if there was a queue. There was a queue, and a busker was playing a mouth organ accompanied by a small mongrel who walked on his hind legs with a cap in his mouth.

'Cute,' said Eliza, dropping a shilling in the cap.

Olive also dropped in a coin and stroked the dog's head. 'I'm taking the stray dog that hangs around Mam's when I move,' she said. 'Joanna fussed over it.'

'Anyway, the queue's moving again,' Eliza interjected.

Ten minutes later they were seated in the auditorium and sharing a bag of chocolate limes, wishing the film would hurry up and start. Otherwise, they were going to be extremely late getting home. Suddenly, to Olive's surprise, she spotted her ex-husband Theo's second wife, Glenys, and wondered what she was doing there.

'Did you see who that was?' asked Eliza, pointing to the woman.

'You mean Theo's wife?' replied Olive.

'Well, that woman certainly looks like her,' said Eliza.

'I thought she was in London with Theo,' whispered Olive.

'So, what's she doing in Liverpool?' asked Eliza.

'Perhaps she's stopping over here before going on somewhere else. Wales or Ireland, maybe.'

'My brother-in-law lives in Colwyn Bay. He adopted Glenys's niece, who's Alfie's half-sister,' said Eliza.

'That's complicated.'

'The war made relationships complicated,' said Eliza.

A youth in the row in front of them shushed them as the lights dimmed. Loud, stirring music drowned out voices as the title *The Ten Commandments* appeared on the screen and Olive felt excitement stir inside her. She had loved films ever since her father had taken her to see one on her seventh birthday. It seemed a long time ago now, but she had never forgotten the magic to be found at the cinema. She had passed that love on to Joanna, so it was not surprising that she was hoping to visit Hollywood while in California.

Olive was still shivering with emotion when they left the cinema.

'Well, do you think Jack will enjoy the film?' she asked.

'That's a daft question,' said Eliza. 'Alfie would enjoy it, too. It's the kind of film that will be reissued again and again.' She paused. 'Are you all right getting the bus to your mams on your own?'

'I'll go to the taxi rank this side of Lime Street railway station and pick one up there,' said Olive. 'You go and catch your bus. I'll be okay.'

They parted. 'I'll give you a ring tomorrow if I hear from Alfie,' called Eliza.

CHAPTER ELEVEN

It was as Olive was waiting in a taxi queue at the station that she heard her name being called. She looked about her and then a woman grabbed her sleeve. 'It's Olive, isn't it?' she said.

Olive stared at her. 'You're Glenys. We thought we saw you in the Gaumont. Did you enjoy the film?'

'Didn't enjoy it when all the first-born sons of the Egyptians were killed.'

'Rameses was warned to let the Hebrews go, and don't forget orders had been given for all the Hebrew baby boys to be killed years before. Moses would have been killed as a baby if he hadn't been found by an Egyptian princess and adopted.'

'Of course. Anyway, I'll tell Theo I saw you when I go back to London. We heard you were going to America.'

'I changed my mind. Joanna's gone, though.'

'All that way on her own?'

'No, she went with Alfie and Jay. He's an American and was in the air force involved in the Berlin airlift. He and Alfie climbed Snowdon together, so Jay suggested they climb some mountains in America together.'

'I hope they enjoy themselves,' said Glenys.

'So, what are you doing in Liverpool?' asked Olive.

'I'm here checking the house is okay.'

'And who's looking after your baby?' asked Olive.

'I've brought our son Paul, he's with Glyn's wife and their little boy and my niece Gwennie.'

'But they live in Colwyn Bay.'

'I know, but when I wrote telling them I was coming to Liverpool, they wrote back that they'd meet me here.'

'What about their B&B? Aren't they busy at this time of year?'

'They've got good staff. A Liverpool woman and her son. He and Gwennie are quite pally. And they're staying at Theo's place here in Liverpool.'

'So how did you manage a trip to the flicks on your own?'

'I promised to look after their little one while they have an outing shopping and to the flicks tomorrow,' said Glenys.

'I see. I'm surprised Theo kept on the Liverpool house now he's working in London and seems settled there.'

'He's thinking of Paul's future and his shares in the slate business. What with the company opening another office in Liverpool.'

'It's a long way off until Paul will inherit Theo's shares.'

'I hope so, but you know men.'

'Not as well as I thought,' said Olive.

'Do you regret not going to America with Joanna?'

Olive shrugged. 'Not really.'

'What do you mean by that?' asked Glenys.

'With me not there, Joanna and Joe have a better chance of forming a good daughter-father relationship, which I had with my father.'

'Yet you weren't at his funeral,' said Glenys.

'That's because I didn't know about it,' said Olive. 'Fortunately, I have lots of happy memories with him.'

She paused as she spotted the taxi. 'This is mine,' she said. 'Can I give you a lift?'

Glenys shook her head. 'No, thanks, I need to drop in at Sayers. Nice seeing you. You know where I am if you'd like to see Paul.'

Before Olive could reply, the taxi driver said, 'Are you getting in, missus?'

'Sorry, mate,' she said, climbing into the back of the taxi. She waved to Glenys as it drove off. Then she gave the driver her mother's address, before leaning back and closing her eyes, wondering what had been in Glenys's mind when she decided to speak to her. It wasn't as if they knew each other well. In truth, they'd avoided each other, so why had she invited Olive to visit the house and meet hers and Theo's baby son? Was it just to show off that she had given him what he most desired? She wondered if Eliza might call in to see Alfie's dead father's brother, Glyn, his wife and their son and his niece, the daughter of Glenys's sister who kidnapped Alfie when he was only a baby. And she ended up in prison. But surely that was in the past now and Glenys could not be holding a grudge against Eliza and Alfie and the niece who had been party to Alfie's rescue.

Olive sighed. She had not been on the scene at the time, as she and Eliza had no longer worked in munitions together. Her thoughts drifted to the first time she had seen baby Alfie and how it had caused her to long for a baby of her own, but she had never imagined she'd become an unmarried mother at the time. Still, marrying Theo had meant she had not had to live with that slur on her name. She wondered if she would receive another letter from Josh or Joe, or both, as well as Joanna. It could be that there were more letters waiting for her right now. Hopefully, her mother wouldn't steam the envelopes open.

She gazed out of the window and realised they had reached Walton, and she would soon be at her destination. Would there be a meal waiting for her? She thought about the film and guessed Dougal would want to know all about it. Olive wondered if her mam had decided when and where to go on a cruise. Perhaps Olive would arrive at her mother's house and discover them perusing the pages of brochures. Olive realised she was on her way to accepting Dougal as part of the family, but he could never replace her father in her heart.

CHAPTER TWELVE

CALIFORNIA

Joanna clung to Alfie's arm as they descended the steps onto the tarmac of San Francisco airport. She was shattered after the voyage across the Atlantic and then a flight from New York, and there was still the journey by car to San Jose to face. Jay's father, Josh, was picking them up at the airport and driving them to Joe's home. She stumbled as they set off towards the buildings, catching up with the stream of other passengers.

'Take it easy,' said Alfie. 'There's no rush.'

'We're going to be in a queue,' she said in a hushed voice. 'It was bad enough in New York. I wish we were in San Jose now.'

'There's no need for you to worry,' said Jay. 'You can take it easy while Alfie and I see to the luggage.'

'I'm not worrying,' she lied. 'I'm just exhausted.'

'You've only just arrived,' said Alfie.

'I know,' she retorted. 'But you're just here to have fun.'

'You're welcome to join us,' said Alfie. 'Isn't that right, Jay?'

Jay shook his head. 'It'll be too much for her. You'll be able to see Mount Tam from San Francisco, so you'll get an idea how high it is, and it's steep.'

'I've climbed Scafell, the highest mountain in England,' she said. 'We went on a school trip to the Lakes and stayed in a hostel.'

'How high?' asked Jay.

'Over three thousand feet,' she replied proudly. 'Snowdon's a bit higher but Ben Nevis is the highest in Great Britain and has more snow.'

'That's Scotland for you,' said Alfie.

'Enough about mountains,' said Jay, ushering Joanna and Alfie ahead of him inside the building.

'It's enormous,' said Joanna. 'But then I've heard and read that everything is bigger in America.'

'You'll get used to it,' said Jay.

Alfie exchanged looks with Joanna, as she found a seat and stretched out her legs. 'I'll stay here while you collect the luggage.'

She continued to sit, watching people and listening to the different American accents, although there were also British, French and Australian accents. No doubt there were some Canadians, but they were so like Americans she couldn't always tell the difference. It seemed an age before Alfie and Jay returned, and even longer going through customs, but eventually they were on the other side and there was a man waving to them.

'There's Pa,' said Jay. 'Wearing the green sweater.'

Joanna realised Jay could not wave back because he was holding their luggage in both hands, so she waved and lengthened her stride to get a closer look. She paused a couple of feet from the man, and they stared at each other. 'Mam was right,' she said. 'Jay does have a look of you.'

'And you have Joe's chin,' said Josh.

Joanna held out her hand. 'How do you do?'

Josh collected himself and took her hand. 'Nice to meet you, Joanna.'

'And you,' she responded in a friendly voice. 'Is my... my father still able to see? I'm in time?'

He nodded. 'Although his sight isn't what it was when I wrote to Olive. He has tunnel vision at the moment.'

Joanna had heard of tunnel vision but despite visiting the library and trying to find out the reasons why people went blind, she was little the wiser.

'You're best asking Joe about it,' said Josh. 'Anyway, how is your mother? I was told various things about her by my son, but somewhere along the line, I think he must have got mixed up.'

'She was going to come but she had an accident, and Nan isn't in the best of health. Although she's just taken in a lodger, who knew my granddad who passed away a short while ago.'

'That must have upset Olive.'

'She's broken-hearted and still cross with Nan, especially as Nan kept his illness from her, as well as his passing and funeral, saying he didn't want her upset.' She paused. 'Mam's bought a house. A friend from the WRAF is going to live with her.'

'A prefab?' said Josh.

'No, a house in Waterloo, near the beach. You can see the Irish Sea from my bedroom in the attic.'

'Isn't Waterloo in London?' Josh felt befuddled.

She shook her flaxen curls. 'That's a different one.'

Jay and Alfie came up to them and placed the suitcases down. 'You two have been talking for ages,' said Jay.

'Joanna's been bringing me up to date about her mother getting a house in Waterloo, by the sea, and about her nan taking in a lodger.'

'I didn't know about the house when I last wrote,' said Jay.

'She hasn't moved in yet,' said Joanna. 'I'll be living with her and her friend Iris when I get back.' She paused. 'Jay, shouldn't you introduce Alfie and your dad to each other? Then let's get on our way.'

'Don't be bossy,' said Alfie, and introduced himself, holding out a hand to Josh.

They shook hands, and Josh picked up one of the suitcases and led the way out to the car park and a cream-coloured Cadillac.

Joanna was just about to say how big it was but bit back the words, not wanting to sound repetitive.

'You can sit in the front with me,' said Josh, staring at her intently. 'You do have your mother's eyes.'

'No, she looks like Joe,' said Jay, opening the door for her.

Joanna hesitated. 'Perhaps you and Alfie would be better sitting in the front so you can get to know each other better,' she suggested to Josh.

He sighed. 'You'll be more comfortable in the front and see more. You can also tell me about your mom's accident.'

She nodded. 'Okay! How long will the journey take?'

'About an hour, depending on the traffic,' he replied.

'That's good.' She settled herself comfortably in the car. 'Do you live close to Joe?'

'About half an hour's drive,' he said, starting the car.

The hood was down and there was a pleasant breeze that whipped her hair and cooled her cheeks. 'What kind of mood will I find him in?' she asked, her voice quivering.

'There's no need for you to worry,' said Josh. 'He was put out when he heard Olive wouldn't be coming, though.'

'She was planning on coming. We'd both got our passports and applied for visas.'

'But she had no intention of staying if she was in the process of buying a house,' he said.

'Of course not! She's been wanting her own place for ages. I'm hoping to go to university, but I'll just have to wait and see how I do in my exams.' She paused. 'I will be living with her during vacations.'

'Naturally,' he said. 'Will you be able to get a grant?'

'I hope so, although Mam says she's planning to help me out and I'll get a part-time job.'

Josh swivelled his head and stared at her briefly. 'What's Olive's job?'

'She's thinking of starting her own business.' Joanna grinned. 'Don't ask what it is. I have the feeling she's still at the thinking stage. I've probably said too much as it is. It's bound to take a lot of money and, no, she hasn't got a sugar daddy.' She closed her eyes.

'What about Theo?' he asked. 'Jay seems to believe they're divorced?'

'I know a divorce is in the process, but Mam hasn't told me if it's finalised yet. He might have mentioned it to Alfie's mother. Theo is related to Alfie.' She paused. 'Alfie's as keen as Jay on climbing mountains. His father was Welsh and there's lots of mountains in Wales.'

'They're talking about Tamalpais State Park,' said Josh. 'You should go there while you're over here.'

'Is that where Mount Tam is?' she asked.

He nodded. 'It's a big climb, but there's also lakes and forest. Plenty of trails to walk if you'd prefer walking to climbing.'

'Are there wild animals? Will I need to be armed?'

'You wouldn't be going on your own,' he said. 'You'd get lost.'

'I mightn't go at all,' she said, stifling a yawn. 'I'll have to spend most of my time with Daddy Joe.'

He smiled. 'How did you feel when Olive told you about him?'

'Stunned, annoyed and disgusted at first. She should have told me ages ago, but I wasn't the only one she didn't tell. And there was a war on…Who's to say I wouldn't have behaved the same if I was in love and believed I might never again see the fella I loved and who loved me. He might have been killed.' She paused. 'Anyway, I'm going to sleep now if you don't mind, while you concentrate on your driving.'

Josh smiled. 'I'll wake you when we arrive. Although you haven't told me about Olive's accident yet.'

'A steery ran into her and damaged her ankle.'

'Does that mean she could always have trouble walking?'

He sounded worried, she thought.

'She's on crutches but can get up and down stairs.' She paused. 'Do you know what a steery is?'

'Tell me?' he asked.

So she told him, and what the injury looked like, and how Jack had found her and pushed her in the steering cart to the police station. 'She's tough, is Mam.' These last words were slurred, and then Joanna dozed, never falling asleep fully, but aware of the scent of pine and of the tang of salt on the breeze that must be coming from the ocean, the Pacific. How many miles was she from home? She thought of her mother, wondering what she was thinking of and whether she and Nan had had any more arguments. Joanna was no longer bothered about any changes Dougal and Nan would make to her bedroom, but began to wonder what Joe's house was like and whether the bedroom allotted to her would be much larger than the two she had slept in when in Liverpool. She thought of Theo and her mother's father, who had been so easy to get on with, and how they'd had fun together. She felt sad that he was no longer part of her life. She remembered the expression on Olive's face when they went to the grave. How the tears had fallen when she placed the flowers in an urn and said that she would see to getting a marble stone engraved with his name, dates, and a verse from the Bible.

Then Joanna felt a touch on her shoulder and the automobile slowing down. 'Wake up,' said Josh. 'We've arrived.'

Joanna was assisted out of the vehicle by Alfie and stared at the large modern house. The walls were painted yellow. On the left-hand side of the cream doorway was a wooden bench, in front of a large picture window, and on the right-hand side of the doorway was a veranda with a climbing plant weaving its way to the top of a trellis. In the doorway stood a man, who was clasping the hand of a little girl who looked to be about ten years old and was shouting, 'Uncle Joe, here's Jay and his pa!'

Joanna decided the man who was leaning on a stick had to be her biological father, so she wasted no time walking towards him. Alfie was following close, as she hurried along the tiled path flanked by fruit bushes and smooth lawns.

'Who's the little girl?' whispered Alfie, reaching for Joanna's hand. He held it tightly, aware that she was trembling as she stopped a couple of feet in front of the man that he presumed was Joe.

'Doris, hush now,' called a woman with greying hair from the other side of the hedge. 'Welcome, folks from the old country. I'm Elsie, and Doris is my granddaughter. I look after her while my daughter is at work. The "uncle" is just a courtesy title.' She paused. 'Come on, Joe, greet your daughter and the young man with her.'

But before she had finished talking, Joanna was holding his arm to steady him and kissing his weather-beaten cheek. 'You have my cleft chin,' he said, peering into her face. Alfie had stepped back, out of the way.

'So she has,' said Elsie, who had made her way into Joe's garden.

'I wish we could have met earlier but it wasn't to be,' said Joe. 'Come on in and have a drink and something to eat. You must be famished after the journey.'

Joanna agreed that she was ready for refreshments and linked her arm through her father's thin one, taking his stick. 'I'm sorry Mam couldn't come but she's really in a state about her father passing away recently.'

'At least she allowed you to come and see me. She should have told me at the time, but I'd have been at a loss what to do. We were going off to fight.' He hugged her against him. 'I only wish my son was here to meet you.'

'I wish that too,' said Joanna. 'Hopefully, we will be able to get out and about while you can still see so you can show me your favourite places and I can take some photos to show Mam.'

'I'm sure Josh and Jay will drive us and show you our stunning scenery and places where nature has torn the earth apart, but you mustn't worry when the ground shakes beneath you.'

'Joe's right,' said Jay. 'We have tremors but they're never serious.'

'One of our teachers has a copy of the painting *Faithful Unto Death*. It shows a Roman soldier on duty when Vesuvius was erupting hundreds of years ago. In the background can be seen fire balls coming through the air. She mentioned the Great Earthquake that struck San Francisco,' said Joanna.

'In 1906,' said Elsie with a shudder. 'Thousands were killed, and buildings toppled, and there were fires all over the place. My grandpa was in the fire service, and he remembers how it took a week or more to put the fires out because so many water pipes were cracked and broken.'

'Did he survive?' asked Joanna.

Elsie nodded. 'Thank the Lord, there hasn't been another like it since.'

'We went to Italy, didn't we, Josh? The Italians' hearts weren't in the fighting and the Germans had invaded,' said Joe.

'Let's change the subject,' said Josh. 'Besides, the scientists can forecast better now when earthquakes and eruptions can be imminent.'

'It must have looked like Liverpool and lots of other ports that were bombed during the war,' said Alfie. 'I mightn't have been here if Jack hadn't rescued Mam and taken her to the hospital. Even after the war, you could still spot houses sliced in half, so you could see bedrooms with wallpaper hanging in strips from walls, a broken bed, wardrobes splintered and lying on their sides.'

'It wasn't just ports,' said Joanna. 'It was towns and cities where there were factories working for the war effort.'

Joe said, 'I remember it. Let's go inside and sit down and eat. I'll show you around the house and garden later.'

Joanna thought of her mother and the house she would soon be moving into and wished she was there with her, but she was aware that her biological father seemed made up to have her company She wondered what Theo thought of her having travelled all this way across the Atlantic to meet Joe. Could it be that he wasn't giving her any thought now he had the son he had always wanted.

Joe drew her into the house and her first impression was of a huge space, as she walked straight into what must have been the living room. At the far end was a kitchen and dining area, with a window fitted into the wall on the left over a sink, and French windows that opened out onto a terrace and garden.

There was little furniture, but what was there appeared comfortable and lacking in sharp edges, and there were no footstools or occasional tables with clutter on them. She did notice a decent-sized radiogram, which must be a blessing to Joe. To the right was a flight of stairs leading to the next floor. There were handrails on both sides.

As Joanna stood, holding her father's arm, Elsie brushed by her and began to remove covers from plates of food and beckoned them over to the table. Joanna was put out and wondered what her mother would have made of the older woman making herself at home in Joe's house. One thing was for sure: Nan was mistaken in thinking that Joe only wanted them to come and see him so they could look after him. Elsie had stepped into the breach by being a good neighbour.

Even so, Joanna was relieved when Elsie left with her granddaughter as, at one point, she seemed about to follow Joanna and Joe on the tour of the house and garden. But before that could begin, Joanna and Joe saw Josh, Jay and Alfie off.

'Will you and Alfie be going climbing tomorrow?' asked Joanna.

'Not this soon,' said Jay. 'Alfie will need to recover from the journey, and I'll have to go and spend a couple of days with Mom. I've been away a long time, and she'll want to check me over and hear all my news. I'm not the best of letter writers.' He grimaced.

'Alfie and I will come over and take you and Joe for an outing,' said Josh.

'That sounds great,' said Joe. 'Joanna and I will have time this evening and in the morning for a good chinwag.'

Joanna agreed, as Alfie was the only link with home, but she knew it was more than that. Anyway, she would see him tomorrow, but for now she would need to stop mooning about him and give all her attention to Joe. She turned and faced him, debating what she should call him. Dad, Pops, Pa. Father sounded too unfriendly. She had called Theo Dad. She settled on Pa and knew she had made the right decision when he smiled.

They went indoors and climbed the stairs, arm in arm, and it was not until they reached what she called the first floor, and he called the second floor, that she asked whether he had given any thought to having a bedroom downstairs.

'You're thinking it'll be easier for me when my sight goes completely,' he said, a break in his voice.

'Yeah.' She followed him into the first room on the right, which held a double bed and was very much a man's room, with fishing rods hanging on the ochre-painted wall and a photograph of a man and a boy holding a large fish.

'That's my son,' he said, tears blocking his throat. 'I should never have let him go with his mother, but she was insistent. Her mother might be old, but she still has a lot of go in her. She could have easily caught a train, and he could have met her at the station, and she could have stayed here for a week or so. I liked her and we got on like a house on fire. From our first meeting I wouldn't have minded if she lived with us, but my wife wouldn't have it. Josh said once it was because her mother would have made her move, and my wife enjoyed playing the invalid.'

Joanna did not comment because she had not met his wife, only saying that she wished she had met her half-brother and asking whether he and Jay had been friends.

'Josh's wife is my cousin and she's clever and wants Jay to follow in her father's footsteps; my uncle is a lawyer and has his own practice. They resent Josh for encouraging Jay to spend so much time on outdoor activities, instead of studying the law and spending time with her and her father, meeting the right people. She says climbing is a dangerous sport. I admit I prefer fishing, which is relaxing, although it has its exciting moments.' He paused. 'But tell me about yourself… What do you enjoy doing and what would you like to do in the future?'

Joanna did not reply immediately, thinking she had no idea what Joe had done for a living before his eyesight had degenerated. 'Couldn't you show me my bedroom first? I'd like to unpack and then we could talk over a coffee and be comfortable downstairs.'

'That sounds a sensible plan,' he said, clutching her arm firmly. 'Elsie thought you'd prefer the guest room. I'd had it in mind you'd prefer my son's room, as it is larger and has a view over the rear garden and the hills and ocean in the distance, but I let her have her way, her being a female, I thought she'd know better what a girl would prefer.'

'That's not necessarily true,' said Joanna. 'I like the thought of sleeping in my half-brother's bedroom. I feel I'd sense his presence there and know better what he was like, rather than having people just talk about him.'

Joe looked pleased by what she had said. 'You must do as you wish; I shall show you both rooms and you can choose.'

'I won't change my mind,' said Joanna, following him out of his bedroom.

She preferred her half-brother's room as soon as she entered it. There was a warm, welcoming feel about it. The closet had been cleared of clothing but contained fishing tackle, and on a shelf there was bed linen, and she guessed she would need to make up the bed. On a wall painted duck egg blue hung a baseball bat and a cap. She touched the cap lightly and then went over to a bookshelf and knelt on the floor, reading the titles of some of the books, such as: the stories of Tom Sawyer and Huckleberry Finn, *Treasure Island*, *The Man in the Iron Mask*, *Kidnapped* and The Hardy Boys series. There were also factual books about the American Civil War, Second World War, as well as books of cartoons and comics. She rose at last and went over to the window; she looked over the garden before lifting her gaze to the far distant hills and then, turning slightly, she caught the gleam of water.

All this time Joe had been sitting silently in a wicker chair, watching her, and only when she went over to the window did he say, 'Well, will this room suit you?'

Joanna turned and held out both hands to him. 'I love it, and I really like it that I've read some of the same books as him. I borrowed them from Alfie. But tell me, Pa, why do you never call my half-brother by his name and refer to him as "my son"?'

He grimaced. 'You'll consider it a stupid reason.'

'Tell me, please?'

Joe clasped her hands firmly. 'I had no say in the matter, and my wife was reading *Gone with the Wind* at the time, so she named him Rhett after the so-called hero. I wasn't best pleased. I wanted to name him Andrew after the saint and my Scottish grandpa who emigrated to Canada but then moved down here. It was too cold up there for Grandmama Elspeth. She had a bit of a chest.'

'I'm sure Mam called me after you,' said Joanna.

Joe squeezed her hands. 'I'm pleased, and I regret not marrying your mother, but my wife was an invalid, and I couldn't bring myself to ask for a divorce.'

'I understand,' she said. 'But surely you could have given him Andrew as a middle name.'

He nodded. 'I was away at the time, and she had him christened Rhett and Harold, after her father, before I returned.'

'I shall always refer to him as my half-brother Andrew,' she said, wanting to please him. 'Now, I'll need to bring up my luggage, as well as make the bed, and I'd like a quick wash and a change of clothes before coffee.'

'You could have a quick shower,' he suggested.

'I've never had a shower,' she said.

He showed her the bathroom and how the shower worked, and then they went downstairs. She left him in the kitchen while she took her luggage upstairs and unpacked a few clothes, made up the bed and then had a shower, which was quicker than a bath, but not as relaxing. She put on clean underwear and a dress in eau-de-nil green with white flowers on it and a white belt. She thought of her mother as she brushed her hair, wondering how she was getting on with Nan and Dougal, and decided she must write to her that evening. Then she returned to the kitchen and made coffee and sandwiches.

She had to admit that it felt strange as they ate and drank, and he asked her about her mother and Theo. She told him about the divorce and brought him up to speed with what had been happening in the past couple of months. They also talked about soccer and other sports, and she told him how she enjoyed swimming. It was then he asked her what she planned to do after she left school, and she told him she would like to go to university and study Pharmacy, but that was a while off yet and, anyway, that would depend on whether she did well in her final exams.

'What about university fees?' he asked.

'I'll have to get a part-time job and Mam might be able to help me,' she replied. 'Alfie's fortunate. He doesn't want to go to university as he inherited shares from his father in the family slate business and has already started work in their office in Liverpool.'

Joe looked interested. 'I used to work for a timber company.'

She said eagerly, 'You mean you were a lumberjack?'

He smiled. 'Do I look like I was strong enough to chop down trees?'

'You could have, once upon a time. when you were young.'

'That's how I started out, along with Josh, but then I decided I'd rather work with wood, so I became a carpenter, not just repairing tables and other furniture and working in the building industry, but also carving items for sale, such as animals and birds.'

'I don't suppose you'll be able to do that when you lose your sight altogether,' she said sympathetically.

'The wife thought I was wasting my time,' he said. 'But I didn't let her put me off. I still love the smooth feel of wood freshly sanded, and the smell of it.'

'I can understand,' she said. 'Do you still have any of the animals you made?'

He nodded and pulled out the chair he was sitting on and took up what she had thought earlier reminded her of a squirrel, but he placed it on the palm of her hand and told her that it was a chipmunk. 'Andrew liked chipmunks, and we had a couple that used to come in the garden. He encouraged them with hazelnuts.' Joanna inspected it intently, stroking and loving the feel of it. 'You can have it. Andrew would want you to keep it,' Joe said huskily.

'I wish I had known him,' said Joanna, stroking the beautifully carved chipmunk.

'His mother would have hated you and your mother. She loved him dearly and was very possessive. It was to be expected, I suppose. She always came first, except when he insisted on going fishing with me once a month. Sometimes she would accompany us, and he would push her in her wheelchair around the lake. He was a good son, and they grew closer during the war, while I was away. I should have insisted he didn't drive all that way to his grandmother's and instead go on the train, but my wife didn't like travelling on public transport.'

Joanna was reminded of her mother and said, 'I must write to Mam and tell her I've arrived safely and that we're getting on like a house on fire.'

'Tell her that I wish her well and hope we can meet again someday.'

'I will,' said Joanna, wondering if it would be possible for him to travel by sea with Josh to Liverpool and surprise her mother. She wouldn't mention it to anyone yet.

She asked him if there was anything else she could do for him before she went to bed and wrote her letter. He shook his head and made his way carefully over to the radio; he switched it on and twiddled with the knob.

She kissed his cheek and wished him a good night and left him sitting comfortably, listening to a radio show. Then she dragged herself upstairs to the bedroom that had once been her half-brother's and she began to write, determined to be positive.

> Dear Mam,
>
> We arrived safely and were met by Josh, who has an attractive face and is taller than me and strong in body. He insisted I sat in the front passenger seat, as I would get a good view of the scenery for the last lap of the journey in his enormous, comfortable Cadillac.
>
> Joe is smaller than Josh but plump and wears glasses. He went on a bit about his wife having been an invalid and him having to care for her, but I got the impression that it was my half-brother who did most of the caring. Anyway, I'm jumping ahead. We got on fine when we met, despite his not being alone. He had a little girl by the hand. Her granny Elsie lives next door and is a good

neighbour to him and had prepared food for us. She looks older than Pa and fusses around him and ate with us and the fellas.

I am sleeping in my half-brother's bedroom, which has a fantastic view. I think Joe mourns his son more than his wife. Alfie is staying at Josh's house; the mountain he and Jay are going to climb is called Mount Tam by the locals. It is not as high as Snowdon, although most things over here are bigger than at home. I must stop saying how enormous everywhere is, but I must tell you Joe's house is larger than Uncle Jack and Aunt Eliza's but not as interesting. He's furnished it to make it safer for him to get around easily, probably, originally, it was planned for his wife's wheelchair.

When you reply to this letter, you must tell me how you are getting on with your house. I will start taking photos. Has your friend Iris arrived? I miss you.

How are Nan and Dougal getting on? Give them my best wishes,

Your loving daughter, Joanna. xxxxx

PS: Joe wishes you well. He also says that he wished you had told him about me from the beginning, although he'd have been lost about what to do, as they were going off to fight in Italy and his wife needed him at home, her being an invalid. She was weak and you were so strong. He's not the dad I imagined.

PPS: I suppose you know he was a lumberjack for a while. Now he carves lovely little animals and has given me a chipmunk that used to be my *half-brother's. He's the only one I regret not having known years ago.*

Joanna folded the two pages of her letter and placed them in the airmail envelope. She would have to buy a stamp and post the letter, once she discovered the whereabouts of the post office.

Josh did phone the following morning about taking them out, but she overheard Joe tell him that he'd had to change the plan, Elsie was going to take Joanna around San Jose as he had an order to finish. It was the first Joanna had heard of that plan, and was disappointed, but she did not complain and thought she would be able to ask Elsie to show her where the post office was. Elsie did not seem pleased, as she would also have to take her granddaughter with her if Joe was working at his carving.

To Joanna's delight, she encountered Alfie while she was out, he was also buying stamps and sending a letter to his mother. When he had arrived at Josh's house, he had been handed a letter from Eliza, informing him that the family from Colwyn Bay were in Liverpool, staying at Theo's house. Theo was still in London, but his new wife Glenys was there checking things, along with the baby. Gwennie, Alfie's half-sister, was there as well and was sorry to have missed him.

It was Olive who had passed on the news, meeting Glenys outside the cinema. Joanna was pleased to hear about the film and mentioned going to Hollywood again. Alfie also was in favour, but after they had posted their letters Elsie joined them and reminded Joanna that there were still places Joe wanted her to see. Alfie suggested he accompany them, only for Jay to turn up to remind him that they had a tennis court booked and were going to be late if they didn't get a move on. Joanna was tempted to accompany them, as she was bored. The only thing of interest Elsie had showed her was the Bank of Italy, the oldest skyscraper in California, built in 1926. She did not tell her how tall it was, but seemed to think Joanna would be awed by the sight since England had no skyscrapers.

Joanna had been impressed but could not resist saying that it was just as well as the Luftwaffe would have destroyed them during the Blitz. After a quick discussion, Elsie told her to go with the young men and watch the tennis, as she had shopping to do. Despite not being a great tennis fan, Joanna enjoyed relaxing in the sunshine. Later, Jay took them to the Egyptian Museum and then to where they could see Mount Tam in the distance, the mountain he and Alfie would be climbing in a few days' time.

Then they escorted her to Joe's house and left her. She found Joe putting his tools away and she asked, 'Did you get all your work finished?'

He went over to a shelf and showed her the family of mountain lions he had carved. She wanted to place her hand on them, but he said sharply, 'Don't touch – the oil in your fingers could mark the wood.'

She backed away. 'I'm sorry. I didn't know.'

'A lot of people don't. But you know now. Did you enjoy your walk?'

She nodded. 'What I would like is to go to a base-ball match. At home I went with my granddad to watch football. We have two of the best teams in the country, Everton and Liverpool.' She sat down.

'I have heard of them, but what about cricket?'

She shook her head. 'Too slow for me. Would you like me to make you something to eat? Or make us a coffee?'

'I'd like that… but do you know how to use the coffee maker? I don't think you do because you didn't use coffee beans yesterday.'

'I'm willing to learn,' she replied. 'We're not great coffee drinkers at home. Tea, that's our tipple, or cocoa. Unless you've some beer in the fridge, or whisky or a soft drink?'

'I'll have a beer – and if you could do me a burger or two?'

She went over to the fridge and took out a beer, found a glass in a cupboard and poured the beer into it, then carried it over to him. She had noticed some Coca-Cola in the fridge and poured herself one. Then she found a box of frozen burgers and some burger buns, and put together three, adding lettuce and coleslaw. She placed two on a plate and gave them to him with a napkin.

He inspected them and asked, 'What about red peppers?'

'I have an allergy to peppers, chilli and paprika. I can't risk touching them.'

He frowned. 'That sounds a mite over-cautious.'

'I don't think so. You've surely heard of a nut allergy and how the smallest amount of nuts can kill? So, Pa, unless you want me collapsing on the floor, you'll have to slice your own red peppers. Sorry,' she said.

'I've never heard the like,' he complained. 'You must be putting it on.'

'Why should I?' she asked, taken aback. 'I've been told that peppers are good for you. I wish I could eat them. Do you want me to bring a couple in their packet and a knife so you could slice them for yourself?'

'I don't want to make a fuss, but I suppose that's the answer if I'm to have red pepper on my burgers.'

She smiled, and taking a length of kitchen roll, she took the peppers out of the fridge, placed them on a plate with a knife and took them to him. 'Enjoy,' she said, and sat down a few feet from him. She then proceeded to eat her burger and wash it down with cola.

There came a knock on the front door, so Joanna said, 'Should I go and see who it is?'

'Of course,' said Joe, and took a bite out of his burger.

'Do I invite them in?' She put her plate on the table and went over to the door.

'If it's Elsie's daughter, tell her to come in. She's most likely come to say hello and welcome you to San Jose.' He sat straighter in his chair and wiped his mouth with his napkin.

Joanna opened the front door to find a quite attractive woman with pale blonde hair who looked to be in her thirties. She was wearing a navy-blue jersey dress trimmed with white. 'I'm Bettina,' she said. 'Elsie's daughter. I felt I must come and say welcome as soon as I knew you'd arrived.'

'Thank you, do come in,' said Joanna. 'Joe and I are just having something to eat. Something more filling than afternoon tea, as I've been out, and he's been working flat out to complete an order.'

'You are a big girl. I thought you were younger.'

'I'm sixteen,' said Joanna, reading the older woman's mind.

'Is your mother tall?'

'She's statuesque, like a Greek goddess or a film star.'

'Interesting,' murmured Bettina, following Joanna into the large living space where Joe was waiting.

'Tina, you're looking happy. Did everything go off well?' he asked.

'It couldn't have gone better. I took your advice, and it worked a treat. Mr Fortescue told me he's going to increase my salary and it's all thanks to you.'

'Joanna, show our guest my latest effort. I know you like my work.'

'You're so patient and talented, Pa,' said Joanna, determined to flatter him before Bettina could. She escorted her to where the carved family of mountain lions were waiting to be collected by their purchaser.

'Does your mother have a job, Joanna?' asked Bettina after her inspection. She'd moved over to Joe and was sitting close to him.

'She's recently left the women's air force and has bought a house near the beach overlooking the Irish Sea. She's going to be busy with the house for the next month or so.'

'Do you have any kin?'

'I have a married uncle, Peter, and he and his wife have two children. My nan is still alive and has a lodger. There is a shortage of housing due to the Blitz, and so many people are emigrating to Australia, Canada and New Zealand – and of course many a young woman has travelled to America as a GI bride. I am hoping to go to university. I was told that one of San Jose's oldest colleges was the first to give degrees to women in California. I think it was Notre Dame. It was probably Jay who mentioned it.'

'You're well informed,' said Bettina. 'Tell me—'

Joe interrupted, 'I think Joanna needs to finish her burger. It's getting cold. Tell me about the meeting, Tina?'

Satisfied, Joanna sat down and picked up her burger, but she had a drink first, as her mouth had gone dry after all her talking. She hoped she had given Bettina plenty to think about, including the possibility of her staying with Joe and applying for Notre Dame. Aware that Bettina and Joe had their heads together and were deep in conversation, she excused herself and went upstairs to have a shower and then read a book about the war between Mexico and California, interested because there were so many Spanish-sounding names that she had noticed.

The next day she and Joe were taken to see the Winchester Mystery House with Jay, who had been there several times. Joe told her that it had been built in Victorian and Gothic style by the rich widow of a Winchester son who had developed the repeating rifle, which became popular with those heading West. She had heard of the Winchester rifle in Western movies. She found it interesting but couldn't believe that the widow had been told by a medium to go to San Jose and build a house there. It took thirty-four years and was built to her design, so it was said. When Joanna first caught sight of it from a distance, she was reminded of an English mansion, but once inside, it was different. It had staircases that led to the roof and windows in the floor. It was rumoured to be haunted.

Naturally, Jay enjoyed it, especially attempting to frighten the life out of her. Joe soon tired of it and persuaded her to go for a walk in the gardens with him. She was surprised when he said in a jokey voice, 'After all, you came all this way to spend time with me and see how enjoyable the American life can be. I'm not short of money and we could go about together. You could see places and describe them to me and write to your mom and make her envious and regret not coming over. We could have got wed. I could make an honest woman of her.'

Joanna remembered that was something she had thought about too, but instead found herself saying, 'Mam would never settle in America. She's a Liverpudlian through and through.'

He stared at her in disbelief. 'I could give her so much. I was given compensation after the accident. It was Josh's fault, and the guilt has never left him.'

'What happened? I know nothing about this.'

He pressed his lips together. 'I don't like talking about it, and doctors were later able to do something to ease the problem.'

'But you fought in the war. How were you able to do that?' she asked.

'Medical science – and I was a backroom boy. Don't mention any of this to Josh… or Jay even? We've put it behind us.'

Joanna assured him that she wasn't in the habit of breaking a confidence. Then she suggested they went and had an ice cream before meeting Alfie and Josh and returning to Joe's. It was decided that the day after tomorrow, they would make the trip together. She did not want to spend too much time alone in his company; she had started to have doubts about him telling the truth about Josh causing an accident. Then him warning her against mentioning it to Josh or Jay. She felt as if he was trying to turn her against Josh.

Once back at Joe's house, Joanna was happy when Elsie and her granddaughter called in, and the woman showed her how to use the coffee machine. She was beginning to think more and more of visiting the film studios and told herself that Joe would not be in favour, but she had not travelled all this way just to see him. So she visited a travel agency later that day and was told she would need to go to Los Angeles; she was given a couple of leaflets and a map, which she placed in her rucksack pocket under her bed.

She was up bright and early the following morning and was relieved that the sky was blue with few clouds. She donned the light trousers her mother had bought her and a short-sleeved T-shirt and the walking shoes she used in Wales or the Lake District. She then threw a light waterproof over her shoulders and went forth to greet Alfie, Jay and Josh.

'Joe will be out in five minutes,' she said, finding it more difficult day by day to call him Pa, as she seldom felt daughterly towards him. Maybe her relationship could be more like that of a niece? But there were men back home who were like uncles to her; and as for fatherly, despite having hurt her, Theo still had a place in her heart, as did Jack.

'Wake up, Joanna!' said Josh, giving her a slight push towards the rear of the car. 'Jay's driving and Alfie's in the front passenger seat. You're sitting in the back with me and Joe,' he added. 'I'll get in first, then you in the middle and Joe last.'

'I wish he'd get a move on,' said Jay, taking her rucksack and placing it in what was called the boot in England but the trunk in America.

'You can't rush him. I wonder when his next visit to the eye specialist is,' she said, making herself comfortable. She overheard Jay say to Alfie, 'When we go climbing on our own, we'll take my smaller runaround, and you can have a go at driving in that for a while.'

Alfie thanked him. Joanna imagined his relief, certain that even if Alfie would enjoy driving the Cadillac, he'd first need to become accustomed to driving on the right-hand side of the road and a vehicle much easier to handle would help with that.

Then Joe climbed into the car with his walking stick, which scraped her ankle. She gasped but used the stick to help him inside. 'You okay?' she said, moving a couple of inches along towards Josh, so there was more space for Joe.

'Thanks,' he said. 'You're a thoughtful daughter.' He eased closer to her and linked his arm through hers. She was now thoroughly squashed and could only see the passing scenery when they left the city by leaning forward and resting her elbows on the tops of the front seats, which meant Joe's arm was dragged forward. She was gazing through the windscreen, but she was concerned that the two in the front might think she wanted to eavesdrop on their conversation. She soon realised that Josh was aware of what was happening as he eased her back, saying he wanted to talk to her.

'So, how is Olive?' he asked.

She was taken aback by his question, believing that Jay had already told him all he needed to know about her mother, so she only said, 'I'll know more when she answers my letter. Maybe I'll receive hers in about a week's time.'

'Does she still keep in touch with her ex-husband?'

She almost asked him why he was interested but decided that could sound rude, so instead she replied, 'She doesn't go out of her way. After all, he works in London, and he has re-married. Occasionally, he writes to me, and he came to my granddad's funeral. He gave Eliza a fiver for me.'

'That was generous of him,' said Josh.

She shrugged. 'There was a time when he believed I was his daughter.'

Several moments passed and it struck her that maybe she should not have mentioned that, because she was aware that Joe had taken a large intake of breath. She waited for him to make a comment, but it was Alfie who said, 'Aunt Olive didn't even tell Mam the truth, and they were close friends. Olive's my godmother.'

'What does it matter now,' said Joanna. 'Mam eventually let the cat out of the bag and told me and Nan and Theo.'

'My stepfather Jack said these things happen in wars. Emotions run high. My dad was killed fighting overseas. He never got to see me,' said Alfie.

'You're saying I'm lucky,' said Joe.

Alfie replied, 'I'm not in your shoes.'

'Let's drop the subject,' said Josh. 'I shouldn't have asked Joanna such a question about her mother.'

'But Mam trusted you,' said Joanna. 'She looked upon you as a friend, as did Joe. You were in a difficult position. You cared about both.'

'I made a promise and should have kept it,' said Josh.

'If you had,' said Joe, 'I'd be more unhappy than I was a short time ago.'

'And I wouldn't be here in stunning California,' said Joanna, throwing her arms in the air and catching both men on their jaws with the backs of her hands. 'Never mind climbing mountains, when am I going to Hollywood and meeting some film stars?'

Then she apologised to Josh and Joe for accidentally hitting them.

'I'm sure you didn't mean it,' said Joe. 'But there'll be no trips to Hollywood. You can't expect Josh or Jay to be ferrying you about all the time.'

'I don't mind, although once I get a job, I won't be able to do it,' said Jay. 'I like films.'

'Me too,' said Alfie. 'I'd like to see the sets and directing.'

'You're on, then,' said Jay. 'But right now, we're heading for the mountains.'

'Yippee-ay-oh!' yelled Alfie.

'I'd also enjoy watching Josh chopping down a tree,' said Joanna.

'I can arrange it,' said Josh. 'But you'll have to do as you're told and stay out of danger, or your pa will have my life. He ignored what I said once and nearly had a nasty accident, if it hadn't been for his son dragging him out of the way.'

'I wished I'd met him,' said Joanna.

'I could do with some wood for my carving,' said Joe, rubbing his chin.

'Here,' said Joanna, 'let me kiss it better, Pa.' She planted a kiss on his jaw.

'What about me?' asked Josh, leaning towards her.

She only hesitated a fraction before brushing his sore jaw with her lips. 'Somehow I must have hit you harder.'

'Peace, all of you,' said Jay.

'Okay,' said Alfie and Joanna.

'We're with you,' said Joe and Josh.

Afterwards peace reigned until Joanna began to sing songs that she had sung as a girl on trips to Blackpool in a charabanc. 'We're off, we're off, we're off in a motor car. Sixty coppers are after us and we don't know where we are…' Then she sang, 'Ten green bottles hanging on a wall…' She paused for a few minutes after the last line to catch her breath, only for Alfie to break into, 'She'll be coming round the mountain when she comes…'

'That's more like it,' commented Jay, joining in.

Not to be outdone, Joanna sang along as well, remembering her mother and granddad singing that song.

'Are you hoping to be spotted and appear in the movies?' asked Joe. 'You haven't got a bad voice, daughter.'

'Thank you, kind sir,' she retorted, bobbing her head in his direction, although she wished he would stop calling her daughter. 'I'll shut up now and save me breath for walking. At least it's not raining.'

'I was just planning to walk up the lower slopes,' said Joe.

'I'll stick with you, then,' she said. 'How much further have we to go?'

'Not far,' said Joe, squeezing her arm against his side.

'Don't believe him,' said Josh. 'He's forgetting another forty miles is more than not far to the English.'

'I had a friend who went to Australia, and he said the road just seemed to go on and on forever,' said Alfie.

'Big country, Australia,' said Jay. 'That's why they have flying doctors.'

'Lots of empty space in the middle,' said Joanna. 'Anyone ever read Nevil Shute's *A Town Like Alice*?'

'I saw the film,' said Alfie. 'Quite a bit of it was set in Malaya. Peter Finch was the Australian hero.'

'The Japanese crucify him, and she believes he's dead but later discovers he's survived and goes to Australia in search of him and finds Alice Springs, which he used to talk about. She must travel miles in her search in Australia.'

'I've seen it too,' said Josh. 'It was called *The Legacy* over here.'

'Anyway...' said Joanna. 'Forty miles shouldn't take too long in this motor. Three-quarters of an hour?'

'Depending on the traffic,' said Jay.

She fell silent, having decided she might have hogged the conversation too much. Closing her eyes, she thought of her mother and whether she had begun ordering furniture for the house in Waterloo, and whether Nan had decided where she wanted to go on a cruise and if Dougal would go with her.

CHAPTER THIRTEEN

LIVERPOOL

JUNE

Olive placed a cup of tea on the coffee table in front of her mother, who was turning the pages of a travel brochure which had a cruise ship on the cover. Olive was sitting on the sofa arm so lowered herself and sat beside her mother so she could see better.

'Have you come to a decision yet?'

'I suppose what's available in September,' replied Flora. 'I fancy a cruise in the Med, but Dougal wants to go to Norway to see the fiords earlier, say August.'

'It was your decision, though, to go on a cruise in the first place,' said Olive, reaching for the paper bag containing two cream cookies that Eliza had dropped in earlier, along with a few groceries. Olive had paid her, but she hadn't stayed long because she had to be home before Jack went to work. He was putting in more hours, due to them being short of manpower because of holidays. Eliza had said she would stay longer when she received a letter from Alfie but would bring the kids with her, as they enjoyed a ride on the bus.

'You are thinking it will be colder in Norway despite it being August?' asked Olive. 'It's a beautiful country and it's light for longer in summer.'

Flora said, 'I know that and it's more expensive. Besides, you could do with my help to move in. What with Joanna in California.'

'Eliza and Jack are going to help me, Mam,' said Olive. 'Lifting and moving furniture will be too much for you or Dougal. I can give you some more money for Norway.'

'You're probably right there about furniture,' said Flora. 'But where are you getting the money from?'

'I won it on the pools,' said Olive in a jokey voice.

Her mother laughed. 'Very funny.'

'I told you I had savings… due to living with you and Dad for years. I owe you both,' she said seriously.

'I'll tell you what I'll do,' said Flora. 'If places are still available for Norway I'll go there. But I don't want your money. It was your dad you owed but he didn't want to take money from you or Joanna. He spoilt the pair of you.'

Olive could barely accept her mother was turning money down and could only believe it was because she felt guilty for not telling her about her father's illness and the funeral. Or that Dougal being a widower with a grown-up son had more money than she and Joanna had believed originally, and he would help her mother out if they went to Norway. Having come to that conclusion, she dropped the subject of money and bit into her cream cookie.

'I wonder when you'll hear from Joanna. She should have arrived in America by now,' said Flora after licking cream from her chin.

'Her letter will take a while to reach here,' said Olive.

'Even by airmail?' said her mother.

'Yes, anyway, if Alfie's letter gets to Eliza first, she'll let us know how things are going,' said Olive.

'Joanna mightn't tell Alfie everything that takes place between her and Joe.' Flora tightened her lips. 'They mightn't take to each other. After all, he had a wife when he was carrying on with you.'

Despite agreeing with her mother, Olive said, 'There was a war on, Mam, and they were thousands of miles away from each other.' She reached for her cup and gulped down a mouthful of tea.

'You're making excuses. Next, you'll be saying she could have been carrying on with someone else like some wives did over here. I could name a couple. Blokes nipping up back jiggers.'

'Enough, Mam,' said Olive. 'Anyway, I was wondering if Dougal has told his son that he's moved in. If he has, I'd like to know, in case he turns up here while you're cruising in Norway.'

'If we go to Norway,' said Flora. 'But I doubt Patrick will turn up here on his own. He's staying with mates in Blackpool.'

'All right, *if*,' Olive smiled. 'But September's a long way off and the pair of you might be ready for a change before then.'

'What d'you mean by that?' asked her mother, bristling.

'Just that you might be ready for a change of air, a holiday. What else would I mean?'

'You know exactly what,' said Flora, getting up. 'Any more snide remarks from you and you won't be welcome here.'

'You're just being touchy,' she said. 'I'll be out of your hair soon enough, Mam. Make the most of my company while you've got it.'

Before Flora could say anything, there was the sound of the front door opening and Dougal called, 'Anyone at home?'

Olive answered, 'In here! You ready for a cup of tea?'

'I'll make it myself, kiddo,' he replied.

'The pot should still be hot; if not, the kettle won't take long to boil,' said Flora. 'But you sit down, darlin', and I'll make it.'

Olive smiled at Dougal as he entered the room. 'I was just asking Mam whether your son knew that you've moved.'

Dougal sat down with a heavy sigh. 'I received a post-card from Blackpool sent to my old address. He must be doing all right.'

Flora glared at Olive. 'She's wondering what to say if he were to turn up here and we'd gone off to Norway.'

A smile lit his face. 'So, you've made up your mind,' he said, sweeping Flora off her feet and kissing her. 'You won't lose by it, sweetheart.'

Then he turned to Olive and said, 'He's not going to turn up here, so don't you be worrying.' He placed Flora gently on her feet, and added, 'I'll sort the cruise out tomorrow, and our passports.'

'It's so exciting,' said Olive. 'I'll leave you two to talk while I go upstairs and finish my library book. It's due up and I want to take it back this evening.'

'It's a good job you're a fast reader,' said her mother. 'It's six o'clock now and the library closes at eight.'

'I know,' said Olive, hurrying out of the kitchen. Hopefully, she wouldn't miss the bus.

She dragged herself upstairs and picked up her library book; she was four pages from the end. She enjoyed savouring the final pages and always read the last two twice. A sigh of satisfaction escaped her, and she removed her bookmark, which had a verse from the Bible in cross-stitch on it. She placed it on the bedside table and then carried the book downstairs and out into the street, reading as she walked. She raced through the pages, only slowing down because a passenger saw her hurtling along and held the bus up for her. She made the library in time and, after handing over her book, she was told she only had five minutes to choose another one. Fortunately, she knew exactly where a book by Ngaio Marsh, which she had not read, was situated and asked the librarian if she could get it for her to save time.

Within ten minutes, Olive had left the library and was waiting at the bus stop to return to her mother's house. She had not been standing there for long when a car drew up.

'Hop in,' said a voice she recognised and had not wanted to hear again. She would have ignored him if he hadn't reached across, opened the passenger door and seized the bag containing her latest library book.

'Don't do that, fool,' she said, swiftly reaching out and resting her hand on the car.

'You're the fool,' said Alan. 'Your mam told me where you were and suggested I bring you home.'

'The bus is here. I don't need a lift,' she said.

'Come on, Olive, be sensible instead of making a scene.'

Out of the corner of her eye she caught a glimpse of the swinging bag holding her library book dangling from his wrist and somehow managed to swing it towards her. He yelped and she stepped back, after having snatched the bag from his grasp. She asked the conductor for help getting aboard. Before Alan could prevent her, the conductor stepped down and helped her up. He swore angrily at Alan, ordering him to skedaddle.

Alan swore back but drove away, much to Olive's satisfaction. She thanked the bus conductor and promised herself that she would learn to drive. Once she arrived at her mother's house, she telephoned Eliza and asked if she could put her up, as she could no longer cope with her mother interfering in her life. When Eliza told her she was welcome, Olive said that she would call a taxi and be with her within the hour. Once she had called a taxi, she told her mother that she was leaving and went upstairs and packed.

Dougal attempted to persuade Olive to change her mind but without success. She asked him, though, if he could see she received the letter that she was expecting from Joanna.

'I'll try and intercept the postman,' said Dougal. 'But you won't cut your mother out of your life altogether, will you?' He took her hand and squeezed it.

'I'll keep in touch,' she replied. 'Tell her I'll see her around.' Olive opened the front door and left, followed by Dougal, carrying her suitcase and bag.

The taxi drew up at the kerb and she made her way carefully to the vehicle as the driver got out and opened a rear passenger door. She waved to Dougal through the open window and then sat back, blinking tears.

Eliza opened the front door a few minutes after the taxi drew up and hurried down the step to take Olive's luggage as the driver helped her out of the taxi. Olive had the money ready and handed it to him with thanks. Then she followed Eliza into the house, where she was welcomed by Beth and led by a tug on her skirt to a comfortable chair, and a cup of cocoa was placed on a coffee table close by.

'I'll take your things up to Alfie's room,' said Eliza.

'Thanks,' said Olive.

Beth said, 'Would you like a buttered scone with your cocoa? I made them with Mam's help.'

'I must have one, in that case,' said Olive, relaxing back in the armchair. She reached for the cocoa cup and took a mouthful. 'Nectar of the gods,' she said.

'What do you mean by that, Aunty Olive?' asked Beth. 'There's only one god.'

'A long time ago the Greeks believed there were many gods and goddesses, and they lived on Mount Olympus in Greece, where they drank nectar, which was believed to taste delicious. There are lots of stories called myths about the Greeks and their gods, which you'll hear about in school when you're much older. Enid Blyton has written a book for children about the myths and the adventures of the ancient Greeks,' said Olive. 'I'll buy you it for Christmas.'

Beth clapped her hands. 'It's a long way off to Christmas.'

'Maybe you can order it from the library this week and your daddy can read it to you sooner,' said Olive. 'Now, where's my scone?'

Beth skipped away to fetch the scone and buttered it and brought it in on a flower-patterned China plate. Then she was chased up to bed.

Eliza came down and sat opposite Olive. 'So, what's happened?'

Olive told her friend all that had taken place that evening.

Eliza said, 'I can understand how you feel about Alan, and your mother trying to push you into a relationship you don't want. Anyway, you'll be moving out soon.'

'I know. The question is, do I give her my new address? I don't want her passing it on to Alan.'

Eliza sighed. 'There's no rush to decide. When you write to Joanna, tell her to address her letters to you at my address and give her your new one as well, and the date you finally decide to move in. Jack and I need to know, and so does your Peter to help you.'

Olive nodded. 'I hope we'll hear from them soon. Did you tell Alfie about me speaking to Theo's new wife, and that her and her family are staying at Theo's Liverpool house? She suggested they'd probably like to see us.'

'Do they want to come here, or do we go there?'

'You could write to them. I can give you the address if you don't remember it. After all, I lived there for several years,' said Olive, stifling a yawn.

'It's probably best they come here,' said Eliza. 'I'll do it this evening. It's a pity Glyn won't be able to see Alfie.' She stood up. 'Anyway, it's time you were in bed. I'll wait up for Jack and tell him you're here. You look tired out.'

Eliza escorted Olive upstairs to Alfie's bedroom, and they made up his bed with fresh linen. 'The guest room is given over to a cousin of Amelia's from Shropshire. She's never been to Liverpool before, and they were close when they were kids. She's just been widowed, and Amelia thought it would be good for her to get away to somewhere she'd never been with her husband.'

'What's her name?' asked Olive.

'Jane Grainger, she lives in Shrewsbury.'

'Doesn't the River Severn run through there and they have a really ancient cathedral?'

Eliza nodded. 'And it's not far from the Welsh border.'

'You'd think she'd rather go to beautiful Wales,' said Olive.

'I think Amelia's going to take her to visit the North Welsh coast, as her cousin has never been that far north,' said Eliza.

'They could stop over at Glyn's B&B in Colwyn Bay,' said Olive. 'Will they go by train?'

'I should think so. She's coming here by train. I've been thinking they could sound Glyn out, when he and his family visit. I'll leave you to get some sleep.' With that, she whisked out of the bedroom, closing the door quietly behind her.

Olive awoke early the next morning, washed and dressed swiftly and went downstairs to make a cup of tea and a slice of toast with real British butter – much better than the margarine used during rationing, which had carried on after the war. She wondered if her daughter was awake, then remembered the times were different. She couldn't remember if Britain was behind or ahead of America. It didn't matter right now – all she cared about was getting her hands on Joanna's letter before her mother did. Hopefully, Dougal would be able to intercept the postman. As it was, a letter from Alfie arrived and Eliza beat Olive to the front door and danced around the lobby, waving it in the air. She only stopped when she was out of breath and Beth stretched over the banister rail and snatched it from her hand.

'Here you are, Aunty Olly, you read it to me!'

'Thank you, but no,' said Olive. 'It would spoil reading Joanna's letter for me… and don't call me Olly!'

'Sorry,' said Beth, handing the letter to her mother.

Eliza ran upstairs and locked herself in the bathroom.

A few minutes later Jack came out of the bedroom and tried the handle of the bathroom door. 'Go away,' called Eliza.

'It's me, don't be long.'

Eliza opened the door. 'I just wanted to read Alfie's letter in peace away from Peter and Beth. I'll go into our bedroom.' She stepped aside, kissed him and rushed to their bedroom. Once inside, she slammed the door shut and placed a chair against it, before stretching out on the bed and opening the envelope.

She took her time reading the letter and some paragraphs she read twice, pleased that he seemed to have enjoyed the journey. He explained that he was looking after Joanna, and that although she and her father appeared to hit it off at first, she seemed to have gone off him a bit. He also mentioned a neighbour called Elsie and a little girl who seemed to be very much at home in Joe's fantastic house.

> *...Which was like something out of the movies, with a veranda – and Josh, Jay and I stayed for something to eat and drink and then left, after arranging to pick up Joe and Joanna to take them out for a trip to the state park where the mountain Jay and I are going to climb is situated. You don't have to worry, it's not as high as Snowdon.*
>
> *I was surprised not to find Jay's mother waiting on the doorstep to welcome us when we arrived at the house. Only later did I discover that she had received a phone call from her father who lives in Los Angeles, and he wasn't well and needed her. She wanted Jay to join her there, as his grandfather had not seen him for an age and wanted to hear all about his time in Europe. I have not been invited along and Jay only expected to be there a few days, so our climb is put back until he returns. So, I can*

see me spending time with Joanna and her father,
who is a wood carver. Joanna and I might try our
hand at it, just for fun. Joanna wants to go to
Hollywood, but I can't see that happening. It's a
heck of a distance but I'd like to make her dream
come true. Joe has still not lost his sight. I wonder
if it was just a ruse to get Joanna and Aunty Olive
here, for reasons he's keeping to himself. I can't say
I like him. She's also feeling homesick and so am
I.

    Lots of love to all, Alfie

Eliza sighed, wishing he had not gone to America. She folded the letter, returned it to its envelope and left it on the dressing table for Jack to read later. She went downstairs and found Olive sitting on the sofa, also reading a letter.

She looked up and said, 'Dougal brought it. Joanna and Joe seem to be getting on fine. He has a posh house like those in the American films. I wonder where he got the money from.' She rubbed the letter across her chin.

'I wouldn't have believed from wood carving,' said Eliza.

'She mentions that, and that it's super that he used to be a lumberjack. He never told me that.' Olive was puzzled. 'I wonder if he's making it up. Sounds more adventuresome than just working for a building company making windows and doors.'

'What else does she say?'

'She mentions the woman next door, who is either a Good Samaritan or otherwise. I wonder how old her daughter is,' said Olive.

'And whether she has a husband or partner,' said Eliza.

'Are we being too suspicious?' Olive wrinkled her brow.

'I'll answer Alfie's letter and mention our thoughts,' said Eliza. 'After all, Joanna felt rejected when Glenys arrived on the scene.'

'I was at fault, too,' said Olive. 'I wasn't fair to my daughter or Theo or Josh and Joe.'

'But Joe deceived you,' said Eliza. 'Just as Alfie's father deceived me.'

'And Josh broke his promise and played on my soft nature. If he hadn't told Joe about Joanna, and us about Joe going blind and his bereavement, we wouldn't be in this tangle.'

'So, what are we going to do? Should I go over there?'

'What about your house?' said Eliza, shaking her head.

Olive sighed. 'How could I forget! I'd like to move in soon.'

'And Joanna wants to go to Hollywood, how about that?'

'She mentioned it when she was over here,' said Olive. 'But will Joe want her to go? I can't remember him ever showing interest in going there.'

Eliza giggled. 'Alfie wants her to go – says he wants to make her dreams come true.'

'Stop it,' said Olive. 'Surely he wasn't planning on them going on their own.'

'We're going round in circles. It's you that says they're like brother and sister. Alfie says Jay's going to see his mother and her father, who's ill. He's told me before that he doesn't get on with Josh and wants his daughter to live with him while Josh is away.'

'It's all Hitler's fault,' muttered Olive. 'So, what am I going to do?'

'You can't go,' Eliza attempted to stifle her giggles. 'You need to start watching your spending and pray that Joe cares more about his daughter than his neighbour, if you want her to fulfil her dream and go to university and become a pharmacist.'

'You're right, of course.' Olive put her head in her hands. 'We were never after his money, but she is his daughter, so he owes her.' Her voice was muffled. 'I didn't want to go, as I no longer love him or want to marry him.'

'He might no longer love you but could be fond enough already of Joanna to suggest she goes to university over there.'

'I doubt she'll be tempted.' Olive lifted her head.

'What about Jay?' said Eliza.

'She likes him but that's all, besides she's too young to marry.' Olive eased herself up from the chair. 'Anyway, I should get going, I planned to go into town to do some shopping.'

'You're not going yet, are you? It's only early. Have another cup of tea and a slice of toast,' Eliza said.

Olive glanced at the clock and sat down again and started to re-read Joanna's letter.

—

After a second breakfast, she decided to change into something smarter, and only then did she phone for a taxi. She went to Philip, Son and Nephew bookshop on Whitechapel and enquired about the Enid Blyton book on Greek myths, as she had decided she should read it herself to make sure it was suitable for Beth. She was pleased on being led to a shelf where there were several books on the subject by a variety of authors, as well as legends and myths of Ireland, Norway and India. She flicked through pages before perusing the section containing detective fiction and choosing a Dorothy Sayers book of short stories. She did not linger for long but bought some postage stamps from the post office and a box of delicious cakes from Marks & Spencer. She then made her way to the bus which would take her to West Derby Road, which was the main road closest to where Eliza lived, hoping she would not bump into Alan. As luck would have it, she did not bump into him, but she spotted him through the window of the bus as the vehicle passed where the prefabs were situated. She turned her head away swiftly, hoping he had not seen her.

She wasted no time leaving the bus but there was no way of her crossing the road swiftly. Then it struck her that she could enter Eliza's by the back garden gate. Hopefully, it was not bolted. It opened smoothly when she lifted the latch and went inside, making her way up the garden. She was about to open the kitchen door when she heard voices, and she froze on recognising Alan's and Eliza's.

Olive was near to collapse but was at a loss what to do. She was desperate for a cup of tea and a sit down. Then she remembered the outside toilet, which had been there for years, and somehow managed to reach it and get inside and close the door. She sank onto the well-scrubbed wooden seat and closed her eyes and told herself that she was an idiot. What was she scared of? How long might she have to stay here? It was then she heard the back gate latch click and heavy footsteps sounding on the garden path. She prayed they would go past but they halted outside, and their owner attempted to open the lavatory door. She hung on to the handle and told them it was occupied.

'Is that you, Olive?' asked Jack.

'Shush!' she said.

'What are you up to?' he whispered. 'This lavatory is for emergencies.'

'Sorry, but Alan is in the kitchen, and I don't want to see him.'

'This is crazy. He can't do anything to you while I'm here. Come out of there now,' said Jack. 'Or I'll force the door open at the count of three. One… Two…'

'Just a mo,' she said, opening the door. 'I'm not going into the house without you.'

'You're nuts,' he said.

'I should have gone to America,' she said, holding onto the door.

'What for? Come out and go into the shed for a few minutes. I won't be long,' said Jack. 'Then we can go in together and you can say we met down Tuebrook, when I was leaving the police station and you were coming out of the cooked meat shop.'

'I've no cooked meat with me,' she said. 'I'll say I popped in to see the house where I once lived and where Glyn, Alfie's uncle, is staying.'

'That sounds better,' said Jack. 'Now vamoose.'

'Vamoose? That reminds me of the Westerns.' She went inside the shed and sat down.

A few minutes later Jack came whistling down to the shed and helped her up and drew her left arm through his right one, and they approached the kitchen door. 'Anyone home?' he shouted.

'You're later than I expected,' said Eliza, coming out of the living room. 'Oh, you've Olive with you.'

'We met in Tuebrook,' said Olive. 'I went to the old house.'

'Alan's here,' Eliza said. 'Come and say hello and have a cup of tea.'

'Thanks,' said Olive. 'Actually, I've been into town to see the solicitor and I bought some cakes on my way back.'

'Come and have tea with me and tell me about your house,' said Alan.

'Beth has her dancing class this evening,' said Eliza. 'She'd love you to go and watch her, Olive.'

'Lovely,' she said.

'She'll like that,' said Jack. 'You can come with me when I pick her up from school.'

'I'll have to be going soon,' grunted Alan. 'I've a date with a woman from work.'

'Oh, what does your son think of that?' asked Olive.

'It's nothing to do with him,' said Alan. 'He's told me he's thinking of going to sea. He'd like to see a bit more of the world.'

'So, who's going to look after you?' Olive asked. 'I mean, he does a lot for you, doesn't he?'

'You can have the job if you like,' he responded. 'Although, there's plenty of women looking for a man, just like after the Great War. There's a shortage, so your loss will be another woman's gain if you aren't interested.'

'Good luck with that,' said Olive. 'I'll pray for her.'

'I'll see you out,' said Jack.

'No need for that,' said Alan, picking up his jacket from the back of the chair. 'I know the way.'

'Ta-ra,' said Olive and Eliza in unison.

Once they heard the front door slam, Jack checked that Alan had truly left the house and joined Olive as she told Eliza that she was divorced and would hopefully soon have the deeds of the house and move in. 'Paying cash was a real help. It's all so exciting. I'll be able to write back to

Joanna with my news and that I hope she and Alfie have a good time in Hollywood and mention that George Biggs is thinking of going to sea.'

'He's doing the right thing,' said Jack. 'He's a good lad.'

'So, are you two really going with Beth to her dancing class?' said Eliza.

'Of course,' said Olive. 'I can't wait, and I want to discuss something with Jack, but don't ask what it is.'

'I don't like secrets,' said Eliza, pulling a face.

'It's nothing for you to worry about,' said Olive. 'I'm not going to write to Joe and suggest he comes over here for Christmas and see my new house.'

Eliza said, 'Is that what he and Joanna would like? Has she mentioned it in her letter?'

'No!' Olive said. 'Now how about a cake?' She reached for the box and opened it.

'Another cup of tea?' asked Jack, picking up the brown teapot.

'Yes, please,' said Olive. 'Unless there's coffee?'

'Coffee it is,' said Eliza, getting to her feet. 'I'll have a cup as well.'

'Let's see the cakes,' said Jack, putting down the teapot. 'I'll have a chocolate éclair.'

'I'll have one of them too,' called Eliza.

'A strawberry and cream tart for me,' said Olive. 'I'll save a custard slice for Beth.'

When they had finished eating and drinking, Jack went upstairs to take a nap. Eliza washed the crockery, and Olive perused Alfie's letter that Eliza passed to her, and was interested, puzzled and pleased to read that he and Joanna were homesick and ready to come home, but not until they had been to Hollywood. Jay had gone with his mother to see his grandfather who was not well and wanted them to go and live with him. Josh had told Olive that his father-in-law had told him to his face that he wasn't good enough for his daughter. Josh was making plans to go to Ireland to see his kin, anyway. Olive rested her cheek in her hand, wondering when he would arrive.

'You're looking serious!' said Eliza. 'You're not worrying about Joanna being homesick and Alfie not liking Joe?'

Olive jumped at the sound of Eliza's voice. She removed her hand and gazed up at her friend. 'I was thinking about Joanna and how mistaken I was believing she and Joe were getting on brilliant.'

'What do you mean?' asked Eliza.

'She's mentioned wishing she had known her half-brother in her letter but never Joe.'

Eliza looked thoughtful. 'Well, if you think about it, that's natural. I mean, there must be lots of children who have half-brothers or half-sisters due to wars and even before then, when more people lost their spouses to illness or accidents and re-married.'

Olive thought about that and how true it was. 'You're right, of course,' she said. 'There must have been many more convenient marriages in the old days.'

'Proper married life must have been lacking for Joe; that could be why he never told you he was married. Joanna wouldn't be here if the pair of you hadn't given in to temptation, as so many other couples did.'

'I gave in,' said Olive, folding her arms across her chest. 'I'm weak. I must admit when I first set eyes on Alfie, I was as jealous as hell. I wanted a baby of my own.'

'So, you got what you wanted.' Eliza smiled. 'But subconsciously you kept that thought to yourself when you gave in to Joe's desire.'

Olive smiled slightly. 'I'm admitting nothing because I hadn't thought it through sensibly at the time and it wasn't the least bit romantic.'

'So, what next?' Eliza asked as Jack entered the room.

'I need to finish hemming the curtains.' Olive grimaced. 'I've left them at Mam's, so I'll have to fetch them.'

Jack said, 'I'll give you a lift.'

'Tomorrow,' said Olive. 'You're tired and I need to go to the bank first and write letters to Joanna and Iris.'

'Can I come to your mother's as well?' said Eliza, taking Alfie's letter from Olive's lap.

'Why not? The more the merrier,' said Olive. 'Besides, this evening I'm going with Jack and Beth to watch her dancing.'

'True,' said Jack. 'That's why I cut my nap short. I suddenly remembered.'

'Had I better change?' said Olive.

They stared at her. Jack shook his head. 'You look fine to me and it's not as if you're going to dance.'

'Will you feel better if you changed?' asked Eliza.

'Probably, but I'd feel as if I should have a bath and wash my hair first.'

'Which would take up more time,' said Jack. 'Go as you are.'

So, that decided, they had another coffee, and Olive washed her face and hands and applied lipstick and left with Jack. It did not take them long to pick up Beth with her tap shoes and costumes from school, and it seemed to Olive scarcely any time before they were seated, and the children were practising their steps to the music of a piano played by the dance mistress. Olive couldn't help thinking of Fred Astaire tapdancing with Ginger Rogers. Olive wondered why Joanna had never wanted dancing lessons when she was younger. Even so, she seemed to enjoy capering about to rock and roll records and skiffle by the likes of Lonnie Donegan. Olive clapped when the act came to an end and wondered about Beth and some of the other children getting parts in a pantomime. Often there would be a scene were villagers would sing and dance. Liverpudlians were fond of singing and dancing and comedy, so loved pantomimes, and they had a choice of at least five theatres in the Christmas season, starring well-known personalities from the radio; two popular performers were Josef Locke, an Irish tenor, and Dorothy Ward who played a principal boy. There were also theatres across the Mersey, in Birkenhead and New Brighton, as well as the seaside resort of Southport.

Fortunately, the evening ended at seven thirty and they went home to French toast and cocoa, and Beth did a tap dance for her mother on the tiled floor, which delighted Eliza. Then, feeling sleepy and ready to nod off, Olive excused herself with thanks and went to bed. She fell asleep with a writing pad and a pen in her hand.

CHAPTER FOURTEEN

CALIFORNIA

Joanna took the blue envelope from her father's hand and, recognising her mother's writing, she placed her mug of coffee on the side table and slit the envelope with a quivering finger. She withdrew several sheets of thin blue paper and smoothed them flat. She started to read and was delighted to be informed that her mother hoped to move in soon. She felt a little sad about the divorce being final, remembering certain happy days. But it came as a surprise to hear that Olive was now living with Eliza and Jack and had been to see Beth tapdancing; also that George Biggs was thinking of going to sea. She wondered what had happened to cause him to do that. Perhaps Alfie would have an idea.

But her mother said no more about George and gave few details about what had happened with Nan. She only told her that she and Nan had fallen out because Nan had interfered in her life once too often, but that her mother and Dougal were getting on fine. Then she went on to ask how it had come about that Joanna was wishing she had met Joe's son, whom she had known nothing about until recently and who wouldn't have known anything of her existence.

Joanna bridled, thinking, and whose fault was that. For a moment she was tempted to tear the letter up. But she read on, and now her mother was asking what she thought about the woman next door to Joe and her granddaughter, and when did she think she would meet the child's mother, and where was the father?

From there Olive went on to say that Joe had never mentioned having been a lumberjack, and she presumed him carving wood was a much more recent occupation. It was only after that she asked why Joanna had not been introduced to Jay's mother. And that she thought the two wives would have been friends, and she would have wanted to help Joe, along with Josh.

Joanna paused, thinking she had never thought of that, but now she did, wondering if Jay and Joe's son had been friends. There had been no mention of such a friendship. Maybe they had been too different, the mothers and the sons. One thing could be said and that was that both mothers and sons had spent a fair amount of time together during the war without a man about the place. How had they felt when their husbands returned from Europe after being parted for so long? Did some resent their husband's authority, while others longed for their men to return?

'So, what does your mother have to say?' asked Joe.

'She asks after you and how are we getting on, as well as mentioning hopefully she'll soon be moving into her own house. She's staying with Alfie's parents. She and Nan have fallen out. Nan is planning to go on a cruise with her lodger but they're not decided whether to go to Norway or the Mediterranean.'

'What about that other bloke Olive knew years ago?'

'He's going out with someone else. His son is thinking of going to sea, just like lots of Liverpool men did for years, and some women.'

'Makes sense,' said Joe. 'Are you still thinking of going to university?'

'If I gain the qualifications,' she replied. 'Would you marry again?'

Joe frowned. 'Why do you ask?'

'I just wondered. You're not that old.'

He smiled. 'I'm going to get myself a dog trained for the blind.'

'It'll be company for you, as well as a help.' She wondered whether to offer her mam's letter for him to read, but there came a knock on the front door and so she went to answer it. She opened the door to see Josh and Alfie standing there.

'Can I help you?' she asked.

'We were wondering if we could help you,' said Josh. 'Can we come in?'

'Of course,' said Joanna. 'I'm sure Joe will be pleased to see you.' She stepped back, opening the door wide.

They followed her to where Joe was sitting near the window overlooking the garden, where many varieties of roses bloomed. Alfie pointed to different ones, saying, 'Mam has that one, it's called "Peace" and unlike some roses, it has a nice scent.'

'It was one of my wife's favourites,' said Joe. 'It only became available after the Second World War.'

'And was aptly named,' said Josh.

'Do you have California poppies?' asked Joanna.

'Mam has tried to grow them,' said Alfie. 'But our weather doesn't suit them. The red ones are no trouble, but she'd like orange and yellow ones.'

'They grow like weeds here,' said Joe. 'That's why they're called California poppies.'

'Red ones grow like that at home,' said Joanna. 'I wonder if I took seeds from those growing here, they just might grow at home in a warm, sheltered spot.'

'Has your mom got a garden at the new house?' asked Josh.

'Yes, and it's not that far from the beach,' she said.

'However interesting all this is,' said Joe, 'why are you here?' Then he surprised Joanna by suddenly changing the subject. 'Would you like a coffee? Joanna, what about it?'

She stood up and went to see to the coffee.

Alfie followed her over. 'Do you want some help?'

'Thanks, so, what are you and Josh here for?' she asked.

'To take you out! Are you percolating the coffee or making instant?' he asked.

'Percolating, that's how Joe likes it,' she said, rolling her eyes.

Alfie took over percolating the coffee, aware she hadn't quite got the hang of it. She thanked him and went over to the cupboards to take out mugs and a plate. She then fetched a tray and placed the mugs on it. She found some biscuits, or cookies as the Americans called them, and emptied them onto a plate, thinking of the cream buns they called cream cookies at home. Then she stepped back as Alfie approached with the percolator and placed it on the tray.

He carried it over and put it on the coffee table, leaving her to pour out the coffee, and Joe and Josh to help themselves to milk and sugar. It was only then she realised she had left the sugar spoons on the worktop. Alfie stood up and fetched them, even as Joe began to tick her off for their absence, which took her by surprise.

'No harm done,' said Alfie and Josh in unison.

'It's taken up time,' said Joe, even as Joanna poured milk into his mug. Alfie was about to hand her a spoonful of sugar, when Joe said, 'I don't take sugar. She knows that.'

'So, what's the fuss about the spoons?' said Alfie, putting the sugar in his own coffee.

Josh nudged him. 'Careful,' he warned.

'I am careful,' he said. 'What a lot of fuss about nothing.'

'You could have spilt the sugar on the table if you weren't careful,' said Joe. 'Besides, I've got to go to the hospital today.'

'You haven't told me about the hospital,' said Joanna, who had seen Josh nudge Alfie and had guessed that he was warning Alfie about the way he was talking to Joe, whose mood had changed. He seemed touchy since the visitors had arrived. What had he and Josh been talking about when she and Alfie were preparing the coffee? Could it be about taking her out?

'Elsie said that she'd accompany me. She was a nurse when she was younger and thinks there is no need for you to come as well. She knows the ropes,' added Joe.

'I see,' said Joanna, thinking she really did. 'That's kind of her.' She changed the subject and spoke to Josh. 'Have you heard from your wife and Jay? Have they arrived safely?'

Josh nodded. 'Jay phoned, told me that the traffic was a nightmare. He's not sure when they'll return, as her father is worse than she thought. He spoke to Alfie as well, suggested he takes you to see the sights.'

'Surely the boy would find our roads difficult to drive on,' said Joe.

'I have my own car at home and I'm not a boy,' said Alfie. 'Besides, he suggested we use the train or coach.'

'I love trains,' said Joanna. 'You don't mind, do you, Pa?' She placed an arm around his neck and kissed his cheek.

'I don't see how I can refuse. I cannot imagine your mother turning the offer down.'

'Me neither,' said Josh. 'And it was my son's suggestion.'

'What about money?' said Joe.

'I'm okay for money,' said Joanna cheerfully. 'Mam saw such a happening and didn't want me cadging from you. As well as that, she suggested I might like to go home by Cunard liner. It's more luxurious. I'm not sure of that. I'd rather save my money for university.'

'I can't afford the time off work with planning to go to Ireland,' said Josh.

'I don't have much time either,' said Alfie. 'But Joanna and I are determined to go to Hollywood studios.'

Joe half-smiled. 'I'm going to miss you, daughter.'

'But you won't be lonely. You've a good neighbour and young company in little Doris and her mother.' She wondered if that was why she had made no mention of her mother's divorce.

His smile deepened. 'She's an interesting child.'

'That's good,' said Joanna. 'Have you tried teaching her how to carve wood?'

'I did, but Elsie almost hit the roof, said it was too dangerous.' He paused. 'I had to agree with her eventually that girls are different to boys.'

'That goes without saying,' said Alfie. 'I have a half-sister at home.'

'I'd have liked a daughter,' said Josh.

'You can't have everything you want in this life,' said Joe.

'I know,' said Josh.

'But at least you both survived the war,' said Alfie. 'My natural father was killed. Luckily, though, Mam met Jack and he's a great stepfather.' He drained his mug. 'Anyway, we'd better be going. Hadn't you better pack a few things, Joanna?'

She nodded and in great excitement and some nervousness, she hurried upstairs, thinking they just might go swimming, as well as climbing the odd mountain, and maybe set foot in Hollywood and see some stars. She thought of her mother having seen Charlton Heston in *The Ten Commandments*. How great it would be to watch a film being made.

She packed a swimming costume and a week's change of underwear, two pairs of pyjamas, a pair of slacks and jeans, four casual tops and two dressy ones, two skirts, a frock, two pairs of nylons, two pairs of ankle socks and a thick pair of walking socks, and one pair of comfortable walking shoes and a pair of high heels. She had no boots, but her shoes were strong brogues bought in Ambleside, in the Lake District. Then she added a waterproof, a woolly hat and gloves, and a cardigan and jacket. Some items were packed in her rucksack, as were her toiletries. She hoped Alfie would remember maps. She packed pens and pencils and writing paper and a couple of novels. She remembered at almost the last minute her passport and purse with cash, and put them in a large handbag with a shoulder strap that she had bought in San Francisco.

She managed with a slight struggle to carry everything downstairs and then Alfie took over while Josh opened the boot and squeezed her luggage inside. Then she kissed

Joe and told him to take care and that she hoped all would go well at the hospital. She would pray for him. A final hug and she climbed into the back of the car and waved goodbye.

He waved back and blew her a kiss and then they were off and straight to the railway station. When they arrived, while Alfie got their tickets, Josh handed her a package. 'Something for the journey,' he said.

She thanked him and he hugged her and told her not to worry about anything but to trust Alfie's good sense and enjoy herself. He would keep an eye out for Joe. Although it probably was not necessary, as that woman next door would be watching out for him. She agreed and thanked him again, and then headed with Alfie to the platform, already worrying about all the stuff she had packed, unable to see how she could manage with less, but how would they manage to carry everything?

They did not have to wait long before their train arrived, and they climbed aboard and found an empty carriage. Alfie stowed their baggage, and they made them-selves comfortable. He had taken several leaflets and a couple of maps from the pocket of his rucksack and handed her one of each. 'I thought you might be in favour of going straight to Paramount Studios where *The Ten Commandments* was made, which our mothers saw recently.'

She stared at him, starry-eyed, and flung her arms about his neck. 'You are a love. I can't wait.'

'I'm glad you're pleased,' he said, removing her arms from about his neck. 'There's no need to choke me to death, though.'

'Sorry,' she said. 'That was the last thing on my mind. Where will we stack our luggage?'

'We'll find somewhere to stay first in Los Angeles and leave it there. After visiting Paramount Studios, we'll see the other sights worth seeing. I'd like to climb the hill where the Hollywood sign is displayed.'

'Me too,' she said, screwing up her face. 'It's just struck me. Doesn't Jay's grandfather live near Los Angeles?'

'You could be right, but we don't have the address, and I don't think his mother would be glad to see us.'

'What about Jay? He'd probably be glad to see us.'

'Maybe, but the granddad mightn't be. Not all Yanks like us Poms.'

'What makes you say that?' she said. 'The few I've met so far have been friendly.'

'We'll just have to wait and see,' said Alfie. 'Anyway, the granddad and Josh don't get on.'

She gave him a puzzled glance. 'You've said that before.'

'Josh told me. You know what fathers can be like with their daughters, and don't always approve of the men they marry.'

'You mean he didn't want his daughter to marry Josh?'

'That's the impression I got when I overheard Josh and his wife arguing. Her father thought Josh beneath her. Not enough money or ambition.'

'She must have been in love with Josh to go against her father.'

'Maybe her mother liked Josh,' said Alfie. 'But she died of a heart attack.'

'You could be right.' Joanna sighed. 'I wonder if he hoped Josh wouldn't return from the war so his daughter and Jay could go and live with him.'

Alfie shrugged. 'Anyway, it's none of our business.'

'I'm not as sure as you. Josh and Mam have kept in touch all these years. His wife wants a divorce. I remember

178

Jay mentioning it back home. They argue a lot. You were there.' Joanna stifled a yawn and stretched and then gazed out of the window at the passing landscape. 'If Mam and Josh realised they were more than friends, would he decide to move to Waterloo?'

'Are you thinking about that because hers and Theo's divorce has gone through?'

She said, 'Your mam told you in her letter?'

Alfie nodded. 'She also mentioned that your mam was hoping to move into her house soon. I'm looking forward to seeing it, with it being not far from the beach. Do you think you'll still want to go to university?'

'It's what I've wanted these last few years and Mam's not against it, although I know she'll miss me, despite having her friend Iris living with her.'

'I wonder if Mam and Jack will take the kids to Anglesey while I'm over here,' he said wistfully.

'You like it that much?' she asked.

He nodded. 'I'd like to have a place there or even just a caravan to have breaks now and again.'

'What if you meet a girl you'd like to marry?' She glanced over her shoulder at him and held her breath.

'I'm in no hurry. I'm only seventeen.'

'Seventeen, you're almost grown up.'

'I'm not ready for the responsibility,' he said.

'During the war, you'd have been called up at eighteen and would have had to grow up quickly.'

'It doesn't bear thinking about,' said Alfie.

'Well, Jay had to join the American forces, and he counts himself lucky that he was flying goods into the American sector in Berlin and not away fighting in Korea.'

'We wouldn't be here if he hadn't been sent to Europe,' said Alfie.

'Or if his dad and Joe hadn't been sent to Britain to help us defeat the Jerries.'

'Enough,' said Alfie, as a smartly dressed middle-aged woman entered the carriage. 'Let's look at this map and trace our journey and then look at the map of Los Angeles.'

'Okay!' Joanna sidled closer and took hold of part of the map that was nearest to her. She was aware of the warmth of his breath on her chin as their heads drew close while they tried to take in as much of the area as possible.

'There's lots of places not far from the ocean,' she said. 'Will the Pacific be warmer the further south we travel? I was told that it's not that warm near San Jose and that it can be foggy.'

Unexpectedly, the woman who had entered the carriage said, 'You're English?'

'We're from Liverpool,' said Joanna. 'You might have heard of our football teams.'

'I sure have. My neighbour has cousins who live in Liverpool. Her husband and mine often discuss soccer. I prefer tennis myself.'

'I've never played,' said Joanna. 'But I always watch Wimbledon on the telly.' She held out a hand. 'I'm Joanna, by the way, and this is my friend Alfie, who can play tennis.'

'I'm Martha.' She shook their hands. 'Have you been staying in San Jose?'

'We still are,' said Alfie. 'We're just going to see some of the sights. Joanna loves the movies, so we're hoping for a tour of Paramount Studios.'

'You'll love it,' said Martha. 'But you mentioned the ocean and whether it would be warmer further south. You bet it is. Santa Monica has a fabulous beach and there's lots to do, but it is expensive to stay there.'

'We were just thinking of swimming and sunbathing,' said Joanna.

'The sun can be very hot. You could just walk around and see the sights, or you could hire bicycles if you're short of time, and you might spot a movie star or two. There are volleyball courts as well. You could watch the play.' She paused. 'I hope you enjoy yourselves whatever you do. I'm off to see my sister. She lives near Monterey. I'll take the bus there. I'll get off at the next station.'

'Thank you,' said Alfie. 'Maybe we'll see you around when we're back in San Jose and we could have a game of tennis.'

'Where are you staying?' she asked.

Joanna gave her Joe's address, adding that Alfie was staying at a different address.

Martha said that Joe's address sounded familiar but that she could not think why, off the top of her head. 'It might come back to me if I don't force it,' she added, getting to her feet when the train began to slow down as they approached a station. The train did not stop long and soon was on its way again.

'She was friendly,' said Joanna. 'Do you think we will see her again?'

'I hope so,' said Alfie. 'I'll enjoy a game of tennis.'

'I've been trying to persuade Joe to take me to a game of baseball, but he doesn't seem keen.'

'Josh would probably take you,' said Alfie, adding, 'I've noticed you don't call Joe Pa anymore.'

'That's because he isn't a dad in my thoughts, and he isn't loving, and I can't believe he ever loved Mam. Josh cared about her more and she must have trusted him, because she was so annoyed with him for breaking his word and telling Joe about me.'

'Mam would like me to call Jack, Dad, because he's been a dad to me. I think he'd like it too,' said Alfie.

'You should do it, then,' she said. 'After all, you're living together as a family now. I doubt Joe, Mam and I will ever do that.' She curled up on the seat like a cat and gazed out of the window. 'Besides, even though California is lovely, it doesn't feel like home.'

'It isn't home, and I'm looking forward to going home. I miss Mam, Dad and the kids.'

'I miss Mam, and I even miss Nan,' said Joanna. 'I wonder if she's gone on her cruise yet and if Dougal's gone with her. Mam said they differed on where to go. And thinking of cruises, I'm looking forward to making the voyage on the ship with you and Josh. I've always felt safe with you both.'

'I hope you'll still feel safe with just me today and in the days to come.'

'Of course I will,' she said. 'I'm glad for this time alone, just the two of us.'

'Josh said Joe isn't pleased but I don't care. Josh thinks it's good for you and Joe to be parted,' said Alfie. 'I think he's regretting breaking his promise to your mam and suggesting you come and visit. I just hope that Jay returns from his granddad's soon, as I'd like to climb a mountain here with him before having to go home.'

She nodded. 'His mother might want him to stay longer if her father is really ill.'

'Jay needs to start looking for a job and working to make money. Josh says he could get him a job with the timber company, but that didn't please Jay's mother. She wants him to work in an office. She knows someone in advertising who would get him in, and he would earn more money, and it would be a clean job, but his grand-father wants him to do law and take over his practice.'

'Joe told me!' exclaimed Joanna. 'Poor Jay.'

'It wouldn't surprise me if he did what I suggested,' said Alfie.

Joanna uncurled herself and put down her legs. 'What's he said to you?'

'He made me promise not to tell anyone.'

'Meanie,' she said. 'I wouldn't tell anyone.'

'You might mean not to,' said Alfie, looking at her fondly. 'But secrets can slip out.'

She pulled a face. 'Are there any secrets you can tell me?'

He pressed his lips tightly together.

She slid along the seat and snuggled up to him. 'Go on, tell me one little secret?'

He coughed before saying, 'Don't try and soft-soap me. It won't work.'

'Why? Aren't I attractive enough?'

He didn't answer.

'Am I too young?'

'Your mam trusts me to take care of you.'

'I'm not asking you to betray her trust. It's not as if I'm a child. Do you know it's not so long ago that a girl could marry at fourteen, and I'm sixteen. Not that I want to get married yet. I've work to do and places to see. But a little kiss would do no harm.'

'So you say. But perhaps that's what Joe said to your mother during the war.'

She drew away from him. 'That's not fair. We wouldn't go that far.'

'You little temptress.' He turned his back on her.

She counted to ten and flung herself at his back. Her arms went round him, and she kissed the nape of his neck and licked his ear before releasing her hold and sitting beside him.

'There, are you tempted?' She winked at him.

He shook his head at her, but before she could move away, he drew her towards him and kissed her lips and pulled her closer, and the kiss deepened. She was in a tizzy, instinctively returning his kiss while at the same time wondering whether she was looking for trouble and should fight him off, although that could put him off her completely. She had always admired him and enjoyed his company, and did not want to lose their friendship. What should she do?

Before she could make up her mind, he raised his head and released her. 'Well?' he asked. 'Where do we go from here?'

'You tell me. You're older and have more experience.'

He looked taken aback. 'More experience of what?'

'Kissing and love,' she replied.

'The two don't necessarily go together,' he said.

'Oh! I see.'

'What do you see?'

'You're warning me off. You don't fancy me.'

'Is that why I kissed you?' His eyes were twinkling.

'You were teaching me a lesson on the dangers of taking kissing seriously.'

'Kissing can be enjoyable.'

She smiled. 'I hope you enjoyed kissing me,' she said. 'I need to learn the difference, as I gather there are kisses and kisses.'

'Time to change the subject,' he said. 'And look forward to the tour round Paramount Studios. Which film would you like to have seen in the making?'

'The one our two mothers saw recently, *The Ten Commandments*. Imagine watching Charlton Heston dividing the Red Sea and them passing through on dry land. And Yul Brynner and his army charging after them and being washed away.'

'Trickery,' said Alfie. 'Yul and the actors wouldn't be washed away and drowned. Too valuable.'

'It's a wonder Jay hasn't thought of becoming an actor. They can earn a lot of money,' she said, darting Alfie a questioning glance.

'I suppose he could be a stuntman,' said Alfie unemotionally.

'Risky,' she mused. 'His mother wouldn't like it.'

'He was in the air force and returned safely,' he said. 'I suppose there was a risk of his plane getting shot down by the Russians.' He paused. 'One thing Jay did tell me, but you already know – his mother is suing for divorce.'

'On what grounds?' she asked.

'You know they argue a lot. And this is America and if you believe the newspapers and the magazines, it's not difficult getting a divorce.'

'Mam and Theo divorced because of his adultery, as you know.'

'I like him,' said Alfie.

'So do I. But you have a stronger reason, he's family.' She gazed out of the window. 'I wonder how much further we have to go,' she mused.

He shrugged and glanced at his watch. 'We won't get there until evening. Why don't you have a nap? You can rest your head on my shoulder.'

She wondered if he expected her to turn down the offer, but she thanked him and made herself comfortable. At first, she was too conscious of his nearness to nod off, but then she relaxed and fell asleep and did not stir until he shook her awake and told her they were in Los Angeles. She eased herself upright and watched as he took down their luggage. She wouldn't allow him to carry it all, so she picked up some of it and followed him out of the station to where he eventually managed to flag down a taxi. The luggage was loaded, and she was assisted into the rear seat, while Alfie climbed into the front seat and had a conversation with the driver. She presumed he was asking for some help to locate reasonably priced places to stay not too far away from Paramount film studios.

Joanna was still half asleep so, despite gazing out of the window at the passing scene, she was too drowsy to take in the names of roads, streets or avenues. Soon, Alfie called to her to wake up and she bumped her head against the window. She cried out and rubbed the bump and forced her eyes wide open. The taxi had stopped, and she could see the building that had caused Alfie such excitement. He and the driver were discussing Alfie getting out and going over to see if he could book tickets for a tour of the studios tomorrow, while the taxi took Joanna and their luggage to a motel further down the road. Alfie didn't want to miss it. He fumbled in his pocket for his wallet, but she brushed his hand away and told him that she had money, and he would need his for the tickets.

She watched him as he crossed the road and went through the gates that led to the Paramount building, and then asked the taxi driver to go on, please, praying there would be vacancies at the motel. She need not have worried; she had enough money to pay the driver and give him a generous tip, and she also managed to reserve two adjoining rooms and pay for them, asking for their luggage to be taken there. Then she washed her hands and face and had a drink of water before going outside to watch out for Alfie. The air was soft and balmy.

Three-quarters of an hour later she saw him jogging in her direction, his jacket flung over his shoulder. She waved to him, and he slowed down as she walked towards him. His face was flushed and sweaty.

'Do you want to go to our rooms first and have a shower and change?' she said. 'Then find somewhere to eat and drink?'

He nodded, smiling as he delved beneath his jacket. He produced a brown paper bag with handles. 'I stopped at a delicatessen on the way and bought some food and drinks.'

'What a good idea! What about the tickets?'

'Cancellations!' He waved them in the air. She made a grab for them and placed them in her handbag. 'Come on,' she said, linking arms with him and pulling him towards their rooms. 'They only had adjoining rooms,' she said.

Alfie raised his eyebrows when he saw that their rooms really were adjoining but made no comment. He went into the room that contained his luggage, and she took the bag of food and drinks into hers and laid everything out on a small table beneath the window. She hadn't realised until then how hungry she was and hoped Alfie would not be long in the shower. While she waited, she changed into a floral summer dress and combed her flaxen hair away from her face, tying it in a ponytail. She fastened dangling topaz earrings, which her mother had given her for her last birthday, to her earlobes. Then there came a knock on the door, and she took a deep breath and called, 'Come in.'

Alfie entered and they smiled approvingly at each other. He was dressed casually in beige slacks and a brown, yellow and white checked cotton shirt with short sleeves.

'You look cool and smart,' she said.

'That dress suits you,' he responded. 'Nice earrings too.'

'Mam told me they were real topaz. I've no idea where topazes come from.'

'A jeweller can probably tell you.'

'It's not one of the top gemstones. I do know it is the November birthstone,' she said. 'But let's forget it and eat.'

He followed her over to the table, where she had moved two easy chairs.

They sat down and helped themselves to crusty rolls, thinly sliced steak and cheese, coleslaw and lettuce. They cut open the crusty rolls and placed the fillings between the two halves and bit into them as if half-starved. Alfie poured himself a beer and she made herself a shandy in a toothbrush glass, washing her food down with several gulps. Then they leant back, and Joanna sighed, but Alfie drained his glass of beer and said, 'I needed that.' He refilled the glass and drank more slowly this time.

After a few minutes, she said, 'So, what time have we to set out in the morning?'

'I'd like to get there by nine thirty. There could be a crowd, and I'd like to have a chat with the tour guide first, if possible.'

'So, we set out at nine to give ourselves enough time to get there. We'll need to be up early if we want to grab breakfast here first,' she said.

'Suits me,' he said. 'At least we don't have to take waterproofs.'

'Suncream, possibly,' she said.

'And sunglasses,' he added.

'We're not going outdoors, are we?' She reached out for a chocolate cupcake. 'I thought the studios would all be undercover.'

Alfie swallowed the last of the contents of his glass. 'The taxi driver told me that Paramount have a ranch outside the city where films are made too, and there are trails and tracks where we could hike.'

'How far is it and how do we get there? I bet they used to make Westerns there,' she said excitedly. 'When I think of the number of Westerns I watched when I was a kid and we'd go to the kids' matinees.'

'And what about space films and comedies and cartoons. I bet the Roadrunner and Coyote cartoons were based on wild animals that live in the wilderness not far from here.'

She nodded. '*Flash Gordon* with Buster Crabbe was a bit frightening at times. I saw one with Mam that had Flash trapped in a place where the walls were coming in on him, as well as the ceiling coming down. I was scared.' Joanna laughed, spluttering out crumbs of chocolate cake.

'Remember Gabby Heyes?' asked Alfie.

'He was an old guy and used to make me laugh,' she said, her eyes dancing. 'As for comedians, I liked Bud Abbott and Lou Costello. Mam would take me to see their films because she liked them,' said Joanna.

'Jack would take me to see Stan Laurel and Oliver Hardy. They were British but also starred in American films.'

'And they'd sing and dance,' said Joanna, standing up as she swallowed the last of the cake. 'Do you remember the "Trail of the Lonesome Pine"? In the Blue Ridge

Mountains of Virginia…' She began to dance. 'I can't remember all the words.'

'Me neither,' said Alfie, getting up and seizing her by the waist and sort of dancing as he recalled Stan and Ollie moving in the film. 'It was funny,' he said. 'And Virginia is in America.'

'But not in California,' she said. 'It's in the southeast of the United States, nearer to the Atlantic than the Pacific. Which reminds me, we've yet to test out the temperature of the water.' She had come to a halt. 'Stan and Ollie danced alongside each other as if doing country dancing.'

'Or barn dancing,' said Alfie, removing his arm from about her waist.

'Harvest supper in the church hall,' she said, nodding. 'Which reminds me, Mam mentioned going to watch Beth dancing. Jack took her with him. I'm glad she's getting out and about.'

'My mam told me about that, and also about seeing Theo's new wife in the cinema.'

'Glenys said your dad's brother and his wife and their son are staying at Theo's house in Liverpool for a few days.'

Alfie shrugged. 'I'd have liked to have seen Uncle Glyn.'

'You could get to his and back in a day in the car,' said Joanna. 'Not like here, where it takes ages unless you're flying.'

'True,' said Alfie. 'But you're enjoying it, aren't you?'

'Up to a point,' she replied. 'You must be a bit fed up with Jay going off with his mother and spoiling your plans.'

'I've got you, and hopefully tomorrow we'll get some climbing in if we get to the Paramount ranch. There's bound to be some hills. Unless you'd rather spend more time in LA, and I'll go climbing on my own.'

'No way,' she said. 'You going alone isn't a good idea. What if you met a bear or were bitten by a rattlesnake? You haven't a gun or a rifle.'

'I've a Swiss army knife,' he said. 'And I'd hardly expect you to suck the poison out if I got bitten by a snake.'

'You're laughing at me,' she said, turning her back on him and picking up a container of what she presumed was coffee. It smelt of coffee. She removed the lid and breathed in the fragrant odour.

He picked up the other container. 'I'm not laughing at you… but you're letting your imagination run away with you.'

She spun round and stared him in the face. 'Next, you'll be saying I've seen too many Westerns. Well, if that were true, I would imagine Roy Rogers or John Wayne or the Lone Ranger to come to your rescue.' Her voice broke on the last two words and tears sprung to her eyes.

'What about Annie Oakley?' he said, placing a hand on her shoulder.

'Who?' she asked, brushing his hand away. She drank some coffee. It was the best she had tasted since arriving in America.

'You saw the film, didn't you? *Annie Get Your Gun* – she was a crack shot. The film came out a few years ago. It was a musical. Not as popular as *Calamity Jane*, I should think. That was another tough woman, and played by Doris Day,' he said.

'I saw it, and I like Howard Keel, who's a good singer.'

'Agreed,' said Alfie. 'So, how about us going to the flicks?'

'You are joking?' she said, moving away from him and sitting down by the window. 'We've tickets for the studios tomorrow and it's too nice to sit in a cinema in the afternoon, so we'll either go to the ranch or find a beach,' she said firmly.

'All right,' he said. 'I meant go to the flicks this evening.'

She glanced at the clock by the bed. 'It's a bit late to be going to the flicks, don't you think? Especially when we've got to be up early tomorrow.'

He glanced at his watch. 'You're right, of course.'

'I would like to try one of those drive-in movie places sometime before we go home,' she said.

'Fine,' he said, moving over to the window and sitting down and reaching for a doughnut. 'We could watch telly here for an hour or so and then go to bed.'

She glanced at the double bed and his eyes followed her. 'Separate rooms, naturally,' he murmured.

'That's why I chose them,' she said. 'Although one room with two beds would have been cheaper.'

'But not advisable,' he said firmly. 'Shall I switch on the telly?'

She nodded and reached for a peach. 'I wonder what's on. Joe laughs like a hyena when Ed Sullivan is on,' she said. 'He must be able to see quite well still.'

'Do you find him funny?' Alfie took an apricot from the packaging on the table. 'There's no oranges.'

'That's because they grow in the gardens,' she said, and saw that there was a film on.

'It looks like an old war film,' said Alfie.

They watched in silence for ten minutes and then Joanna said, 'Isn't that John Wayne?'

'I think you're right,' said Alfie. 'Hard to tell with that flying helmet on. It's not a film I've ever seen.'

'I don't really like war films,' she said a few minutes later. 'And isn't that Robert Ryan? He's a real toughie.'

'I'll change the channel,' said Alfie. 'Although, I'd like to know what it's called.'

They discovered later it was called *Flying Leathernecks*, although by then they were watching a show about stars and their movies, in particular Dean Martin and Jerry Lewis. They showed a scene from *Scared Stiff*.

'I've seen that film,' said Alfie. 'It's a mixture of comedy, horror and musical.'

'Where was it on?' she asked.

'The Forum, on the corner overlooking part of Lime Street.'

She yawned and stretched. 'I've never been in there.'

'You sound tired,' he said. 'You'd better kick me out.'

'Fine chance of that,' she said. 'Have another cake and a can of soda and walk out. Whoever wakes first tomorrow rattles the door handle to wake the other.'

'Will do,' he said. 'Good night.'

'God bless,' she said, stifling a yawn.

CHAPTER FIFTEEN

Joanna cleared everything from the table, placed some things in the rucksack and others in the wastebin, had a quick wash, cleaned her teeth, and climbed into bed. She mumbled a prayer asking God to keep her mam secure and happy, and that she and Josh would be nice to each other when he visited. She would like to be there and push them together.

She rolled onto her side and prayed for safe travelling for Alfie and herself. She stared drowsily at the door that separated her from Alfie. She had enjoyed the evening and wondered if they would get to see an outdoor movie. Did it mean they would have to hire an automobile for a day and visit a few places while they had it? She would discuss it with him in the morning. She wondered whether he was sleeping in pyjamas with long bottoms or shorts and a T-shirt. It was still quite warm, and she hoped she'd be able to sleep. She closed her eyes and thought of swimming in cool waters, then unexpectedly she thought she heard someone shout, 'Shark!' Why was it she could think of bears and the poisonous rattlesnake and not of the dangers of sharks?

She would speak of that to Alfie in the morning; in the meantime, she told herself to think of something pleasant, such as his kiss. Her lips still tingled from the memory of it. The shark vanished from her thoughts, and she pictured herself back home on the beach at Waterloo, playing rounders with Alfie, George, John and Mary while her mother and Alfie's mother lazed on towels in the palest of suns, shouting encouragement, even as Jack helped Beth and her little brother Peter build a sandcastle. She saw them carrying buckets down to the sea but knew they were safe because there were no sharks lurking there.

She drifted into sleep and only stirred when she heard the rattle of the doorknob and Alfie calling that it was time to rise and shine.

'Coming!' she called. 'Just give us a few minutes.' She forced her eyelids open and climbed out of bed. She gave herself a lick and a promise, as her nan would have said, and dressed in clean underwear, shorts and a T-shirt, socks and her brogues, and threw a cardigan over her shoulders. She combed her hair and tied it up. Then she checked she had her sunglasses and a clean handkerchief, as well as a sunhat. Finally, she called, 'I'm ready.'

The dividing door opened, and Alfie entered. He also wore shorts and a T-shirt but also a leather jacket and a baseball cap and sunglasses. On his feet he wore socks curled over the tops of his boots. His hair was damp and curled as if he had just come out of the shower.

'I dreamt we were on Waterloo beach playing rounders with friends and the mums, and Jack was there building a sandcastle with Beth and Peter. I felt safe thinking there were no sharks in the water,' she said.

'You're not worrying about sharks now, are you?' He seized her by the shoulders and shook her gently. 'This doesn't mean I have to buy a speargun, does it?' he added.

'It could be useful against bears and snakes, too,' she said, grabbing a handful of his orange T-shirt to stop him from shaking her. It worked, but now he took hold of her wrist and held her at arm's length.

'Listen to me, Joanna, there wouldn't be people in the water if there were sharks in the vicinity. There'll have been warnings put in place, and lifeguards.' He paused. 'Now grow up and stop imagining danger everywhere.' His grip slackened. 'Let's go and have breakfast and get to Paramount Studios and find out if we can get to the ranch this afternoon.'

She raised her wrist to her mouth and sucked it. 'Sorry if I hurt you,' he said, and taking hold of her hand, he lifted it and kissed the red marks on her wrist. 'Mam always used to kiss hurts better.'

'Mine too,' she said, her voice wobbling.

'See, we have a lot in common,' he said, and led her by the hand to the dining room.

They ate several maple syrup pancakes with a glass of orange juice and a cup of coffee before fetching rucksacks, leftover food, and a couple of bottles of cold drinks and walking poles. Then they headed for the studios. They walked as Joanna wanted to have a closer look at the stores and houses, and where the stops were for public transport.

They arrived at the studios in plenty of time for the start of the guided tour, and that enabled Alfie to question the guide about Paramount Ranch, of tracks for hiking and if the old Western town and circuits where movies were made still existed. There was plenty of parking if you hired a car. He showed them where they could obtain maps and information brochures, such as directions and hours of opening. Then he excused himself as more people turned up and he gathered everyone together.

When they were witnesses to a movie being created, Joanna would have liked Alfie to take photos, but it wasn't allowed, and they all had to keep quiet and stay out of shot. It wasn't as exciting as she had thought it would be, and she did not recognise any of the actors or actresses as famous.

She was relieved when it came to an end, and they could escape the group and leave to go and find a car hire place. Alfie had decided that a car would be much more convenient to get about and easy to drop off at the motel when the time was up. She left it to him to sort it out, with the help of one of the couples in the group, Heather and Robbie McGregor, who looked to be in their forties and were from Canada. The husband had spent some time in Britain during the war and his parents were from Scotland. They were friendly, and when Alfie told them of his and Joanna's plans to visit the Paramount Ranch, they decided to visit it too, offering Alfie and Joanna a lift in their car.

They accepted but insisted on paying for the fuel. At first their offer was turned down, but Joanna told them they wouldn't go with them if they didn't allow them to pay. That settled, the two men put their heads together and consulted a map which Alfie had bought, and soon they were on their way, with Alfie acting navigator at the front and Joanna and Heather in the back conversing about where they lived, family and their visit so far to America.

Heather told Joanna they were from Calgary, in Alberta, and Joanna told her they were from Liverpool.

'Famous football team,' said Heather instantly. 'Robbie's parents were from the Isle of Mull, in the Hebrides. He used to talk of Liverpool men coming for the fishing.'

'It's a long way, but then we have plenty of Scots in Liverpool. Most come from Greenock to work in the Tate and Lyle sugar mill because theirs closed, but some come from Glasgow and are sailors. They work on the docks or in shipyards in Birkenhead, the other side of the Mersey. What does your husband do?' asked Joanna.

'He's in the mounted police. His dad was a policeman.'

'Alfie's stepfather is a policeman. His natural father was killed in the war.'

'How do they get on?' asked Heather.

'Great. Alfie never knew his father.'

'What about your parents?'

Joanna hesitated. 'They met in the war in Liverpool but parted. I'm over here seeing my dad. He lives in San Jose, near San Francisco. My mother is Alfie's godmother. Our families are very close. Mam was going to come over, but she bought a house, so I came over with Alfie and Jay, the son of a friend who Mam met in the war. Jay had been with the American air force in Europe during the Berlin airlift.'

'Robbie was in the air force and remembers some Brits coming over to Canada for training during the war.'

'My mother was with the WRAF for a while, but she worked in munitions at the beginning of the war, with Alfie's mam.'

'The war changed so much,' said Heather. 'I lost a younger brother. He was in the navy and was killed when his ship was torpedoed. His wife's parents were dead, and she has no other family. She works in a hospital in Calgary now and was supposed to come away with us but had to put it off for a fortnight. She's joining us in Santa Monica in a couple of days.'

'She's lucky to have you,' said Joanna.

'She's told us that,' said Heather.

'We were planning on spending some time in Santa Monica,' said Alfie, who had been half-listening to their conversation. 'Then returning to San Jose before going home at the end of July. I have work and Joanna is beginning to feel homesick.'

Joanna said, 'It's true, and Mam has just moved into another house, and I can't wait to join her.'

'What about your father over here?' asked Robbie.

'He doesn't need me. He's getting a dog, and he has good neighbours. I never planned on staying for good.'

'So, how are you travelling home?' asked Heather.

'We'll fly to San Francisco from San Jose and then take a train to New York and then take a ship to Ireland and then to Liverpool,' said Alfie. 'A friend from San Jose is travelling with us to visit relatives in Ireland.'

'We came to Canada by ship from Glasgow,' said Heather. 'We were visiting my sister-in-law and decided to stay.'

Joanna changed the subject. 'Have we much further to go, Alfie?'

Alfie checked the map once more and traced the road with a finger. 'Not much further.'

She was pleased that he was proved right, and in no time at all a parking place was found and they were following a signpost to the Western village.

Joanna said, 'It looks just like the movies.'

'Of course it does, noggin,' said Alfie. 'Otherwise, it wouldn't be here.'

'Don't call me noggin,' she retorted. 'I don't know where you get that from.'

'Sorry,' he said meekly. 'It just came into my head.' He seized her hand. 'Shall we get on?'

They began to run, carefully avoiding people who got in their way, until they reached the wooden sidewalk in front of the swing doors that led into the saloon. Heather and Robbie followed more sedately.

Alfie pushed open one of the doors and led the way in. Joanna followed closely, as the saloon was noisy and smoky. A piano was playing, and feet were tapping. She hung on to the back of Alfie's leather jacket as he led the way to the bar and elbowed his way to the front, leaving it to Joanna to make their excuses while he ordered two sarsaparillas.

As he did so, she looked at the mirror behind the bartender and saw a face she recognised. 'Jay!' she shouted. 'What are you doing here?'

He looked surprised but pleased. 'I've never been before and as Granddad and Mom were going to a meeting, I decided to drive here. It isn't that far from his place.'

Alfie had now noticed Jay, and he wasted no time paying for the sarsaparillas and getting away from the bar. Joanna had taken one of the drinks and, seeing as there were no tables to be had, she waved to Heather and Robbie and indicated they were going outside where the air was fresher.

Joanna and Alfie found a place on the wooded sidewalk where they could sit down and drink their sarsaparillas. They had not been sitting there long when they were joined by Jay, who immediately asked what they were doing there.

Alfie explained and was just telling him about the Scots Canadian couple, when they turned up. They told the group that they had just been turned out of the saloon, although others had been taken on as extras and had gone with a couple of women to be fitted up for costumes.

Alfie made the necessary introductions.

'There's going to be a gunfight,' said Robbie. 'I'd have liked to see it.'

'I wouldn't,' said Heather, shivering. 'Someone might get hurt.'

'Don't be daft,' said her husband. 'There won't be real bullets. They'll only be acting.'

'Can you be sure of that?' said Joanna, draining her glass of sarsaparilla. 'Someone might get hurt when falling to the floor pretending to have been shot.'

'I've never thought of that,' said Heather.

'They won't have been shot, though,' said Jay.

'I'd like to go and see the church and ranch house and then go on a hike into the hills,' said Joanna.

'There's also stables and a bunkhouse,' said Alfie.

'Are there horses?' asked Robbie. 'I wouldn't mind a ride in the hills.'

'You have to pay to hire them,' said Alfie. 'I'd rather walk.'

'Me too,' said Joanna and Heather.

'We can split up,' said Jay. 'I'd like a ride, so I'll go with Robbie.'

'Has your dad ever been here, Jay?' asked Joanna.

He nodded. 'Mom didn't come, though. She went shopping instead. She's a city girl.'

'I think Mam would have liked it,' said Joanna.

That settled, Jay went off with Robbie to see about horses while the other three headed for the church and ranch house.

Joanna enjoyed visiting both buildings, especially the kitchen in the ranch house, although she wouldn't have swapped a 1958 kitchen for the picturesque Western one of the old days. The women must have really worked their fingers to the bone. She had to admit that she had enjoyed going into the saloon, re-imagining the past where many a gunfight had broken out over a game of cards, and where women had sung and danced on the stage, kicking up their legs to the whistles and whoops of the patrons.

When they left the building, they decided not to wait around for Robbie and Jay to make an appearance but to head for the hills after fetching what they needed from Robbie's automobile.

Alfie checked out the various trails and suggested the one called Coyote Canyon, which was moderate and not too long. 'If we're fortunate we might see not only a coyote but a roadrunner too.'

The three of them set off and were content to set their pace to Heather's, as she liked to take her time to see the flowers and any wildlife. It was she who spotted a coyote, which she thought at first was a half-starved wolf, until shown a photograph in a booklet. They never completed the whole track, as they began to tire, and the time was getting on. They were also hungry and thirsty, as they had drunk all their water, so they turned back, and it did not seem to take them as long. Alfie had taken their hands and helped them both along; Joanna had loved the feel of his strong fingers laced with hers.

They found Jay and Robbie sitting on folded blankets in the car, eating hamburgers and drinking beer out of bottles. 'Did you enjoy your ride?' asked Heather.

'Did you enjoy your walk?' asked Jay, shifting on the folded blanket as if uncomfortable.

Joanna nodded. 'But we're tired now, and hungry and thirsty. Where did you get the hamburgers, and do they have doughnuts and lemonade?'

Jay gave them directions, and Alfie went with her while Heather sat down next to her husband and cadged a bite of his hamburger. It was not long before Joanna and Alfie returned with several burgers, a paper bag full of dough-nuts and bottles of drink.

It was not until they were all sated that Jay talked about the conversation between him and Robbie.

'You know how I've been trying to decide what to do to earn a living?'

Alfie and Joanna nodded.

'Robbie's been telling me about him being a Mountie. I haven't mentioned to anyone before, but I had thought of being a cop, although Mom wouldn't like it.'

'But you'd like to be a Mountie, and you think she'd accept that?' said Alfie.

'No, but it's time I stopped thinking of others and did what I wanted. She wants to divorce Dad and move to Los Angeles to live with Granddad. She's told Dad it's too quiet where he lives and that he needs to see a bit of life. I think that's a good idea, but I don't want to carry on living with them.'

'So, you're going to apply to be a Mountie?' said Joanna.

He nodded. 'I'll speak to Dad first. I'll go back home with you two on the train. I'll leave the car for Mom.'

'We're going back in a few days,' said Alfie. 'Then we're going to sail home soon after. We're both homesick and I've got work.'

'And I've exams and I need to do well if I want to get into university,' said Joanna.

'What do you want to study?' asked Heather.

'Pharmacy,' she replied. 'I'm interested in medicine and particularly what makes people better.'

'You didn't consider being a nurse or even a doctor?' asked Robbie.

'I don't believe I'd make a good nurse,' she said. 'And I've heard it takes seven years to be a qualified doctor.'

'And costs a lot of money,' said Jay. 'You can make a good living over here, though.'

'We have the National Health Service now,' said Alfie. 'Doctors can still earn a decent income.'

'How do you know?' asked Jay.

'I've several Welsh mates and they have a couple of doctors in their rugby team. They work damn hard, but they love their job, say it's rewarding.'

'Let's change the subject,' said Heather. 'Time's marching on.'

Jay checked his watch. 'I'd best go. I told Mom where I was going, and she stressed that I wasn't to be late, as they were having guests.'

'See you tomorrow, then,' said Robbie.

'You bet,' said Jay. 'I'm not going to allow them to persuade me that they need me.'

'You're best coming to our motel first,' said Alfie. 'We'll meet up with Robbie and Heather and their sister-in-law in Santa Monica at the pier.'

A time was decided on and Alfie wrote directions for Jay to find their motel, and they parted ways.

Robbie dropped Alfie and Joanna off at their motel. Joanna thanked him, and Alfie handed over a bit more money for petrol, or gas as they called it in America. Then they went to their rooms, showered, changed and then went for something to eat.

They had French fries, baked beans and ham fritters, and for dessert cookie butter ice-cream cake washed down by coffee. 'That was delicious,' said Joanna, stretching and yawning.

'Tired?' said Alfie.

She nodded. 'And I feel like I've caught the sun. I should have put more Nivea cream on.'

'Do you want to go and sit in the gardens in the shade somewhere or go to our rooms and rest and watch something on TV?'

'Let's go in the garden for half an hour or so,' she said. 'Then you can watch the news while I have a rest on my bed and then we'll see if there's a film on one of the channels,' she answered.

'Suits me,' he said.

So out into the gardens they went, and in no time at all Joanna had dozed off listening to the twitter of birds and the distant sound of traffic and people calling. She became fully awake after Alfie stroked her cheek with a yellow California poppy. She brushed it away at first, thinking it was a crawly, only to realise her mistake when she felt something touch the corner of her mouth. Then she opened her eyes and saw Alfie's blue eyes laughing into hers as he tickled her nose with the flower.

'You beast,' she said. 'I was lovely and relaxed.'

'I wanted to talk,' he said.

'About Jay wanting to be a Mountie?' she said, and yawned.

'I think it will suit him, but it's him wanting to get away from his mam and granddad and leave the country that strikes me as interesting, but not surprising. Being in the forces suited him for a while. He's a man of action, so he doesn't need smothering by his mother and granddad.'

'Don't you think he should have stayed in the air force?'

'No, he wouldn't have had the freedom to move about.'

'You think he'll be happier in the Mounties?'

'He'll only find out by trying it out,' said Alfie.

'Are you happy doing what you're doing?' she asked.

'I've only just started, so I'm seeing how it goes. I'm not unhappy, and I've got to support myself and hopefully a wife and family one day.'

'You probably won't have to do it on your own. Some women are working after they're married these days, and I think the numbers will increase,' she said.

'Who'll look after the children?' he asked, frowning.

'Perhaps they won't start working until the children go to school, and maybe they'll work only part-time,' she suggested thoughtfully.

'All right,' he murmured. 'I guess you've overheard women talking about this.'

'Hmm! Although, wives have always done some kind of work to boost the family's income. For years they worked from home, taking in washing, or doing sewing, or they went out cleaning or cooking. And up in Lancashire and Yorkshire they worked in the cotton and wool mills, and before that they worked at spinning and weaving at home.'

Alfie shook his head. 'You've made your point, but I don't really need a history lesson. You haven't mentioned the wives who gut fish in fishing ports like Fleetwood in Lancashire.' He paused. 'Anyway, it's years off before I plan on marrying. It's the wars that caused people to rush into marriage.'

She sighed. 'How did we get started on this subject?'

'Jay, jobs and money,' he said. 'I wonder if he'll ever settle down.'

'You mean get married?' she murmured, a twinkle in her eyes.

'Don't start again or...' he warned.

'Or what?' She stood up. 'I think I'll walk to the front and watch the sea. Maybe I'll even have a paddle.'

'A paddle?' Alfie rose. 'You're going to walk all that way and just have a paddle?'

'It'll cool me down and I can get out quick if a shark arrives on the scene, although that's unlikely, so you said.'

'You're crazy. You've been yawning your head off and you're going to go for a walk. You were talking about watching a film earlier.'

She yawned again.

'See!' he said. 'You're exhausted.'

'Are you coming with me?'

'Nope!' He closed his eyes. 'Take a stick with you and if a shark comes after you with his mouth wide open, jam the stick in it so he can't close his jaws. Either that or hit him hard on his snout with the stick and make a run for it.'

'Ha ha! You think you're so funny!' She was so annoyed with him for not coming with her and making a joke about her fear of sharks that she broke a narrow branch from a shrub and poked him in the stomach with it and then ran away, still clutching it.

She half-expected him to give chase but he didn't and that caused her disappointment and anger. She marched out of the gates and crossed the road, certain that there would be a way to the sea by cutting through an opening between some of the buildings. Soon she caught sight of the Pacific and hurried towards it. Finding a flat rock, she made herself as comfortable as possible sitting on it with her back against another rock. She gazed out over the waves to where there were two yachts scurrying before the breeze, which had cooled down now it was evening. She thought about how her mother walked to the beach between Waterloo and Crosby to watch the sun go down. There was an area where on a clear day one could see the peaks of Snowdon. She felt a yearning for home, despite the beauty she had seen that day and the pleasure she had felt meeting new people, and the fun she had experienced at Paramount Studios and Ranch with Alfie and the others.

She moved and took a couple of photographs with her camera, before putting it away and heading down to the water where grown-ups and children still played in the waves. She removed her pumps and socks, fastened the laces together and slung them round her neck. Then she walked into the water. It was cool but still held a hint of warmth from the sun. Suddenly, she felt sorry for Alfie, wishing that he was with her, enjoying the sea, the feel of the sand between one's toes and the fresh air with no sign of a shark to be seen. She wished she had her swimming costume with her, as she would have enjoyed a swim.

She turned and splashed out of the waves and trod through the sand back to her rock, where she waited for a short while for her feet to be dry enough to brush most of the sand off. Then she pulled on her pumps, not bothering with her socks, which she stuffed in a pocket before making her way to the motel. There was no sign of Alfie in the garden, so she went to her bedroom.

She could hear a television, so she opened the connecting door and slipped into Alfie's room, where she found him sitting up against the pillows, asleep. As much as she wanted to wake him, she left him to rest. She went and showered in her own bedroom and changed out of her slightly sandy clothes to fresh underwear and skirt and blouse, before returning to watch the rest of the film while stretching out beside the still slumbering Alfie.

She might have dozed off, but the film had enough excitement, romance and fantasy to keep her awake and absorbed, so much so that she was even unaware when Alfie woke and lay unmoving, watching her staring at the screen. It was not until the music signalled the end of the film and she breathed such a great sigh of satisfaction that she became aware he was staring at her.

'I'm sorry I fell asleep and missed some of the film,' he said. 'How long have you been here?'

She looked at him. 'You were asleep when I came in and I thought of waking you, but I didn't like disturbing you.'

'Pity! How was the sea?'

'No sharks! I wished you were with me and I'd taken me cozzie. I felt quite homesick, thinking of Mam and our beaches back home.'

'So, our plans haven't changed?'

'No,' she said. 'Should I make some drinking chocolate?'

'You can make it up here?'

'There are some sachets in my rucksack.'

'Great, I don't feel like moving.'

'Lazybones!' she said, blushing. She slid off the bed and went over to put water in the kettle and then went through into her bedroom and returned with what she needed. She made two cups of drinking chocolate and placed them on the bedside table with a packet of custard creams she had brought with her from home and sat on the bedcovers next to Alfie. Only when both were sitting up against the pillows did she hand him his cup. He was beneath the covers and a white cotton vest covered his chest. He took a deep gulp of his drinking chocolate before asking whether she had paddled.

'Of course, I didn't go all that way for nothing, although watching the sun going down was worth the effort.'

'You must be tired out?' he said.

'A bit, but I didn't go all the way down the main road, I cut through an opening on the other side and came to a stretch of beach that probably ran all the way to the harbour at Los Angeles.'

'You could have been on Long Beach,' he said, taking a custard cream from the packet she offered. 'You're going to have to get some sleep. Jay will be here in the morning.'

'I will, but can I finish my drink first?'

'Of course. Are you warm enough?'

She nodded and glanced at the television screen. 'Another film's coming on. Would it be all right if I stayed and watched it? I don't think they are as long as the main feature at home.'

'No, they were the B movie. You really got your money's worth,' he said.

'And continuous performances so if you'd missed some of the film you could catch up on it,' she said, smiling. 'Neither Nan and Granddad nor Theo and Mam had a telly, so we watched the Queen's Coronation at the flicks. I love the Queen, she's lovely.'

'And she worked during the war when she was a princess and in her late teens, driving and even doing mechanic work when her father was still King.'

'Now she's a queen and a mother, as well as being head of the Commonwealth,' said Joanna.

'I saw her once in the flesh,' said Alfie. 'I was with Mam in either Dale Street or Islington I think, and Jack had told Mam the time the King's car would be passing along there if she wanted to have a look. Mam lifted me up on her shoulders. I was only little, and she wanted me to be able to say that I'd seen the King at that time.'

'I wish I had,' said Joanna with a sigh. 'I was probably too young.'

'It must have been before 1952 because the King died in February of that year,' said Alfie.

'Your mam might remember,' she said.

'Maybe, or Jack,' he said. 'But what does it matter?'

'I think it's interesting.' She reached for a biscuit. 'Had you started school?'

'You could ask your mam, she might have gone to see the royals.'

'I wonder what Josh thinks of Britain having a royal family,' she said.

'I doubt he thinks about it. I've never heard him discuss American politics. Or wave the flag like lots of them do. Changing the subject, I think I need to write to Mam soon because she needs to know we'll be coming home sooner.'

'I'll write to mine as well,' said Joanna. 'They'll need to know we're stopping off in Ireland with Josh. Anyway, let's stop talking so we can watch the film.' She drained her cup. 'Do you want another drink?' She made to get off the bed.

'No, you stay where you are,' he said. 'I'll make them.'

She was about to shout, 'No!' but saw that he was decent in a pair of pyjama trousers and so she remained silent.

When the film finished, she rose from the bed, took their cups and washed them and the spoons before tidying everything away. She wiped the top of the bedside cabinet and said, 'Good night, God bless,' and kissed his cheek. Before she could draw away, he kissed her gently on the mouth. 'Thanks for the drinks and your company. Much appreciated.'

'I'd best go,' she said huskily.

'You're right,' he said. 'Sleep tight and check you haven't forgotten anything.'

'I'll leave the biscuits for you,' she said. 'I know you like custard creams.'

She hurried out before her emotions got the better of her and closed the door. She threw herself face down on the bed and smothered her sobs, wishing she was old enough for them to get married and dreading that he could get called up for his National Service next year. She sniffed back her tears and threw aside the pillow and got out of bed. She splashed water on her face and then dried it. She undressed and put on her pyjamas. Then she went over to the window and gazed out. The sky had clouded over, and a wind had got up and was tossing the branches of the trees. She thought that it did not look like it was going to be a good day for Santa Monica tomorrow. She climbed into bed and prayed that all would be fine between her and Alfie. But maybe even now he was regretting the kiss he had given her and telling himself that her mother would have a fit if she knew they had lain on a bed together and kissed. They had grown up almost like brother and sister once their mothers had met up again towards the latter half of the war.

But she no longer felt sisterly towards him and she was convinced that since they had come to America, his feelings towards her had changed too. That kiss had affected them both and might have gone further if she had not come to her senses and recalled what some of the girls in school said during break about snogging and necking and tongues. Some had giggled and one had warned them about giving into temptation and letting a bloke go too far and possibly getting into trouble.

Immediately, Joanna had crept away and now her thought was of her mother, who had believed herself in love with GI Joe, not knowing he was married. Yet if she had not given in to him then, she would not have given birth to a daughter.

Shouldn't Josh have told her of Joe being married earlier? What a tangle it was! How was he to know her relationship with Joe had gone so far, though, until Olive had told him of the baby? Was it possible Josh had liked her mother from the beginning but, being married, he had not seduced her? Then he could not break the connection and continued to care about how Olive and her daughter were managing.

One thing was for sure: it was Josh who had kept in touch with her mother, not Joe. She thought of Jay and what he had told Alfie about his parents forever arguing and now divorce proceedings.

She punched her pillow and turned over and told herself that she must act normally in the morning. She must also remember to write a letter to her mother about returning home earlier and Josh travelling with them to visit Ireland.

CHAPTER SIXTEEN

Jay arrived at the motel early the following morning and had breakfast with them. He seemed tight-lipped when he arrived, carrying a suitcase and a rucksack.

Alfie raised his eyebrows. 'You managed to get away?'

'I'm here, aren't I?' said Jay. 'I didn't say, "So long!" I just left a note, saying I was going to see Dad and will give him her letter, and then I will be going to Canada.'

'I'd like to see Canada,' said Joanna.

'Another time,' said Alfie. 'Josh was going to book our tickets home when he books his.'

Joanna said, 'I'd forgotten about that.'

'You can visit once I've settled, sometime in the future,' said Jay.

'I'll see what Mam says,' she said, glancing at Alfie.

'I'd better get saving,' he murmured, winking at her.

'Now we'd best get a move on,' said Jay. 'We need to get to the station to catch the train to Santa Monica. I'm glad the weather's cleared up.'

No time was wasted and soon they were on the train and looking forward to a swim in the Pacific Ocean. They left their suitcases in the left luggage.

They had no difficulty finding Robbie and Heather and their sister-in-law, Fiona, who was blue-eyed with flaxen hair and a perfectly oval face, slightly sunburnt. She was wearing a sundress in orange and yellow and seemed friendly. She had a pleasant voice, but her accent was difficult to pin down.

Jay wasted no time shaking hands with her and getting into conversation after having been introduced by Heather. Joanna and Alfie also exchanged greetings and explanations with Fiona, before following the others to a spot on the beach, which was not crowded. Fiona had claimed a place with several rugs and towels. Soon Alfie and Joanna had removed their top clothes and folded them in their rucksacks, and clad in trunks and bikini, they headed for the sea. She couldn't help but admire his body.

Alfie was in first and, once up to his waist, he encouraged Joanna to come further in, as it was warm and safe. 'Trust me,' he called.

And not wanting to be thought a cowardly custard, she plunged into the shallow water and pulled herself along, aware of the hot sun on her shoulders, until she was able to grasp his ankles. She would have brought him down if he had not seized her shoulders and they both toppled over. Their heads emerged from the surface of the water, coughing and spluttering, top to tail.

'You idiot,' spluttered Joanna. 'I wasn't going to hurt you. It was just going to be a bit of fun. Help me up?'

'I'm not sure I can,' said Alfie. 'I can only see your feet. I hope a shark doesn't turn up now.'

'Very funny,' she gasped, tempted to bite him.

'Then you've got what you wanted, a bit of fun,' said Alfie. 'Now shut up while I free my feet from this seaweed.'

Joanna tried to think about that, but her brain seemed to have stopped working and maybe that was because she was having difficulty keeping her head above water. She felt a hysterical giggle burst in her throat and thought she was going to choke. Then, unexpectedly, she became aware that she was being rolled over and twisted round. Her head was being raised higher out of the water, and not only her head, but most of her body. She couldn't think how Alfie had managed it, but somehow she was staring down into his face, and they were chest to chest, which she found quite thrilling.

'How?' she choked on the word.

He shrugged, nearly unsettling her. 'I told you to trust me. I'm double-jointed and was once a gymnast, but don't push your luck too far again. I'm not Houdini or Superman.' He paused. 'Now let's have a swim.' He rolled her off him and swam away.

She watched him for a couple of minutes before following him, wondering if he was telling the truth. She'd never heard that he was double-jointed, but she thought she could remember having been told he had been in the school gymnastic team.

The rest of the day was calm and restful, and nobody must have been taking notice of what they were doing in the water. At the end of the day, they all had dinner at the hotel where Fiona was staying, and Robbie and Heather booked a room there as well. But Alfie, Joanna and Jay stayed in a motel, as they could not afford the hotel prices.

They all stayed just a couple more days and went for a ramble in the hills, before heading for San Jose. By then it was obvious that Jay and Fiona had hit it off and that they did not want to part. They all went to Josh's house first and Jay introduced Fiona, Robbie and Heather to him. Then Jay told Josh of his intention to join the Canadian mounted police and that he and Fiona really liked each other. He also handed his mother's letter to his father. Josh made an appointment with his lawyer the following day.

While Josh was seeing his lawyer about a divorce, Joanna and Alfie visited Joe, who was pleased to see his daughter and asked her if she'd enjoyed seeing more of California. She asked him how he had got on at the hospital and was told it was possible there might be an operation that could mean he wouldn't go completely blind.

She threw her arms round him and told him she could not be more delighted and hopefully she could come and visit him sometime in the future and celebrate. She had packed the rest of her clothes and the presents for her mother and Nan. Of course she would keep in touch and knew he would be well looked after by Elsie and her daughter. He asked her what she thought of Fiona; as his cousin, Jay's mother was concerned and a little more than upset about her son moving to Canada. His mother and grandfather had possessed such hopes for him of climbing higher in the job market.

Joanna told him that Fiona was a lovely person whose ambition was to help people, much like Joe's next-door neighbour, Elsie.

A fortnight later Josh, Jay, Alfie and Joanna were booked into a hotel in San Francisco, as were Robbie, Heather and Fiona.

The following day those bound for Canada said their farewells, and Jay hugged Josh and Alfie, and kissed Joanna.

Josh, Alfie and Joanna took the train to New York, where they boarded the liner to Cobh, near Cork. The three of them stood at the rail, gazing down at the crowds waving.

'I wonder when we'll see the old country again,' said Josh.

'America is not the old country,' said Joanna. 'It's the new world.'

'The old country is the United Kingdom,' said Alfie, taking a last look at the New York skyline and reaching for Joanna's hand. 'I'm looking forward to seeing some of Ireland, but I can't wait to see the Liver birds. I'll truly feel home then.'

'Me too,' she said. 'I'm pleased I met Joe, and I enjoyed seeing the sights of San Jose and the Paramount film studios and the ranch, though.'

'And rambling and swimming in the Pacific,' murmured Alfie, slipping an arm about her waist. 'But we never went to the top of the Empire State Building or saw a famous film star,' he added.

'We never saw a shark or a bear or a rattlesnake, thank God,' she said, with a shudder. 'But we did see a coyote and the inside of an old Western saloon, and we've lots of photographs and met lots of friendly people.'

'So, you enjoyed your visit,' said Josh. 'No regrets?'

'I have a few. I wished Mam was there sometimes, but she didn't need to be there for me to know she and Joe would never have been suited, and if they were to have married, they would have broken up and she'd have returned to Liverpool.'

'What about her ex-husband, Theo?' asked Josh hesitantly.

'Their marriage didn't last. Anyway, you're best talking about it to Mam when you see her again.'

There was silence then, except for the cry of birds and the slap of waves against the hull, and they turned and made their way to the prow of the ship heading into the Atlantic.

Two days later, the liner had left the coastline of America and the sea was reasonably calm; the air was mild and the sky a pale blue with a scattering of white clouds edged with grey. There were scarcely any other ships, and Joanna was hoping for a smooth crossing, regardless of what she had overheard some sailors say about tornadoes and hurricanes across the eastern part of America storming into the Atlantic. After all, having grown up in Liverpool, she was no stranger to winds blowing slates from roofs and ships colliding in the Irish Sea; there was many a buoy marking the site of wreckage in the estuary of the Mersey or the river itself. She had decided that while it was dry and not too windy, she would play deck quoits with Alfie, while Josh was getting exercise jogging around the deck or swimming in the pool. He was a very good swimmer, and it came as no surprise to see him donning a wetsuit, an aqualung, weight belt and mask and taking to the pool when it was vacant.

He told her and Alfie that he was training for when he would join his Irish kin underwater, fishing for scallops.

'I've never heard of them,' she said.

'They're difficult to catch,' said Josh. 'I'll do a drawing of the shell. Mussels are easier and that's why there are so many mussel men in the area where my cousin lives.'

When Joanna saw his drawing of a scallop shell, she was reminded of the shell brooch that pilgrims wore. Alfie shook his head. 'I think you're mistaken. They're cockleshells, which are much more plentiful. You can find the shells on most beaches on Merseyside and collect cockles and cook them yourself by boiling them in a big pan. Didn't you ever go camping in Moreton and go cockling?'

She shook her head. 'I wonder if our Peter ever went with his mates before I was born?'

'Ask him. He couldn't always be watching football.'

She nodded. 'I wonder if he ever went with Mam's younger brother and me dad.'

Josh said, 'I'm hungry.'

'Me too,' she said, watching Alfie help Josh off with his aqualung.

'It's really heavy,' said Alfie. 'I wouldn't mind having a go, though. I've seen blokes on Anglesey going in on Trearddur Bay. They have a boat, only the size of a rowing boat, but with an outboard engine. I spoke to one of them and he told me they belonged to the Liverpool Aqua Club. They train at Queens Drive swimming baths.'

'You should look them up in the telephone book,' suggested Joanna. 'See if they have women members and I could join as well.'

'Wait until we get home,' said Alfie. 'I've work and you've studying.'

Joanna's spirits dropped. 'Don't remind me. But we'll still have some free time. Although...' She paused and fiddled with her hair.

'Although what?' asked Josh.

She sighed. 'Nothing,' she said.

'It must have been something,' said Alfie.

'It can wait until we get home.' She turned away and gazed over the surface of the sea in the direction of America. 'I'd like to see a movie after lunch. It looks like it's clouding over.'

'Then let's get under cover,' said Alfie, putting his arm around her and ushering her to the nearest stairway. 'Are you coming, Josh?'

'You go ahead,' he said. 'I'll follow on.'

'We're going to have to change. We'll meet you in the small dining room,' said Joanna.

It didn't take her long to choose a mauve skirt and cream taffeta blouse that she had bought in New York when shopping. She had dressed and was just fastening beige low-heeled shoes, when there was a knock on her cabin door.

'Are you ready?' called Alfie.

'Almost.' She glanced at the porthole and saw that it was still dull outside but at least it was not raining. She picked up a poncho she had bought in a shop in Los Angeles, swung it around her shoulders and unlocked the door.

'Are you warm enough?' he asked with a grin. 'We're not going outside, you know. Where did you get the poncho?'

'We might change our minds after seeing the film… Decide we need some fresh air,' said Joanna. 'You've got a sweater on over your shirt and have changed out of shorts.'

'I felt the plush seats could itch my legs in shorts,' he said. 'That's a nice skirt you're wearing. Is it new?'

She nodded. 'So is the blouse. I bought them in New York, in Macy's. Did you buy anything new when we were there?'

'Only for Peter and Beth. I didn't need any more clothes. I bought an action figure for Peter and a Barbie doll with a whole load of dresses, and even make-up, for Beth.'

'Don't you think Beth's a bit old for dolls?'

'Not this one,' he said. 'It's incredible the toys they have over here, even though it's a while off Christmas.'

'New York gets lots of tourists. I've heard some of the rich come from England for special occasions.'

'Blinking heck!'

'They probably save up for a year or more, or it's a special offer. Anyway, I'm starving so let's get a move on or Josh will be there before us,' she said.

He rolled his eyes at her. 'He's got to pack up his diving gear and put it away. I really would like to have a go.'

'It could be that we'll need life jackets if the weather gets worse,' she said, hugging herself. 'Remember we had life-jacket practice on the voyage out.'

'You do know that part of the *Titanic*'s problem was that they didn't have enough lifeboats,' said Alfie. 'After that a new law was brought in, stating that there had to be sufficient lifeboats for everyone on the ship.'

'But what if the ship sank before everybody was able to get into boats?'

'You really are cheerful, aren't you?' he said, pulling a face.

'I was also thinking of the *Lusitania*. Not all survived.'

'That was bombed during the war, so sank quicker. Now can we change the subject? I promise I won't leave the ship without you, and don't forget that technology, such as the wireless, is more advanced these days. There's radar for instance.'

'Of course,' she said.

'At least you haven't mentioned sharks,' murmured Alfie.

'Pig,' she said, digging him in the ribs with her elbow. He put both his arms around her, imprisoning her. 'Bully,' she said.

'Another word out of you,' said Alfie, 'and I'll forget I'm a gentleman and close your mouth.'

'I'll—' Before she could say another word, he covered her mouth with his. She stopped struggling as he released his grip on her arms and, as the kiss deepened, she reached up and fastened her arms around his shoulders and linked her hands at the back of his neck.

The kiss seemed to go on forever and they only drew apart when a voice said, 'I thought you would have saved a table by now.'

'Sorry,' said Joanna, blushing. Alfie was holding her hand, and his chin was resting on the top of her head. She added, 'We found a better way of ending a disagreement than continuing to insult each other.'

'I'm glad it worked for you. It never did with my wife, that's why we've settled on a divorce for incompatibility,' said Josh.

'I'm so glad,' said Joanna. 'I'd much prefer having you for a stepfather than Joe for a father.'

'I hope your mother feels like that,' said Josh. 'I've wasted so much time and been an idiot where Joe was involved.' His expression was grim.

'You were too thoughtful where he was involved,' said Alfie. 'Sometimes you must put yourself first. Jay reckons Joe played on your guilty feeling over that so-called accident with the tree, when really it was his own fault for not heeding your warning.'

'I felt to blame because I encouraged him to take on the work, as he hadn't worked since we were demobbed. He used his wife's illness as an excuse, even though most of the time his son did the caring and work about the house, as well as the neighbour. As it was, he received compensation for another accident and some money from a charity.' He paused. 'I suppose I shouldn't be telling you this, as he is your father, Joanna.'

'I know what it's like to shut something up inside you because you feel you can't talk about it to anyone,' she said, 'Mam feels the same. You both need to unburden yourselves.' She fell silent.

'Time to go and eat,' said Alfie. 'I'm starving.'

'Me too,' said Josh.

'And me,' said Joanna in a small voice.

Without delay the three of them hurried to the smaller dining room, relieved to find there was still plenty to eat on the buffet table: salad, sliced cold meat, game pie, smoked salmon and tuna, sweetcorn and peas in mayonnaise, baked potatoes, as well as fresh fruit salad.

Joanna helped herself to a baked potato, salad and smoked salmon. The men went for the cold meat and game pie. The three of them had fresh fruit salad afterwards and then coffee, before heading for the cinema where the American musical *Gigi* was showing.

'I missed it when it came out in Liverpool,' said Joanna. 'It mightn't be to your tastes, but it is set in Paris,' she added.

'I quite like musicals,' said Alfie.

'People were raving over it,' said Josh. 'So I went to see it a few months ago with a friend and his two daughters. It's colourful and funny in places and the songs are good. Even so, I'll give it a miss and go and watch *Vertigo* in the other cinema. It's an Alfred Hitchcock one and James Stewart is in it. Besides, you two young ones might enjoy some time on your own.'

So, they went their separate ways and when Joanna and Alfie came out of the cinema and saw Josh playing chess with another male passenger, they decided to go to the rear of the ship and see if the sun was going down. There was a sliver of silver and orange edging a clump of grey-black cloud, but that was all there was to see.

Alfie's arm went round her, and he kissed her cheek. She shifted closer to him, and a delicious thrill passed through her as he pressed tiny kisses down the side of her face. She half-expected his hands to roam her body, but he only placed them either side of her face. He brought her closer still, eased her lips apart with his tongue and ravished her mouth. The tip of his tongue dallied with hers and she was amazed how much she liked it. She had heard some of the girls at school talk about tongues and now she was no longer ignorant. Then he drew away and licked her ear.

She giggled. 'You're not thinking of eating me, are you?'

'No, that would be a waste when there are more pleasant things for us to share,' he said, and kissed her lips gently. 'I think we'd better go inside. I thought I felt rain.'

'Do you want to come to my cabin?' she said.

'Best not,' he said, taking her hand and moving towards a stairway.

'You're thinking of my mam,' she murmured, liking the feel of his strong fingers curled around hers.

'I made her a promise.'

'She thinks I'm a child,' she said crossly, swinging their arms together.

'Perhaps, but she also doesn't want you to make a mistake and lose your dream of going to university and you know what else.'

She hesitated before saying, 'I think I love you. I've so enjoyed being in your company and doing things we both enjoy together.'

'So have I, but I must make a living and save money to get married. You'll need training to get a decent job. We're going to have to wait to get married, anyway.'

'You mean until I'm twenty-one, because Mam won't give her permission?' She clung to him. 'That's five years away.'

'I know. It'll be a test to see if our love is real,' he said. 'Give it a year and they'll see we're serious, and your mam will relent.'

She picked up on some words he mentioned. 'You said "our love", so you do love me?'

'I couldn't not love you.'

'What about Gretna Green?'

'I wondered when you'd say that.' He squeezed her hand.

Joanna said, 'Then I didn't disappoint you.'

'No, you never do.'

'We'd best go and do something where we won't be tempted.'

'Do you like jigsaws?' he teased.

'I do. They're good for the brain, but I'm not used to sharing.'

'It'll be a lesson for the two of us, then,' he said. 'Now let's get in, out of the rain.'

'I think the wind is getting up too.' She snuggled up to him. 'Let's hope it passes.' He ushered her out of the wind and cold.

Soon they were sitting down with Josh and some other passengers, though, some tables were empty, no doubt because some passengers were feeling seasick. She could hear the wind whistling and the banging of loose items as the deck tipped this way and that. She said loudly, 'I'm reminded of crossing the Mersey from New Brighton to Liverpool on the ferry. There were that many people on it that I thought the boat would topple over. It was scary but the boat reached the Pier Head, and we all safely disembarked.'

'Thanks for that,' said Josh. 'Think positively, that's the thing.'

Some passengers said they were going to bed, but Alfie and Joanna found a thousand-piece jigsaw of a harbour in Cornwall and, after dividing it in two, set out to attempt to complete it over the next two days. Josh sat near them, reading an Agatha Christie novel from the ship's library.

They finally called it a night at eleven o'clock and went to bed. Both Alfie and Joanna chose a book from the library. Alfie escorted Joanna to her cabin and offered to stay with her. She accepted but he took a blanket from the bed and settled in a chair.

Fortunately, the wind dropped halfway through the night and the rain lashing on the porthole slackened. The following morning there were patches of blue between the clouds but the relief everyone experienced passed, as the wind increased again, and waves slapped against the hull of the ship.

There was a message broadcast by the captain during lunch, saying that there would be a lifeboat drill at three o'clock, as there was a storm surge coming from the east coast of Maryland, blown by a hurricane, but there was no need to panic as they were getting closer and closer to Mizen Head, the Land's End of Ireland. They would need to keep their distance because of rocks, though, and go round the coast in an easterly direction to Cobh.

They decided to go on deck and watch what was going on. They had their cameras with them. Time passed by quickly and soon evening approached. The rain had stopped but there was a three-quarter moon, and stars could be seen blazing in the expanse of midnight blue sky between clouds.

'It's not a bad night,' said Alfie, as they strolled arm-in-arm along the second highest deck.

'But there's still danger,' said Joanna. 'I wonder where Josh is?' Then suddenly she spotted him on a lighted deck where one of the operations was taking place. Josh was wearing his wetsuit with a life jacket and the light picked up the sheen of water on the rubbery material. She took a photograph but realised she was too far away and pointed him out to Alfie. They moved closer where they could take another shot, even as the ship appeared to tilt.

They leant over the side of the ship, and she waved and called down to Josh. He looked about him and then she shifted over a little more and shouted his name, while waving both arms as he gazed up. At that moment Alfie's flash went off. She was startled and overbalanced. She attempted to grab the side of the boat, but her fingernails only scraped the painted wood; she tried to hook a foot over the rim of the side, but it was wet, and she cried out and felt the damp air rushing past her. Even as she fell, she attempted to slow herself down, but she was flailing and could not feel the side of the ship. Finally, she felt the cold water enveloping her legs and skirt.

Alfie's heart was in his mouth, but he told himself to keep calm as he swung his camera so that it dangled from the back of his neck. He clambered over the side of the ship and clung on for a few seconds, dangling in space, before letting go and plunging after her. He banged his arm and his head, and then his camera, against one of the lifeboats, which swayed slightly away from him. He prayed he wouldn't hit another. The pain was intense, and he thought he was going to lose consciousness, but he fought against the darkness that threatened to overtake him and thought he could hear Joanna calling him. She was still alive, he told himself, and he must stay awake. Suddenly, he became aware of men shouting and a boat being set adrift, then he was fighting to keep his head above water as his damaged arm dangled uselessly at his side and he watched with blurred vision as Josh swam with Joanna towards the drifting boat.

Josh pushed her up and, with force, over the side and into the boat. Then he turned and, with difficulty, he swam towards Alfie, who gasped, 'I think I've broken my arm.'

Josh managed to get a hold on Alfie and dragged him to the boat, where somehow Joanna assisted him in helping Alfie to get on board. Joanna looped the strap on his camera around her wrist, and, they were clinging to each other, water streaming from their sodden clothing.

–

A thankful Josh relaxed his grip and leant back in the water, only to find himself struggling to stay afloat, despite the life jacket. He attempted to shout but water filled his mouth, and he felt himself being carried away by the current, as he spat out water. Suddenly he could see Olive's face and hear her calling him. Eventually, he managed to keep his head and shoulders above water and realised he had been carried a fair distance away from the liner; all he could see was a glow in the sky where the liner and the harbour had been. He could only hope and pray that Alfie and Joanna would have realised that they could not see him nearby and called for help.

In the meantime, he had to stay afloat, lying on his back so he wouldn't tire himself out. He turned his aching head and glanced to where he reckoned the coast was. It was then he realised that he was some distance away from a barren stretch of rocky cliffs that he recalled the liner steaming past. He felt something hard and jagged scrape his cheek and would have grabbed the rock, but it slid away. He could see the odd light in the distance. A smallholding or a farm perhaps. He began to sing 'Eternal Father, Strong to Save' but his voice faltered as he no longer had the breath to sing and so he just floated, glad of his wetsuit and life jacket, praying he would soon be found.

CHAPTER SEVENTEEN

WATERLOO

JULY/AUGUST

Olive sat on the arm of the chair and lifted her eyes from her sewing to stare out of the window and over the back garden, and wondered what her daughter would think of it. Her last letter had told her about the size of gardens and parks she had visited in America, as well as the landscape they'd admired as they had travelled by train to Los Angeles to visit Paramount Studios and the Ranch in the hills. She had also enthused about the food, especially the thickness of the steaks. She had mentioned a Scottish married couple from Canada and how the husband and Jay had gone horse riding while she, Alfie and the wife, Heather, had walked one of the many trails and seen a coyote. No rattlesnakes, thank God.

Then had come the news she had been waiting for, positive news. She and Alfie were homesick and had decided to come home earlier, Josh was catching the ship at the same time but stopping in Ireland to see his kinfolk, so she and Alfie would disembark there too, and see a bit of the country. As for Jay, he must be in Canada, training to be a Mountie while staying in Calgary with the couple they'd met.

Olive shoved the needle in the curtain material and placed it on the arm of the chair. She decided to go for a walk to the beach and look at the sea and maybe collect shells, wondering what Josh would tell her in his letter when it eventually arrived. At least he had her new address. She thought of Jay, guessing father and son would miss each other, but no doubt Josh would be pleased he had started out on a career and was becoming independent.

In the meantime, she must make everything ready for Joanna's return. Surely it wouldn't be long now. She thought of her mother and Dougal, sailing in the Mediterranean. The Norway cruise had been fully booked, so Flora had got her way. Olive put her jacket on and left the house. It was then that her neighbour, Mike, caught up with her and asked where Iris was that morning.

Olive shrugged. 'I'm not sure. She could be doing voluntary work, helping with children during the school holidays while their mothers are at work.'

'I wondered if she'd gone away with that bloke who's always hanging around, watching your house.'

'You mean Alan, I suppose. I've told her to give him the old heave-ho, but she tells me I'm a dog in the manger. Just because I don't want him, shouldn't prevent him and her getting together. I've told her she's deceiving herself, though, and he's just hanging about to annoy me. If she doesn't stop encouraging him, then she can go home to her mother, and I'll have the police on him.'

'And what did she say to that?' he asked.

'She doesn't believe me.' She paused. 'Anyway, I can't stand here gossiping. I've places to go and things to do.'

'Sorry for keeping you,' he said. 'I'll keep my eye open for him and warn him off.'

She sighed. 'I'd rather you keep out of it. He's not a nice man.'

'Okay! But I'm always here if you need me.'

She thanked him, but hurried away, hoping that he wasn't going to prove a nuisance. She appreciated his kindness but despite his offers of help and his good looks, she wanted to manage her own problems and didn't want another man in her life, bar Josh. She considered Joanna's letter and her plans for her return journey. She really hoped Josh would come to Liverpool with them. She wondered if she would recognise him now, and him her. Was it possible that Alfie might have taken a photo of him chopping down a tree when he had shown him and Joanna the safest way to do so? It would be a real action shot. She decided to go and visit Eliza.

Olive was glad to find Jack at home, in the garden, mending the swing which the children so enjoyed. Eliza had gone shopping, so Olive made two cups of tea and went out to him and the children. 'Time for a break,' she said. 'Did Eliza get a letter from Alfie?'

He nodded and sipped the tea and asked if there were any biscuits. 'I'll check the tin,' she said. 'Does he mention Josh coming over to Ireland on the same ship and the three of them stopping off there?'

'Yeah! Now go and get the biscuits, *please*?'

'All right, keep your hair on.' She went into the kitchen and brought out the tin, holding her face up to the sun as she stepped off the step. She took the lid off the tin and offered it to him. 'There's nothing in there,' he said. 'She's going to have to stock up on custard creams before Alfie arrives home.'

'I could go and get you a packet of dark chocolate digestives if you like,' she said. 'Save you waiting, and it won't take me long if I don't bump into you-know-who.'

'Alan,' he said.

'He's being a real pain. Forever hanging around my house, making up to Iris, and she's delighted with that, whatever I say.'

'Keep your mouth shut if you want to get rid of him,' said Jack. 'Now go and get me biscuits. I'll give you the money when you get back. I want to finish this job before the kids start nagging me to hurry up.'

'I'm going, I'm going,' she said, sauntering down the garden and out the back gate.

She wasted no time going to the nearest grocer's shop down Rocky Lane, not wanting to risk bumping into Alan if she went the other way.

As it was, she saw Alan's son, George, crossing the road towards her while she waited at the kerb to cross in the opposite direction. 'You're home?' she said, before adding, 'Daft question.'

'Not really,' he said. 'Dad's place is no longer home. I've got a one-roomed flat in Bootle, but I decided I should go and see how Dad is doing. Take him out for a pint and a pie before he starts moaning I don't give him anything.' He paused. 'Are you here seeing Eliza?'

'Yeah, but don't tell your dad you've seen me.'

'Have you moved into your new house?'

She nodded. 'I have a woman friend staying with me and he's forever hanging around.'

'Has he finished with the other one he had?'

'I presume so,' she said. 'Anyway, it's good to see you, but I'll have to be on my way.'

She waved but he placed a hand on her arm. 'How's Joanna?'

'Still in America, but she'll be coming home soon. Had a letter from her a short while ago. She and Alfie have been to Los Angeles.'

'It's all right for some,' he said. 'I don't suppose you've seen Mary?'

'She could be on holiday with her gran in Colwyn Bay. Drop in and see Eliza after you've seen your dad. She'll know.'

'I might just do that,' he said, smiling.

'Ta-ra,' she said, hurrying away.

When she arrived back with the biscuits, it was to find Eliza and the children home.

'First things first,' said Jack, holding out his hand. 'Biscuits.'

She gave the chocolate digestives to him, and he gave her the money.

'So, what do you want?' asked Eliza, beginning to unpack her shopping.

'Someone to talk to,' replied Olive.

'What about Iris?'

'Jack told me to keep my mouth shut.' Olive took a digestive from Jack's packet on the table. 'I'll let him tell you. I'm fed up with the subject. Instead, I'll tell you that I've just met George, he's home and was asking about Mary. I thought she might have gone to Colwyn Bay to see her gran. Anyway, he might drop in after he's seen his dad.'

'Anything else?' asked Eliza.

'Did Alfie mention about him and Joanna going to Ireland with Josh before the three of them come over here?'

Eliza nodded.

Olive lowered her eyes. 'She said he's going to write to me.'

'Why, if he's coming over?'

Olive said, 'Maybe he finds it easier to write things he finds difficult to say face to face.'

'What about that neighbour of yours?'

'You mean Mike? He wants to be my knight in shining armour and challenge Alan.' She groaned.

'Regretting moving?' said Eliza.

'No, maybe I just need a holiday.'

'Can you afford one?'

'I could probably afford one in a tent in Wales. Anything more expensive and I won't be able to help Joanna through university.'

'Perhaps she'll change her mind about going or not get the results she needs,' said Eliza.

'We'll know when they arrive home,' interrupted Jack. 'Anyway, she might be able to get a grant.'

'Put it out of your mind,' said Eliza. 'What are you going to do now?'

'I think I'll go for a walk in the park,' she said.

'Can I come with you?' asked Beth. 'We could feed the ducks.'

'Has your mam got any stale bread?' asked Olive.

'You can take the last two slices of that loaf from yesterday,' said Eliza. 'Don't be long.'

'Am I staying for dinner?' asked Olive. 'If so, I'll buy some iced fingers, if the bakery has any left.'

'Fine, you can stay,' said Eliza. 'Jack will run you home.'

'I'm on lates, remember,' he said.

'Sorry,' she said.

'Don't be worrying about me,' said Olive.

'Don't go trying to kick a football, though,' said Jack.

'I'm not an idiot,' said Olive tartly. 'My foot is still a bit sore.'

He raised his eyebrows.

'Don't say it,' she warned him, shrugging on her jacket.

'Perhaps we should hire a rowing boat,' suggested Beth.

'Certainly not,' said her mother. 'You're feeding the ducks, that's all. Aunty Olive's not made of money.'

Beth gazed at her father. 'Da-ad, how about it?'

'Don't you dare, Jack,' said Eliza, watching him dig a hand into his trouser pocket. 'You spoil her.'

'She's the only daughter I have,' he said. 'And she's a good girl.'

'I didn't say she wasn't, but she should wait until she gets her pocket money.'

'But Aunty Olive won't be here then,' said Beth.

'That's enough,' said Eliza crossly.

'This is all my fault,' said Olive. 'I should go home.'

'No,' said Beth, seizing her hand. 'We can hire a rowing boat another time. Just because Mam's a meanie, we can't let the ducks go hungry.'

'Don't be cheeky to your mother,' said Jack, withdrawing his empty hand from his pocket. 'Say you're sorry.'

Beth crossed over to Eliza and hugged her and whispered, 'Sorry, Mam.'

'Just don't say it again.' Eliza ruffled her daughter's hair.

'Maybe I should have admitted I can't row in the first place,' said Olive, biting her lower lip.

'Let's forget it,' said Jack. 'I'll teach Beth to row the next fine day I'm off work.'

Olive was about to say Beth wasn't strong enough, only to decide to keep her mouth shut, as it was up to her goddaughter's parents to decide that. 'Come on, Beth! Let's go and feed the ducks.'

Beth collected the stale bread and followed Olive out of the house and across the road to Newsham Park. 'Have you a park near your new house, Aunty Olive?'

'There's Marine Park and Adelaide Garden not far from the seafront, but there's no swings or a seesaw or a maypole like there is in Sheil Park. But then, we have the beach and further along to the north there's Crosby swimming pool, and even further along is Formby and Freshfield, with sandhills and woods with red squirrels and rabbits.'

'How far away are the woods with the squirrels?'

'It's quite a walk, but a short train journey, just three or four stops.'

'What about swimming in the sea?' asked Beth.

'Lots of people do swim in the sea but it's cold.'

'You've swam in the sea?'

'Yeah! It didn't feel as cold when I was a kid. Dad used to say kids don't feel the cold the same as adults. But I enjoy paddling and jumping the waves, despite the cold.'

'Could I come and stay with you for one day and sleep over and go to the beach with you, please?'

'If your mam and dad agree,' replied Olive. 'There was something else me and my brother Peter used to do as kids and that was roll or jump down the sandhills. You must be careful, though, you need to watch out for broken glass people might have left around instead of taking it home and putting it in a bin. You also need to watch out for sinking sand. It's just in patches, not all over the beach or near the sandhills. Anyway, I'll be keeping my eye on you and the tide.'

Olive thought of something else they could do if Beth came to stay but decided to keep quiet about that and, taking the child's hand, she hurried her along the grass in the direction of the bridge over the lake. There were some children playing rounders and she would have stopped and watched them for a while, but Beth hurried her past them, and soon they were on the bridge, gazing down at the ducks and the occasional pair of swans with growing cygnets.

'Oh, aren't they sweet,' said Beth, standing on tiptoe so she could rest her arms on the wrought iron bridge and heave herself up to get a closer look at the birds.

'I presume you mean the cygnets,' said Olive, smiling.

'Is that what baby swans are called?' said Beth.

Olive nodded. 'You like birds?'

'I like birds and animals. I'd like to be a vet or perhaps a zookeeper.'

'Have you mentioned that to your dad or mam?'

Beth shook her head. 'I told Alfie, and he said I needed to do well at school and when I went up into junior school I should talk to my class teacher about it, as well as mam and dad.'

'Maybe you should talk to your mam and dad first,' said Olive. 'Not just yet, but in a few years' time.'

'Is that because I'm only young and a girl?'

'I say it because your dad and mam can probably find out more about it than you can. Although, my daughter Joanna has been wanting to go to university and she's going to do something about it when she arrives home.'

'What if she wants to get married?' asked Beth.

'We'll have to wait and see.' Olive took some bread from the bag and said, 'Time to feed the ducks and swans, don't you think?'

Beth took the bread from Olive and tossed it down to the birds. 'Being grown-up and marrying a prince... Life must have been easier for Cinderella. She'd have plenty of money and be able to do what she liked.'

Olive shook her head. 'She'd have a job to do. Just think of our Queen.' She threw some bread to the swans.

Beth held out a hand for more bread. 'She doesn't have to do housework. She has servants to clean the palace.'

'She still has work to do: lots of government documents to read and respond to, as well as countries to visit and people to listen to and advise.'

'She wears lovely clothes and jewels, and rides horses. One of her horses ran in the Grand National.'

'The horse that won this year was Mr What and its owner was Irish,' said Olive.

'Dad said he wished he'd backed it because it was 18 to 1,' said Beth.

Olive handed her the last of the bread and suggested it was time to go back. Beth tossed the bread to the birds and blew a kiss as well. Then they turned away and headed for home.

They arrived at the house just as George Biggs did. 'You've arrived here early,' said Olive.

'Dad wasn't in,' said George. 'So I decided to come here.' He opened the gate for them.

They passed through, thanking him, and Beth said, 'It's nice to see you again. Where have you been?'

'Gibraltar,' he replied, watching her remove a door key from her pocket and turning it in the keyhole with difficulty. 'Here, let me do it.'

Beth moved to one side and watched him turn the key without difficulty. 'Thanks,' she said. 'Come in and tell me about Gibraltar.' She led the way inside.

Olive and George followed her, and the sitting-room door opened.

'You're back,' said Eliza, gazing at the three figures.

'Look, it's George,' said Beth. 'He's home from Gibraltar and he's going to tell me all about it.'

'Good to see you, George,' said Eliza. 'We were just about to eat. Would you like to join us?'

'Will you have enough?' he asked, swinging his kitbag onto the floor.

Jack, who had come to see who it was when he heard a male voice, picked up the kitbag and placed it behind the sofa, out of the way.

'Good to see you, lad. I take it you haven't seen your dad yet?'

'He was out. I might leave calling on him until tomorrow and go straight to my flat in Bootle when I leave here.'

'We could get a taxi between us,' said Olive, suddenly recalling that George enjoyed cooking.

'Jack would have given you a lift,' said Eliza. 'Only, he has to go to work.'

'No trouble,' said George. 'Sharing a taxi with Olive is fine by me.'

Olive smiled, hoping that his father was not hanging around her house.

Beth fetched cutlery for George, and they all sat down at the dining table. She suggested he sit next to her so he could continue to tell her about Gibraltar. Jack shook his head. 'He's sitting between your mother and me. I'll have to leave soon for work. He can talk to you later.'

'Does that mean I don't have to go to bed as early?' she asked.

George said, 'I'll talk loudly so you can all hear me. You need your beauty sleep, Beth. And I'll have to leave at a reasonable time with Olive, because my landlady doesn't know I'm back.'

Beth's face fell but she said, 'Will you call in and see us tomorrow after you've visited your dad?'

'I'll do my best,' he said, picking up a spoon and fork and dipping both into the bowl of scouse.

Jack pushed the jar of pickled beetroot towards him and waited until George had eaten at least half of his dinner before asking about his voyage to Gibraltar and whether there had been any trouble.

'We were transporting soldiers and sailed from Portsmouth and into the Atlantic, and down the coast of France and it became a bit rough then.'

'The Bay of Biscay?' said Jack.

George raised his eyebrows. 'A lot of the soldiers were seasick, but I wasn't. I put it down to trips on the ferry across the Mersey when the boats were packed in summer with people, and it was going up and down like crazy.'

'What is there to see and do in Gibraltar?' asked Beth.

'The weather's nice and as a tourist you can swim in the sea and there's caves to explore, and there's a street where you'd think you were in Britain. Lots of Brits live there and there are lovely flowers and birds and countryside. There's also bands and parades by the British and Gibraltar military that stir the senses.'

'I like the sound of a band marching,' chorused Olive, Eliza and Beth.

'I even enjoy the Boys' Brigade band when they march, and the Sally Army,' said Beth.

'I'd better be going soon,' said Olive, thinking she wanted to get home before Iris.

'Me too,' said George. 'I'll just finish me scouse.'

'I'll phone for a taxi,' said Olive.

'There's a card with a number by the phone,' said Eliza.

Olive made the call, and a taxi arrived ten minutes later.

Beth whispered to Olive as she kissed her good night, reminding her about her desire to come to stay with her.

'I won't forget, which reminds me. Did Alfie enclose any photos?' said Olive, hugging Beth.

'A couple, one at the ranch and one of Josh chopping down a tree,' said Eliza. 'I'll get them out when next I see you.'

Olive would have liked to see them there and then but thanked her friend and left with George.

Olive was glad when the taxi took them the long way around so she had time to talk to George about her business plan and ask him if he would be interested in working for her as a chef. 'I don't expect you to answer right away. It's a bit of a way off yet. I'm also thinking of asking Mary whether she would be interested in working for me as she has some experience working in the tearoom where her gran lives in Colwyn Bay.'

His face lit up. 'I'm planning on seeing her soon. I'll sound her out, if you like?'

He tapped the taxi driver on the shoulder. 'This is where I get out, mate.' He handed Olive some money.

She thanked him and said, 'I'll be in touch.'

When the taxi dropped Olive outside her house and she paid the driver, she was relieved to see there was no sign of Alan's car outside. She hurried up the path and opened the front door with her key.

It was then that she saw the cigarette butts in the ashtray and became angry and suspicious. Instead of calling out Iris's name, she crept upstairs, having removed her shoes.

'Iris?' she shouted.

'I'm in bed,' called Iris. 'Come in.'

Olive pushed open the door and went inside. Iris was sitting up in bed, reading. 'No Alan?' said Olive.

'Oh, he's been, and I invited him in but only to watch telly and have a snog. That's as far as I'd let him go,' said Iris. 'I might fancy him, but I'm not besotted. If he wants me, then he'll have to put a gold band on the third finger of my left hand and have the priest declare us man and wife in church. I do want to get married. I don't want to go back to my mum's.'

Olive sank onto the bed. 'You amaze me.'

'I told him I don't come cheap.'

'What did he say to that?'

'That I'd led him on.' She sighed. 'I told him he was easily led and that he could have scarpered.'

Olive felt a giggle rising in her throat. 'What did he do?'

'I remembered Mike next door and mentioned going to get him if he didn't stop messing me about. He said I wouldn't dare so I screamed, and he left but he forgot his coat.'

Olive couldn't restrain her laughter.

'Stop laughing,' said Iris. 'This is serious.'

Eventually Olive got control of herself. 'So, do you think he'll be back for his coat?'

'I'm not going to take it. I might post it and see what his next move is.'

'You don't think it's over between you?'

'I'm not going to pursue him and have him say I wanted him back.' Iris smiled. 'I'd love to see his face, though, when the postman arrives with his coat.'

'I'd love to know what your game is,' said Olive.

'Marriage! But he needs to be taught a lesson.' Iris closed her book. 'Shut the door on your way out. I'm tired.'

'You haven't asked how my day was,' said Olive.

'How was your day?' Iris closed her eyes.

'I went to Eliza's; I took my goddaughter to feed the ducks. I'm going to have her to stay over here for a day and a night. Also, Alan's son is home, but he has his own place now. He will probably call in on his dad tomorrow,' said Olive, digging Iris in the ribs.

'Let's hope that doesn't change my plans,' said Iris.

'The ball's in your corner. Good night. God bless.'

CHAPTER EIGHTEEN

Olive closed the bedroom door behind her and went to bed. She spent a short time thinking of Iris and Alan, and then of Josh; she still had not received his letter. Perhaps he would not come to Liverpool after all. She felt a twinge of sadness; she thought of George and Mary and her business. She wondered what Joanna would think and whether it would change her daughter's plans. She had missed her; it had only been a few years ago when Joanna was as young as Beth… Olive fell asleep thinking of having Beth over and taking her to the beach and Freshfield Woods and seeing the squirrels and, if they were lucky, the natterjack toads in the pool among the sandhills.

–

The following morning Olive had a phone call from Eliza, asking whether she had really invited Beth to go and stay with her.

'I did,' answered Olive. 'I had been thinking of Joanna and how she used to enjoy such outings. Beth is my goddaughter and yet I've spent such little time with her. I know I should have asked you first but what with George turning up, I forgot.'

'It's fine,' said Eliza. 'And you'll be interested to know that Milly phoned me, and I asked about Mary, and she is staying with her grandmother in Colwyn Bay.'

'I'll mention it to George if I hear anything from him,' said Olive.

'Was Alan at yours when you arrived home?'

'No, but he had been, and him and Iris had a bit of a falling out. Only time will tell if they get back together again,' she said. 'Anyway, let me know when Beth can come and stay?'

'Will do,' said Eliza and put the phone down.

Olive made herself a coffee, and with it to hand she settled on a bedroom for Beth to sleep in. The curtains needed hemming and the bed needed making.

As she shortened the curtains, her thoughts kept returning to Josh and why he had taken such an interest in her relationship with Joe. He had never talked about his own marriage. He had been friendly with her, so much so that she had told him about being pregnant with Joe's baby. It was odd. She still felt muddled up. She dug her needle into the pincushion and admitted that she had no cause to judge Josh or Joe, when she had kept the truth about Joanna's father from those who had a right to know. She set the curtain aside and decided she needed some exercise, so she put on her hat and coat. Only when she opened the front door did she realise how windy it was, but she would not let that put her off. She would go down to the front and watch the waves.

As she left the house, the wind caught the door and snatched it out of her hand, slamming it shut. She drew in a shuddering breath and thought she must be quite mad going out in this weather. There could be loose slates whipped from roofs that could knock her unconscious, or broken branches. She remembered windy days from her childhood and how she and her brother would go out with their father. He would hold them both by the hand

and sing, 'Windy weather, frosty weather, when the wind blows, we all blow together,' and they would laugh and laugh until they cried and clutched each other.

The memory brought tears as well as a smile to her face and she thought of her brother Peter: it seemed a long time since they had seen each other. He had not visited their mother while she had been staying there or even been in touch.

Perhaps she should go and visit him and his family, as she had said she would ages ago. Surely he wouldn't turn her away from the front door. She changed direction and headed towards the bus stop. She stopped on the way and bought a tin of chocolate biscuits, thinking it best not to go empty-handed. It was possible her brother might not be working. He was a mariner and worked on the banana boats.

She had to change buses a couple of times but eventually she arrived in Kirkdale, not far from Waterloo Road, which was commonly called the dock road. She turned up one of many terraced streets with a pub on the corner and was partly blown along until she arrived at her brother's rented home. Fortunately, it was still standing, unlike many of the houses in the neighbourhood which had been damaged or destroyed in the Blitz.

She knocked on the door with her fist, as the doorknocker had long gone in an appeal for metal during the war. It was a few minutes before she heard scurrying and a child's voice calling to her mother. The door opened and her niece Brenda and sister-in-law Eleanor stood there.

'Good God, where did you blow in from?' asked Eleanor, who was wearing a floral pinny and a headscarf covering her hair in curlers.

'I have my own place in Waterloo. Mam has got a lodger but has gone on a cruise in the Mediterranean with him. I was thinking of you all, so I decided to come and see you. I did wonder if our kid might be on shore leave. Lousy weather.'

'Thinking of the weather, you'd better come in so I can shut the door, and the house doesn't get cold.'

'Sorry,' said Olive, stepping inside and following her sister-in-law and niece along the lobby. They reached a back room where a toddler was asleep on the sofa, surrounded by cushions to prevent him from rolling off.

'How's Joanna getting on? Has she left school and found herself a job?'

Olive hesitated, pondering on truth or lie. 'She's in America.'

'You're joking!'

'God's honest truth!' Olive crossed her heart. 'She's gone with Eliza's son Alfie and an American friend, Jay.'

'That must have cost a bit.'

'I won on the pools,' said Olive. 'And she got herself a part-time job for a while.'

'Honest to God? You really won on the pools?'

'Cross my heart and hope to die if I dare tell a lie.'

'I can hardly believe it.' Her sister-in-law put the kettle on the coal fire in the black leaded grate. 'Cup of tea?'

'Thanks. I thought she needed her chance, so she's gone over there to get a feel of the place. She's coming home soon.'

At that moment the toddler woke up, and no more questions were asked. Olive made the tea and produced the tin of biscuits while her sister-in-law tended her son.

Olive's niece Brenda came over to her and said, 'Can I have a biccie, please?'

The lid was removed, the tin offered to the little girl. Her mother said, 'She'll be forever trying to make up her mind. You're best picking one and giving it to her.'

Olive did so and then took a plate from the sideboard cupboard and placed it on a table alongside the tin, adding several more biscuits to it.

'If you want another biscuit, you ask for it and I will get the plate down and give you one,' said Olive to her niece.

'Larry has one, too, please?' asked Brenda, gazing up at Olive from pleading hazel eyes.

'Not yet,' said her mother. 'And no more for you until after lunch.'

Olive thought for a moment that her niece was going to cry, but she scrubbed her eyes and said, 'Can I choose two and put them on a saucer and watch them in case all the biscuits go before we can have ours?'

Olive gazed at Eleanor. 'What do you say?'

'I say she can put two biscuits on a saucer, and I will put it on the sideboard out of temptation's way.'

'Agreed,' said Olive. 'We all have to learn patience.'

Brenda's face was a picture of indignation when the saucer and biscuits were taken from her and placed on the sideboard, along with the tin and the plate.

Then she lay on the floor and drummed her heels on the linoleum, but her mother ignored her and signalled for Olive to do the same. 'She'll stop eventually.'

'It's my fault,' said Olive.

The kitchen door opened, and her brother entered.

'I didn't hear you come in, love,' said his wife.

'I'm not surprised, considering the noise this one is making,' he said, nudging his daughter with his foot. Then he lifted her arm and took one of the biscuits from the saucer, popping it in his mouth.

Brenda roared, 'That's Larry's.'

'He can have the other one,' mumbled her daddy.

'But that's mine,' she said.

He stared at Olive. 'Hallo, stranger. Where have you been all this time?'

'Mam didn't tell you two, then?' she asked, despite knowing the truth.

'What didn't she tell us?' He placed his daughter on a chair.

'I've bought a house in Waterloo.'

His eyebrows rose. 'You're joking!'

'No, although I never knew I was so funny. I should be on the telly.'

'What other jokes have you told?' asked her brother.

'She's won the pools and Joanna's in America,' said his wife, handing his son to him and forcing them into an armchair.

'I know the latter,' he said, planting a raspberry kiss on his son's neck. 'I was talking to Jimmy, Milly's husband. She'd seen Eliza, Olive's friend, and she was telling her that Joanna had gone to California with Eliza's son Alfie and the son of some American soldier who Olive had met during the war.'

'It is no joke that Joanna is in California, but she'll be coming home soon with Alfie, and Jay's father. He will be dropping off in Ireland where he has kin. His son Jay has gone to Calgary, in Canada, to join the Mounties.'

'Milly's half-Irish, so Jimmy told me. Her mother lives over there.'

'Shut up, both of you,' said Eleanor. 'I've a casserole in the oven and it's time I took it out before it's ruined.'

Olive sat down beside Peter and added, 'So, how is it you were talking to Milly's husband?'

'Is it true you've won the pools?' said her brother.

She nodded as she took his son from him and kissed Larry's cheek. 'But a lot of it has gone. Like I said, I've bought a house in Waterloo, between Seaforth and Crosby.'

'I know where it is. You must have won a few thousand.'

'I haven't told anyone the amount. It's my inheritance from Dad; he gave me his numbers and told me to take over and that they'll come up one day.'

'You're joking!'

'If anyone says that to me again, I'll scream. I intended telling him when I arrived home, but then I received the letter telling me he was dead and about the funeral. Too late!' Tears glistened in her eyes. 'Mam threw it in my face that he'd left everything to her. I couldn't care less about his will. What hurt me was her keeping his illness and funeral from me. It was cruel, but I'm no angel or saint. I've kept things from family and friends.'

'Okay, don't get yourself upset. It'll put you off your food. So, when are you going to invite us to your place for a meal?'

'When Joanna comes home,' she answered. 'Now tell me why you were talking to Jimmy?'

'You know Jimmy's in the building industry?'

'He's a bricklayer,' she said, wondering where this was going.

He nodded. 'Well, there's a lot of rebuilding being done by the Council and new private houses going up, and I asked what the chances of me getting a job in the industry were, as I want to be at home more to help with the kids and see more of my dear wife. So, I'll only be a labourer to start with but eventually I'll climb the ladder and be a journeyman brickie.'

'That's brilliant,' said Olive. 'But won't you miss going to the glorious Caribbean and bringing home coconuts, shells, rum and bananas?'

'Not as much as I miss my family,' he said, blowing a kiss to his wife.

She returned his kiss and asked when he would be starting his new job. Also, she asked if the ship's master knew he was quitting.

'I've already spoken to him. He wasn't pleased, said I was a good worker, but he wished me luck.'

'That's good,' said Olive. 'I'd like my own business. I was thinking about going to America at one time with Joanna,' she said. 'There was a point when I was torn in two. To go or not to go, that was the question.' She sighed. 'I needn't have worried. She seems to be managing all right. I'd dreamt of her being caught in a gun fight.'

'Watching too many Westerns,' said her brother.

She stuck her tongue out at him. 'You're as bad as Jack,' she said.

'What kind of business?' he asked.

'A café or restaurant.' She paused. 'Jack made me see sense about America. Also, if you haven't heard, Theo and I are divorced and Mam has a lodger, Dougal.'

He frowned. 'He knew Dad.'

'He's Irish, a widower, and was unhappy in his lodging, so Mam told him he could have Joanna's room while she was in America. I decided to buy a house and have a friend come and lodge with me as she was unhappy at home.'

'You're as bad as Mam, listening to sob stories,' he said.

'You haven't heard the worst,' said Olive. 'Alan Biggs, who I once had a crush on years ago, started hanging around and got too fresh; that was before Iris came to stay. I told him to get lost, but he started up again and got round Iris, and she thinks him the bees' knees. She realised her mistake, though, when he tried it on, and I'm hoping he's got the message and stays away, but I'm not completely convinced he will. She believes that her playing hard to get will encourage him to propose marriage.'

'I'll come and see him off,' Peter said.

She held up a hand as if to ward him off. 'My next-door neighbour is raring to have a go at him, but I've told him to keep out of it, as he could get hurt.'

'I'm your brother and it's up to me to look out for you. It's what Dad would want, so no arguing.'

Olive groaned. 'I shouldn't have told you. Your place is here, with your wife and children. What if he hurt you and you couldn't work?'

'You should have more faith in me,' he said sulkily.

'It has nothing to do with faith,' she told him.

'Have you spoken to Eliza about him?' he asked.

She did not answer.

'I bet you have,' he said. 'She'd tell Jack.'

'I've had enough help from Jack. The last man who would have helped me was Dougal, when I was still living with Mam. She was encouraging Alan.'

'Does she know about your win on the pools?'

'I eventually told her when I mentioned I was buying a house. She'd told Joanna and me that she was going to spend the money she had tucked away on a cruise and leave us nothing. That we'd had enough from her.'

'What about me and the kids?' he asked.

'You'll have to take that up with our mother. Did you get a mention in Dad's will?'

'No, but he had slipped some money to us as a family when he first became ill and told me not to mention it to Mam. I presumed he had seen you all right. What a marriage theirs was!'

'You know she never recovered from her brother being killed,' said Olive. 'She allowed grief to blight her life.'

'So, what comes next? What is Joanna going to do when she arrives home?'

'She hopes eventually to become a pharmacist, but she would need to go to university and get a degree in the subject. And to go to university she will need to get good grades in certain subjects. If she doesn't get them at the first shot, she needs to go to a college of further education or night school.'

'What if she meets someone and decides to get married?'

'These days a married woman doesn't have to stay at home and be a housewife. Since getting the vote and after two world wars, it's not just single women who have gone out to work. So, studying and training doesn't always get wasted,' said Olive. 'Naturally, some married women want to give up their jobs and care for their husbands and the house, and the children, if they come along. But maybe they can get a part-time job to help with family expenses and for holidays.'

'They'll take away men's jobs,' said her brother.

'Rubbish,' she said. 'There's thousands of jobs that women are naturally good at, and men wouldn't touch.'

'We'll see,' he said. 'And there's some husbands who won't want their wives going out to work,' he added quickly. 'I'm not one of them, as long as the kids aren't neglected and my dinner's ready when I come home from work.'

Olive noticed that her sister-in-law had remained silent throughout the conversation. But she decided not to mention it, as it could be that she had mixed feelings on the subject and did not want to be accused of sitting on the fence. Anyway, the topic was dropped. She decided that if her business got off the ground, Eleanor could work part-time for her and bring the kids along. It was then she remembered that she needed to finish shortening the curtains so decided to go home. She explained why she had to cut her visit short but promised she wouldn't be a stranger and would let them know when Joanna was home.

Her brother saw her out and said, 'Don't forget to let me know if that bloke continues to harass you and your friend?'

'I won't, and good luck with the new job.'

'I might pop in later,' he said. 'I'll come for tea.'

She nodded and hurried away to catch a bus to South Road. She did some shopping, popping into Woolworths to buy another reel of cotton and a bucket and spade for Beth to use on the beach. She wouldn't allow her to take them home but would insist they remained in her house to use when next she visited. That way Brenda could use them when she came to visit too.

When Olive arrived home, there were two envelopes on the doormat and a postcard from Palma Nova, Majorca. She was glad that her mother and Dougal were enjoying themselves.

For an instant she felt she had missed something. Her mother's handwriting was terrible, so she read it again more slowly, and this time realised that her mother and

Dougal had got married. She placed the postcard against the clock on the mantelpiece, before slitting open the envelope postmarked Liverpool and withdrawing a letter suggesting she come for an interview on Wednesday at 10am the following week. Immediately, she felt pleased and wondered what to wear, though she felt a little apprehensive and then decided she did not have the time for the job if she was going to start up her own business.

She opened the other blue airmail one, but it was not in her daughter's handwriting. It contained an international bank draft for £500, signed by Joe. But she soon realised the letter had been written by Josh, as Joe's eyesight was worse. The letter explained Joe would soon have an operation, but not only that: he was engaged to the daughter of his next-door neighbour, and they would be getting married soon. He had enjoyed Joanna's visit and would miss her, but he understood why she wanted to return home. He had enclosed the £500 to help with her studies. He hoped she would keep in touch and that one day they would meet again. He wished Olive every blessing and asked her to listen to Josh and give him every chance, as he was a decent guy, now free to listen to his heart.

She was dumbfounded and could not help wondering whether it was Josh who had added those last few sentences. She felt as if she wanted to cry and crushed the letter in her hand.

She decided not to answer, as it was likely that Josh, Joanna and Alfie had already left America, and she didn't know where Josh's Irish relatives lived. She considered whether Milly and Mary had gone over to Ireland. She was hopeful she'd see George before he went back to sea. All this coming and going when one lived in a port, with family spread near and far. Her thoughts soon returned to

Josh: she had liked and trusted him, and he had let her down. She did her best to dismiss him from her mind, to go for a walk on the sands and collect shells. Then she saw a poster outside the cinema and decided immediately to go and see it as it was one of those fantasy adventure films.

She enjoyed fantasy films, so she checked opening times and prices and hurried home for a cup of tea and a snack. Happily, there was nobody loitering outside. It had slipped her mind that she had intended to shorten curtains. She decided to do them in the evening.

The sky had clouded over, so she headed for the cinema in plenty of time, imagining there would probably be a queue, which turned out to be the case, but it was not too long. When she got inside, she was pleased to see there were a fair number of decent seats, so she chose one in the middle stalls and made herself comfortable, and she dozed off despite a certain amount of noise from the audience, especially from children cheering on the hero and booing the baddies.

Olive took her time leaving the cinema, but once outside, she wasted no time hurrying home. She would need to prepare a meal for Iris and herself, as well as her brother, in case he turned up. She tried to remember what there was in the larder and the fridge that would not take long and finally settled on a kind of corned beef hash. For pudding she baked a strawberry jam tart to serve with custard that she would make later. Easy-peasy, as Joanna would say.

The table was set for three and she was just putting the finishing touches to dinner, when there came a knocking at the door. She went to see who it was, hoping it was not Alan playing tricks, and found Milly's daughter, Mary, on the step.

'Hello, Mary, this is a surprise, but it's nice to see you. I thought you were going to Dublin?'

'I couldn't go. Granny took ill. She's been taken into hospital now. Eliza told me you wanted to speak to me, so I thought I'd come and look you up. I'd heard you'd moved, and I was nosey and wanted to see the house, as well as finding out what George had to say. Dad has gone to Colwyn Bay now and is staying in Gran's place so he can visit her and be there for her when she is allowed out of hospital. He's written to his aunt in Essex, who is Gran's only sister, hoping she'll come over and look after her when he must go back to work. I'll be going to work too.'

'Well, sit down and I'll tell you what I discussed with George.'

Mary glanced about her and, seeing the table was set, said, 'You're about to eat, I should go.'

'No, sit down. I'll make a cup of tea, and we can talk while having it,' said Olive. 'I'm ready for a cuppa. I haven't long been in. I went to the pictures this afternoon.'

'What did you see?' Mary followed her into the kitchen.

Olive returned Mary's smile and told her about the film, all the while thinking what a nice-looking girl she was with auburn hair and brown eyes and skin that was fine as rose petals. She also had a kind nature, always willing to help, even before being asked.

'I met George by accident, and he told me that he wanted to see you, as he hadn't heard from you. He has moved to Bootle. I don't have the address, but I have an idea where he lives.' She paused, thinking she heard a key in the front door. 'That will be my friend Iris,' she said.

'I'd best go,' said Mary, getting to her feet.

'No, wait. Go into the kitchen. I heard a man's voice. Keep quiet while I get rid of him.' The man's voice did not sound like her brother's. 'It's best he doesn't see you here.' She pushed Mary into the kitchen and pulled the door to. Just in time.

Iris entered, with Alan a few feet behind. 'What are you doing here?' asked Olive. 'You're not welcome.'

'I was invited in,' said Alan with a swagger. 'There's no way that you can throw me out.'

'So you say. But I can set the police on you.'

'She won't like you doing that, and if you've been thinking of getting the bloke next door, forget it. He's not in.'

'No, I was thinking of my brother, He's itching to knock your block off.'

Alan glanced around. 'I can't see any sign of him.' He went over to the kitchen door and pushed it, but it scarcely budged.

'Get away from there,' shouted Olive. 'If you don't want a punch in the face.'

Alan hesitated, then turned when he heard a knock on the front door. 'Dad,' said George. 'I've been told you've been wearing your welcome out here.'

'I've heard the same,' said a voice that Olive recognised even more.

'Well, here you are, brother mine. Could you get rid of this unwelcome visitor, please?'

'With pleasure,' said both men, seizing Alan by the upper arms.

CHAPTER NINETEEN

'Leave him alone!' cried a furious female voice. Iris forced her way past Olive. 'Bullies!' she said accusingly. 'He's mine and I'll deal with him as I see fit. Isn't that true, Alan?' She swung her handbag, and the three men ducked. She seized Alan's arm and drew him down the step. 'We're going home, and I'll cook you a nice meal and we'll drop in at the off-licence and buy a couple of bottles and relax and make plans for the wedding.'

'She's crazy,' said George.

'No, she's just in love,' said Olive. 'She'll tame him and be able to tell her mother that she's got a man at last and won't be coming home.' She paused. 'Now let's go inside and have a cuppa and something to eat.'

The two men followed her into the sitting room, where they found Mary placing a knitted tea cosy over the teapot. On seeing them, she removed it and poured tea into four cups.

'I've been looking for you,' she said to George.

He returned her smile. 'I've been wanting to see you as well. Never expected to find you here.'

She passed him a cup of tea and their fingers touched, and they stilled. Olive found herself watching them and suddenly she was thinking of that first time she had met Josh at the Grafton, when he'd picked her up from the floor. She had felt there was something special about him then.

'Help yourself to milk and sugar,' said Olive, going over to the sideboard and taking out an extra plate and cutlery. Then she brought in the frying pan and shared the corned beef hash on the plates, accompanied by a sliced and buttered loaf placed on a large plate in the middle of the table.

They sat down and her brother asked, 'Is there any more HP sauce… please?'

Olive fetched a new bottle and returned to the table and said to Mary, 'Iris won't be staying. I think most likely she'll be back for her stuff tomorrow.'

'Good luck to her,' said her brother Peter. 'She might have a screw loose, but she has plenty of guts.'

'She's the type of wife Dad needs,' said George. 'I hope they'll make a success of their life together.'

'I'm pleased,' said Olive. 'He's out of my hair and I've my guest room back. I don't think I'll rush to get another lodger. Besides, it shouldn't be long before Joanna is home.' She dipped a spoon into the corned beef hash, savoured it and commented, 'This isn't bad.'

'It's very tasty,' said George. 'We should open a café, Olive.'

'That's my idea,' she responded. 'I have been offered a job, but opening a café sounds better.'

'You'd have to give up the sea,' said Mary.

'One more trip,' said George, 'to make some money.'

'I could be your waitress,' suggested Mary.

'Eleanor could help part-time too,' said Olive, looking at her brother. 'This isn't going to happen overnight. We must make proper plans.'

'You need funding and the right place,' said Peter, bringing them down to earth.

'There's no rush if George is going back to sea,' said Mary. 'We work and save, look around for a place where there's passing trade but not too much competition.'

'You're thinking of the place where your granny works in Colwyn Bay,' said Olive. 'Well, we've the seaside here and not everybody can afford holidays away, or even a day trip to Southport or New Brighton.'

'Teenagers,' said George.

'Music,' said Mary. 'Jukeboxes, records.'

'What about live music?' said Olive. 'I remember the Queen's Coronation and street parties, a piano. Now there's cafés in Liverpool with jukeboxes where records are played because music has changed, and parents don't always want to listen to rock 'n' roll at home.'

'You haven't heard of the Cavern?' asked George.

'No, I used to dance at the Grafton. It's where I first met Josh,' she said dreamily. 'Where is the Cavern and what is it?'

They all stared at her.

'It started out as a jazz club last year but now rock 'n' roll and skiffle have taken over. It's in Mathew Street in the cellar of an old warehouse. It's off North John Street. Some of the lads from school used to talk about it. They were thinking of getting together a group and hoping to get a booking.'

'This is all very interesting,' said Olive. 'But it's not what we want. The jukebox idea is worth thinking about, but how much would one of them cost?'

'Something to find out,' said Mary.

'Kitchen equipment and furniture and the like for the café need to come first,' said Olive and George at the same time.

'We'd have to get a till and a coffee machine,' said Olive.

'There's a lot to think about,' said Mary. Then she asked, 'Does anyone want another cup of tea?'

'I'd like a beer,' said the two men.

'I'd like a Babycham,' said Mary.

Olive found her purse and withdrew a five-pound note. 'I really should be saving this, but we should make a toast. I'll have a Cherry B.' She handed the money to George and said, 'There's an off-licence on South Road. You shouldn't have any trouble finding it.'

'I know where it is,' he told her.

'I'll go with you,' said Mary. 'I need some fresh air.'

The two young ones left.

'I'll wash the dishes,' said Olive, clearing the table. 'There's still a jam tart and custard for dessert but I don't think that'll go with the drinks. I suppose you could take half of it home.'

'Thanks,' her brother said, following her into the kitchen. 'Are you going to show me over the house?'

'Let me see to the dishes first. I'm supposed to have been hemming curtains this evening.'

'I'll give you a hand if you like while we're waiting.'

'Before or after seeing over the house?' she asked. She was still waiting for him to answer as he dried the dishes and looked miles away. 'You can leave them,' she said. 'I'll see to them later.'

'Okay,' he said, hanging the tea towel on a hook.

'Come on, then,' she said, leading the way.

She showed him the parlour. 'Nice size,' he commented. 'Do you really believe that you'll go ahead with your plan for a café?'

She shrugged. 'Only time will tell, and I don't want to discuss it anymore this evening.'

'Okay, I'll shut up.'

They left the parlour, and she led the way upstairs, pausing on the landing in front of the nearest door on the left. She threw it wide open. 'Bathroom and lavatory.'

'Nice,' he said.

She closed the door and walked along the landing to the door facing them, which was her bedroom.

'Good size and excellent furniture, and I like the size of the bed. No single for you.'

'I like plenty of room and after sleeping in a single while in the WRAF and at Mam's, I decided to spoil myself. Now stop bouncing on it. It's not a trampoline.'

'Do you think you'll ever get married again?' He smoothed the candlewick bedspread.

'Only time will tell.' She left the bedroom and showed him the other two rooms – one was small and sparsely furnished, with no curtains at the window; the other was rectangular and bigger, with twin beds and a pale oak double wardrobe and dressing table which showed signs of having been used. She paused. 'I think I heard a knock at the door, The sooner Iris collects her things and returns her door key, the better.'

'What if he comes as well? Should I stay around for a while?'

'They won't be back tonight, and you should go home,' said Olive. 'It's probably George and Mary back with the drinks.'

'Okay, if you're sure,' he said, heading for the stairs. She followed him.

'There's just one thing. My godchildren, Beth and Peter, are coming to stay for a night soon. It made me think that my other godchild might like to come too, if she doesn't throw a tantrum.'

'Oh, you've remembered Brenda is your goddaughter,' he said, shrugging on his jacket.

'I've been busy, and I hadn't heard from you,' she said, flushing.

'Okay, understood. Are you sure you can cope?'

'I hope so. I have got a daughter.'

'This will be two.' He looked doubtful. 'I'll see what the wife says. We can arrange it when you have a date.'

'They can play with each other and bring a toy, and I'll buy a few toys for them as well. In fact, there might be some of Joanna's old toys at Mam's. I've still got a key.'

'Do you know when she'll be back from the cruise?' he asked.

'She shouldn't be long now. I'll probably go to hers tomorrow.' She paused. 'Did she send you a postcard?'

'She sent the kids one but none of us could understand her writing.'

'She and Dougal got married.'

He whistled. 'Doesn't surprise me.' He paused. 'I'll see you at theirs tomorrow, in case you need help carrying things.'

'All right, I'll aim to get there about twelve. I'll get some sausage rolls and a couple of oranges and a jar of coffee on the way, and we can have lunch there.'

She opened the front door and George and Mary entered and placed the bottles on the table in the kitchen. Olive produced glasses and a bottle opener and they sat down and made a toast to Olive's business and a happy future.

Then Olive saw them out and got on with the hemming, hoping she would be able to cope with her two goddaughters and getting her business off the ground.

–

The following day she was up early, and, after breakfast, she left the house and caught a train to Balliol station, where she changed to catch a train for Aintree. She walked from there to her mother's house and let herself in.

She switched on the gas oven and placed the sausage rolls inside on a baking tray; she lit a gas ring to heat the kettle. She glanced at the clock, convinced her brother would arrive in the next quarter of an hour. So she sat down, having decided it would be better to stay downstairs and wait for the kettle to boil rather than go upstairs first.

She turned off the oven ten minutes later and made herself a mug of instant coffee. Then she heard a knock at the door and went to let her brother in.

'You're just in time,' she said.

He followed her through to the kitchen, gazing about him. 'Nothing's changed.'

'The gas cooker is new since you last visited.' She made him a coffee. 'She only uses it when she doesn't have the coal fire lit.' She placed the sausage rolls on plates, passed him a jar of Branston Pickle and went into the back room to sit down. 'So, is Brenda coming to stay today?'

He nodded as he opened the jar. 'Can you pick her up?'

She shook her head. 'I spoke to Jack on the phone, and he said he can pick her up in his car, or you could drop her off at theirs. You know where they live. It will save him time and petrol.'

'Tight thing!'

'He isn't tight! That was my idea,' she said. 'They're going away soon and he's really busy until then.'

'Lucky them! Where are they going to?' He spooned Branston Pickle onto his plate and dipped the end of a sausage roll into it.

'Anglesey! They're going to meet Alfie and Joanna off the Dublin ferry, and then will stay with them on Anglesey for a few days and return home with them.'

'Why didn't they come straight home to Liverpool from America?'

'Because they fancied a look at Ireland. Josh has family there and they can stay with them and be shown around,' said Olive. 'I'll leave you and go to see what I can find in the way of toys.'

She left her brother to finish his coffee, closed the door behind her and carefully climbed the stairs. She went into the bedroom that had been Joanna's and opened a cupboard in an alcove. As she had suspected, there were several dolls and a bag of dolls' clothes, a fluffy pink elephant, several wooden jigsaws, several cloth books, some building bricks, a skipping rope with bells attached, a couple of rubber balls, and a little clown that rolled over and bobbed up again. She piled everything onto the bed and headed downstairs for some carrier bags, which were usually stored in a drawer in the kitchen.

She beckoned her brother to follow her upstairs and he did so without delay. When he saw the toys on the bed, he whistled. 'Gosh, she kept all these!' He picked up the clown. 'I know who'll love this. Our Larry.'

'You can put it in a separate bag and give it to him on the sly when you get home to pick up Brenda and take her to Jack's. I'll head home with the rest, but you'll have to carry them as far as the railway station for me.'

'Okay,' he said, stuffing the dolls in the bag with the clothes, and the clown in another bag.

She placed the two balls in her pockets and the rest into bags and carried them downstairs. She left a note on the table for her mother and then they left.

Fortunately, Olive had some help getting on and off trains and as soon as she arrived home, she placed everything on the sofa. Then she rested for several minutes, before making herself a gin and tonic and a cheese butty. Only after she had downed them did she find a large cardboard box to store the toys, pushed it under the table and concealed it with a tablecloth.

She'd been back in the house half an hour, when there came a knock on the door, and she hurried to open it. Alan stood there and only then did she remember about Iris's stuff. 'Where's Iris?' she asked.

'I thought she'd be here,' he said.

'Well, she's not,' said Olive. 'She left with you, so she doesn't live here anymore.'

'I've come for her things.'

'But you don't seem to know where she is, so why should I give you them?' She made to close the door, but he put his foot in it. She placed her whole weight against the door and slowly it moved, and he yelped. 'You're not coming in,' she said firmly.

'What's going on here?' demanded a man's voice.

'Getaway,' panted Alan. 'This is none of your business.'

Olive felt the door give and she fell backwards as Alan was lifted away, his feet dragging along the ground until he was shoved against the gate.

'Now stay there and don't move,' ordered the stranger. 'You okay, Ma'am?' The man turned to face her and reached down a hand. She gripped it, wonderingly. It had been so long since she had seen Josh that she couldn't tell if this man might be him, although he couldn't be – surely he hadn't arrived in Liverpool already? She allowed herself to be lifted to her feet.

'Who are you?' she asked, attempting to pull her hand free as she gazed up into his weather-beaten face. There was something familiar about his features, but she could not swear on the Holy Bible that she recognised him.

'I'm Daniel O'Grady and I believe you knew my cousin, Josh.'

She caught the hint of an Irish accent in his voice. 'You said *knew*. Where is Josh?'

'That's the problem. We don't know. The ship got into difficulties, and he managed to help the two younger ones into a boat, but when they turned to help him, there was no sign of him.'

Olive was stunned and could not speak. It was then she heard not only Alan's voice but Iris's too. Then Jack arrived with Beth, Peter and Brenda.

'What's going on?' asked Iris. 'Alan, you are here. I told you I wouldn't be long. I only went to the shops. I told you to wait for me.'

'You were ages,' he said, falling into her arms. 'Let's get your stuff and get away from here. It's madness.'

Olive found her voice. 'You stay here, Alan. Iris can go and fetch her belongings. I have other guests to see to.' Her thoughts were in a whirl, but she knew she had to get rid of Alan and Iris and see to the girls before anything else. She took hold of her godchildren' hands and led them into the house. Jack stayed outside, keeping a watch on Alan.

CHAPTER TWENTY

She took the children into the back room and gave them the box of toys; they could play while she went upstairs. 'Do you need any help?' she asked Iris. 'Are you still going with Alan?'

Iris nodded. 'Thanks for having me and see you some time.' She placed clothes in a suitcase and swept toiletries and cosmetics from the dressing table into a holdall, as well as a few knick-knacks.

Olive followed her downstairs and said, 'Goodbye and good luck.' She watched her and Alan until they were out of sight. Then she drooped her head on Jack's shoulder. He placed an arm around her waist, and they went inside to find Daniel kneeling on the floor with Beth, Peter and Brenda, helping them with a wooden jigsaw.

Olive sank onto the sofa, stretched out and put her feet up on a cushion. 'Make a pot of tea, please?' she said to Jack.

Daniel continued to play with the children but glanced at Olive every few minutes. 'Joanna and Alfie said you and Josh were pretty friendly.'

'Yes,' she said huskily. 'Is a search being made for him?'

'Of course, it's been some time but there's always hope, and we can pray to our Lady, St Patrick and St Christopher and our Lord.'

She nodded, thinking of Jesus calming the storm and of Jonah being swallowed by the whale and washed ashore. She must have faith that Josh would survive. She thought of her daughter and Alfie and asked whether they had been hurt.

'A few scrapes and bruises, and Alfie broke his arm, and of course, they're in shock.' He paused. 'The family decided that I should come over and let you and Alfie's mammie know what had happened while the search is ongoing. The coastguard and the Garda have also joined it, and a helicopter should soon be available, but Josh isn't the only one missing. It was a real bad storm in the Atlantic, off America's east coast, a few days ago, the ship nearly made it to Cobh, but the wind got up and changed direction. Fortunately, Josh is wearing a wetsuit because he'd been practising in the liner's swimming pool on his way here. Apparently, he also has a life jacket on. Other lifeboat stations have been informed, so with all those out looking for him and helping the liner in distress, matters shouldn't be as bad as they could have been.'

Olive turned to Jack. 'Are you wanting to go over there?' she asked, a tremor in her voice.

He nodded. 'We've been advised to wait until morning and see if any ships or plane companies want to risk it. What we need is for the wind to drop.'

'I presume they've tried to phone,' said Olive.

'Some lines are down in Ireland, so it's a case of wait, be patient and pray.'

Olive sighed. 'I obviously chose the wrong weekend for the children to come and stay and play on the beach.'

'You can probably phone Eliza from here,' said Jack, coming in with the kettle. 'But what's the point? Best to try in the morning.'

She nodded, watching him pour the tea and thinking the children probably needed a drink and a snack. She had to get up and make them something herself, and the two men as well. She would offer Daniel a bed for the night. Unless he had already booked a room in a bed and breakfast in Liverpool. As it was, he accepted her offer to stay, but said that he would sleep on the sofa downstairs, as the children would need the beds. Jack looked at her askance but made no comment.

Olive got little sleep that night, unable to stop imagining Josh struggling to swim and to keep his head above water in enormous waves, but the children were also restless and eventually she brought them into bed with her and told them old familiar fairy tales. Eventually, they drifted off and she relaxed and prayed, not only for Josh's safe return but also for her daughter's and Alfie's recovery, as well as for all those in peril on the sea. Then she realised she was singing in a low voice, 'Eternal Father, strong to save, whose arm hath bound the restless wave…' and tears were trickling down her cheeks. She stopped singing and instead hummed the words until finally she fell asleep.

She was roused by something poking her cheek. Alarmed, she struggled to move away from whatever it was, only to realise there was someone else in the bed, jammed up against her other side. She forced open her eyes and, now fully awake, remembered that Brenda and Beth were in bed with her. She raised her arms and stretched, before the events of the previous evening came to her, and she felt sick and began to pray fervently for Josh. She removed Brenda's elbow from the side of her face and looked towards the window, where she saw that the sun was shining through a gap in the curtains.

She thought of Daniel downstairs and wondered if he was awake. She shoved the bedcovers down with her feet and her goddaughters moaned and scrabbled with their fingers, searching for their warmth. 'Wake up, girls,' she said.

Brenda's eyes opened slowly but Beth's flew open, and she stared at Olive. 'I'm hungry,' she said. 'Have you got cornflakes, Aunty Olive?' She sat up. 'Are we going to the beach today?'

'Later,' replied Olive. 'I've things to do first.'

'Get washed, dressed, have breakfast and clean teeth,' said Beth, turning on her side and sliding off the bed.

Brenda said, 'I don't want to get up. I want Angela, my dolly, and my daddy.'

'Don't you want to go to the beach and make a sand-castle?' said Beth. 'It'll be fun.'

'Your daddy is busy today. As for Angela, we'll find her soon.'

'I want her now,' said Brenda, folding her arms across her chest and jutting out her bottom lip.

'After breakfast, as long as there's no tantrums from you, miss,' said Olive firmly. 'I also have something new for you both if you behave yourselves while I'm busy.'

'Can't we know what it is now?' asked Beth eagerly.

'No, I want it to be a surprise,' said Olive. 'Now move yourselves or the day will be over before we can get to the beach.'

They removed their nighties and went to the bath-room. Brenda needed help to fasten her shoes a little later and Beth asked Olive to do up the top two buttons on the back of her frock. That done, she woke Peter and left them to eat their breakfasts. Having seen no sign of Daniel, she went in search of him. She decided he must have gone for a walk along the beach. So she phoned Eliza; the call was answered immediately. But it was obvious that Eliza was hoping to hear from someone else.

'Sorry, Eliza, but it's me, Olive. I gather you haven't any fresh news of Josh.'

'We do have. He was spotted by a dog walker from the top of a cliff.' She paused and Olive's heart lifted. Eliza continued, 'The moon was up, and she wasted no time finding a phone box and getting in touch with the coastguard, explaining where she had seen a swimmer in difficulty. The coastguard phoned various stations, who got in touch by radio with the various lifeboat captains, relaying information, and Josh was found and taken to the nearest hospital near Bantry Bay. He's had a bang on the head; he'll be okay but will have to rest. Alfie and Joanna have been informed at the hospital in Dublin and are so relieved. Alfie is feeling much better this morning and is not in pain. Joanna is by his bedside and they've their heads together, talking in low voices. A nurse suspects they're plotting how to get Alfie out of the hospital, so they see Josh as soon as possible. There's talk of flights resuming from RAF Valley airport in Anglesey because there's been more than one ship in distress in the Irish Sea, and Jack and I have hopes of getting a flight from Speke to Dublin this afternoon.' She hesitated. 'Are you all right to keep Beth and Peter with you a bit longer?'

'Of course, although I wish I was going with you to Ireland,' said Olive. 'Give my love to Joanna and Alfie. And Josh, when you see him. Has anyone thought of letting Jay know what's happened?'

'The family think best not to tell him.'

'Daniel says if I give him Jay's phone number then he'll phone him.'

'I have a phone number where he can be reached,' said Eliza.

'Give it to me.' Olive picked up the pencil and small pad by the phone and heard her name being called. 'I'm here,' she shouted. 'Where are you?'

'In the kitchen with the children,' Daniel answered.

Olive wrote down the number and then put the receiver down and wasted no time joining Daniel in the kitchen. He was making proper coffee, and the children had finished their breakfasts and were drinking orange juice, which Daniel must have found in the fridge and poured out for them.

'I spoke with Eliza on the phone,' she said. 'She and Jack are hoping to fly to Dublin later today.' She paused. 'Will you try and get a flight and go home to Ireland? Josh has been spotted and is in a hospital near Bantry Bay.'

'I'll think about it. I don't like leaving you on your own and having to cope with the kids. Unless your brother could come here to pick up his daughter today?'

She put a hand to her head. 'I can't remember what he said. There was so much going on.'

'Perhaps if I stay until he comes,' said Daniel. 'I could phone Jay in California if you give me the number. That's if it'll help you.'

'Jay isn't in America but in Canada. I've the number. It's by the phone, with the name of the couple he's staying with. What time is it over there?' she asked. 'I promised Brenda to find her doll Angela that she brought from home.'

Daniel glanced at his watch thoughtfully. 'They could still be in bed. Maybe we should wait a bit longer.'

'I should phone a bit later. You're a stranger to them. We could sort the children out first,' she said.

'Maybe the doll went into the cardboard box with all the other toys and dolls,' he said.

'You're most likely right.'

Followed by the three children, Olive went into the sitting room and emptied the contents of the box onto the rug. She snatched up a doll that looked the least like an Angela. The little girl hugged it to her and kissed its face.

'What about the new things you've got for us, Aunty Olive?' asked Beth.

Impatiently, Olive went over to a cupboard and took some buckets and spades from the top shelf, her mind full of thoughts of Josh as the girls danced up and down beside her. 'They're great,' said Daniel, picking up one of the metal spades and clanging it against a colourfully painted bucket. 'Let's go down to the beach and make a sandcastle and collect shells to decorate it.'

'And fetch water to make a moat for it,' said Beth.

'I'll not be coming with you yet,' said Olive, searching the childrens' luggage and taking out their bathing costumes. 'I have to make a phone call and prepare a picnic.' She handed several towels and well-worn blankets to Daniel. 'I'll be as quick as I can.'

The children heaved happy sighs as they set off at a run, but Daniel gave them a stern look that brought them to a swinging halt. They struggled only for a moment and then froze when Olive shouted, 'What did I say to you?'

They stared at her dumbly.

'Do I have to say it again? Are you deaf?'

They shook their heads.

'Good,' she said. 'What must you do?'

'Behave ourselves,' they said in unison.

'Don't let your mind wander! There are patches of sand which are like mud on the beach, and you can sink in them and get stuck. So, stop when told and you also must watch out for the tide, as the water can come in quickly and go out quickly, and you don't want to be swallowed up by it. So, you stay close to Daniel.' Despite it being August, the sea was likely to be terribly cold and they could catch hypothermia.

Olive hurried indoors, picked up the phone and followed the instructions Eliza had given her, dialling carefully. She sighed with relief when, after ten minutes, a familiar voice answered and asked who was speaking. She replied, 'Jay, it's Olive, and I feel you must know—'

'Is that really you, Olive? What's wrong? Where are you phoning from? Ireland? I thought Pa might have rung me.' His voice sounded strained. 'Are you two together? Is Pa still asleep? Suffering from jet lag?'

'What are you thinking?' she said. 'He travelled by ship. Now shush and listen. Firstly, don't be panicking. There's been an accident off the coast of Ireland. Josh saved Joanna's and Alfie's lives before being swept away by currents and vanishing. Thankfully, he was spotted by a dog walker on a cliff around the coast and she called for help.' Olive sniffed back tears. 'He was rescued and is in hospital and is going to be okay. His kin were involved in the search for him. I'm home but will fly to Dublin soon. It was me who decided to get in touch with you, as I think it'll do Josh good to see you. Others did not want to upset you, but I reckon I know you and Josh better than your Irish kin.' She paused to blow her nose.

Jay said, 'Thanks a lot for getting in touch. God bless you and safe journey.'

She echoed his words and blew a kiss down the phone. Then she phoned her brother and explained the situation and he promised he would come and pick his daughter up about three o'clock that afternoon.

Then she went and made some egg butties, and packed them with bottles of cream soda, packets of marshmallows, chocolate digestives and sausage rolls from Satterthwaite. After changing into a sundress, she made her way to the beach, feeling as if she was walking on air.

Olive sat back against a rucksack containing extra towels. She did not take out her book straightaway but told Daniel what Jay had said and of her new plan to go to Ireland. She felt certain that Amelia would care for Beth and Peter. She would phone her now and did so and promised to let her know once she had the time of her flight to Ireland.

Then she watched the children making a sandcastle, often lifting her eyes to gaze out to sea. There were several people in the water, some jumping the waves rolling onto the beach. Some were swimming and a couple of teenagers were in the water throwing a beachball to each other.

After a while she reached for her book and began to read. But she couldn't concentrate because she kept thinking of Josh. She finished reading at the end of the chapter, suddenly aware that she couldn't hear the childrens' chatter. She lifted her eyes to search the beach and scanned the water's edge for signs of Daniel, Beth, Peter and Brenda.

Then she spotted Daniel. He had rolled up his trouser legs and was up to his calves in water. She realised after a few minutes that he was talking to a young woman.

She experienced a spurt of anger. Where were the children? Then she spotted Brenda not so very far away from him, sitting on the wet sand just out of reach of the waves. She was fiddling with something in her bucket. Beth and Peter soon approached her, each with something clutched in their hands and the three started chatting. Then Beth went over to Daniel and pulled on his trouser leg, lifted the bucket and pointed up the beach, indicating something. He ruffled her hair and then continued to speak to the young woman. Minutes later, the five of them came up the beach towards Olive. She noticed that the girls were carefully carrying a bucket each. She rose from the blanket and reached inside the rucksack to get several towels ready. The buckets were placed by the sandcastle and Olive gazed at them and saw that they contained water and shells.

Daniel said, 'They've done well. But I must introduce my cousin to you, Olive. This is Kathy. She lives over here.'

Kathy nodded. 'He's been telling me about his cousin on his mother's side, Josh, and him being a friend of yours that you met during the war.'

'Yes, he was in the American army based at Aintree Racecourse,' said Olive. She draped towels about the girls' shoulders and rubbed them vigorously one at a time.

Kathy and Daniel turned away and moved a little apart, speaking in low voices.

Olive wondered if she should have asked Kathy to tea but at that moment Daniel turned towards her and said, 'I hope you won't mind if I go home with Kathy to see her family.'

'Of course not.' She gave all her attention to the children, and they ate the picnic she'd prepared. Then, after lining the bottom with shells, they poured water in the moat. They collected more shells before packing up and going back to the house where she found her brother sitting on the front step, smoking a cigarette. Daniel was talking to him.

Brenda ran to her father with her bucket full of mainly cockle shells. Peter said, 'Wait!'

Olive's heart sank. 'What is it?'

'Joanna's been trying to phone you but without any luck.'

'What's happened? Has Josh had a relapse?' She clasped her hands tightly together.

'She just wanted to hear your voice.'

Olive smiled. 'She'll hear it soon enough. Are you taking Brenda home? I want to be here if Joanna phones again.'

He smiled. 'Too right, but if anything bothers you, get in touch.'

'I will. There's also the possibility that Mam and Dougal will be in touch.'

'Let us know if they are.' He stood up and called his daughter. 'Come on, kid. Time to go home.'

The girl pouted. 'I don't want to go home.'

'Now none of that,' he said. 'Or Aunty Olive won't have you stay again.'

'But Beth and Peter aren't going home,' she said.

'That's because their mam and daddy are going to Ireland,' said Olive. 'You be a good girl for your daddy, and you can come again.' She picked up Angela and handed the doll to her and gave her one of the jigsaws to take home with her. 'You show your mam how clever you are.'

'Thank you,' said Brenda, holding her face up for a kiss.

Olive kissed her niece and her brother. 'I'll be in touch,' she said.

'Thanks for having her. Ta-ra!'

She saw them out and returned to the other children to find Beth clasping the telephone receiver.

'What are you doing?' asked Olive, taking the receiver from her and replacing it.

'I want to speak to Mammy and Daddy.'

'They're not at home. You must have heard me say so.'

'They might have come back,' said Beth.

'We don't want them going to Anglesey without us,' said Peter.

'If you were listening, you'd know they've gone to see Alfie in Ireland and bring him home.'

'What about your Joanna? Will they bring her home to you too?' said Beth.

'Possibly!'

At that moment the telephone rang.

Olive made a grab for it, brushing Beth's hand away. She stumbled slightly over the telephone numbers because they were still new to her. 'Who's this speaking?' she asked.

'Mam, is that you? You sound weird.'

Olive felt tears well in her eyes. 'It is me. Is that you, Joanna?'

'Yeah, it's me. Oh, I need you, Mam. I've missed you.'

Olive sat down abruptly. 'I've missed you as well.'

CHAPTER TWENTY-ONE

'Where are you speaking from?' asked Olive when she got her emotions under control.

'Bantry Hospital. It's on the south-west coast of Ireland in County Cork. The nearest airport is Cork. Josh was spotted by a dog walker and flown here, airlifted from a lifeboat,' said Joanna. 'He's a real hero, Mam, and can swim like a fish. You should have seen him in the pool on the ship. Alfie was keen to learn but aqualungs aren't cheap. He's seen divers all kitted up going on dives in Trearddur Bay. He spoke to one of them and was told that there's an Aqua Club in Liverpool. I bet Josh would enjoy going along to that and diving off Anglesey.'

'Stop rabbiting on! I know Josh has been found and is in hospital. I thought he was in Dublin hospital.'

'No, that's where Alfie is. Josh is here in Bantry, Cork.'

'Do you think he's still planning to come to Liverpool.'

'I'm sure he's impatient to see you and the new house, but he's going to have to stay in Ireland for a while, so you're going to have to come over here if you want to see him earlier.'

'What are you going to do with me and Peter?' interrupted Beth.

Olive thought quickly. 'I'm droping you both home and Amelia will look after you. Is that all right with you?'

Beth nodded. 'Should I pack my things?'

Olive said, 'That's a good girl. Did you hear all that?' she said to her daughter.

'I did,' replied Joanna happily.

'Well, get off the phone then, so I can phone the airport.'

'Okay, see you soon, Mam. Love you lots.'

'I love you too.' Olive blew a kiss down the phone before replacing the receiver and looking up the phone number for Liverpool airport.

She was soon told that flights to Cork only departed from Cardiff. She would be best flying to Dublin from Liverpool and then continuing by train or bus to Cork. There was a flight at eleven fifty-five in the morning and it took only an hour. Olive booked a seat, then brought down her holdall and began to pack. She found her passport, uncertain whether she needed it for Ireland. She remembered purchasing it for America and reminded herself she should visit the bank as soon as they opened to get a taxi to the airport.

She had difficulty getting any sleep but at least it meant she didn't oversleep. She rose at six o'clock, had a quick bath and got dressed. Once they'd had breakfast, she took an old favourite book from the bookshelf and read for a while but couldn't concentrate. Before leaving the house, she popped a note through her neighbour's door, informing him that she was going to Ireland for a fortnight and asking if he could please keep an eye on the house?

Then she and Beth left, not forgetting an umbrella; they didn't call Ireland the Emerald Isle for nothing. She did not visit the bank but decided to go to the money exchange when she arrived at the airport, and felt a spurt of excitement as she hailed a taxi on South Road and climbed inside with Beth.

She gave Eliza's address, 'And then Liverpool airport, please,' she said, making herself comfortable on the back seat and placing her holdall next to her.

She closed her eyes and prayed for Josh, rejoicing that soon she would see him and her daughter, and possibly Eliza and Jack, who were staying with Milly's mother and stepfather in Dublin.

As it was, only Jack and Jay were waiting for her at the airport after she landed in Dublin. She saw the two men coming towards her and she started to run. Jay took the holdall from her.

'Take it easy. We don't want any more accidents,' he said, hugging her.

Jack said, 'Beth?'

'Missing you and Eliza and Alfie, of course. She's safely with Amelia now.'

'Good, thanks for having her. You managed both girls?'

'Yeah! With a lot of bribery. I found a cupboard of Joanna's old toys and dolls, and bought them buckets and spades, and we built a sandcastle on the beach.'

They came to customs and although she produced her passport, the officer barely looked at it and waved them through. Jack led her to the hire car, where Joanna was waiting for them.

She opened the car door for her mother, who fell into her arms, and they hugged each other, before holding each other at arm's length and studying each other intently.

Olive said, 'You've a faint tan but are pale underneath it and you've shadows beneath your eyes. Not surprising, considering the terrible time you've been through.'

'Look on the bright side, Olive. She and Alfie have survived,' said Jack.

'Josh's condition is still serious but he's going to be all right if he does as he's told,' said Joanna. 'I overheard the doctor in Bantry talking to a Garda and the lifeboat men who rescued him. Unfortunately, the liner's half-underwater, so a lot of our stuff is lost, except for what we were wearing. But fortunately, no lives were lost.

'As for Josh, he was being carefully nursed night and day for a couple of days, mumbling incoherently and yelping in pain, despite them giving him medication. He does have a head injury and that could have caused temporary amnesia.

'Then, yesterday he apparently spoke clearly for a brief time and said mine and Alfie's names before drifting away again. That's why his cousin was allowed to bring me to see him. When he next came to, he asked for you and Jay.'

'Did he recognise you when he saw you?' asked Olive, trembling.

'He smiled and then closed his eyes.' Joanna's lips quivered. 'It doesn't make sense, Mam. How can he remember some things and not others?'

'It's a mystery but let's think about it,' said Jack. 'Somehow, despite the bang on his head and his other scrapes and cuts, it could be that he's managed to link your name and that of Alfie with Jay and Olive.'

'But why?' asked Joanna.

'Well, your name and Alfie's are linked together because he's spent quite a bit of time with the two of you over the last couple of months, and rescued you,' said Jay.

'Let's drop the subject for now,' said Jack, 'and get to Bantry hospital.'

They asked a taxi driver waiting outside the station in the hope of picking up a fare and he wrote down directions on the back of an envelope. Even so, they went the wrong way but eventually found the hospital. They asked directions for Josh's room, as it was still visiting hours. Olive rushed ahead. A nurse was in the room, and she would have turned her away if they hadn't explained that she was the Olive that Josh had been asking for.

She asked the nurse how Josh was getting on and was told she could not stay long, as he mustn't get excited. The nurse then talked to the others, saying they were to stay outside.

Olive sat on the chair next to Josh's bed and gazed at the yellowing bruises on his face. He was looking older but there were signs of that younger Josh she had met at the Grafton. She swallowed the tears blocking her throat and gently touched his hand that lay on the counterpane. She noticed his fingernails were chipped and some of the skin was torn away.

'Josh!' she said huskily. 'It's Olive. You wanted to see me.'

His eyelids slowly opened. 'I can't see you clearly.'

'I'm Olive. We met in the Grafton during the war.' She felt a salty tear on her lip and licked it away. 'I'm Joanna's mother. Don't you recognise me?'

'You can't be here. You couldn't come because you'd bought a house near Liverpool. You and Joe didn't suit. I was a fool. Jay's mother told me so, said I should have kept away. I was saying your name in my sleep. She...' His voice tailed off.

Jay had slipped into the room and sat at the foot of the bed, gazing down at his father. 'Dad, wake up! I'm here. Jay, your son. What were you thinking, playing the hero again?'

The nurse came in. 'Your time's up,' she said.

'I need another five minutes,' stressed Olive. 'He's confused. I need to reassure him.' She clung to his hand even as his eyes opened and he said, 'You're not my son. You're…'

'Olive,' she finished the sentence for him and moved to make room for Jay. 'Here's your son.'

'You've exhausted him,' said the nurse. 'Now let go of his hand.' Her Irish accent was stronger as she seized Olive's shoulders and pulled her away. But Josh's fingers wouldn't let go, even as Jay moved the nurse aside. She seized his sleeve. 'Holy Mary, Mother of God. Never in all my born days have I had to act in such a way.' The nurse turned her head. 'You, Meester, help me here and drum some sense into her head.'

'Didn't you hear, nurse?' said Jay.

Olive's hand fell to her side and the nurse stumbled backwards; Jack had entered the room and caught her before she could hit the floor. Olive was struggling to keep the tears at bay, but she held her head high and breathed in deeply.

'My dad has been asking for her and me,' said Jay. 'Now give us ten minutes and then we'll get out of your way.'

Olive decided to stay out of the way and give Jay some time alone with his father. The nurse said to him, 'You're a Yank.'

'That's right, he is,' said Olive. 'Just like your patient here. I'll be back, love,' she called to Josh. Only then did she allow the tears to fall.

Jay remained in the room and sat by the bed. 'Dad!' he murmured. 'I'm here thanks to Olive and nobody's going to shift me.'

'You are his son,' said the nurse.

'Sure am, and his next of kin. He and Mom are going through a divorce.'

Joanna put her arms around her mother and hugged her. 'Come on now, Mam. He'll get better and be himself once more and you can talk to each other without interruptions.'

Olive hiccoughed as she attempted to control herself. Jack came out of the room and put his arms about both mother and daughter and ushered them out of the building to the car, where he told them to get inside and wait for him. He was going to see what happened next between Jay and the nurse and would advise him to ask to see the specialist.

'He's not well enough to be allowed out yet and will need to be kept quiet, warm and rested,' said Jay when he returned.

'So, I can't take him home with me yet?' said Olive sadly.

Jay said, 'Sorry, although I'm convinced he'd love that.'

She smiled. 'How long can you stay? I presume your relatives can put you up for a while.'

He nodded. 'But I can stay for longer than a few days. I'm getting married in a month's time and I've just started a new job in a new country.'

'Congratulations,' said Olive, kissing his cheek. 'I can stay here as long as your father needs me.'

'I'd expect no less,' said Jay, placing an arm about her shoulders. 'I spoke to the specialist about you, told him that you and Dad are going to be married, so you can see him anytime. I told him how you'd met during the war but were parted and lost touch but were brought together when I came over to Liverpool.'

'Near enough to the truth,' she said huskily, deeply touched by his words.

'This is all very well,' said Joanna, with tears in her eyes. 'They've a lot of time to make up for and it could be that here in Ireland they'll have that time. While I go and look after the house and do some studying and keep my eye on Nan and my step-granddaddy.'

'You'll also have to look after the dog,' said Olive. 'He is yours after all and I can only hope that he's still around when you and Alfie get back home. With a bit of luck, my neighbour or our Peter will have remembered about him.'

'I'm sure me and Alfie will be happy to take the dog for walks on the beach.'

Jay said wearily, 'Can we talk about all this over a meal and a drink? I'm starving. I can't remember when I last had something to eat.'

'Good idea,' said Jack, making a move. 'I also need to meet Eliza and take Joanna to the hospital in Dublin to see Alfie.'

'Food first,' said Olive, 'before we split up.'

So they found the nearest pub still serving food and ordered Irish stew for the men and the speciality of the house: mussels in a secret recipe that Olive guessed contained whisky, cream, seaweed, a hint of garlic and the secret ingredient. While they waited inside, a plate of soda bread thickly spread with creamy Irish butter was placed in the middle of the table. It was not easy having a conversation, because there was a lot of chatter going on, as well as singing from a couple of men playing a penny whistle and a fiddle on a small stage in a corner of the room.

Olive signalled to her daughter that they should go outside with their drinks and food, where there were tables and chairs and pots with shrubs and flowers. They sat down at a table. 'Let's eat first, then I want to tell you about an idea George, Mary and I had.'

Joanna stared at her. 'Are we talking about that business you mentioned? One for you to invest some of your winnings in?'

'Yeah, a café not far from my house and the Mersey. Just before I left to come here, I spotted an unusual building that could be made into what I want, but what with all that's been happening, it slipped my mind.'

'Which makes me wonder where Josh fits into your plans?' asked Joanna. 'And my going to university?'

'I just want you to get together with George, Mary and her grandmother when you get home and show them the place I'm considering. See whether they think if it'll do and then I'll put an offer in for it. George is a good cook, so he'll be our chef. Eleanor wants a part-time job – and I'm sure Nan and Dougal would like to make a bit of extra money if we're short of staff at times. Mary and her gran have had experience in catering. You're in charge until I come home with Josh. I'll discuss my idea once he's feeling better and I know what he wants to do with the rest of his life. We haven't even discussed marriage yet and whether he's happy to live in Waterloo or wants to go back to California. If he wants to still be a lumberjack, could he find such work in Britain, I wonder.'

'Give him time, Mam. It's a lot for him to think about. You both need a holiday and time together to have some fun and get used to each other.'

'You're growing up and talking sensibly. Here's to us and a happy future!' Olive raised her glass of shandy and clinked it with her daughter's. They were on their way back inside when the rest of their party began to make their way outside. Jack said, 'It's time to make a move. I need to pick up Eliza from Milly's mother's and stepfather's house in Dublin, so we can visit Alfie in the hospital. I presume you'll be coming with us, Joanna?'

She nodded. 'That's all right with you, isn't it, Mam?'

'Of course,' said Olive. She took her daughter aside, giving her some money, and the spare key to her house. 'Buy yourself some clothes to replace those you lost. You'll need a suitcase as well. I'll be visiting Josh again and have Jay to keep me out of mischief.' She kissed her daughter. 'Give my love to Alfie.'

'Will do. Thanks, Mam,' said Joanna. She kissed her and left with Jack.

'We'll be seeing one of Dad's cousins at the hospital, and he'll give us a lift back to his place afterwards,' said Jay. 'It's his sons who are members of the lifeboat crew. Dad's cousin used to be one of them, but his wife told him it was time he quit. After all, he has enough on his plate with the mussel fishing and, more recently, scallops as well.'

'So, they live near the sea?' she said.

'That's what I've been told, but they also have some land where they have chickens and a pig and grow some veggies. It makes me wonder how Dad ended up working as a lumberjack.'

'Bigger country, more trees and demand for wood,' suggested Olive. 'So, what shall we do before we go to the hospital?'

'Would you like to have a look in St Anne's Church? It's very old and from the top is a fantastic view from the eight bells platform. You could even have a go at ringing the bells. It also has a liar clock.'

'Why is it called "liar"?'

'Because it has four faces and from certain angles it can look like it's telling a different time.'

'Confusing,' she said. 'I'd like to go into a church and pray.'

So Jay took out a map of the city and they headed in the direction of the church. 'The bells are eighteenth century.'

'How do you know all this?' she asked.

'Dad had a travel book and forgot to pack it. I picked it up and slipped it into my rucksack and forgot to give it back, but I remembered it after your phone call and started reading it on the plane.' He took a slim volume out of his pocket and handed it to her.

She flicked through the pages, pausing now and then to look at a photograph. 'Can I borrow it so I can read it in bed tonight?'

'Sure,' said Jay. 'Maybe tomorrow we could find another place to visit after seeing Dad.'

Olive nodded. 'Perhaps after visiting St Anne's, we could find somewhere to have a coffee,' she suggested.

'That's fine by me,' he said. 'But we'll need to keep our eye on the time.'

'Not by the liar clock, though,' she said.

He nodded and laughed. 'Must take a photo of its four faces and the view if we have time to go up there.'

She agreed and glanced in a shop window while Jay figured out the way to their destination. Her eyes rested on several colourful stuffed leprechauns, and she thought how much her goddaughters would like them. She tapped Jay on the shoulder and told him she wanted to go in the shop. She added, 'Have you thought your dad is going to need clothes to replace those he's lost?'

'Thanks for reminding me,' he said. 'I thought of it and then forgot. We'll do that tomorrow.' He went in the shop with her and bought a leprechaun for his fiancée, saying, 'She'll say I'm mad, but she'll still like it.'

They left the shop, and it was not long before they came to St Anne's and went inside. It was empty so they had a quick stroll around, their footfalls echoing, and found a suitable pew, where they sat for a moment. They knelt and prayed for Josh to recover soon, so he could leave hospital, and for Alfie's broken arm to knit, so he could return home and get back to work.

Olive prayed that Joanna would be able to perform the tasks she'd asked of her, and have done well in the exams she had sat before going to America. She also prayed for Joe and his new wife, the passengers and crew on the liner. Lastly, she prayed for herself and her relationship with Josh, that they would come together in love and forgiveness and understanding.

She rose from her knees and at the last minute remembered her mother and Dougal and wished them well and lots of happiness. She sat back in the pew and glanced at her watch.

Jay said, 'Time to make a move, find a coffee shop and then a shop that sells goodies and magazines. Tomorrow we mustn't forget to buy Dad some clothes.'

Olive nodded and, humming a hymn, she made her way to the back of the church, picked up St Anne's Church magazine from a table and pushed a banknote in the collection box. Jay also dropped money in and left the church, having decided they had no time to go and look at the view.

There was a river running up through the middle of the road and several bridges crossing it to different streets. They set off in the direction of the hospital along a bustling road, and, having discovered an attractive coffee shop, they went inside and were fortunate enough to be served straightaway and were in and out quickly, conscious of the time. They found a fruit shop and chose a few bananas, an orange and a bunch of grapes. Then they hurried on and soon the hospital was within sight. They passed through the gates and Jay said, 'There's Dad's cousin, Callum.' He waved and so did Olive, even as she prayed she could get some time alone with Josh.

She was delighted when they found Josh sitting up, reading a book. They were told by a different nurse that only two visitors were allowed at one time, but she would let it pass this once, due to the circumstances and as long as they didn't over-excite the patient.

Callum said, 'I'll just stay for ten minutes and then leave you two to tell Josh your plans.'

Jay and Olive thanked him, and she went forward and kissed Josh's cheek and said, 'Hello, love. I was here before, but you were out of it. It's Olive.'

'I thought I dreamt you were here. I'm so glad to see you.' He reached out and took her hand and drew her closer. 'I hope you're going to stay for a while. Now give me a proper kiss.' She did not hesitate but pressed her lips against his. The kiss seemed to go on forever and only ended when Callum coughed. Then she stepped back so he could speak to Josh. They shook hands and to her surprise began to talk about the storm and the damage it had caused to the vegetable garden and the trees, the mussel beds, and the local football match.

Then Josh asked which trees were lost. Callum said, 'The old oak we used to climb as kids and the apple tree that never produced much in the way of fruit.' He sighed. 'I'd like your help when you get out of here.'

'I can give twenty-four hours but then I'm having a real holiday and taking Olive to see more of Ireland. Do you fancy that idea, sweetheart?' Josh shot her a beseeching glance.

Then a smiling Jay said, 'I'll give you a hand, Dad, with the tree. I've never forgotten what you taught me in my teens… and surely Callum's sons can help. But like you, I can't stay much longer.'

Josh added, staring at Callum, 'We treat that venerable oak with respect. No chopping it up for firewood but use it for making furniture.'

'All right, I'm with you. I was considering using it for a boat.'

'Discuss it with your lads first,' said Josh. 'They're more involved than I am.'

Callum nodded. 'You're right. I'll leave you now to discuss things with Jay and your lady friend.'

Jay said, 'I'm thirsty.' And followed him out.

Olive waited until they had left before moving over to the bed. Josh beckoned her closer.

'Lady friend?' she murmured, resting her hand on the bedcover.

He dropped the book he had been reading and covered her hand with his own. 'You're my friend and a lady,' he said. 'He's being tactful. It's ages since we've seen each other, and he doesn't know yet about my divorce.'

He stared at Olive and beckoned her even closer. He told her that Alfie would be allowed to leave Dublin hospital the following day. They would give him a note for a doctor in a Liverpool hospital about removing the cast in a few weeks. Josh said that Alfie and Joanna had grown closer so she would want to go with him. They were extremely fond of each other and not like a brother and sister. He knew it because he had seen it in their eyes and behaviour.

'Why are you telling me this? I thought we were going to talk about us and having a holiday together here in Ireland. I don't want to be just your lady friend.'

'And I don't want to be the fancy man who never was,' he said. 'I love you, but I let you slip through my fingers. I should have told you the truth about Joe from the beginning. I want you now. We could go through a private ceremony, just the two of us here. It did happen years ago, when couples could not afford a marriage licence,' he said.

'You mean I'll be your common-law wife?' said Olive.

'Just while we're on holiday over here, to make us feel joined as one in God's eyes. We can make our promise and then have a church wedding and a party with our families and friends when I know my divorce is final. I believe Jay's mother is making me wait for the divorce papers for spite. I have sent a sharp letter to my lawyer who's in my father-in-law's clique.'

'You're saying you're not going back to California?'

'What for? There's nothing for me over there. If I cross the Atlantic, it'll be to go to Canada to visit Jay, and I'd want you with me as my wife.'

'When do we start?' She kissed him.

'As soon as I can get out of here,' said Josh.

Olive considered what Joanna had said about giving Josh time, but she reasoned that he had made his decision, and the rest could come later.

She felt that Joanna must already believe that real love would find its way. Her mother and Dougal had got married with no family there, and she decided to ask Joanna to visit her mother's house and make sure the place looked nice and there was plenty of food in. She could congratulate them and bring them up to date with everything that had happened, including the café, and invite them to dinner at her house where she hoped she and Josh would be settled soon.

As it was, Josh could not leave the hospital as soon as they wanted, but he was allowed out the day Jay left to be reunited with Fiona in Canada and to finish his training. He promised to return to Liverpool with Fiona for Josh and Olive's wedding. Callum had picked the three of them up from the hospital and took them to the harbour to wave Jay off after a meal at Callum's and for Josh to inspect the old oak tree.

It was not the first time Olive had visited Callum's smallholding, which had a fair amount of land grazed by cattle and where he grew vegetables. The house itself was whitewashed stone, with two front windows adorned with pretty window boxes painted green. There was a dairy where butter and cheese were made, and a henhouse, a barn and a pigsty. Also, outside was a privy and two water butts. The yard was wet and scattered with straw and seeds and muck.

Olive was told they were too far away from the mains, so water was fetched from a nearby river, but there was also a water tank on the tiled roof, which had a pipe running to a tap in the kitchen sink. There was a huge fireplace where a fire burnt brightly every day; a large black cooking pot was hanging over it. She could hear bubbling and smell stew. There was a tabby cat on a rug in front of the hearth.

There were two bedrooms upstairs and one downstairs where the boys slept, as they were up early to see to the beasts.

Josh took the clothing that Jay and Olive had bought him into the downstairs bedroom and chose navy-blue cotton trousers and a woollen plaid shirt to wear. Then he went into the kitchen, where he was just in time to see Olive coming downstairs from the bedroom she had shared with the daughter of the house. Olive was dressed in a cream long-sleeved blouse and a plain red skirt with ankle socks and brown brogues.

'You both look nice,' said Mary. 'The stew will be ready soon but you've time to go outside where Callum is waiting to show you Old Venable.'

So, Josh and Olive joined Callum and his sons at the site at the edge of a field where an enormous oak tree lay on the grass. Leaves and acorns and broken twigs and smashed branches lay scattered about, and roots stuck upwards in a tangled widespread mess.

Josh patted the split trunk. 'It's a bloody shame,' he muttered. 'You're not going to be able to rush the job if you want to make the most of the wood. There are companies who would pay good money for oak.'

Callum said, 'I want to use some of it myself. I thought I mentioned it to you. A pastime for the dark nights.'

'I won't be here,' said Josh.

'And you need to recover your strength,' said Olive.

'I could advise you which part of the tree is best for what you want to make,' offered Josh. 'I was thinking of setting out this afternoon for our holiday around Ireland and returning here before we take the ferry to Liverpool, and give you a hand then. Your boys could help you with the sawing. I'll leave you with measurements and design.'

He held out his hand to his cousin, which he grasped firmly, and they agreed. Josh winked at Olive. 'It'll be fine, darling, I promise.'

She raised her eyebrows. 'Cross your heart?'

'I swear it.' He lifted her hand to his lips and kissed each finger.

Then they had a meal with Callum, Mary and their sons and daughter.

Josh's and Olive's few essentials, as well as clothes, were put in the rucksacks. Once ready, they said their thanks, hugged and kissed, climbed into the hire car and settled back comfortably, holding hands.

'Do you want me to take you to the cabin first, Cousin Joshua? You'll be needing to get the fire lit and settle in for the night and tomorrow explore the area. Aunty Bridget has placed some books of interest for you to share and there is food and drinks and milk in the cool box,' said Michael, the eldest son.

'Is there oil and matches?' asked Josh, giving Olive a sidelong glance.

She met his eyes, wondering what this was all about a cabin and oil and matches?

And then, kissing the tip of her nose, he said, 'I'm hoping, sweetheart, you'll enjoy the surprise. There are plenty of beautiful places in Ireland and I decided I didn't want to show you the top tourist locations first, such as Blarney Castle and its kissing stone.'

'So, where are you taking me?' she asked, kissing his chin.

'Aunty Bridget's cabin, which is a few hours' drive, was built by a professor at Trinity College in Dublin, who suddenly decided he wanted to live the simple life. He'd met a woman, and she felt the same, so he resigned his post. Bridget got pregnant. He had the cabin built, but not being close enough to have electric, main drains and gas put in cheaply, they really did live the simple life.'

Olive drew back her head. 'When was this, and were they really related to your family? Alfie calls me Aunty Olive but I'm not an aunt by blood.'

'It was an honorary title and was only given to her after the professor passed away. He ate a poisonous plant.'

'Am I right in thinking she didn't die as well?' said Olive.

'She had more sense,' said Michael. 'She looked to the sea for her food, even her veggies.'

'Seaweed,' said Olive. 'I had seaweed at a pub in Bantry. It was in a wonderful sauce and with mussels.' She paused. 'So, what happened to Bridget and her child after her husband passed away? Did the child go to school?'

'No, Bridget taught her at home. She did have a wireless run by battery. And she learnt from that as well and was kept up to date,' said Josh.

'What did they do about clothes?' asked Olive.

'They knitted, crocheted and sewed their own,' said Josh.

'I think you're having me on,' said Olive, punching him lightly on the jaw. 'They'd need money to buy wool, cotton, needles and the like.'

'We're here. It's the furthest I can take you in the car,' said Mick. 'The daughter was in her teens when she had the brilliant idea of renting the cabin to holidaying fishermen who couldn't afford a hotel and didn't need much, only to get away somewhere quiet and cheap where the fishing was good.'

They got out of the car and took their baggage from the boot. Olive gazed about her. The car was parked on the road. 'Where is it?'

'This way,' said Josh, following in his cousin's tracks between shrubs, low-growing flowering plants and trees. Soon the road was out of sight and within less than half an hour there was the gleam of water through the trees, and she spotted a timber and stone one-storey building. A yellow gleam of light shone through a window, lifting Olive's spirits, and when the door opened at the lightest touch, she squeezed Josh's hand as he drew her inside.

'I'll be leaving you, then,' said Michael. 'And be back the day after next to move you on. We can't chance leaving a hired car where it is.'

Olive wondered where they would be going to but, for now, she was happy to stay at the cabin alone with Josh. 'I should imagine this is like what the early settlers in the New World built.'

'Not quite,' said Josh. 'There's more to this cabin than meets the eye. I never forgot meeting you,' he said as soon as they were alone, reaching out and taking her left hand. 'I swear I fell in love with you the moment I helped you to your feet. Then your friend turned up and brought me to my senses. I was married and I didn't want to behave like some married servicemen did and commit bigamy or pretend to be free.'

She nodded and said, 'As it was, we became friends. You must have noticed there are bunk beds in here? Are we expected to sleep in them?'

He did not reply.

'If you were thinking of some loving, you should have arranged a double bed and our pre-wedding ceremony.'

'Joanna said we were to have fun and so...'

'You decided we'd do some play acting,' she said, her lips twitching.

'You're so clever,' he said. 'During the Californian gold rush in the late 1840s there were simple cabins like this one built. A lot of the miners wouldn't have been the lowest of the low because to leave Ireland they'd have needed money for their fare.'

'And those that couldn't, stayed in Liverpool where they knew they'd be fed. Some had family there,' she said.

Josh brought her against him and silenced her with a kiss. 'Enough of the history lesson,' he murmured against her lips. 'There is another room to this cabin, but we should wait until we've had supper, so you can lay the table. We could do with some flowers as a centrepiece, but we don't want to make the same mistake as the professor.'

'Of course not, although did the professor really exist?' she asked, kissing his cheek.

He raised a sooty eyebrow. 'Read the book *The Magical Tales of Ireland*.'

'Does it tell the reader about leprechauns?' She picked up a book from a shelf, but he took it from her.

'Don't start messing about. Food and drink first and then the ceremony, and if you wish we can try out the bottom bunk bed.'

'You're teasing me,' she said, setting plates and cutlery and glasses on the table.

Josh proceeded to place plastic containers on the table and spoon out sliced beef, potatoes in their jackets, whole carrots and Yorkshire pudding and gravy.

'I don't believe it,' she said, sitting down as he poured wine into their glasses.

'If we were in a hotel, they wouldn't feed us better. The beef is Irish, and so are the potatoes and carrots.'

'What about the Yorkshire puddings?' she asked, putting butter on her split potato.

'Eat,' said Josh. 'Enjoy.'

Olive had a feeling that the pudding would be apple pie and cream, and she was right, and the pastry was delicious. She cleared her plate. 'My compliments to the cook,' she said.

'I should think so,' he said. 'Now for the ceremony.'

'What about the dishes?' she asked, getting to her feet.

'We'll put them in the sink with water and leave them for now,' said Josh.

He had removed his jacket and was wearing navy blue trousers and a blue shirt that she remembered buying for him and which was open at the neck. He held a book of Celtic blessings. She remembered seeing one in the cathedral on the Isle of Iona in Scotland.

She could hardly believe he had gone to so much trouble. 'Shouldn't I change?' she asked. 'You've changed.'

'No, I got splinters on the other shirt,' he said. 'This is a simple ceremony. You can get all dollied for the legal ceremony in your parish church. Now we are just going to stand and take each other for husband and wife to love and to cherish until death us do part.'

This they said and then unexpectedly he took a small box from his pocket which contained a silver ring formed in the shape of a Celtic knot heart. She was almost overcome by his thoughtfulness.

He placed it on the third finger of her left hand and said, 'Until it is replaced by a blessed wedding band of gold.'

They kissed long and passionately and then he pulled back a curtain to reveal a door that led into another room painted white, in the middle of which there was a carved wooden bed made up with clean white sheets, a couple of patterned wool blankets and an eiderdown of flower-sprinkled green silk. On the wall opposite the bed was a painting of a ship in full sail heading towards the sunset.

'I can hardly believe this,' she said, squeezing his hand.

'It's magic, isn't it?'

'If one believes in magic,' she said.

'If not magic, what about dreams coming true? Shall we?' he said, drawing back the bedcovers.

They undressed and climbed into bed, reached out for each other and made love.

Olive wondered if it was too late for her to have Josh's baby. She would be forty in just over a year. She hated it that just then her mother invaded her thoughts, but what did it matter if Flora counted the months from the wedding to the day of the birth.

CHAPTER TWENTY-TWO

LIVERPOOL

SEPTEMBER

'It feels strange,' Joanna said, placing her suitcase on her bed, along with the envelopes she had picked up from the mat when she'd arrived home. She had not come straight home but had stayed at Eliza's and Jack's house after the journey from Dublin. Alfie had run her home this morning. They had walked along the beach for some fresh air and to discuss the task her mother had set her, as well as their own future. Since their near-death experience in Ireland, they both felt their former plans were no longer viable, whatever their parents thought. Joanna was determined not to be parted from Alfie; he felt the same and would back her up all the way.

She felt a damp nose force itself into her hand as she opened the first envelope, and placed its contents on the bed as she stroked the dog, who had been cared for by their next-door neighbour while her mother was in Ireland.

Joanna and Alfie had been kissing while they said goodbye, when a voice said, 'So, you're back?' She had almost jumped out of her skin, but then saw that it was their neighbour, holding a dog's collar. 'Your mam forgot about him.'

'She'll be mortified,' stuttered Joanna as she and Alfie sprang apart. 'Thanks for looking after him,' she added, taking the lead from him and a tin of dog food. 'Mam's staying on a bit longer in Ireland.'

'Did you have a good trip?'

'It had its up and downs,' she said. 'Tell you about it another time. Can't stop.' She shot a glance at Alfie. 'Thanks for the lift. Look after yourself and see you soon.'

Alfie smiled. 'Give me a ring if you get stuck.'

'Thanks,' she said, smiling. 'I have to go in, lots to do, including feeding the dog.'

Alfie climbed into the car and drove off with care. He thought of Josh, who had saved his and Joanna's lives, and sent up a prayer for him and Olive, his godmother. He briefly touched the Saint Christopher's medal she had bought him for his seventeenth birthday in May. That had really been the beginning of his and Joanna's adventure, which had resulted in them growing closer than they had ever been.

He thought of his father and the secret he had kept for years, until events had forced the truth to emerge in a dangerous and dramatic way. He wondered how many children born during the war and shortly after had been raised in such a way… He had been fortunate in having been told the truth about his natural father, and that later his mother had married Jack, who could not have been a better stepfather. He recalled the times they'd been so happy together as a family, even more so after his half-sister Beth was born.

Alfie found his thoughts drifting but was roused by the blare of a horn and swerved in time to avoid a crash. His heart was racing, and he drew up at the side of the road and stayed there until he calmed down. Eventually, his thoughts took off in a different direction and he thought of Joanna and whether she had fed the dog, and if they should have a dog or cat when they were husband and wife, sooner rather than later. Having children would wait until they were comfortably settled.

—

Joanna had fed the dog and was reading the mail; some letters were addressed to her mother, but she read them because they might involve the task Olive had set her. But first things first, she needed to check out Nan and Dougal, who according to Olive had got married while on the cruise. What reasons could they have for being so secretive? Anyway, she still needed to talk to them and see if they would be interested in her mother's idea for a café. Then she remembered that her mother had told her to leave them till last. First, she should trace George and Mary and see if they were still interested in being part of her mother's scheme. She decided to phone the estate agent first, saying she would bring her mother's letter with her and the deposit for the key.

Having done that and having the key, she phoned Mary, who told her that she was still interested and so was her grandmother who worked in a café in Colwyn Bay. As for George, she felt certain he'd be interested, although he was still at sea but should be home any day now.

'Bring him then, if he's home. The thing is,' said Joanna, 'Mam spotted a place that was out of the ordinary. She thought it would do but she's still in Ireland and she's concerned somebody else could get it before she can, so she wants those interested – such as you, George and your gran, if she's better, to come and have a look. If more of you think it will do, then I'll let her know and she'll buy it, and we can start organising the necessary alterations.'

'Can me and my gran come to your mam's house tomorrow morning and go and have a gander?' said Mary.

'Sure,' said Joanna, starting to feel excited.

'What if it needs some building work done to it?' asked Mary.

'I'll put it to me mam,' said Joanna, feeling slightly worried. Would her mam have enough money to pay builders?

It was Eliza who came up with the name of a builder who could be interested and told Alfie, who wasted no time in asking his stepfather, Jack. Ben had been a brick-layer but now owned his own building company, so Alfie wanted to know if he would be interested in giving the building a look over. Jack told him that he would find the number in the address book by the phone.

Joanna set about making a shopping list: coffee, tea, sugar, butter, bread, lamb chops, chicken, bacon, eggs, scones, strawberry jam, cream, cocoa, crumpets, Persil washing powder, Fairy liquid, soap, potatoes, carrots, apples, oranges, grapes, bananas, onions, Oxo… that would have to do for now. No, also more milk, and cooking oil and dog food too.

She hurried to the estate agent's and then to the Co-op and to a few more shops. When she could carry no more, she made her way home, thinking she would have to be up early in the morning.

As it was, as soon as Joanna had finished her breakfast and taken the dog for a walk, Mary, her grandmother, George, Alfie and Ben the builder were waiting for her outside the house. She apologised and invited them inside, showing them into the living room. With Mary's help, she served cups of tea and biscuits and told them to follow her to the building which her mother had her eye on.

It was a tall building with several floors. The top had large glass windows and Mary's grandmother said, 'It reminds me of a lighthouse and a windmill. There's a fair amount of space at the front that is concreted and grassed over. I wonder if the sea once came up this far.'

'What an oddity,' said Ben. 'I wonder when it was built and by whom.'

'Surely it must get a mention in a local history book somewhere,' suggested George. 'One sees strange buildings abroad in Europe or even down south.'

'Chairs and tables could be placed outside for grown-ups to have a drink and a snack if they don't want a proper meal inside,' said Mary.

'Let's go inside,' said Joanna, brandishing the key.

'Let's see whether it's any good for what Mam wants,' Joanna said. She led the way and soon discovered that the space was larger than she had thought from outside, realising that an extension had been built on.

Joanna and her would-be helpers wandered around the space. Then she went upstairs, followed by Mary, George and Alfie; there was a decent living space, including a bathroom and separate lavatory. Ben inspected the very top space and then went downstairs and outside in search of a ladder, which he used to inspect the roof, the guttering and drainpipes.

'It's so different from any other eating and entertaining place I've ever seen,' said Joanna.

'We love it,' said Mary and George. 'We'd love to live here.'

After a discussion with the group and a talk with Ben, Joanna went and spoke to the estate agent and told her that she would be getting in touch with her mother. After taking a builder's advice, she would be recommending that her mother get home and have another look at it and a good think about whether to go ahead and buy it.

CHAPTER TWENTY-THREE

DUBLIN

SEPTEMBER

'Are you liking it here?' asked Josh. 'Or would you prefer being at the cabin?'

Olive's shoulder brushed his arm. 'What a question! The cabin will always be a magical place for me. It was a shame, though, that we never caught any fish ourselves for our dinner. And cooked them over a fire under the stars.'

'Well, we'll see what the hotel will be serving this evening. But for now, we'd best put a move on if we're to see the Book of Kells in Trinity College.' He hurried her out of St Stephen's Green and to Trinity College, where it had been on display in the Old Library since the nineteenth century.

'It hasn't always been here, has it?' said Olive, gazing in awe at the beautiful colourful illustration in the open pages of the handwritten Latin script of the gospels.

'You tell me?' he said.

'I'm not sure but when I went on retreat to a priory in Alnmouth, near Alnwick Castle in Northumberland, we had an outing to the Isle of Iona where there was a manuscript very like this one. Although, it could be a copy or just similar.'

'Whatever,' said Josh, placing his arm about her shoulders. 'It's fantastic that it's still in such condition. But one can only gaze at it for so long and wonder, before making room for someone else. Besides, I'm hungry and it's time to go and get changed for dinner and have a drink.'

They left the college and walked to their hotel overlooking St Stephen's Green and wasted no time going up to their bedroom, kicking their shoes off and undressing and putting on dressing gowns and drinking cups of tea, lying on their bed.

Olive finished her tea first and went to run a bath. 'How tired are we?'

'I don't know how tired you are,' said Josh. 'It depends on what you have in mind. I do want to go down and have dinner.'

'I meant do you want to go to a theatre or a pub, where there's music or there might be dancing downstairs, or are you tired enough to go to bed and talk?'

He hesitated. 'What do you want to talk about?'

'We'll see what comes naturally,' she said. 'It's no time now to find we've run out of things to say to each other.'

'The bath will be getting cold,' he said, taking her hand and dragging her from the bed. She left him and added bubble bath and tested the water before switching off the taps and removing her dressing gown. She slid into the water with a sigh of pleasure because it was still deliciously warm.

The door opened and Josh entered. He gazed down at her and smiled. 'May I?' he said.

'Still a gentleman, Josh,' she said.

'Well?' he asked.

Her eyes danced. 'You may.' She moved over slightly as he removed his dressing gown and slid into the other end of the bath.

He tickled her toes. After a few minutes she splashed him. Then she pinched his big toe. 'Stop messing,' she cried. 'I thought you were hungry, so we can't stay long in the bath.'

'I am hungry.' He bit her toe.

'Stop it,' she giggled. 'We don't want to miss dinner, besides—'

There came a knock at the door.

They froze and then came a voice. 'Some mail was delivered at reception for you.'

Olive called, 'We'll pick it up when we come down for dinner.'

'I wonder who it's from,' said Josh, reaching for Olive.

She slipped down into his arms. 'It can wait. Just ten minutes more. The water's so lovely.' Olive made herself comfortable, enjoying the warm, sweet-smelling security of his strong arms about her.

Josh planted a kiss on the side of her neck. 'I knew I was lovestruck when I couldn't stop thinking about your eyes... they're the colour of cornflowers. Your friend at the Grafton obviously knew how I felt when she saw you and I in a clinch. She could read my expression. I badly wanted to kiss your sweet lips and to go further, as I felt a connection between us. And that couldn't be, so it was for the best she was there.'

'You mean because you were married?'

'Yeah!' Josh kissed her again and sighed. 'I never thought I'd see you again, but I knew your name and I dreamt about you.' He paused. 'Then you walked into the Blue Anchor pub, and I could scarcely believe it.'

'You acted as if you'd never seen me before, despite having held me in your arms longer than necessary. I was hurt, especially when you did not react when Joe made a play for me and asked for a date.'

'I should have told you then that Joe is my wife's cousin.'

'Why didn't you? I know because Joanna told me, but Joe never mentioned it.'

'I can't say that surprises me, but he knew I'd never grass on him unless absolutely necessary.' He paused. 'I've always believed Joe was her spy. Our marriage was a mistake, and a divorce would have been a natural progression, only Deirdre didn't want me having access to our son, so she was on the lookout for anything that would blacken my name. Her father is a lawyer, and we've never had time for each other.'

'How did you ever get as far as marrying her?'

'She was a bit of a rebel in those days, and I was different to the class of boy she usually mixed with, so at her suggestion we ran away and married by special licence in New Mexico.'

'I thought there was no class system in America,' she said, nudging him in the ribs, but his skin was slippy so her elbow had little effect. 'But you're separated now,' she added.

'Of course, or we wouldn't be here. Jay is going to visit my lawyer with a letter and a cheque for payment from me, demand the divorce papers, then send them to me at Jack's and Eliza's. Is that enough now? Can we go and eat?'

'You've no questions for me?'

'Later,' he said, lifting her up and kissing between her shoulder blades.

He pulled out the plug and then they rubbed themselves dry, combed their hair and dressed and hurried downstairs.

They went to reception and picked up the mail addressed to Olive. It had been forwarded from Callum's address. They found a table, sat down and perused the menu before ordering a drink. Then Olive opened the envelope and withdrew four sheets of paper.

'It is a message from Joanna about the building I was interested in. She thinks I should buy it,' said Olive. 'I mentioned to you about investing some of my winnings in a café or a restaurant which could provide an income for us and jobs for the likes of Mary and George, who want to get married.'

'I don't remember,' he said, running a hand through his damp hair.

She reached out a hand to him. 'You weren't listening.'

'There's been a lot happening. Does this mean we have to return to Liverpool sooner than planned?'

'Not necessary,' she replied. 'I can telephone or write to my bank, the estate agent and my solicitor and we can stay a few days longer if that's what you want.' She covered his hand with hers. 'You can read the letter and check out the forms if you like.'

He shook his head and took a mouthful of Guinness. 'No need, and from what you say, I think it wiser if we go home and you sort everything out on the spot. We can always return to Ireland another time. After all, we've our other wedding to sort out and our second honeymoon.'

She leant across the table and kissed him. 'And there's Christmas, but first there's another question-and-answer session we need to sort out.'

'Shall we order another drink first and take it upstairs?' he suggested.

So, that's what they did, and once settled comfortably in bed, he said, 'Why did you marry Theo? I have an idea, but I'd rather you told me.'

'I needed to prevent my mother from calling me and my baby all sorts of nasty names, and also to help Theo, who was hurting because he loved someone else but couldn't see a way ahead to sorting matters out so they could be together.'

'Marrying you seems an odd way of doing so.'

'I agree but it's the past now and they're together and have the son they both wanted.'

'You never loved him?'

'No!' They hugged each other tightly.

'Next question?' she asked.

'Why didn't you come to California with Joanna?'

'I didn't want to see Joe, although I felt sorry for him, and I believed it only right that I should be honest with Joanna. Theo told me not so long ago that he had guessed Joanna wasn't his daughter, but he was good to her and provided her with a father figure.' She kissed his cheek. 'I would have liked to see you, but you were still married, and I was unsure why you were still writing to me' She hugged him. 'I did wonder whether it was because you cared about how I was managing to cope with Joe's daughter.'

Josh nodded.

'I didn't know that you were aware I had married Theo.'

Josh pressed a kiss on the top of her head. 'When Joe's wife and son were killed, he went to pieces and received little support from my wife and her father, but knowing what I did I thought it would help him to meet the daughter he knew nothing about.' He paused and took a deep breath. 'I was unaware at the time that he was connecting to his neighbour's daughter, but that blood connection still meant a lot to him. And it proved so, and I don't regret getting in touch with you about that. I had always planned to meet up with you again and that was partly the reason I planned the trip to Ireland, especially when I heard that you and Theo were getting a divorce.' He paused again. 'I admit that Alan arriving on the scene was a shock but that did not last.'

They both took deep breaths. Then Josh rose and picked up the phone and ordered a small bottle of champagne and two packets of crisps.

'You'd better also remember to cancel our room and have our bill ready in the morning,' said Olive.

'Will do,' he said, blowing her a kiss.

'And do you really want champagne?'

Josh said, 'Just to toast us.'

'Then order a pale beer as well,' she said.

That done, the pair of them went and sat by the window and gazed out over Dublin at night while toasting each other.

'Should we order tickets for the ferry to Liverpool?' said Olive. 'That's if you don't mind going by sea?'

Josh shook his head. 'I'm looking forward to seeing the Liver birds.'

'Spoken like a true Liverpudlian,' she said, laughing and throwing her arms round him. 'I'm wondering whether I should ask Dougal to give me away instead of my brother, as a gesture that will speak to my mam of welcome and that we are family and should forgive and forget the hurt we caused each other.'

'You think your brother will be okay with that?'

'As long as I explain,' she said. 'Besides, his daughter will be one of my bridesmaids.'

'What about Alfie and Joanna?'

She stared at him. 'What about them?'

'You've talked about helping Mary and George, who love each other and want to get married. What about supporting your daughter? She and Alfie love each other.'

'What are you saying? What happened in California?' She drew away from him, but he reached for her hand and held it tightly.

'Not what you could be thinking. Give the pair of them credit. They weren't going to let you down. No doubt they kissed. But they were responsible for themselves and that meant they looked at each other differently, and Joanna realised that she was no longer a child but on the verge of womanhood and what she wanted out of life had altered. Even you treated her as a grown-up by asking her to set in motion your plan for the café… restaurant. Whatever!'

'You're not suggesting I allow her to get married?' she said weakly.

'No, but if she speaks to you about Alfie and how much they'll miss each other if she goes away to university, and how they'd like to get married, you could suggest an engagement and setting a possible date for her to look forward to.'

Olive began to think about the future. What if she and Josh were to have a baby?

'What are you thinking?' asked Josh.

'You don't want to know,' replied Olive.

'Family?' said Josh.

She nodded. 'I should ring Joanna and let her know we'll be home tomorrow.'

EPILOGUE

DECEMBER 1958

'What does Eliza say?' asked Olive.

'Why don't you ask her?' said Joanna.

'Has Alfie mentioned to her about getting engaged?' Olive lifted her veil and stared at her daughter.

'She thinks we'll suit but that we should wait until I'm eighteen to get married.'

'Alfie will be nineteen. If you have a two-year engagement.'

'It seems ages away.' Her tone was terse.

'He'll have finished his National Service by then. Although there is talk about ending National Service.'

Joanna put a hand to her head. 'I don't want to think about it.'

'Well, don't.' Her mother placed an arm around her shoulders and hugged her. 'I know it's tough, sweetheart. But be positive. I've heard it said that if women were in charge there would be no wars, is that true? How many mothers would fight to defend their children to the death?' Olive thought of the child she was carrying and wondered what Josh would feel when she told him. She wanted to get further on before doing so, concerned that she might miscarry at her age.

'Shush now,' she said, hearing her daughter sniff. 'It's my wedding day. We can't read the future, so live just for the moment and make the most of it.'

'Nan and Dougal have arrived and so have Uncle Peter and Eleanor and the kids,' said Joanna. 'And Jay and Fiona are at Eliza's and Jack's, so Josh is made up they've got here in time.'

'What about Beth?'

'Uncle Pete picked her up. Eleanor is seeing to dressing the girls.'

There was a knock on the bedroom door. 'Can I come in?' called Flora.

'Of course you can, Mam,' answered Olive. 'Is Dougal all right? Not nervous?'

'No, he has nerves like steel. Although, Dougal's son Patrick is in the back garden smoking a ciggie. He wasn't sure he'd be welcome at the wedding.'

'He's family,' said Olive. 'And we have other Irish family here: Josh's cousin Callum, his wife Mary and their sons Michael and Dermot, and daughter Ruth.'

'Dougal told him that, but I think he wants to hear it from you,' said her mother, feeling the material of Olive's cream wedding gown. 'You do look nice.'

'Thanks, so do you, Mam.'

'This is my wedding suit,' said Flora, smoothing the sunshine yellow skirt. 'I bought it in Majorca.'

'Great,' said Joanna. 'I wouldn't mind going there.'

'Save your pennies, then,' said Nan, glancing at her gold watch. 'Time you were ready. I think I've just heard a car draw up outside.'

Joanna went over to the window and gazed out. 'Nan's right, Mam.'

'I'll go down and see to the buttonholes, shall I?' said Flora.

'Thanks, Mam,' replied Olive. 'Don't forget your stepson, Patrick. Mam, why didn't you tell me ages ago that you knew Dougal's wife?'

Flora sighed. 'Secrets and lies! He married my best friend Val. She knew I fancied him. He and your dad and her and me used to make up a foursome. Not as in two couples, but just as friends. Then she started sucking up to him after his father vanished, offering to help with the kids. I couldn't help, even if I'd wanted to because my dad was going through that bad time having his leg amputated and Mam was pregnant. Eventually, I had to give up going out and for a while I hardly saw them, although your dad used to call in at ours and stay and talk to my dad, so Mam and me could go out. Then Dougal's mam and the kids went to Ireland and eventually your dad told me when he came back from a football match that Dougal and Val were getting married.' She paused. 'A month later your dad proposed, and we got wed a month after that. Your dad was a good man, and I was a selfish madam. I should have given him more love, but I never forgot Dougal.'

Her mother kissed her cheek and left the bedroom. Olive followed shortly after, blinking back tears, wishing she had never pried into her mother's past.

She met Joanna on the stairs, who said, 'You look lovely, Mam. I'll go and get your bouquet and see to Brenda and Beth and our posies and take them downstairs.'

'Thanks, love, but I'm coming down now.'

Olive removed her Celtic ring from the third finger on her left hand and placed it momentarily on her right hand, smiling as she remembered Josh putting it in place.

Then as she heard footsteps, she said a quick prayer and opened the door to her stepfather.

'You look smart,' she said.

'You look beautiful,' said Dougal. 'I never thought I'd walk a bride down the aisle. I didn't even get the opportunity with my sisters.'

'Just make sure I don't trip.' She placed her hand on his sleeve and thought of her dad for a moment and how he'd be glad for her to be marrying a good man, as well as be happy for her mother. Dougal handed Olive her bouquet, and they climbed into the wedding car.

When the car drew up outside the church, Olive could not help remembering when she had arrived here in a wheelchair with Joanna pushing her. She felt so much happier now, knowing Josh was waiting for her in front of the altar ready for this part of the journey through life together.

As the organ burst into the wedding march, Josh and his best man Jay turned their heads and stared up the aisle that was flanked by pews filled by friends and family. Everyone was looking at the beautiful bride, whose gaze was fixed on her groom as she approached on her stepfather's arm. The organ fell silent.

'So here we are at last,' said Josh in an undertone as Olive came to a halt beside him in front of the communion rail. 'You look a dream in shimmering cream.' He reached out and took her hand and held it firmly.

'You look pretty good yourself. Smart suit,' she whispered. 'Give us a kiss.'

'Don't tempt me,' he retorted in a low voice. 'Later.'

The young curate's lips twitched and then he adopted a serious expression. 'Dearly beloved, we are gathered here in the sight of God and the face of this congregation to join this man and this woman in the bonds of holy matrimony. If anyone can show just cause, why they cannot lawfully be joined together, then confess it now or forever hold your peace.'

Josh held his breath, thinking even at this time that Joe might suddenly spoil this moment for him. When nobody spoke, he told himself how foolish he was for fearing such an interruption, but it proved how much he loved this woman at his side.

The curate asked, 'Joshua Graham, wilt thou have this woman to be thy wedded wife, to live together after God's ordinance in the holy estate of matrimony? Wilt thou love her, comfort her, honour and keep her in sickness and in health; and forsaking all others keep thou only unto her, if ye both shall live?'

'I will,' said Josh loudly, his voice echoing around the sacred building.

'Who gives this woman to this man?'

Dougal stepped forward and placed Olive's hand in Josh's.

Olive was thinking of those moments when she and Josh had spoken those simple vows in the log cabin in Ireland. The curate asked for the ring and Josh placed the plain golden band on her finger.

'Forasmuch as Joshua Graham and Olive Florence have consented together in holy wedlock and have witnessed the same before God and this company and thereto have given and have pledged their troth either to the other and have declared the same by the giving of a ring and by the joining of hands; I pronounce that they be man and wife together, in the name of the Father and of the Son and the Holy Ghost Amen.'

Then, smiling, he said to Josh, 'You may kiss the bride.'

Olive knew by that smile that the curate had heard them whispering earlier. As Josh kissed her long and deep, she was wondering whether his 'worse' moment was going to be that evening – had he forgotten to book them a honeymoon?

Everything was going well: they had signed the register, the organist had played the right wedding music, and all had arrived at the wedding reception safely. Most of the guests had exclaimed in surprise when they set eyes for the first time on the building Olive had bought to become her café/restaurant. It had been a bit of a rush to get it ready for the wedding reception, but family and friends had set to with gusto. Now speeches had been applauded, and thanks had been heartfelt.

Olive made up her mind to broach the subject of the honeymoon after they had cut the wedding cake, and everyone seemed happy and chatty.

Jay, Alfie and Joanna were squabbling light-heartedly over what record to play first when Josh went over and insisted on Elvis's 'Love Me Tender', 'Because Olive and I won't be here later when the smoochy music will be played.'

Olive waited for him to mention the word 'honey-moon', but all he did was to approach her and ask her for that dance. He swept her into his arms and sang the words of the song in her ear, and she knew he was going to keep her waiting until they were out of there and on the way to wherever he had chosen.

But before that took place, everyone gathered outside to wave them off. There were some who had their minds on finding the best place to catch the bride's bouquet as she took up her stance, closed her eyes and tossed it high in the air, hoping for the best. Being tall, she could see over many a head and was satisfied to see Mary catch the bouquet with the help of George. It seemed only fair, as they were going to oversee the catering for the café/restaurant and moving into the top floor of the building.

Once they were in the car, Olive said, 'I need to change out of my wedding dress and collect my luggage.'

'Of course, I'm an idiot,' said Josh.

'No, I should have taken my stuff with me to the reception earlier.'

They were soon at the house where she changed with his help, and she handed her luggage to him. She hurried to the car, impatient to know where they were going. She soon realised they were heading north, so she said, 'Blackpool!'

He grinned. 'Guess again.'

'Morecambe?'

He shook his head.

'York? Scotland?'

'No. Nearer.'

'Windermere?'

'You're getting warmer.'

'You mean Grasmere, where Wordsworth's buried and lived in a cottage and there's a little shop that sells home-made gingerbread?'

'No,' he said. 'You're not far off, though.'

'Coniston, where Donald Campbell attempted to beat the water speed record.'

'How do you know all these places?' he asked.

'Ancestry. I've traced my family tree and in so doing visited towns, villages, seaside, churches, libraries and cemeteries.'

He shook his head. 'The town has a theatre by the lake and a factory that makes writing implements. There, I've given you two clues.'

'Pencils...' she said. 'Keswick. They have a museum, as well as a factory, lovely scenery and a lake, Derwent Water, where you can take a boat trip, and it stops at certain places so you can get off and have a walk and also get back on. There's also a market twice a week and places to stay and eat. It also has a cinema, and an ancient stone circle a short distance outside the town. Oh, I forget to mention it also has a chocolate shop.'

'You sound like a holiday brochure.' He chuckled. 'How did your family end up in Liverpool?'

'Looking for work or marrying.'

'I like it.'

'You've obviously put a lot of time in finding a lovely and interesting place for our honeymoon.'

'Of course I did, O ye of little faith. That's going to be the last secret of importance I'll keep from you.'

'You mean no surprise birthday presents or treats?'

'Don't be picky, you know what I mean.'

'You're not keeping your plan for us to climb England's highest mountain on our honeymoon a secret, are you?'

'No! But I did want to keep a secret until Christmas.'

She sighed. 'Too busy. You'll be sorry if you don't tell me tonight.'

'I'll give you a clue. What do we decorate and put a star or an angel on at Christmas?'

'A Christmas tree.'

'And what did I have to do with trees?'

'You chopped them down.' Her eyes widened.

'I did more than that. I was a forester.'

'You're a tease. Are you telling me you've got a job?'

'I applied to the National Trust and explained my situation and my experience. I knew they had a lot of woodland and they're giving me a trial, starting with Freshfield Woods.'

'You're kidding me! I had thought we might both have to work in the café part-time.'

'Are you calling me a liar?'

'No, there has to be trust where there's love.' She kissed his cheek. 'You'll have your reward later, love.'